William Henry Wilkins, Isabel Burton

The Romance of Isabel, Lady Burton

Vol. 1

William Henry Wilkins, Isabel Burton

The Romance of Isabel, Lady Burton
Vol. 1

ISBN/EAN: 9783337349240

Printed in Europe, USA, Canada, Australia, Japan

Cover: Foto ©Andreas Hilbeck / pixelio.de

More available books at **www.hansebooks.com**

THE ROMANCE OF

ISABEL LADY BURTON

THE STORY OF HER LIFE

TOLD IN PART BY HERSELF
AND IN PART BY
W H WILKINS

WITH PORTRAITS AND ILLUSTRATIONS

VOLUME I

NEW YORK
DODD MEAD & COMPANY
1897

University Press
John Wilson and Son Cambridge U S A

To

HER SISTER

MRS. GERALD FITZGERALD

I DEDICATE THIS BOOK

PREFACE

L ADY BURTON began her autobiography a few
months before she died, but in consequence
of rapidly failing health she made little progress with
it. After her death, which occurred in the spring of
last year, it seemed good to her sister and executrix,
Mrs. Fitzgerald, to entrust the unfinished manuscript
to me, together with sundry papers and letters, with
a view to my compiling the biography. Mrs. Fitzgerald wished me to undertake this work, as I had the
good fortune to be a friend of the late Lady Burton,
and one with whom she frequently discussed literary
matters ; we were, in fact, thinking of writing a
romance together, but her illness prevented us.

The task of compiling this book has not been an
easy one, mainly for two reasons. In the first place,
though Lady Burton published comparatively little,

she was a voluminous writer, and she left behind
her such a mass of letters and manuscripts that the
sorting of them alone was a formidable task. The
difficulty has been to keep the book within limits.
In the second place, Lady Burton has written the
Life of her husband ; and though in that book she
studiously avoided putting herself forward, and gave
to him all the honour and the glory, her life was so
absolutely bound up with his, that of necessity she
covered some of the ground which I have had to go
over again, though not from the same point of view.
So much has been written concerning Sir Richard
Burton that it is not necessary for me to tell again
the story of his life here, and I have therefore been
able to write wholly of his wife, an equally congenial
task. Lady Burton was as remarkable as a woman
as her husband was as a man. Her personality was
as picturesque, her individuality as unique, and,
allowing for her sex, her life was as full and varied
as his.

It has been my aim, wherever possible, throughout
this book to let Lady Burton tell the story of her
life in her own words, and keep my narrative in the
background. To this end I have revised and in-
corporated the fragment of autobiography which was

cut short by her death, and I have also pieced together all her letters, manuscripts, and journals which have a bearing on her travels and adventures. I have striven to give a faithful portrait of her as revealed by herself. In what I have succeeded, the credit is hers alone : in what I have failed, the fault is mine, for no biographer could have wished for a more eloquent subject than this interesting and fascinating woman. Thus, however imperfectly I may have done my share of the work, it remains the record of a good and noble life—a life lifted up, a life unique in its self-sacrifice and devotion.

Last December, when this book was almost completed, a volume was published calling itself *The True Life of Captain Sir Richard F. Burton*, written by his niece, Miss Georgiana M. Stisted, stated to be issued "with the authority and approval of the Burton family." This statement is not correct—at any rate not wholly so ; for several of the relatives of the late Sir Richard Burton have written to Lady Burton's sister to say that they altogether disapprove of it. The book contained a number of cruel and unjust charges against Lady Burton, which were rendered worse by the fact that they were not made until she was dead and could no longer defend herself. Some of these attacks were so paltry and malevolent, and so utterly foreign to Lady Burton's generous and truthful character, that they may be dismissed with contempt. The many friends who knew and loved her have not credited them for one moment, and the animus with which they were written is so obvious that they have carried little weight with the general public. But three specific charges call for particular refutation, as silence on them might be misunderstood. I refer to the statements that Lady Burton was the cause of her husband's recall from Damascus ; that she acted in bad faith in the matter of his conversion to the Roman Catholic Church ; and to the impugning of the motives which led her to burn *The Scented Garden*. I should like to emphasize the fact that none of these controversial questions formed part of the original scheme of this book, and they would not have been alluded to had it not been for Miss Stisted's unprovoked attack upon Lady Burton's memory. It is only with reluctance, and solely in a defensive spirit, that they are touched upon now. Even so, I have suppressed a good deal, for there is no desire on the part of Lady Burton's relatives or myself to justify her at the expense of the husband whom she loved, and who loved her. But in vindicating her it has been necessary to tell the truth. If therefore, in defending Lady Burton against these accusations, certain facts have come to light which would otherwise have been left in darkness, those who have wantonly attacked the dead have only themselves to blame.

In conclusion, I should like to acknowledge my indebtedness to those who have kindly helped me to make this book as complete as possible. I am especially grateful to Mrs. Fitzgerald for much encouragement and valuable help, including her reading of the proofs as they went through the press, so that the book may be truly described as an authorized biography. I also wish to thank Miss Plowman, the late Lady Burton's secretary, who has been of assistance in many ways. I acknowledge with gratitude the permission of Captain L. H. Gordon to publish certain letters which the late General Gordon wrote to Sir Richard and Lady Burton, and the assistance which General Gordon's niece, Miss Dunlop, kindly gave me in this matter. My thanks are likewise due to the Executors of the late Lord Leighton for permission to publish Lord Leighton's portrait of Sir Richard Burton; to Lady Thornton and others for many illustrations; and to Lady Salisbury, Lady Guendolen Ramsden, Lord Llandaff, Sir Henry Elliot, Mr.

W. F. D. Smith, Baroness Paul de Ralli, Miss Bishop, Miss Alice Bird, Madame de Gutmansthal-Benvenuti, and others, for permission to publish sundry letters in this book.

W. H. WILKINS.

8, MANDEVILLE PLACE, W.,
April, 1897.

CONTENTS OF VOL. I

BOOK I

WAITING

xiii

LIST OF ILLUSTRATIONS

VOL. I

BOOK I
WAITING
(1831—1861)

I have known love and yearning from the years
Since mother-milk I drank, nor e'er was free.

ALF LAYLAH WA LAYLAH
(*Burton's "Arabian Nights"*).

.

CHAPTER I

BIRTH AND LINEAGE

Man is known among men as his deeds attest,
Which make noble origin manifest.

ALF LAYLAH WA LAYLAH
(*Burton's "Arabian Nights"*).

ISABEL, Lady Burton, was by birth an Arundell of Wardour, a daughter of one of the oldest and proudest houses of England. The Arundells of Wardour are a branch of the great family of whom it was sung:

Ere William fought and Harold fell
There were Earls of Arundell.

The Earls of Arundell before the Conquest are somewhat lost in the mists of antiquity, and they do not affect the branch of the family from which Lady Burton sprang. This branch traces its descent in a straight line from one Roger de Arundell, who, according to *Domesday*, had estates in Dorset and Somerset, and was possessed of twenty-eight lordships. The Knights of Arundell were an adventurous race. One of the most famous was Sir John Arundell, a valiant

3

commander who served Henry VI. in France. The
grandson of this doughty knight, also Sir John
Arundell, was made a Knight Banneret by Henry VII.
for his valour at the sieges of Tiroven and Tournay,
and the battle that ensued. At his death his large
estates were divided between the two sons whom
he had by his first wife, the Lady Eleanor Grey,
daughter of the Marquis of Dorset, whose half-sister
was the wife of Henry VII. The second son, Sir
Thomas Arundell, was given Wardour Castle in
Wiltshire, and became the ancestor of the Arundells
of Wardour.

The House of Wardour was therefore founded by
Sir Thomas Arundell, who was born in 1500. He
had the good fortune in early life to become the
pupil, and ultimately to win the friendship, of Cardinal
Wolsey. He played a considerable part throughout
the troublous times which followed on the King's
quarrel with the Pope, and attained great wealth and
influence. He was a cousin-german of Henry VIII.,
and he was allied to two of Henry's ill-fated queens
through his marriage with Margaret, daughter of
Lord Edmond Howard, son of Thomas, Duke of
Norfolk. His wife was a cousin-german of Anne
Boleyn and a sister of Catherine Howard. Sir Thomas
Arundell was a man of intellectual powers and administrative ability. He became Chancellor to Queen
Catherine Howard, and he stood high in the favour
of Henry VIII. But in the following reign evil
days came upon him. He was accused of conspiring
with the Lord Protector Somerset to kill the Earl of

Northumberland, a charge utterly false, the real reason of his impeachment being that Sir Thomas had been chief adviser to the Duke of Somerset and had identified himself with his policy. He was beheaded on Tower Hill a few days after the execution of the Duke of Somerset. Thus died the founder of the House of Wardour.

In Sir Thomas Arundell's grandson, who afterwards became first Lord Arundell of Wardour, the adventurous spirit of the Arundells broke forth afresh. When a young man, Thomas Arundell, commonly called "The Valiant," went over to Germany, and served as a volunteer in the Imperial army in Hungary. He fought against the Turks, and in an engagement at Grau took their standard with his own hands. On this account Rudolph II., Emperor of Germany, created him Count of the Holy Roman Empire, and decreed that "every of his children and their descendants for ever, of both sexes, should enjoy that title." So runs the wording of the charter.[1] On Sir Thomas Arundell's return to England a warm dispute arose among the Peers whether such a dignity, so conferred by a foreign potentate, should be allowed place or privilege in England. The matter was referred to

[1] The name of Arundell of Wardour appears in the official Austrian lists of the Counts of the Empire. The title is still enjoyed by Lord Arundell and all the members of the Arundell family of both sexes. Lady Burton always used it out of England, and took rank and precedence at foreign courts as the Countess Isabel Arundell (of Wardour). She used to say, characteristically : " If the thing had been bought, I should not have cared ; but since it was given for a brave deed I am right proud of it."

Queen Elizabeth, who answered, "that there was a close tie of affection between the Prince and subject, and that as chaste wives should have no glances but for their own spouses, so should faithful subjects keep their eyes at home and not gaze upon foreign crowns ; that we for our part do not care that our sheep should wear a stranger's marks, nor dance after the whistle of every foreigner." Yet it was she who sent Sir Thomas Arundell in the first instance to the Emperor Rudolph with a letter of introduction, in which she spoke of him as her "dearest cousin," and stated that the descent of the family of Arundell was derived from the blood royal. James I., while following in the footsteps of Queen Elizabeth, and refusing to acknowledge the title conferred by the Emperor, acknowledged Sir Thomas Arundell's worth by creating him a Baron of England under the title of Baron Arundell of Wardour. It is worthy of note that James II. recognized the right of the title of Count of the Holy Roman Empire to Lord Arundell and all his descendants of both sexes in a document of general interest to Catholic families.

Thomas, second Baron Arundell of Wardour, married Blanche, daughter of the Earl of Worcester. This Lady Arundell calls for special notice, as she was in many ways the prototype of her lineal descendant, Isabel. When her husband was away serving with the King's army in the Great Rebellion, Lady Arundell bravely defended Wardour for nine days, with only a handful of men, against the Parliamentary forces who besieged it. Lady Arundell then delivered up

WARDOUR CASTLE.

[*Page* 6.

the castle on honourable terms, which the besiegers broke when they took possession. They were, however, soon dislodged by Lord Arundell, who, on his return, ordered a mine to be sprung under his castle, and thus sacrificed the ancient and stately pile to his loyalty. He and his wife then turned their backs on their ruined home, and followed the King's fortunes, she sharing with uncomplaining love all her husband's trials and privations. Lord Arundell, like the rest of the Catholic nobility of England, was a devoted Royalist. He raised at his own expense a regiment of horse for the service of Charles I., and in the battle of Lansdowne, when fighting for the King, he was shot in the thigh by a brace of pistol bullets, whereof he died in his Majesty's garrison at Oxford. He was buried with great pomp in the family vault at Tisbury. His devoted wife, like her descendant Isabel Burton, that other devoted wife who strongly resembled her, survived her husband barely six years. She died at Winchester; but she was buried by his side at Tisbury, where her monument may still be seen.

Henry, third Lord Arundell, succeeded his father in his titles and honours. Like many who had made great sacrifices to the Royal cause, he did not find an exceeding great reward when the King came into his own again. As Arundell of Wardour was one of the strictest and most loyal of the Catholic families of England, its head was marked out for Puritan persecution. In 1678 Lord Arundell was, with four other Catholic lords, committed a prisoner to the Tower,

upon the information of the infamous Titus Oates and
other miscreants who invented the "Popish Plots."
Lord Arundell was confined in the Tower until 1683,
when he was admitted to bail.   Five years' imprisonment for no offence save fidelity to his religion and
loyalty to his king was a cruel injustice ; but in those
days, when the blood of the best Catholic families
in England ran like water on Tower Hill, Lord
Arundell was lucky to have escaped with his head.
On James II.'s accession to the throne he was sworn
of the Privy Council and held high office.   On King
James's abdication he retired to his country seat,
where he lived in great style and with lavish hospitality.   Among other things he kept a celebrated pack
of hounds, which afterwards went to Lord Castlehaven,
and thence were sold to Hugo Meynell, and became the
progenitors of the famous Quorn pack.

Henry, the sixth Baron, is noteworthy as being the
last Lord Arundell of Wardour from whom Isabel
was directly descended (see p. 9), and with him our
immediate interest in the Arundells of Wardour ceases.
Lady Burton was the great-granddaughter of James
Everard Arundell, his third and youngest son.   Her
father, Mr. Henry Raymond Arundell, was twice
married.   His first wife died within a year of their
marriage, leaving one son.   Two years later, in 1830,
Mr. Henry Arundell married Miss Eliza Gerard, a
sister of Sir Robert Gerard of Garswood, who was
afterwards created Lord Gerard.   The following year,
1831, Isabel, the subject of this memoir, was born.

I have dwelt on Lady Burton's lineage for several

Table showing the descent of Isabel Lady Burton from Henry, sixth Lord Arundell of Wardour, and her kinship to the present Peer.

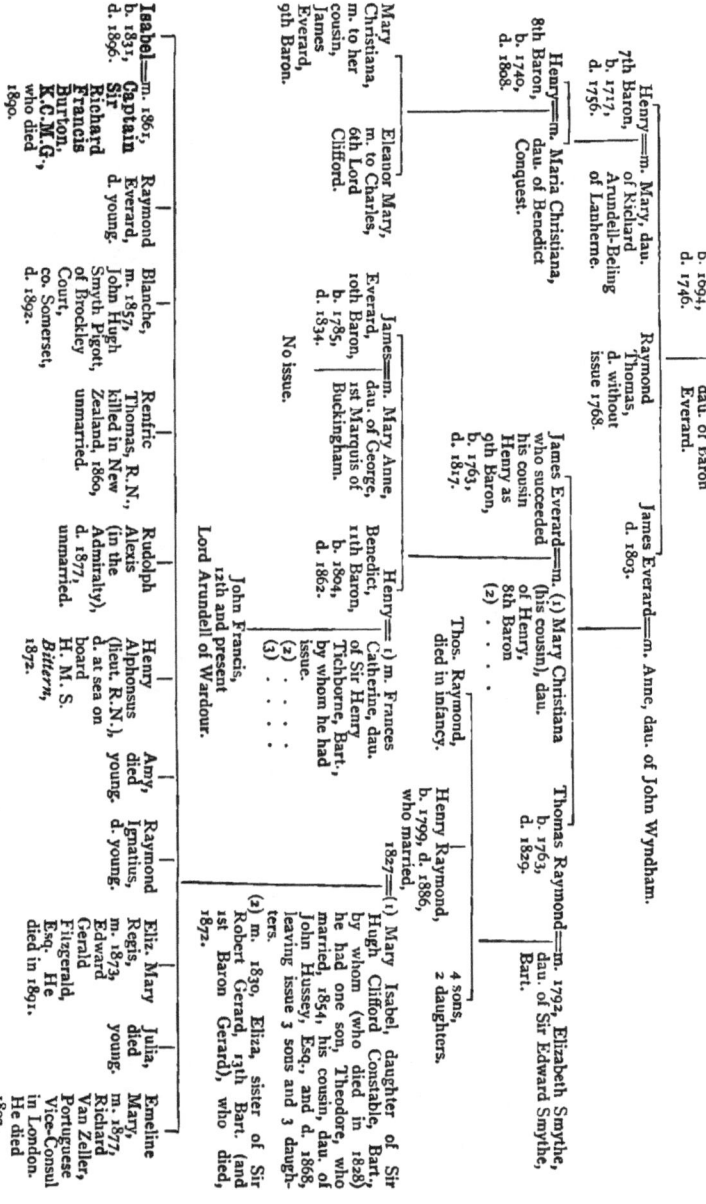

reasons. In the first place, she herself would have wished it. She paid great attention to her pedigree, and at one time contemplated writing a book on the Arundells of Wardour, and with this view collected a mass of information, which, with characteristic generosity, she afterwards placed at Mr. Yeatman's disposal for his *History of the House of Arundell.* She regarded her forefathers with reverence, and herself as their product. But proud though she was of her ancestry, there never was a woman freer from the vulgarity of thrusting it forward upon all and sundry, or of expecting to be honoured for it alone. Though of noble descent, not only on her father's side, but on her mother's as well (for the Gerards are a family of eminence and antiquity, springing from the common ancestor of the Dukes of Leinster in Ireland and the Earls of Plymouth, now extinct, in England), yet she counted it as nothing compared with the nobility of the inner worth, the majesty which clothes the man, be he peasant or prince, with righteousness. She often said, " The man only is noble who does noble deeds," and she always held that

> He, who to ancient wreaths can bring no more
> From his own worth, dies bankrupt on the score.

Another reason why I have called attention to Lady Burton's ancestry is because she attached considerable importance to the question of heredity generally, quite apart from any personal aspect. She looked upon it as a field in which Nature ever reproduces herself, not only with regard to the physical organism, but also the psychical qualities. But with it all she was no pessimist, for she believed that there was in every man an ever-rallying force against the inherited tendencies to vice and sin. She was always " on the side of the angels."

I remember her once saying : " Since I leave none to come after me, I must needs strive to be worthy of those who have gone before me."

And she was worthy — she, the daughter of an ancient race, which seems to have found in her its crowning consummation and expression. If one were fanciful, one could see in her many-sided character, reflected as in the facets of a diamond, the great qualities which had been conspicuous in her ancestors. One could see in her, plainly portrayed, the roving, adventurous spirit which characterized the doughty Knights of Arundell in days when the field of travel and adventure was much more limited than now. One could mark the intellectual and administrative abilities, and perhaps the spice of worldly wisdom, which were conspicuous in the founder of the House of Wardour. One could note in her the qualities of bravery, dare-devilry, and love of conflict which shone out so strongly in the old Knight of Arundell who raised the sieges of Tiroven and Tournay, and in " The Valiant " who captured with his own hands the banner of the infidel. One could see the reflex of that loyalty to the throne which marked the Lord Arundell who died fighting for his king. One could trace in her the same tenacity and devotion with which all her race has clung to the ancient faith and which sent one of them to the Tower. Above all one could trace her likeness to Blanche Lady Arundell,

who held Wardour at her lord's bidding against the
rebels.   She was like her in her lion-hearted bravery, in
her proud but generous spirit, in her determination
and resource, and above all in her passionate wifely
devotion to the man to whom she felt herself " destined
from the beginning."

In sooth they were a goodly company, these Arundells
of Wardour, and 'tis such as they, brave men and good
women in every rank of life, who have made England
the nation she is to-day.   Yet of them all there was
none nobler, none truer, none more remarkable than
this late flower of their race, Isabel Burton.

CHAPTER II[1]

As star knows star across the ethereal sea,
So soul feels soul to all eternity.

B LESSED be they who invented pens, ink, and
paper !
I have heard men speak with infinite contempt of
authoresses. As a girl I did not ask my poor little
brains whether this mental attitude towards women
was generous in the superior animal or not ; but I
did like to slope off to my own snug little den, away
from my numerous family, and scribble down the
events of my ordinary, insignificant, uninteresting life,
and write about my little sorrows, pleasures, and
peccadilloes. I was only one of the " wise virgins,"
providing for the day when I should be old, blind,
wrinkled, forgetful, and miserable, and might like such
a record to refresh my failing memory. So I went
back, by way of novelty, beyond my memory, and
gleaned details from my father.

[1] The greater part of Book I. is compiled from Lady Burton's
unfinished autobiography, at which she was working the last few
months of her life. The story is therefore told mainly in her own
words.

For those who like horoscopes, I was born on a Sunday at ten minutes to 9 a.m., March 20, 1831, at 4, Great Cumberland Place, near the Marble Arch. I am not able to give the aspect of the planets on this occasion ; but, unlike most babes, I was born with my eyes open, whereupon my father predicted that I should be very " wide awake." As soon as I could begin to move about and play, I had such a way of pointing my nose at things, and of cocking my ears like a kitten, that I was called " Puss," and shall probably be called Puss when I am eighty. I was christened Isabel, after my father's first wife, *née* Clifford, one of his cousins. She died, after a short spell of happiness, leaving him with one little boy, who at the time I was born was between three and four years old.

It is a curious fact that my mother, Elizabeth Gerard, and Isabel Clifford, my father's first wife, were bosom friends, schoolfellows, and friends out in the world together ; and amongst other girlish confidences they used to talk to one another about the sort of man each would marry. Both their men were to be tall, dark, and majestic ; one was to be a literary man, and a man of artistic tastes and life ; the other was to be a statesman. When Isabel Clifford married my father, Henry Raymond Arundell (of Wardour), her cousin, my mother, seeing he was a small, fair, boyish-looking man, whose chief hobbies were hunting and shooting, said, " I am ashamed of you, Isabel ! How can you ? " Nevertheless she used to go and help her to make her baby-clothes for the coming boy. After Isabel's death nobody, except my father, deplored her

so much as her dear friend my mother ; so that my
father only found consolation (for he would not go
out nor meet anybody in the intensity of his grief)
in talking to my mother of his lost wife. From
sympathy came pity, from pity grew love, and three
years after Isabel's death my mother and my father
were married. They had eleven children, great and
small ; I mean that some only lived to be baptized and
died, some lived a few years, and some grew up.[1]

To continue my own small life, I can remember
distinctly everything that has happened to me from
the age of three. I do not know whether I was
pretty or not ; there is a very sweet miniature of me
with golden hair and large blue eyes, and clad in a
white muslin frock and gathering flowers, painted by
one of the best miniature painters of 1836, when
miniatures were in vogue and photographs unknown.
My mother said I was " lovely," and my father said I
was " all there " ; but I am told my uncles and aunts
used to put my mother in a rage by telling her how
ugly I was. My father adored me, and spoilt me
absurdly ; he considered me an original, a bit of
" perfect nature." My mother was equally fond of
me, but severe—all her spoiling, on principle, went to
her step-son, whose name was Theodore.

When my father and mother were first married,
James Everard Arundell, my father's first cousin, and
my godfather, was the then Lord Arundell of Wardour.
He was reputed to be the handsomest peer of the
day, and he was married to a sister of the Duke of

[1] Two only now survive : Mrs. Fitzgerald and Mrs. Van Zeller.

Buckingham. He invited my father and mother, as
the two wives were friends, to come and occupy one
wing of Wardour immediately after their marriage,
and they did so. When James Everard died, my
parents left Wardour, and took a house in Montagu
Place at the top of Bryanston Square, and passed their
winters hunting at Leamington.

We children were always our parents' first care.
Great attention was paid to our health, to our walks,
to our dress, our baths, and our persons; our food
was good, but of the plainest; we had a head nurse
and three nursery-maids; and, unlike the present,
everything was upstairs—day nurseries and night
nurseries and schoolroom. The only times we were
allowed downstairs were at two o'clock luncheon (our
dinner), and to dessert for about a quarter of an hour
if our parents were dining alone or had very intimate
friends. On these occasions I was dressed in white
muslin and blue ribbons, and Theodore, my step-
brother, in green velvet with turn-over lace collar
after the fashion of that time. We were not allowed
to speak unless spoken to; we were not allowed to
ask for anything unless it was given to us. We
kissed our father's and mother's hands, and asked
their blessing before going upstairs, and we stood
upright by the side of them all the time we were in
the room. In those days there was no lolling about,
no Tommy-keep-your-fingers-out-of-the-jam, no Dick-
crawling-under-the-table-pinching-people's-legs as nowadays. We children were little gentlemen and ladies,
and people of the world from our birth; it was the

old school. The only diversion from this strict rule was an occasional drive in the park with mother, in a dark green chariot with hammer-cloth, and green and gold liveries and powdered wigs for coachman and footman : no one went into the park in those days otherwise. My daily heart-twinges were saying good-night to my mother, always with an impression that I might not see her again, and the other terror was the old-fashioned rushlight shade, like a huge cylinder with holes in it, which made hideous shadows on the bedroom walls, and used to frighten me horribly every time I woke. The most solemn thing to me was the old-fashioned Charley, or watchman, pacing up and down the street, and singing in deep and mournful tone, " Past one o'clock, and a cloudy morning."

At the age of ten I was sent to the Convent of the Canonesses of the Holy Sepulchre, New Hall, Chelmsford, and left there when I was sixteen. In one sense my leaving school so early was a misfortune ; I was just at the age when one begins to understand and love one's studies. I ought to have been kept at the convent, or sent to some foreign school ; but both my father and mother wanted to have me at home with them.

I want to describe my home of that period. It was called Furze Hall, near Ingatestone, Essex. Dear place ! I can shut my eyes and see it now. It was a white, straggling, old-fashioned, half-cottage, half-farmhouse, built by bits, about a hundred yards from the road, from which it was completely hidden by trees. It was buried in bushes, ivy, and flowers. Creepers

covered the walls and the verandahs, and crawled in
at the windows, making the house look like a nest ;
it was surrounded by a pretty flower garden and
shrubberies, and the pasture-land had the appearance
of a small park.   There were stables and kennels.
Behind the house a few woods and fields, perhaps
fifty acres, and a little bit of water, all enclosed
by a ring fence, comprised our domain.   Inside the
house the hall had the appearance of the main cabin
of a man-of-war, and opened all around into rooms
by various doors : one into a small library, which led
to a pretty, cheerful little drawing-room, with two
large windows down to the ground ; one opened on
to a trim lawn, the other into a conservatory ; another
door opened into a smoking-room, for the male part of
the establishment, and the opposite one into a little
chapel ; and a dining-room, running off by the back
door with glass windows to the ground, led to the
garden.   There was a pretty honeysuckle and jessamine
porch, which rose just under my window, in which
wrens and robins built their nests, and birds and bees
used to pay me a visit on summer evenings.   We had
many shady walks, arbours, bowers, a splendid slanting
laurel hedge, and a beautiful bed of dahlias, all colours
and shades.   A beech-walk like the aisle of a church
had a favourite summer-house at the end.   The pretty
lawn was filled, as well as the greenhouse, with the
choicest flowers ; and we had rich crops of grapes, the
best I ever knew.   I remember a mulberry tree, under
the shade of which was a grave and tombstone and
epitaph, the remains and memorial of a faithful old

NEW HALL, CHELMSFORD.

[*Page* 18.

dog ; and I remember a pretty pink may tree, a large white rose, and an old oak, with a seat round it. Essex is generally flat ; but around us it was undulating and well-wooded, and the lanes and drives and rides were beautiful. We were rather in a valley, and a pretty road wound up a rise, at the top of which our tall white chimneys could be seen smoking through the trees. The place could boast no grandeur ; but it was my home, I passed my childhood there, and loved it.

We used to have great fun on a large bit of water in the park of one of our neighbours,—in the ice days in winter with sledges, skating, and sliding ; in the summer-time we used to scamper all over the country with long poles and jump over the hedges. Nevertheless, I had a great deal of solitude, and I passed much time in the woods reading and contemplating. Disraeli's *Tancred* and similar occult books were my favourites ; but *Tancred*, with its glamour of the East, was the chief of them, and I used to think out after a fashion my future life, and try to solve great problems. I was forming my character.

And as I was as a child, so I am now. I love solitude. I have met with people who dare not pass a moment alone ; many seem to dread themselves. I find no greater happiness than to be alone out of doors, either on the sea-beach or in a wood, and there reflect. With me solitude is a necessary consolation ; I can soothe my miseries, enjoy my pleasures, form my mind, reconcile myself to disappointments, and plan my conduct. A person may be sorrowful without

being alone, and the mind may be alone in a large
assembly, in a crowded city, but not so pleasantly.   I
have heard that captives can solace themselves by
perpetually thinking of what they loved best ; but there
is a danger in excess of solitude, lest our thoughts
run the wrong way and ferment into eccentricity.
Every right-minded person must think, and thought
comes only in solitude.   He must ponder upon what
he is, what he has been, what he may become.   The
energies of the soul rise from the veiled obscurity
it is placed in during its contact with the world.
It is when alone that we obtain cheerful calm-
ness and content, and prepare for the hour of
action.   Alone, we acquire a true notion of things,
bear the misfortunes of life calmly, look firmly on
the pride and insolence of the great, and dare to
think for ourselves, which the majority of the great
dare not.   When can the soul feel that it lives, and is
great, free, noble, immortal, if not in thought?   Oh !
one can learn in solitude what the worldly have no
idea of.   True it is that some souls capable of reflection plunge themselves into an endless abyss, and
know not where to stop.   I have never felt one of
those wild, joyous moments when we brood over our
coming bliss, and create a thousand glorious consequences.   But I have known enough of sorrow to appreciate rightly any moment without an immediate care.
There are moments of deep feeling, when one must
be alone in self-communion, alike to encounter good
fortune or danger and despair, even if one draws out
the essence of every misery in thought.

I was enthusiastic about gypsies, Bedawin Arabs, and everything Eastern and mystic, and especially about a wild and lawless life. Very often, instead of going to the woods, I used to go down a certain green lane ; and if there were any oriental gypsies there, I would go into their camp and sit for an hour or two with them. I was strictly forbidden to associate with them in our lanes, but it was my delight. When they were only travelling tinkers or basket-menders, I was very obedient ; but wild horses would not have kept me out of the camps of the oriental, yet English-named, tribes of Burton, Cooper, Stanley, Osbaldiston, and one other tribe whose name I forget. My particular friend was Hagar Burton, a tall, slender, handsome, distinguished, refined woman, who had much influence in her tribe. Many an hour did I pass with her (she used to call me " Daisy "), and many a little service I did them when any of her tribe were sick, or got into a scrape with the squires anent poultry, eggs, or other things. The last day I saw Hagar Burton in her camp she cast my horoscope and wrote it in Romany. The rest of the tribe presented me with a straw fly-catcher of many colours, which I still have. The horoscope was translated to me by Hagar. The most important part of it was this :

" You will cross the sea, and be in the same town with your Destiny and know it not. Every obstacle will rise up against you, and such a combination of circumstances, that it will require all your courage, energy, and intelligence to meet them. Your life will be like one swimming against big waves ; but

God will be with you, so you will always win. You will fix your eye on your polar star, and you will go for that without looking right or left. You will bear the name of our tribe, and be right proud of it. You will be as we are, but far greater than we. Your life is all wandering, change, and adventure. One soul in two bodies in life or death, never long apart. Show this to the man you take for your husband.—HAGAR BURTON."

She also prophesied :

" You shall have plenty to choose from, and wait for years ; but you are destined to him from the beginning. The name of our tribe shall cause you many a sorrowful, humiliating hour ; but when the rest who sought him in the heyday of his youth and strength fade from his sight, you shall remain bright and purified to him as the morning star, which hangs like a diamond drop over the sea. Remember that your destiny for your constancy will triumph, the name we have given you will be yours, and the day will come when you will pray for it, long for it, and be proud of it."

Much other talk I had with Hagar Burton sitting around the camp-fire, and then she went from me ; and I saw her but once again, and that after many years.

This was the ugliest time of my life. Every girl has an ugly age. I was tall, plump, and meant to be fair, but was always tanned and sunburnt. I knew my good points. What girl does not ? I had large, dark blue, earnest eyes, and long, black eyelashes and eyebrows, which seemed to grow shorter the older I got. I had

very white regular teeth, and very small hands and
feet and waist ; but I fretted because I was too fat
to slip into what is usually called "our stock size,"
and my complexion was by no means pale and interesting enough to please me. From my gypsy tastes
I preferred a picturesque toilette to a merely smart
one. I had beautiful hair, very long, thick and soft,
with five shades in it, and of a golden brown. My
nose was aquiline. I had all the material for a very
good figure, and once a sculptor wanted to sculpt me,
but my mother would not allow it, as she thought
I should be ashamed of my figure later, when I had
fined down. I used to envy maypole, broomstick girls,
who could dress much prettier than I could. I was
either fresh and wild with spirits, or else melancholy
and full of pathos. I wish I could give as faithful
a picture of my character ; but we are apt to judge
ourselves either too favourably or too severely, and so
I would rather quote what a phrenologist wrote of me
at this time :

"When Isabel Arundell loves, her affection will be
something extraordinary, her devotion great—in fact,
too great. It will be her leading passion, and influence
her whole life. Everything will be sacrificed for one
man, and she will be constant, unchangeable, and jealous
of his affections. In short, he will be her salvation or
perdition ! Her temper is good, but she is passionate ;
not easily roused, but when violently irritated she
might be a perfect little demon. She is, however, for-
giving. She is full of originality and humour, and her
utter naturalness will pass for eccentricity. She loves

society, wherein she is wild and gay ; when alone, she is thoughtful and melancholy. She is ambitious, sagacious, and intellectual, and will attract attention by a certain simple dignity, by a look in her eye and a peculiar tone of her voice. To sum her up : Her nature is noble, ardent, generous, honourable, and good-hearted. She has courage, both animal and mental. Her faults are the noble and dashing ones, the spicy kind to enlist one's sympathies, the weeds that spring from a too luxuriant soil."

Thus wrote a professional phrenologist of me, and a friend who was fond of me at the time endorsed it in every word. With regard to the ambition, I always felt that if I were a man I should like to be a great general or statesman, to have travelled everywhere, to have seen and learnt everything, done everything ; in fine, to be the Man of the Day !

When I was between seventeen and eighteen years of age, we left Furze Hall and went to London. The place in which we have passed our youthful days, be it ever so dull, possesses a secret charm.

I performed several pilgrimages of adieu to every spot connected with the bright reminiscences of youth. I fancied no other fireside would be so cosy, that I could sleep in no other room, no fields so green. Those who know what it is to leave their quasi-native place for the first time, never to return; to know every stick and stone in the place for miles round, and take an everlasting farewell of them all ; to have one's pet animals destroyed ; to make a bonfire of all the things that one does not want desecrated by stranger hands;

to sit on some height and gaze on the general havoc ;
to reflect on what is, what has been, and what may
be in a strange world, amidst strange faces ; to shake
hands with a crowd of poor old servants, peasants, and
humble friends, and not a dry eye to be seen,—those
who have tasted something of this will sympathize with
my feelings then. "Ah, miss," the old retainers said,
"we shall have no more jolly Christmases ; we shall
have no beef, bread, and flannels next year ; the hall
will not be decked with festoons of holly ; there will
be no more music and dancing!" "No more snap-
dragons and round games," quoth the gamekeeper ;
and his voice trembled, and I saw the tears in his
eyes and in the eyes of them all.

So broke up our little home in Essex, and we went
our ways.

CHAPTER III

Society itself, which should create
Kindness, destroys what little we have got.
To feel for none is the true social art
Of the world's lovers.

BYRON.

I WAS soon going through a London drilling. I was very much pleased with town, and the novelty of my life amused me and softened my grief at leaving my country home. I greatly disliked being primmed and scolded, and I thought dressing up an awful bore, and never going out without a chaperone a greater one. Some things amused me very much. One thing was, that all the footmen with powdered wigs who opened the door when one paid a visit were obsequious if one came in a carriage, but looked as if they would like to shut the door in one's face if one came on foot. Another was the way people stared at me ; it used to make me laugh, but I soon found I must not laugh in their faces.

We put our house in order ; we got pretty dresses, and we left our cards ; we were all ready for the season's campaign. I made my *début* at a fancy ball

26

at Almack's, which was then very exclusive. We went under the wing of the Duchess of Norfolk.

I shall never forget that first ball. To begin at the beginning, there was my dress. How a girl of the present day would despise it! I wore white tarlatan over white silk, and the first skirt was looped up to my knee with a blush rose. My hair, which was very abundant, was tressed in an indescribable fashion by Alexandre, and decked with blush roses. I had no ornaments ; but I really looked very well, and was proud of myself. We arrived at Almack's about eleven. The scene was dazzlingly brilliant to me as I entered. The grand staircase and ante-chamber were decked with garlands, and festoons of white and gold muslin and ribbons. The blaze of lights, the odour of flowers, the perfumes, the diamonds, and the magnificent dresses of the cream of the British aristocracy smote upon my senses ; all was new to me, and all was sweet. Julian's band played divinely. My people had been absent from London many seasons, so at first it seemed strange. But at Almack's every one knew every one else ; for society in those days was not a mob, but small and select. People did not struggle to get on as people do now, and we were there by right, and to resume our position in our circle. There is much more heart in the world than many people give it credit for—at any rate in the world of the gentle by birth and breeding. Every one had a hearty welcome for my people, and some good-natured chaff about their having " buried themselves " so long. I was at once taken by the hand, and kindly greeted by many. Some great personage, whose name I forget,

gave a private supper, besides the usual one, to which
we were invited ; and in those days there were polkas,
valses, quadrilles, and galops. Old stagers (mammas)
had told me to consider myself very lucky if I got
four dances, but I was engaged seven or eight deep
soon after I entered the ballroom, and had more
partners than I could dance with in one night. Of
course mother was delighted with me, and I was
equally pleased with her : she looked so young and
fashionable ; and instead of frightening young men
away, as she had always done in the country, she
appeared to attract them, engage them in conversation, and seemed to enjoy everything ; she was such
a nice chaperone. I was very much confused at the
amount of staring (I did not know that every new
girl was stared at on her first appearance) ; and one
may think how vain and incredulous I was, when I
overheard some one telling my mother that I had been
quoted as the new beauty at his club. Fancy, poor
ugly me !

I shall not forget my enjoyment of that first ball.
I had always been taught to look upon it as the
opening of Fashion's fairy gates to a paradise ; nor
was I disappointed, for, to a young girl who has
never seen anything, her first entrance into a brilliant
ballroom is very intoxicating. The blaze of light and
colour, the perfume of scent and bouquet, the beautiful
dresses, the spirited music, the seemingly joyous multitude of happy faces, laughing and talking as if care
were a myth, the partners flocking round the door to
see the new arrivals—all was delightful to me. But

then of course in those days we were not born *blasé*,
as the young people are to-day.

And I shall never forget my first opera. I shall
always remember the delights of that night. I thought
even the crush-room lovely, and the brilliant gaslight,
the mysterious little boxes, with their red-velvet
curtains, filled with handsome men and pretty women,
which I think Lady Blessington describes as " rags
of roues, memoranda books of other women's follies,
like the last scene of the theatre ; they come out in gas
and red flame, but do not stand daylight." I do not
say that, but some of them certainly looked so. The
opera was *La Sonambula*, with Jenny Lind and Gardoni.
When the music commenced, I forgot I was on earth ;
and, so passionately fond of singing and acting as I
was, it was not wonderful that I was quite absorbed
by this earth's greatest delight. Jenny's girlish figure,
simple manner, birdlike voice, so thrilling and so full
of assion, her perfect acting and irresistible love-
making, were matchless. Gardoni was very handsome
and very stiff. The scene where Gardoni takes her
ring from her, and the last scene when he dis-
covers his mistake, and her final song, will ever be
engraven on my memory ; and if I see the opera
a thousand times, I shall never like it as well as
I did that night, for all was new to me. And after
—only think, what pleasure for me !—there came
the ballet with the three great stars Amalia Ferraris,
Cerito, and Fanny Essler, whom so few are old enough
to remember now. There are no ballets nowadays
like those.

This London life of society and amusement was delightful to me after the solitary one I had been leading in the country. I was ready for anything, and the world and its excitement gave me no time to hanker after my Essex home. The rust was soon rubbed off; I forgot the clouds; my spirit was unbroken, and I lived in the present scrap of rose-colour. They were joyous and brilliant days, for I was exploring novelties I had only read or heard of. I went through all the sight-seeing of London, and the (to me) fresh amusement of shopping, visiting, operas, balls, and of driving in Rotten Row. The days were very different then to what they are now : one rose late, and, except a cup of tea, breakfast and luncheon were one meal ; then came shopping, visiting, or receiving. One went to the Park or Row at 5.30, home to dress, and then off to dinner or the opera, and out for the night, unless there was a party at home. This lasted every day and night from March till the end of July, and often there were two or three things of a night. I was tired at first ; but at the end of a fortnight I was tired-proof, and of course I was dancing mad. The Sundays were diversified by High Mass at Farm Street, and perhaps a Greenwich dinner in the afternoon.

I enjoyed that season immensely, for it was all new, and the life-zest was strong within me. But I could not help pitying poor wall-flowers—a certain set of girls who come out every night, who have been out season after season, and who stand or sit out all night. I often used to say to my partners, " Do go and dance with So-and-so " ; and the usual rejoinder was, " I really would do anything to oblige you, but I am sick of seeing those girls." In fact, we girls must not appear on the London boards too often lest we fatigue these young coxcombs. London, like the smallest watering-place, is full of cliques and sets on a large scale, from Billingsgate up to the throne. The great world then comprised the Court and its *entourage*, the Ministers, and the *Corps Diplomatique*, the military, naval, and literary stars, the leaders of the fashionable and political world, the cream of the aristocracy of England ; and—at the time of which I write—the old Catholic cousinhood clan used to hold its own. You must either have been born in this great world, or you must have arrived in it through aristocratic patronage, or through your talents, fame, or beauty. Nowadays you only want wealth ! There were some sets even then which were rather rapid, which abolished a good deal of the tightness of *convenance*, whose motto seemed to be *savoir vivre*, to be easy, fascinating, fashionable, and dainty as well as social.

I found a ballroom the very place for reflection ; and with the sentiment that I should use society for my pleasure instead of being its slave, I sometimes obstinately would refuse a dance or two, or sitting-out and talking, in order to lean against some pillar and contemplate human nature, in defiance of my admirers, who thought me very eccentric. I loved to watch the intriguing mother catching a coronet for her daughter, and the father absorbed in politics with some con-temporary fogey ; the old dandy with his frilled shirt

capering in a quadrille the steps that were danced in
Noah's ark ; the rouged old peeress, whom you would
not have taken to be respectable if you did not happen
to know her, flirting with boys.   I saw other old
ones, with one foot in the grave, almost mad with
excitement over cards and dice, and every passion,
except love, gleaming from their horrid eyes.   I saw
the rivalry amongst the beauties.   I noted the brainless
coxcomb, who comes in for an hour, leans against the
door, twirls his moustache, and goes out again—a sort
of "Aw! the Tenth-don't-dance-young-man!"; the
boy who asks all the prettiest girls to dance, steps on
their toes, tears their dresses, and throws them down ;
the confirmed, bad, intriguing London girl, who will
play any game for her end ; and the timid, delighted
young girl, who finds herself of consequence for the
first time.   I have watched the victim of the heartless
coquette—the young girl gazing with tearful, longing
eyes for the man to ask her to dance to whom she
has perhaps unconsciously betrayed her affection ; she
in her innocence like a pane of glass, the other
glorying in her torture, dancing or flirting with the
man in her sight, only to glut her vanity with another's
disappointment.   I have watched the jealousy of men
to each other, vying for a woman's favour and cutting
each other out.   I have heard mothers running down
each other's daughters, dowagers and prudent spinsters
casting their eyes to heaven for vengeance on the
change of manners—even in the Forties!—on the
licence of the day, and the liberty of the age!   I
have heard them sighing for minuets and pigtails, for I

came between two generations—the minuet was old
and the polka was new ; all alike were polka mad,
all crazed with the idea of getting up a new fast style,
but oh ! lamblike to what it is now ! I watched the last
century trying to accommodate itself to the present.

One common smile graced the lips of all—the
innocent, the guilty, the happy, and the wretched ; the
same colour on bright cheeks, some of it real, some
bought at Atkinson's ; and, more wonderful still, the
same general outward decorum, placidity, innocence,
and good humour, as if prearranged by general consent.
I pitied the vanity, jealousy, and gossip of many
women. I classed the men too : there were many
good ; but amongst some there were dishonour and
meanness to each other, in some there were coarseness
and brutality, and in some there was deception to
women ; some were so narrow-minded, so wanting in
intellect, that I believed a horse or a dog to be far
superior. But my ideal was too high, and I had not
in those days found my superior being.

I met some very odd characters, which made one
form some rather useful rules to go by. One man I
met had every girl's name down on paper, if she
belonged to the *haute volée*, her age, her fortune,
and her personal merits ; for he said, " One woman,
unless one happens to be in love with her, is much
the same as another." He showed me my name
down thus : " Isabel Arundell, eighteen, beauty,
talent and goodness, original—chief fault £0 0*s*. 0*d*. ! "
Then he showed me the name of one of my friends :
" Handsome, age seventeen, rather missish, £50,000 ;

she cannot afford to flirt except *pour le bon motif,*
and I cannot afford, as a younger brother, to marry
a girl with £50,000.   She is sure to have been brought
up like a duchess, and want the whole of her money
for pin-money—a deuced expensive thing is a girl
with £50,000!"   Then   he   rattled   on   to   others.
I told him I did not think much of the young men
of the day.   "There now," he answered, "drink of
the spring nearest to you, and be thankful; by being
too fastidious you will get nothing."

I took a great dislike to the regular Blue Stocking;
I can remember reading somewhere such a good
description of her :   "One who possesses every quali-
fication to distinguish herself in conversation, well
read and intelligent, her manner cold, her head cooler,
her heart the coolest of all, never the dupe of her
own sentiments; she examined her people before she
adopted them, a necessary precaution where light is
borrowed."

A great curiosity to me were certain married people,
who were known never to speak to each other at
home, but who respected the *convenances* of society so
much that even if they never met in private they
took care to be seen together in public, and to enter
evening parties together with smiling countenances.
Somebody writes :

> Have they not got polemics and reform,
> Peace, war, the taxes, and what is called the Nation,
>   The struggle to be pilots in the storm,
> The landed and the moneyed speculation,
>   The joys of mutual hate to keep them warm
> Instead of love, that mere hallucination?

What a contrast women are! One woman is "fine
enough to cut her own relations, too fine to be seen
in the usual places of public resort, and therefore of
course passes with the vulgar for something exquisitely
refined." Another I have seen who would have sacrificed all London and its "gorgeous mantle of purple
and gold" to have wedded some pale shadow of
friendship, which had wandered by her side amid her
childhood's dreary waste. And oh! how I pity the
many stars who fall out of the too dangerously attractive
circle of society! The fault there seems not to be
the sin, but the stupidity of being found out. I say
one little prayer every day: "Lord, keep me from
contamination." I never saw a woman who renounced
her place in society who did not prove herself capable
of understanding its value by falling fifty fathoms
lower than her original fall. The fact is, very few
people of the world, especially those who have not
arrived at the age of discretion, are apt to stop short
in their career of pleasure for the purpose of weigh-
ing in the balance their own conduct, enjoyments, or
prospects; in short, it would be very difficult for any
worldly woman to be always stopping to examine
whether she is enjoying the right kind of happiness
in the right kind of way, and, once fallen, a woman
seems to depend on her beauty to create any interest
in her favour. I knew nothing of these things
then; and though I think it quite right that women
should be kept in awe of certain misdemeanours, I
cannot understand why, when one, who is not bad,
has a misfortune, other women should join in hounding

her down, and at the same time giving such licence
to really bad women, whom society cannot apparently
do without. 'Tis "one man may steal a horse, and
another may not look over the hedge." If a woman
fell down in the mud with her nice white clothes on,
and had a journey to go, she would not lie down and
wallow in the mud ; she would jump up, and wash herself clean at the nearest spring, and be very careful
not to fall again, and reach her journey's end safely.
But other women do not allow that ; they must haul
out buckets of the mud, and pour it over the fallen
one, that there may be no mistake about it at all.
Then men seem to find a wondrous charm in poaching
on other men's preserves (though a poacher of birds
gets terrible punishments, once upon a time hanging),
as if their neighbours' coverts afforded better shooting
than their own manors.

When I went to London, I had no idea of the matri-
monial market ; I should have laughed at it just as
much as an unmarrying man would. I was interested
in the fast girls who amused themselves at most extraordinary lengths, not meaning to marry the man ; and
at the slower ones labouring day and night for a
husband of some sort, without any success. I heard
a lady one day say to her daughter, "My dear, if you
do not get off during your first season, I shall break
my heart." Our favourite men joined us in walks
and rides, came into our opera-box, and barred all the
waltzes ; but it would have been no fun to me to have
gone on as some girls did, because I had no desire to
reach the happy goal, either properly or improperly.

Mothers considered me crazy, and almost insolent, because I was not ready to snap at any good *parti* ; and I have seen dukes' daughters gladly accept men that poor humble I would have turned up my nose at.

> What think'st thou of the fair Sir Eglamour ?
> As of a knight well spoken, neat and fine ;
> But were I you he never should be mine.

Lots of such men, or mannikins, affected the season, then as now, and congregated around the rails of Rotten Row. I sometimes wonder if they are men at all, or merely sexless creatures—animated tailors' dummies. Shame on them thus to disgrace their manhood ! 'Tis man's work to do great deeds ! Well, the young men of the day passed before me without making the slightest impression. My ideal was not among them. My ideal, as I wrote it down in my diary at that time, was this :

" As God took a rib out of Adam and made a woman of it, so do I, out of a wild chaos of thought, form a man unto myself. In outward form and inmost soul his life and deeds an ideal. This species of fastidiousness has protected me and kept me from fulfilling the vocation of my sex—breeding fools and chronicling small beer. My ideal is about six feet in height ; he has not an ounce of fat on him ; he has broad and muscular shoulders, a powerful, deep chest ; he is a Hercules of manly strength. He has black hair, a brown complexion, a clever forehead, sagacious eyebrows, large, black, wondrous eyes—those strange eyes you dare not take yours from off them—with long

lashes.   He is a soldier and a *man* ; he is accustomed
to command and to be obeyed.   He frowns on the
ordinary affairs of life, but his face always lights up
warmly for me.   In his dress he never adopts the
fopperies of the day, but his clothes suit him—they
are made for him, not he for them.   He is a thorough
man of the world ; he is a few years older than myself.
He is a gentleman in every sense of the word—not
only in manners, dress, and appearance, but in birth
and position, and, better still, in ideas and actions; and
of course he is an Englishman.   His religion is like
my own, free, liberal, and generous-minded.   He is by
no means indifferent on the subject, as most men are ;
and even if he does not conform to any Church, he
will serve God from his innate duty and sense of honour.
The great principle is there.   He is not only not a
fidgety, strait-laced, or mistaken-conscienced man on
any subject ; he always gives the mind its head.   His
politics are conservative, yet progressive.   His manners
are simple and dignified, his mind refined and sensitive,
his temper under control ; he has a good heart, with
common sense, and more than one man's share of
brains.   He is a man who owns something more than
a body ; he has a head and heart, a mind and soul.
He is one of those strong men who lead, the master-
mind who governs, and he has perfect control ·over
himself.

"This is the creation of my fancy, and my ideal
of happiness is to be to such a man wife, comrade,
friend—everything to him, to sacrifice all for him, to
follow his fortunes through his campaigns, through

his travels, to any part of the world, and endure any amount of roughing. I speak of the ideal man 'tis true, and some may mock and say, ' Where is the mate for such a man to be found ? ' But there are ideal women too. Such a man only will I wed. I love this myth of my girlhood—for myth it is—next to God ; and I look to the star that Hagar the gypsy said was the star of my destiny, the morning star, which is the place I allot to my earthly god, because the ideal seems too high for this planet, and, like the philosopher's stone, may never be found here. But if I find such a man, and afterwards discover he is not for me, then I will never marry. I will try to be near him, only to see him, and hear him speak ; and if he marries somebody else, I will become a sister of charity of St. Vincent de Paul."

CHAPTER IV

BOULOGNE: I MEET MY DESTINY

(1850—1852)

Was't archer shot me, or was't thine eyes?
ALF LAYLAH WA LAYLAH
(*Burton's " Arabian Nights "*).

THE season over (August, 1850), change of air,
sea-bathing, French masters to finish our education,
and economy were loudly called for ; and we turned our
faces towards some quiet place on the opposite shores
of France, and we thought that Boulogne might suit.
We were soon ready and off.

We had a pleasant but rough passage of fifteen
hours from London.   While the others were employed
in bringing up their breakfasts, I sat on deck and
mused.   Suddenly I remembered that Hagar had told
me I should cross the sea, and then I wondered why
we had chosen Boulogne.   I was leaving England for
the first time ; I knew not for how long.   What should
I go through there, and how changed should I come
back ?   I had gone with a light heart.   I was young
then ; I loved society and hated exile.   I had written
in my diary only a little time before : " As for me, I
am never better pleased than when I watch this huge

game of chess, Life, being played on that extensive chess-
board, Society." I never felt so patriotic as that first
morning on sea when the white cliffs faded from my
view. We never appreciate things until we lose them,
and I thought of what the feelings of soldiers and
sailors must be, going from England and returning
after years of absence.

At length the boat stopped at the landing-place at
Boulogne, and we were driven like a flock of sheep
between two ropes into a *papier-maché*-looking building,
whence we were put into a carriage like a bathing-
machine, and driven through what I took to be mews,
but which were in reality the principal streets. I
recognize in this reflection the prejudiced London
Britisher, the John Bull ; for in reality Boulogne was
a most picturesque town, and our way lay through
most picturesque streets. After driving up the hilly
street, and under an archway, in the old town, we
came to a good, large house like a barn, No. 4, Rue
des Basses Chambres, Haute Ville, Boulogne-sur-Mer.
The rooms were chiefly furnished with bellows and
brass candlesticks ; there was not the ghost of an armchair, sofa, ottoman, or anything comfortable ; and the
only thing at all cheery was our kinswoman, Mrs.
Edmond Jerningham, who, apprised of our arrival, had
our fires lighted and beds made. She was cutting bread-
and-butter and preparing tea for us when we came
in, and had ready for us a turkey the size of a fine
English chicken. This banquet over, we all turned
into bed, and slept between the blankets.

Next morning our boxes were still detained at the

custom-house, and my brothers and sisters and myself got some bad tea and some good bread-and-butter, and sat round in a circle on the floor in our night-gowns, with our food in the middle. Shortly after we heard a hooting, laughing, and wrangling in a shrill key, "Coralie, Rosalie, Florantine, Celestine, Euphrosine!" so I pricked up my ears in the hopes of seeing some of those pretty, well-dressed, *piquante* little *soubrettes* of whom we had heard mother talk, when in rolled about a dozen harpies with our luggage. At first I did not feel sure whether they were men or women; they had picturesque female dresses on, but their manners, voices, language, and gestures were those of the lowest costermongers. They spoke to me in *patois*, which I did not understand, and seemed surprised to see us all in our nightgowns, forgetting that we had little else to put on till they had brought the luggage. I gave them half a crown, which they appeared to think a great deal of money, and it inspirited them greatly. They danced about me, whirled me round, and in five minutes one had decked me up in a red petticoat, another arrayed me in her jacket, and a third clapped her dirty cap on my head, and I was completely attired *à la marine*. I felt so amused by the novelty of the thing that I forgot to be angry at their impertinence, and laughed as heartily as they did.

When they were gone, we set to work and unpacked and dressed, and by the afternoon were as comfortable as we could make ourselves; but we were thoroughly wretched, though mother kept telling us to look at

the beautiful sky, which was not half as blue or bright
as on the other side of the water. We sauntered out
to look at the town. I own my first impressions of
France were very unfavourable ; Boulogne looked to
me like a dirty pack of cards, such as a gypsy pulls
out of her pocket to tell your fortune with. The
streets were irregular, narrow, filthy, and full of open
gutters, which we thought would give us the cholera.
The pavement was like that of a mews ; the houses
were unfurnished ; the sea was so far out from our part
of the town that it might as well not have been there
—and such a dirty, ugly-looking sea too, we thought !
The harbour was full of poisonous-looking smelling
mud, and always appeared to be low water. The
country was dry, barren, and a dirty brown (it was a
hot August) ; the cliffs were black ; and there was not
a tree to be seen—I used to pretend to get under a
lamp-post for shade. Every now and then we had
days of fine weather, with clouds of dust and sirocco,
or else pouring rain and bleak winds. From mother's
talk of the Continent we expected at least the comforts
of Brighton with the romance of Naples ; and I shall
never forget our feelings when we were told that, after
Paris, Boulogne was the nicest town in France. Now
I imagine that ours are the feelings of every narrow-
minded, prejudiced John Bull Britisher the first time
he lands abroad. It takes him some little time to
thoroughly appreciate all the good things that he does
get abroad, and to be fascinated with the picturesque-
ness, and then often he returns home unwillingly.

We had a cheap cook, so that our dinners would

have been scarcely served up in my father's kennel at home. When I had eaten what I could pick out by dint of shutting my eyes and forcing myself to get it down, I used to lie down daily on a large horsehair sofa, such as one sees in a tradesman's office, and sometimes cry till I fell asleep; I felt so sorry for us all.

The most interesting people in Boulogne were the *poissardes*, or fisherwomen; they are of Spanish and Flemish extraction, and are a clan apart to themselves. They are so interesting that I wonder that no one has written a little book about them. They look down on the Boulognais; they are a fine race, tall, dark, handsome, and have an air of good breeding. Their dress is most picturesque. The women wear a short red petticoat, dark jacket, and snowy handkerchief or scarf, and a white veil tied round the head and hanging a little behind. On *fête* days they add a gorgeous satin apron. These costumes are expensive. Their long, drooping, gold earrings and massive ornaments are heirlooms, and their lace is real. The men wear great jack-boots all the way up their legs, a loose dark jacket, and red cap; they are fine, stalwart men. They had a queen named Carolina, a handsome, intelligent woman, with whom I made great friends; and also a captain, who had a daughter so like me that when I used to go to the fish-market at first they used to chaff me, thinking she had dressed up like a lady for fun. They also have their different grades of society; they have their own church, built by themselves, their separate weddings, funerals, and christenings. They do not marry out of their own tribe or associate with the townspeople. Their language has a number of Spanish and Latin words in it. They have a strict code of laws, live in a separate part of the town on a hill, are never allowed to be idle, and are remarkable for their morality, although by the recklessness of the conduct and talk of some of the commoner ones you would scarcely believe it. If an accident does occur, the man is obliged to marry the girl directly. The upper ones are most civil and well spoken, and all are open-hearted and not grasping. There is a regular fleet of smacks. The men are always out fishing. The women do all the work at home, as well as shrimping, making tackle, marketing, getting their husbands' boats ready for sea, and unloading them on return ; and they are prosperous and happy. The smacks are out for a week or ten days, and have their regular turn. They have no salmon, and the best fish is on our side of the water. The lowest grade of the girls, who serve as kinds of hacks to the others, are the shrimping girls ; they are as vulgar as Billingsgate and as wild as red Indians. You meet them in parties of thirty or forty, with their clothes kilted nearly up to their waists and nets over their backs. They sing songs, and are sure to insult you as you pass ; but they make off at a double quick trot at the very name of Queen Carolina.

At Boulogne the usual lounge, both summer and winter, was the Ramparts, which were extremely pretty and picturesque. The Ramparts were charming in summer, with a lovely view of the town ; and a row down the Liane, or a walk along its banks, was not to be despised. There were several beautiful country walks in summer. The peasants' dances, called *guinguettes*, were amusing to look at. The hotels and *table d'hôtes* were not bad. The ivory shops in the town were beautiful ; the bonnets, parasols, and dresses very *chic* ; the bonbons delicious. The market was a curious, picturesque little scene. There were pretty *fêtes*, religious and profane, and a capital carnival.

The good society we collected around us ; but it was small, and never mixed with the general society. The two winters we were there were gay ; there was a sort of agreeable *laissez aller* about the place, and the summers were very pleasant. But mother kept us terribly strict, and this was a great stimulant to do wild things ; and though we never did anything terrible, we did what we had better have left alone. For instance, we girls learned to smoke. We found that father had got a very nice box of cigars, and we stole one. We took it up to the loft and smoked it, and were very sick, and then perfumed ourselves with scent, and appeared in our usual places. We persevered till we became regular smokers, and father's box of cigars disappeared one by one. Then the servants were accused ; so we had to come forward, go into his den, make him swear not to tell, and confided the matter to him. He did not betray us, as he knew we should be almost locked up, and from that time we smoked regularly. People used to say, "What makes those Arundell girls so pale? They must dance too much." Alas, poor things ! it was just the want of these innocent recreations that drove us to so dark a deed !

I have already said that we were taken to Boulogne for masters and economy. Our house in the Haute Ville was next to the Convent, and close to the future rising—slowly rising—Notre Dame. My sister Blanche and I gradually made up our minds to this life, our European Botany Bay. We were not allowed to walk alone, except upon the Ramparts, which, however, make a good mile under large shady trees, with views from every side—not a bad walk by any means. Mother, my sister Blanche, and I used to walk once daily up the lounge, which in fine weather was down the Grande Rue, the Rue de l'Ecu, the Quai to the end of the pier and back ; but in winter our promenade may be said to be confined to the Grande Rue. There we could observe the notorieties and eccentricities of the place. There might be a dozen or more handsome young men of good family, generally with something shady about money hanging over them, a great many pretty, fast girls and young married women, a great deal of open flirtation, much attention to dress, and plenty of old half-pay officers with large families, who had come to Boulogne for the same reasons as ourselves. If there were any good families, they lived in the Haute Ville, and were English ; there were, in fact, half a dozen aristocratic English families, who stuck together and would speak to nobody else. I have learnt since that often in a place one dislikes there will arise some circumstance that will prove the pivot on which part, or the whole, of one's life may turn, and that scene, that town, or that house will in after-years retain a sacred place in one's heart for that thing's sake, which a gayer or a grander scene could never win. And so it was with me.

At this point it is necessary to interrupt Isabel's auto-biography, to introduce a personage who will hereafter play a considerable part in it. By one of those many coincidences which mark the life-story of Richard and Isabel Burton, and which bear out in such a curious manner her theory that they "were destined to one another from the beginning," Burton came to Boulogne about the same time as the Arundells. This is not the place to write a life of Sir Richard Burton—it has been written large elsewhere,[1] so that all who wish may read ; but to those who have not read Lady Burton's book, the following brief sketch of his career up to this time may be of interest.

Richard Burton came of a military family, and one whose sons had also rendered some service both in Church and State. He was the son of Joseph Netterville Burton, a lieutenant-colonel in the 36th Regiment. He was born in 1821. He was the eldest of three children ; the second was Maria Catherine Eliza, who married General Sir Henry Stisted; and the third was Edward Joseph Netterville, late Captain in the 37th Regiment (Queen's), who died insane. Colonel Burton, who had retired from the army, and his wife went abroad for economy when Richard was only

---

[1] *Life of Sir Richard Burton,* by Isabel his wife.

a few months old, and they settled at Tours. Tours
at that time contained some two hundred English
families, who formed a society of their own. These
English colonies knew little of Mrs. Grundy, and
less of the dull provincialism of English country towns.
Thus Richard grew up in a free, Bohemian society,
an influence which perceptibly coloured his after-life.
His education was also of a nature to develop his
strongly marked individuality. He was sent to a
mixed French and English school at Tours, and he
remained there until his father suddenly took it into
his head that he would give his boys the benefit of
an English education, and returned to England. But,
instead of going to a public school, Richard was sent
to a private preparatory school at Richmond. He
was there barely a year, when his father, wearying of
Richmond and respectability, and sighing for the
shooting and boar-hunting of French forests, felt that
he had sacrificed enough on account of an English
education for his boys, and resolved to bring them
up abroad under the care of a private tutor. This
resolution he quickly put into practice, and a wandering
life on the Continent followed, the boys being educated
as they went along. This state of things continued
till Richard was nineteen, when, as he and his brother
had got too old for further home training, the family
broke up.

Richard was sent to Oxford, and was entered at
Trinity College, with the intention of taking holy
orders in the Church of England. But the roving
Continental life which he had led did not fit him for

the restraints of the University. He hated Oxford, and he was not cut out for a parson. At the end of the first year he petitioned his father to take him away. This was refused ; so he set to work to get himself sent down—a task which he accomplished with so much success that the next term he was rusticated, with an intimation that he was not to return. Even at this early period of his life the glamour of the East was strong upon him ; the only learning he picked up at Oxford was a smattering of Hindustani ; the only thing that would suit him when he was sent down was to go to India. He turned to the East as the lotus turns with the sun. So his people procured him a commission in the army, the Indian service, and he sailed for Bombay in June, 1842.

He was appointed to the 14th Regiment, Bombay Native Infantry, and he remained in India without coming home for seven years. During those seven years he devoted himself heart and soul to the study of Oriental languages and Oriental habits. He passed in ten Eastern languages. His interest in Oriental life, and his strong sympathy with it, earned him in his regiment the nickname of " the white nigger." He would disguise himself so effectually that he would pass among Easterns as a dervish in the mosques and as a merchant in the bazaars. In 1844 Richard Burton went to Scinde with the 18th Native Infantry, and was put on Sir Charles Napier's staff. Sir Charles soon turned the young lieutenant's peculiar acquirements to account in dealing with the wild tribes around them. He accompanied his regiment to Mooltan to

RICHARD BURTON IN 1848 IN NATIVE DRESS.   [*Page* 50.

attack the Sikhs. Yet, notwithstanding all these unique
qualifications, when Richard Burton applied for the
post of interpreter to accompany the second expedition
to Mooltan in 1849, he was passed over on account
of a feeling against him in high quarters, on which
it is unnecessary here to dwell. This disappointment,
and the mental and physical worry and fatigue which
he had undergone, broke down his health. He applied
for sick leave, and came home on a long furlough.

After a sojourn in England, he went to France
(1850) to join his family, who were then staying at
Boulogne, like the Arundells and most of the English
colony, for change, quiet, and economy. Whilst at
Boulogne he brought out two or three books and
prepared another. Burton took a gloomy view of his
prospects at this time ; for he writes, " My career in
India has been in my eyes a failure, and by no fault
of my own ; the dwarfish demon called ' Interest ' has
fought against me, and as usual has won the fight."
There was a good deal of prejudice against him even
at Boulogne, for unfounded rumours about him had
travelled home from India.

Burton, as it may be imagined, did not lead the life
which was led by the general colony at Boulogne.
" He had a little set of men friends," Isabel notes ;
" he knew some of the French ; he had a great
many flirtations—one very serious one. He passed
his days in literature and fencing. At home he was
most domestic ; his devotion to his parents, especially
to his sick mother, was very beautiful." At this time
he was twenty-eight years of age. The Burton family

belonged to the general English colony at Boulogne ;
they were not intimate with the *crème* to whom the
Miss Arundells belonged ; and as these young ladies
were very carefully guarded, it was some little time
before Richard Burton and Isabel Arundell came
together.   They met in due season ; and here we
take up the thread of her narrative again.

One day, when we were on the Ramparts, the vision of
my awakening brain came towards us.   He was five feet
eleven inches in height, very broad, thin, and muscular :
he had very dark hair ; black, clearly defined, sagacious eyebrows ; a brown, weather-beaten complexion ;
straight Arab features ; a determined-looking mouth and
chin, nearly covered by an enormous black moustache.
I have since heard a clever friend say that " he had
the brow of a god, the jaw of a devil."   But the most
remarkable part of his appearance was two large, black,
flashing eyes with long lashes, that pierced one through
and through.   He had a fierce, proud, melancholy
expression ; and when he smiled, he smiled as though
it hurt him, and looked with impatient contempt at
things generally.   He was dressed in a black, short,
shaggy coat, and shouldered a short, thick stick, as if
he were on guard.
   He looked at me as though he read me through
and through in a moment, and started a little.   I was
completely magnetized ; and when we had got a little
distance away, I turned to my sister, and whispered to
her, " That man will marry me."   The next day he
was there again, and he followed us, and chalked up,

THE RAMPARTS, BOULOGNE.

[*Page* 52.

"May I speak to you?" leaving the chalk on the
wall; so I took up the chalk and wrote back, "No;
mother will be angry"; and mother found it, and was
angry; and after that we were stricter prisoners than
ever. However, "Destiny is stronger than custom."
A mother and a pretty daughter came to Boulogne
who happened to be cousins of my father's; they
joined the majority in the society sense, and one day
we were allowed to walk on the Ramparts with them.
There I met Richard again, who (agony!) was flirting
with the daughter. We were formally introduced,
and his name made me start. Like a flash came back
to me the prophecy of Hagar Burton which she had
told me in the days of my childhood in Stonymoore
Wood: "*You will cross the sea, and be in the same
town with your Destiny and know it not. . . . You
will bear the name of our tribe, and be right proud of
it.*" I could think of no more at the moment. But
I stole a look at him, and met his gypsy eyes—those
eyes which looked you through, glazed over, and saw
something behind; the only man I had ever seen,
not a gypsy, with that peculiarity. And again I
thrilled through and through. He must have thought
me very stupid, for I scarcely spoke a word during that
brief meeting.

I did not try to attract his attention; but after
that, whenever he came on the usual promenade, I
would invent any excuse that came ready to take
another turn to watch him, if he were not looking.
If I could catch the sound of his deep voice, it seemed
to me so soft and sweet that I remained spellbound,

as when I hear gypsy music. I never lost an opportunity of seeing him, when I could not be seen ; and as I used to turn red and pale, hot and cold, dizzy and faint, sick and trembling, and my knees used to nearly give way under me, my mother sent for the doctor, to complain that my digestion was out of order, and that I got migraines in the street ; he prescribed me a pill, which I threw in the fire. All girls will sympathize with me. I was struck with the shaft of Destiny, but I had no hope, being nothing but an ugly schoolgirl,[1] of taking the wind out of the sails of the dashing creature with whom Richard was carrying on a very serious flirtation.

The only luxury I indulged in was a short but heartfelt prayer for him every morning. I read all his books, and was seriously struck, as before, by his name, when I came to the book on *Jats in Scinde*. The Jats are the aboriginal gypsies in India.

The more I got to know of Richard, the more his strange likeness to the gypsies struck me. As I wrote to the *Gypsy Lore Journal* in 1891, it was not only his eyes which showed the gypsy peculiarity ; he had the restlessness which could stay nowhere long, nor own any spot on earth, the same horror of a corpse, deathbed scenes, and graveyards, or anything which

---

[1] It is necessary here to defend Lady Burton against herself. She was certainly not " ugly " ; for she was—a friend tells me who knew her at this time—a tall and beautiful girl, with fair brown hair, blue eyes, classic features, and a most vivacious and attractive manner. Nor could she correctly be called a " schoolgirl"; for though she was taking some finishing lessons in French, music, etc., she was more than nineteen years of age, and had been through a London season.

was in the slightest degree ghoulish, though caring
little for his own life, the same aptitude for reading
the hand at a glance. With many he would drop
their hands at once and turn away, nor would anything
induce him to speak a word about them. He spoke
Romany like the gypsies themselves. Nor did we
ever enter a gypsy camp without their claiming him.
"What are you doing with that black coat on?" they
would say. "Why don't you join us and be our king?"
Moreover, Burton is one of the half-dozen distinctively
Romany names ; and though there is no proof whatever
of his Arab or Romany descent, the idea that he had
gypsy blood is not to be wondered at. He always
took a great interest in gypsy lore, and prepared a book
on the subject. He wrote many years later : " There
is an important family of gypsies in foggy England,
who in remote times developed our family name.
I am yet on very friendly terms with several of these
strange people ; nay, a certain Hagar Burton, an old
fortune-teller (*divinatrice*), took part in a period of my
life which in no small degree contributed to determine
its course."

My cousin asked Richard to write something for me
at that time ; he did so, and I used to wear it next
my heart. One night an exception was made to
our dull rule of life. My cousins gave a tea party
and dance, and the "great majority" flocked in, and
there was Richard like a star among rushlights ! That
was a night of nights ; he waltzed with me once,
and spoke to me several times, and I kept my sash
where he put his arm round my waist to waltz, and

my gloves, which his hands had clasped. I never wore them again. I did not know it then, but the "little cherub who sits up aloft" was not only occupied in taking care of poor Jack, for I came in also for a share of it. I saw Richard every now and again after that, but he was of course unconscious of my feelings towards him. And I was evidently awfully sorry for myself, since I find recorded the following moan:

"If kind Providence had blessed me with the man I love, what a different being I might be! Fate has used me hardly, with my proud, sensitive nature to rough the world and its sharp edges, alone and unprotected except by hard and peremptory rules."

So I thought then; but I have often blessed those rules since. A woman may have known the illusions of love, but never have met an object worth all her heart. Sometimes we feel a want of love, and a want to love with all our energies. There is no man capable of receiving this at the time, and we accept the love of others as a makeshift, an apology, to draw our intention from the painful feeling, and try to fancy it is love. How much in this there is to fear! A girl should be free and happy in real and legitimate love. One who is passionate and capable of suffering fears to risk her heart on any man. Happy is she who meets at her first start the man who is to guide her for life, whom she is always to love. Some women grow fastidious in solitude, and find it harder to be mated than married. Those who fear and respect the men they love, those whose judgment and sense confirm their affection, are lucky. Every one has some mysterious and singular idea respecting his destiny. I asked myself then if I would sacrifice anything and everything for Richard, and the only thing that I found I could not sacrifice for him would be God; for I thought I would as soon, were I a man, forsake my post, when the tide of battle pressed hardest against it, and go over to the enemy, as renounce my God. So having sifted my unfortunate case, I soon decided on a plan of action. I could not push myself forward or attract his notice. It would be unmaidenly—unworthy. I shuddered at the lonely and dreary path I was taking; but I knew that no advantage gained by unworthy means could be lasting or solid; besides, my conscience was tender, and I knew that the greatest pleasure unlawfully obtained would eventually become bitter, for there can be no greater pain than to despise oneself or the one we love. So I suffered much and long; and the name of the tribe, as Hagar Burton foretold, caused me many a sorrowful and humiliating hour; but I rose superior at last. They say that often, when we think our hopes are annihilated, God is granting us some extraordinary favour. It is said, " It is easy to image the happiness of some particular condition, until we can be content with no other " ; but there is no condition whatever under which a certain degree of happiness may not be attained by those who are inclined to be happy. Courage consists, not in hazarding without fear, but in being resolutely minded in a just cause.

> Marvel not at thy life; patience shall see
> The perfect work of wisdom to her given;
> Hold fast thy soul through this high mystery,
> And it shall lead thee to the gates of heaven.

The days at Boulogne went slowly by. We used to join walking or picnic parties in summer, and generally have one of our pleasant big teas in the evening. I joined in such society as there was in moderation, and I became very serious. The last summer we had many friends staying with us ; the house was quite like a hotel. We much longed to go to Paris ; but in the winter poor little baby died, and mother had no spirits for anything. This last winter (1851-52), during the time of the *coup d'état*, there were eighteen hundred soldiers billeted on Boulogne ; and the excitement was great, crowds of people were rushing about to hear the news, and vans full of prisoners passing by. They were very violent against the English too ; we had our windows broken occasionally, and our pet dog was killed. Carolina, the Poissarde queen, told us that if the worst came to the worst she should send us across to England in her husband's fishing-smack. Boulogne was a droll place ; there was always either something joyous, a *fête*, or some scandal or horror going on. It was a place of passage, constant change of people, and invariably there was some excitement about something or other.

Our prescribed two years were up at last, and we all agreed that anything in London would be preferable to Boulogne. We began quietly to pack up, pay our debts, and make our adieux. We were sorry to leave our little circle ; they were also sorry to part from us ; and the tradespeople and servants seemed conscious that they were about to lose in a short while some honest and safe-paying people—not too frequent in Boulogne

—and were loud in their regrets. I had many regrets
in leaving, but was delighted at the prospect of going
home, and impatient to be relieved of the restraint I
was obliged to impose on myself about Richard. Yet
at the same time I dreaded leaving his vicinity. I was
sorely sorry, yet glad. All the old haunts I visited
for the last time. There were kind friends to wish
good-bye. I received my last communion in the little
chapel of Our Lady in the College, where I had so
often knelt and prayed for Richard, and for strength
to bear my sorrow as a trial from the hand of God,
as doubtless it was for my good, only I could not see
it. When one is young, it is hard to pine for something, and at the same time to say, " Thy will be done."
I always prayed Richard might be mine if God willed
it, and if it was for his happiness.

I said good-bye to Carolina, the queen of the fisherwomen ; she reminded me strangely of Hagar Burton,
my gypsy. I wondered how Hagar would tell her
prophecies now ? " Chance or not," I thought, " they
are strange ; and if ever I return to my home, I will
revisit Stonymoore Wood, though now alone ; for my
shaggy Sikh is dead, my pony gone, my gypsy camp
dispersed, my light heart no longer light, no longer
mine." I would give worlds to sit again on the
mossy bank round the gypsy fire, to hear that little
tale as before, and be called " Daisy," and hear the
prophecy of Hagar that I should take the name of the
tribe. I listened lightly then ; but now that the name
had become so-dear I attached much deeper meaning
to it.

At last the day was fixed that we were to leave
Boulogne, May 9, 1852, and I was sorely exercised
in my mind as to whether or no I should say good-
bye to Richard ; but I said to myself, " When we leave
this place, he will go one way in life, and I another ;
and who knows if we may ever meet again ? " To
see him would be only to give myself more pain, and
therefore I did not.

We walked down to the steamer an hour or two
before sailing-time, which would be two in the morning.
It was midnight ; the band was playing, and the
steamer was alongside, opposite the Folkestone Hotel.
It was a beautiful night, so all our friends collected
to see us off, and we walked up and down, and had
chairs to remain near the band. When we sailed, my
people went down to their berths ; but I sat near the
wheel, to watch the town as long as I could see the
lights, for after all it contained all I wanted, and who
I thought I should never see more. I was sad at
heart ; but I was proud of the way in which I had
behaved, and I could now rest after my long and
weary struggle, suffering, patient, and purified ; and
though I would rather have had love and happiness,
I felt that I was as gold tried in the fire. It is no
little thing for a girl to be able to command herself,
to respect herself, and to be able to crush every petty
feeling.

When I could see no more of Boulogne, I wrapped
a cloak round me, and jumped into the lifeboat lashed
to the side, and I mused on the two past years I had
been away from England, all I had gone through, and all

the changes, and especially how changed I was myself;
I felt a sort of satisfaction, and I mused on how much
of my destiny had been fulfilled. Old Captain Tune,
who had become quite a friend of ours at Boulogne,
came up, and wanted me to go below. I knew him
well, and was in the habit of joking with him, and I
told him to go below himself, and I would take care of
the ship ; so instead he amused me by telling me stories
and asking me riddles. The moon went down, and
the stars faded, and I slept well ; and when I awoke
the star of my destiny, my pet morning star, was
shining bright and clear, just " like a diamond drop
over the sea." I awoke, hearing old Tune say, " What
a jolly sailor's wife she would make ! She never changes
colour." We lurched terribly. I jumped up as hungry
as a hunter, and begged him to give me some food, as
it wanted four hours to breakfast ; so he took me down
to his cabin, and gave me some hot chops and bread-
and-butter, and said he would rather keep me for a
week than a fortnight. It blew freshly. I cannot
describe my sensations when I saw the dear old white
cliffs of England again, though I had only been away
two years, and so near home. The tears came into
my eyes, and my heart bounded with joy, and I felt
great sympathy with all exiled soldiers and sailors, and
wondered what face we should see first. Foreigners
do not seem to have that peculiar sensation about
home, or talk of their country as we do of ours ; for
I know of no feeling like setting one's foot on English
ground again after a long absence.

CHAPTER V

FOUR YEARS OF HOPE DEFERRED

(1852—1856)

I was fancy free and unknew I love,
But I fell in love and in madness fell;
I write you with tears of eyes so belike,
They explain my love, come my heart to quell.

ALF LAYLAH WA LAYLAH
(*Burton's " Arabian Nights"*).

ON leaving Boulogne, Isabel saw Richard Burton no more for four years, and only heard of him now and again from others or through the newspapers. She went back to London with her people, and outwardly took up life and society again much where she had left it two years before. But inwardly things were very different. She had gone to Boulogne an unformed girl ; she had left it a loving woman. Her ideal had taken form and shape ; she had met the only man in all the world whom she could love, the man to whom she had been "destined from the beginning," and her love for him henceforth became, next to her religion, the motive power of her actions and the guiding principle of her life. All her youth, until she met him, she had yearned for something, she hardly knew what. That something had come to her, sweeter than all her young imaginings, glorifying her life and flooding her soul with radiance. And after the light there had come the darkness ; after the joy there had come keenest pain ; for it seemed that her love was given to one who did not return it—nay, more, who was all unconscious of it. But this did not hinder her devotion, though her maidenly reserve checked its outward expression. She had met her other self in Richard Burton. He was her affinity. A creature of impulse and emotion, there was a certain vein of thought in her temperament which responded to the recklessness in his own. She could no more stifle her love for him than she could stifle her nature, for the love she bore him was part of her nature, part of herself.

Meanwhile she and her sister Blanche, the sister next to her in age, had to take the place in society suited to young ladies of their position. Their father, Mr. Henry Raymond Arundell, though in comfortable circumstances, was not a wealthy man ; but in those days money was not the passport to society, and the Miss Arundells belonged by birth to the most exclusive aristocracy of Europe, the Catholic nobility of England, an aristocracy which has no parallel, unless it be found in the old Legitimist families of France, the society of the Faubourg St. Germain. But this society, though undoubtedly exclusive, was also undoubtedly tiresome to the impetuous spirit of Isabel, who chafed at the restraints by which she was surrounded. She loved liberty ;

her soaring spirit beat its wings against the prison-
bars of custom and convention ; she was always
yearning for a wider field. Deep down in her heart
was hidden the secret of her untold love, and this
robbed the zest from the pleasure she might otherwise
have taken in society. Much of her time was spent
in confiding to her diary her thoughts about Richard,
and in gleaning together and treasuring in her memory
every scrap of news she could gather concerning him.
At the same time she was not idle, nor did she pine
outwardly after the approved manner of love-sick
maidens. As the eldest daughter of a large family
she had plenty to do in the way of home duties, and
it was not in her nature to shirk any work which came
in her way, but to do it with all her might.

The Miss Arundells had no lack of admirers, and
more than once Isabel refused or discouraged advan-
tageous offers of marriage, much to the perplexity of
her mother, who naturally wished her daughters to
make good marriages ; that is to say, to marry men
of the same religion as themselves, and in the same
world—men who would make them good husbands in
every sense of the word. But Isabel, who was then
twenty-one years of age, had a strong will of her own,
and very decided views on the subject of marriage,
and she turned a deaf ear to all pleadings. Besides,
was she not guarded by the talisman of a hidden
and sacred love ? In her diary at this time she
writes :

" They say it is time I married (perhaps it is) ; but
it is never time to marry any man one does not love,

because such a deed can never be undone. Richard
may be a delusion of my brain. But how dull is reality !
What a curse is a heart ! With all to make me
happy I pine and hanker for him, my other half, to
fill this void, for I feel as if I were not complete. Is
it wrong to want some one to love more than one's
father and mother—one on whom to lavish one's best
feelings? What will my life be alone ? I cannot marry
any of the insignificant beings round me. Where are
all those men who inspired the *grandes passions* of
bygone days ? Is the race extinct ? Is Richard the
last of them ? Even so, is he for me ? They point
out the matches I might make if I took the trouble,
but the trouble I will not take. I have no vocation
to be a nun. I do not consider myself good enough
to offer to God. God created me with a warm heart,
a vivid imagination, and strong passions ; God has
given me food for hunger, drink for thirst, but no
companion for my loneliness of heart. If I could
only be sure of dying at forty, and until then preserve
youth, health, spirits, and good looks, I should be
more cheerful to remain as I am. I cannot separate
myself from all thought of Richard. Neither do I
expect God to work a miracle to make me happy.
To me there are three kinds of marriage : first,
worldly ambition ; that is, marriage for fortune, title,
estates, society ; secondly, love ; that is, the usual pig
and cottage ; thirdly, life, which is my ideal of being
a companion and wife, a life of travel, adventure, and
danger, seeing and learning, with love to glorify it ;
that is what I seek. *L'amour n'y manquerait pas !*

"A sailor leaves his wife for years, and is supposed to be unfaithful to her by necessity. The typical sportsman breakfasts and goes out, comes home to dinner, falls asleep over his port, tumbles into bed, and snores till morning. An idle and independent man who lives in society is often a *roué*, a gambler, or drunkard, whose wife is deserted for a *danseuse*.

"One always pictures the 'proper man' to be a rich, fat, mild lordling, living on his estate, whence, as his lady, one might rise to be a leader of Almack's. But I am much mistaken if I do not deserve a better fate. I could not live like a vegetable in the country. I cannot picture myself in a white apron, with a bunch of keys, scolding my maids, counting eggs and butter, with a good and portly husband (I detest fat men!) with a broad-brimmed hat and a large stomach. And I should not like to marry a country squire, nor a doctor, nor a lawyer (I hear the parchments crackle now), nor a parson, nor a clerk in a London office. God help me! A dry crust, privations, pain, danger for him I love would be better. Let me go with the husband of my choice to battle, nurse him in his tent, follow him under the fire of ten thousand muskets. I would be his companion through hardship and trouble, nurse him if wounded, work for him in his tent, prepare his meals when faint, his bed when weary, and be his guardian angel of comfort—a felicity too exquisite for words! There is something in some women that seems born for the knapsack. How many great thoughts are buried under ordinary circumstances, and splendid positions exist that are barren of them—

thoughts that are stifled from a feeling that they are too bold to be indulged in! I thank God for the blessed gift of imagination, though it may be a source of pain. It counteracts the monotony of life. One cannot easily quit a cherished illusion, though it disgusts one with ordinary life. Who has ever been so happy in reality as in imagination? And how unblessed are those who have no imagination, unless they obtain their wishes in reality! I do not obtain, so I seek them in illusion. Sometimes I think I am not half grateful enough to my parents, I do not half enough for them, considering what they are to me. Although we are not wealthy, what do I lack, and what kindness do I not receive? Yet I seem in a hurry to leave them. There is nothing I would not do to add to their comfort, and it would grieve me to the heart to forsake them; and yet if I knew for certain that I should never have my wish, I should repine sadly. I love a good daughter, and a good daughter makes a good wife. How can I reconcile all these things in my mind? I am miserable, afraid to hope, and yet I dare not despair when I look at the state of my heart. But one side is so heavy as nearly to sink the other, and thus my *beaux jours* will pass away, and my Ideal Lover will not then think me worth his while. Shall I never be at rest with him to love and understand me, to tell every thought and feeling, in far different scenes from these—under canvas before Rangoon—anywhere in Nature?

" I would have every woman marry; not merely liking a man well enough to accept him for a husband, as

some of our mothers teach us, and so cause many
unhappy marriages, but loving him so holily that,
wedded or not wedded, she feels she is his wife at heart.
But perfect love, like perfect beauty, is rare. I would
have her so loyal, that, though she sees all his little
faults herself, she takes care no one else sees them ; yet
she would as soon think of loving him less for them
as ceasing to look up to heaven because there were a
few clouds in the sky. I would have her so true, so
fond, that she needs neither to burthen him with her
love nor vex him with her constancy, since both are
self-existent, and entirely independent of anything he
gives or takes away. Thus she will not marry him
for liking, esteem, gratitude for his love, but from the
fulness of her own love. If Richard and I never
marry, God will cause us to meet in the next world ;
we cannot be parted ; we belong to one another.
Despite all I have seen of false, foolish, weak attach-
ments, unholy marriages, the after-life of which is
rendered unholier still by struggling against the inevitable, still I believe in the one true love that binds
a woman's heart faithful to one man in this life, and,
God grant it, in the next. All this I am and could
be for one man. But how worthless should I be to
any other man but Richard Burton! I should love
Richard's wild, roving, vagabond life ; and as I am
young, strong, and hardy, with good nerves, and no fine
notions, I should be just the girl for him ; I could
never love any one who was not daring and spirited.
I always feel inclined to treat the generality of men
just like my own sex. I am sure I am not born for

a jog-trot life; I am too restless and romantic. I
believe my sister and I have now as much excitement
and change as most girls, and yet I find everything
slow. I long to rush round the world in an express ;
I feel as if I shall go mad if I remain at home. Now
with a soldier of fortune, and a soldier at heart, one
would go everywhere, and lead a life worth living.
What others dare I can dare. And why should I
not? I feel that we women simply are born, marry,
and die. Who misses us ? Why should we not have
some useful, active life? Why, with spirits, brains,
and energies, are women to exist upon worsted work
and household accounts ? It makes me sick, and I
will not do it."

In the meantime Richard Burton, all unconscious
of the love he had inspired, had gone on his famous
pilgrimage to Mecca. As we have seen, he was home
from India on a long furlough ; but his active mind
revolted against the tame life he was leading, and
craved for adventure and excitement. He was not
of the stuff to play the part of *petit maître* in the
second-rate society of Boulogne. So he determined
to carry out his long-cherished project of studying
the "inner life of Moslem," a task for which he
possessed unique qualifications. Therefore, soon after
the Arundells had left Boulogne, he made up his mind
to go to Mecca. He obtained a year's further leave
to carry out his daring project. In 1853 he left
England disguised as a Persian Mirza, a disguise
which he assumed with so much success that, when

he landed at Alexandria, he was recognized and blessed
as a true Moslem by the native population. From
Alexandria he went to Cairo disguised as a dervish,
and lived there some months as a native. Thence he
travelled to Suez, and crossed in an open boat with a
party of Arab pilgrims to Yambú. The rest of his
dare-devil adventures and hair-breadth escapes—how
he attached himself to the Damascus caravan and
journeyed with the pilgrims to Mecca in spite of the
fiery heat and the scorching sands, how he braved
many dangers and the constant dread of " detection "
—is written by him in his *Pilgrimage to Mecca and El
Medinah*, and is touched upon again in Lady Burton's
Life of her husband. The story needs no re-telling
here. Suffice it to say that Burton was the first man
not a Mussulman who penetrated to the innermost
sanctuary of Moslem, and saw the shrine where the
coffin of Mohammed swings between heaven and earth.
He did the circumambulation at the Harem ; he was
admitted to the house of our Lord; he went to the
well Zemzem, the holy water of Mecca; he visited
Ka'abah, the holy grail of the Moslems, and kissed the
famous black stone ; he spent the night in the Mosque ;
and he journeyed to Arafat and saw the reputed tomb
of Adam. He was not a man to do things by halves,
and he inspected Mecca thoroughly, absolutely *living
the life* of the Mussulman, adopting the manners,
eating the food, wearing the clothes, conforming to
the ritual, joining in the prayers and sacrifices, and
speaking the language. He did all this, literally
carrying his life in his hand, for at any moment he

BURTON ON HIS PILGRIMAGE TO MECCA. 	[*Page* 70.

might have been detected—one false step, one hasty
word, one prayer unsaid, one trifling custom of the
shibboleth omitted, and the dog of an infidel who had
dared to profane the sanctuary of Mecca and Medinah
would have been found out, and his bones would
have whitened the desert sand. Quite apart from
the physical fatigue, the mental strain must have been
acute. But Burton survived it all, and departed from
Mecca as he came, slowly wending his way with a caravan across the desert to Jeddah, whence he returned up
the Red Sea to Egypt. There he sojourned for a space ;
but his leave being up, he returned to Bombay.

The news of his marvellous pilgrimage was soon
noised abroad, and travelled home ; all sorts of rumours
flew about, though it was not until the following year
that his book, giving a full and detailed account of his
visit to Mecca, came out. Burton's name was on the
lips of many. But he was in India, and did not come
home to reap the reward of his daring, nor did he
know that one faithful heart was full of joy and
thanksgiving at his safety and pride at his renown.
He did not know that the " little girl " he had met
now and again casually at Boulogne was thinking of
him every hour of the day, dreaming of him every
night, praying every morning and evening and at the
altar of her Lord, with all the fervour of her pure soul,
that God would keep him now and always, and bring
him back safe and sound, and in His own good time
teach him to love her. He did not know. How
could he ? He had not yet sounded the height, depth,
and breadth of a woman's love. And yet, who shall

say that her supplications were unheeded before the throne of God ?   Who shall say that it was not Isabel's prayers, quite as much as Richard Burton's skill and daring, which shielded him from danger and detection and carried him safe through all ?

In Isabel's diary at this time there occurs the following note :

" Richard has just come back with flying colours from Mecca ; but instead of coming home, he has gone to Bombay to rejoin his regiment.   I glory in his glory. God be thanked ! "

Then a sense of desolation and hopelessness sweeps over her soul, for she writes :

" But I am alone and unloved.   Love can illumine the dark roof of poverty, and can lighten the fetters of a slave ; the most miserable position of humanity is tolerable with its support, and the most splendid irksome without its inspiration.   Whatever harsher feelings life may develop, there is no one whose brow will not grow pensive at some tender reminiscence, whose heart will not be touched.   Oh if I could but go through life trusting one faithful heart and pressing one dear hand !   Is there no hope for me ?   I am so full of faith.   Is there no pity for so much love ?   It makes my heart ache, this future of desolation and distress ; it ever flits like the thought of death before my eyes.   There is no more joy for me ; the lustre of life is gone.   How swiftly my sorrow followed my joy !   I can laugh, dance, and sing as others do, but there is a dull gnawing always at my heart that wearies me.   There is an end of love for me, and of all the

bright hopes that make the lives of other girls happy
and warm and pleasant."

Burton did not stay long at Bombay after he rejoined
his regiment. He was not popular in it, and he disliked the routine. Something of the old prejudice
against him in certain quarters was revived. The
East India Company, in whose service he was, had
longed wished to explore Harar in Somaliland,
Abyssinia; but it was inhabited by a very wild and
savage people, and no white man had ever dared to
enter it. So it was just the place for Richard Burton,
and he persuaded the Governor of Bombay to sanction
an expedition to Harar ; and with three companions,
Lieutenant Herne, Lieutenant Stroyan, and Lieutenant
Speke, he started for Harar.

From her watch-tower afar off, Isabel, whose ceaseless
love followed him night and day, notes :

"And now Richard has gone to Harar, a deadly
expedition or a most dangerous one, and I am full of
sad forebodings. Will he never come home ? How
strange it all is, and how I still trust in Fate ! The
Crimean War is declared, and troops begin to go out."

When Burton's little expedition arrived at Aden
en route for Harar, the four men who composed it
parted and resolved to enter Harar by different ways.
Speke failed ; Herne and Stroyan succeeded. Burton
reserved for himself the post of danger. Harar was
as difficult to enter as Mecca; there was a tradition
there that when the first white man entered the city
Harar would fall. Nevertheless, after a journey
of four months through savage tribes and the desert,

Burton entered it disguised as an Arab merchant, and stayed there ten days.[1]   He returned to Aden.   Five weeks later he got up a new expedition to Harar on a much larger scale, with which he wanted to proceed Nilewards.   The expedition sailed for Berberah. Arriving there, the four leaders, Burton, Speke, Stroyan, and Herne, went ashore and pitched their tent, leaving the others on board.   At night they were surprised by more than three hundred Somali, and after desperate fighting cut their way back to the boat.   Stroyan was killed, Herne untouched, and Speke and Burton wounded.

A little later the following note occurs in Isabel's diary :

"We got the news of Richard's magnificent ride to Harar, of his staying ten days in Harar, of his wonderful ride back, his most daring expedition, and then we heard of the dreadful attack by the natives in his tent, and how Stroyan was killed, Herne untouched, Speke with eleven wounds, and Richard with a lance through his jaw.   They escaped in a native dhow to Aden, and it was doubtful whether Richard would recover.   Doubtless this is the danger alluded to by the clairvoyant, and the cause of my horrible dreams concerning him about the time it happened. I hope to Heaven he will not go back !   How can I be grateful enough for his escape ! "

Burton did not go back.   He was so badly wounded that he had to return to England on sick leave, and sorely discomfited.   Here his wounds soon healed, and

[1] *Vide* Burton's *First Footsteps in Africa.*

he regained his health. He read an account of his journey to Harar before the Royal Geographical Society; but the paper attracted little or no attention, one reason being that the public interest was at that time absorbed in the Crimean War. Strange to say, the paper, until it was over, did not reach the ears of Isabel, nor did she once see the man on whom all her thoughts were fixed during his stay in England. It was of course impossible for her to take the initiative. Moreover, Burton was invalided most of the time, and in London but little. His visit to England was a short one. After a month's rest he obtained leave—after considerable difficulty, for he was no favourite with the War Office— to start for the Crimea, and reached there in October, 1854. He had some difficulty in obtaining a post, but at last he became attached to General Beatson's staff, and was the organizer of the Irregular Cavalry (Beatson's Horse : the Bashi-bazouks), a fact duly noted in Isabel's diary.

The winter of 1854-55 was a terrible one for our troops in the Crimea, and public feeling in England was sorely exercised by the account of their sufferings and privations. The daughters of England were not backward in their efforts to aid the troops. Florence Nightingale and her staff of nurses were doing their noble work in the army hospitals at Scutari ; and it was characteristic of Isabel that she should move heaven and earth to join them. In her journal at this time we find the following :

" It has been an awful winter in the Crimea. I have given up reading the *Times* ; it makes me so miserable,

and one is so impotent. I have made three struggles
to be allowed to join Florence Nightingale. How I
envy the women who are allowed to go out as nurses!
I have written again and again to Florence Nightingale;
but the superintendent has answered me that I am too
young and inexperienced, and will not do."

But she could not be idle. She could not sit with
folded hands and think of her dear one and her brave
countrymen out yonder suffering untold privations,
and do nothing. It was not enough for her to weep
and hope and pray. So the next thing she thought
of was a scheme for aiding the almost destitute wives
and families of the soldiers, a work which, if she had
done nothing else, should be sufficient to keep her
memory green, prompted as it was by that generous,
loving heart of hers, which ever found its chiefest
happiness in doing good to others. She thus describes
her scheme :

" I set to work to form a girls' club composed of
girls. My plan was to be some little use at home.
First it was called the 'Whistle Club,' because we
all had tiny silver whistles ; and then we changed it
to the 'Stella Club,' in honour of the morning star—
my star. Our principal object was to do good at home
amongst the destitute families of soldiers away in the
Crimea ; to do the same things as those we would have
done if we had the chance out yonder amongst the
soldiers themselves. We started a subscription soup-
cauldron and a clothing collection, and we got from
the different barracks a list of the women and their
children married, with or without leave. We ascertained

their real character and situations, and no destitute
woman was to be left out, nor any difference made
on account of religion. The women were to have
employment ; the children put to schools according to
their respective religions, and sent to their own churches.
Lodging, food, and clothes were given according to
our means, and words of comfort to all, teaching the
poor creatures to trust in God for themselves and their
husbands at the war—the only One from whom we
could all expect mercy. We undertook the wives and
families of all regiments of the Lifeguards and Blues
and the three Guards' regiments. We went the rounds
twice a week, and met at the club once a week. There
were three girls to each locality ; all of us dressed
plainly and behaved very quietly, and acknowledged
no acquaintances while going our rounds. We carried
this out to the letter, and I cannot attempt to describe
the scenes of misery we saw, nor the homes that we
saved, nor the gratitude of the soldiers later when they
returned from the war and found what we had done.
It has been a most wonderful success, and I am very
happy at having been of some use. The girls responded
to the rules, which were rigorously carried out ; and
when I look at my own share of the business, and
multiply that by a hundred and fifty girls, I think
the good done must have been great. In ten days,
by shillings and sixpences, I alone collected a hundred
guineas, not counting what the others did. My beat
contained one hundred women of all creeds and situations, and about two hundred children. I spared no
time nor exertions over and above the established rules.

I read and wrote their letters, visited the sick and
dying, and did a number of other things.

"I know now the misery of London, and in making
my rounds I could give details that would come up
to some of the descriptions in *The Mysteries of Paris*
or a shilling shocker. In many cellars, garrets, and
courts policemen warned me not to enter, and told
me that four or five of them could not go in
without being attacked ; but I always said to them,
'You go to catch some rogue, but I go to take the
women something ; they will not hurt me ; but I should
be glad if you waited outside in case I do not come
out again.' But the ruffians hanging about soon
learnt my errand, and would draw back, touch their
caps, move anything out of my way, and give me a
kind good-day as I passed, or show me to any door
that I was not sure of. Some people have been a little
hard on me for being the same to the fallen women as
to the good ones. But I do hate the way we women
come down upon each other. Those who are the
loudest in severity are generally the first to fall when
temptation comes : and who of us might not do so
but for God's grace ? I like simplicity and large-minded
conduct in all things, whether it be in a matter of
religion or heart or the world, and I think the more
one knows the simpler one acts. I have the consolation of knowing that all the poor women are now doing
well and earning an honest livelihood, the children
fed, clothed and lodged, educated and brought up in
the fear and love of God, and in many a soldier's
home my name is coupled with a blessing and a

prayer. They send me a report of themselves now once a month, and I love the salute of many an honest and brave fellow as he passes me in the street with his medal and clasps, and many have said, ' But for you I should have found no home on my return.' "

After the fall of Sebastopol the war was virtually at an end, and the allied armies wintered amid its ruins. The treaty of peace was signed at Paris on March 30, 1856. Five months before the signing of the treaty Richard Burton returned home with General Beatson, his commander-in-chief, who was then involved in an unfortunate controversy. An evil genius seemed to follow Burton's military career, and it pursued him from India to the Crimea. He managed to enrage Lord Stratford so much that he called him " the most impudent man in the Bombay army." He was certainly one of the most unlucky, even in his choice of chiefs. Sir Charles Napier, under whom he served in India, was far from popular with his superiors ; and General Beatson was always in hot water. The Beatson trial was the result of one of the many muddles which arose during the Crimean War ; it took place in London in the spring (1856), and Burton gave evidence in favour of his chief. But this is by the way. What we are chiefly concerned with is the following line in Isabel's diary, written soon after his return to England :

" I hear that Richard has come home, and is in town. God be praised ! "

That which followed will be told in her own words.

CHAPTER VI

RICHARD LOVES ME

(1856—1857)

Daughter of nobles, who thine aim shalt gain,
Hear gladdest news, nor fear aught hurt or bane.

ALF LAYLAH WA LAYLAH
(*Burton's "Arabian Nights"*).

NOW this is what occurred. When Richard was well home from the Crimea, and had attended Beatson's trial, he began to turn his attention to the " Unveiling of Isis " ; in other words, to discover the sources of the Nile, the lake regions of Central Africa, on which his heart had long been set ; and he passed most of his time in London working it up.

We did not meet for some months after his return, though we were both in London, he planning his Central African expedition, and I involved in the gaieties of the season ; for we had a gay season that year, every one being glad that the war was over. In June I went to Ascot. There, amid the crowd of the racecourse, I met Hagar Burton, the gypsy, for the first time after many years, and I shook hands with her. " Are you Daisy Burton yet ? " was her

first question. I shook my head. "Would to God
I were!" Her face lit up. "Patience; it is just
coming." She waved her hand, for at that moment
she was rudely thrust from the carriage. I never saw
her again, but I was engaged to Richard two months
later. It came in this wise.

One fine day in August I was walking in the
Botanical Gardens with my sister. Richard was there.
We immediately stopped and shook hands, and asked
each other a thousand questions of the four intervening
years; and all the old Boulogne memories and feelings
returned to me. He asked me if I came to the
Gardens often. I said, "Oh yes, we always come and
read and study here from eleven to one, because it is
so much nicer than studying in the hot room at this
season." "That is quite right," he said. "What are
you studying?" I held up the book I had with me
that day, an old friend, Disraeli's *Tancred*, the book
of my heart and taste, which he explained to me. We
were in the Gardens about an hour, and when I had
to leave he gave me a peculiar look, as he did at
Boulogne. I hardly looked at him, yet I felt it, and
had to turn away. When I got home, my mind was
full of wonder and presentiment; I felt frightened and
agitated; and I looked at myself in the glass and
thought myself a fright!

Next morning we went to the Botanical Gardens
again. When we got there, he was there too, alone,
composing some poetry to show to Monckton Milnes
on some pet subject. He came forward, and said
laughingly, "You won't chalk up 'Mother will be

angry,' as you did when you were at Boulogne, when
I used to want to speak to you." So we walked and
talked over old times and people and things in general.

About the third day his manner gradually altered
towards me ; we had begun to know each other, and
what might have been an ideal love before was now
a reality. This went on for a fortnight. I trod
on air.

At the end of a fortnight he stole his arm round
my waist, and laid his cheek against mine and asked
me, " Could you do anything so sickly as to give up
civilization? And if I can get the Consulate of Damascus,
will you marry me and go and live there ? " He said,
,' Do not give me an answer now, because it will mean
a very serious step for you—no less than giving up
your people and all that you are used to, and living
the sort of life that Lady Hester Stanhope led. I see
the capabilities in you, but you must think it over."
I was long silent from emotion ; it was just as if the
moon had tumbled down and said, " You have cried
for me for so long that I have come." But he, who
did not know of my long love, thought I was thinking
worldly thoughts, and said, " Forgive me ; I ought not
to have asked so much." At last I found voice, and
said, " I do not want to think it over—I have been
thinking it over for six years, ever since I first saw
you at Boulogne. I have prayed for you every morning
and night, I have followed all your career minutely,
I have read every word you ever wrote, and I would
rather have a crust and a tent with you than be queen
of all the world ; and so I say now, ' Yes, *yes*, YES ! ' "

I will pass over the next few minutes. . . .

Then he said, "Your people will not give you to me." I answered, "I know that, but I belong to myself—I give myself away." "That is all right," he answered ; "be firm, and so shall I."

I would have suffered six years more for such a day, such a moment as this. All past sorrow was forgotten in it. All that has been written or said on the subject of the first kiss is trash compared to the reality. Men might as well undertake to describe Eternity. I then told him all about my six years since I first met him, and all that I had suffered.

When I got home, I knelt down and prayed, and my whole soul was flooded with joy and thanksgiving. A few weeks ago I little thought what a change would take place in my circumstances. Now I mused thus : "Truly we never know from one half-hour to another what will happen. Life is like travelling in an open carriage with one's back to the horses—you see the path, you have an indistinct notion of the sides, but none whatever of where you are going. If ever any one had an excuse for superstition and fatalism, I have. Was it not foretold ? And now I have gained half the desire of my life : he loves me. But the other half remains unfulfilled : he wants to marry me ! Perhaps I must not regret the misery that has spoilt the six best years of my life. But must I wait again ? What can I do to gain the end ? Nothing ! My whole heart and mind is fixed on this marriage. If I cared less, I could plan some course of action; but my heart and head are not cool enough. Providence and fate must decide my future. I feel all my own weakness and nothingness. I am as humble as a little child. Richard has the upper hand now, and I feel that I have at last met the master who can subdue me. They say it is better to marry one who loves and is subject to you than one whose slave you are through love. But I cannot agree to this. Where in such a case is the pleasure, the excitement, the interest? In one sense I have no more reason to fear for my future, now that the load of shame, wounded pride, and unrequited affection is lifted from my brow and soul. He loves me—that is enough to-day."

After this Richard visited a little at our house as an acquaintance, having been introduced at Boulogne ; and he fascinated, amused, and pleasantly shocked my mother, but completely magnetized my father and all my brothers and sisters. My father used to say, " I do not know what it is about that man, but I cannot get him out of my head; I dream about him every night."

Richard and I had one brief fortnight of uninterrupted happiness, and were all in all to each other; but inasmuch as he was to go away directly on his African journey with Speke to the future lake regions of Central Africa, we judged it ill advised to announce the engagement to my mother, for it would have brought a hornets' nest about our heads, and not furthered our cause—and, besides, we were afraid of my being sent away, or of being otherwise watched and hindered from our meeting ; so we agreed to keep it a secret until he came back. The worst of it all was, that I was unable, first, by reason of no posts from a certain point, and, secondly, by the certainty of having his letters opened and read, to receive many letters from him, and those only the most cautious ; but I could write to him as freely as possible, and send them to the centres where his mail-bags would be sent out to him. All my happiness therefore was buried deep in my heart, but always was chained. I felt as if earth had passed and heaven had begun, or as if I had hitherto been somebody else, or had lived in some other world. But even this rose had its thorn, and that was the knowledge that our marriage seemed very far off. The idea of waiting for willing parents and a grateful country appeared so distant that I should scarcely be worth the having by the time all obstacles were removed. Richard too was exercised about how I should be able to support his hard life, and whether a woman could really do it. Another sorrow was that I had to be prepared to lose him at any moment, as he might have to quit at a moment's notice on receiving certain information.

I gave him Hagar Burton's horoscope, written in Romany—the horoscope of my future. One morning (October 3) I went to meet him as usual, and we agreed to meet the following morning. He had traced for me a little sketch of what he expected to find in the lake regions, and I placed round his neck a medal of the Blessed Virgin upon a steel chain, which we Catholics commonly call " the miraculous medal." He promised me he would wear it throughout his journey, and show it me on his return. I had offered it to him on a gold chain, but he said, " Take away the gold chain ; they will cut my throat for it out there."

He showed me the steel chain round his neck when he came back ; he wore it all his life, and it is buried with him.   He also gave me a little poem :

> I wore thine image, Fame,
> Within a heart well fit to be thy shrine;
> Others a thousand boons may gain—
>   One wish was mine:
>
> The hope to gain one smile,
> To dwell one moment cradled on thy breast,
> Then close my eyes, bid life farewell,
>   And take my rest!
>
> And now I see a glorious hand
> Beckon me out of dark despair,
> Hear a glorious voice command,
>   " Up, bravely dare !
>
> And if to leave a deeper trace
> On earth to thee Time, Fate, deny,
> Drown vain regrets, and have the grace
>   Silent to die."
>
> She pointed to a grisly land,
> Where all breathes death—earth, sea, and air;
> Her glorious accents sound once more,
>   " Go meet me there."
>
> Mine ear will hear no other sound,
> No other thought my heart will know.
> Is this a sin ? " Oh, pardon, Lord !
>   Thou mad'st me so!"
>
>   R. F. B.

The afternoon on which I last met him was the afternoon of the same day. He came to call on my mother. We only talked formally. I thought I was going to see him on the morrow. It chanced that we were going to the play that night. I begged of

him to come, and he said he would if he could, but
that if he did not, I was to know that he had some
heavy business to transact. When I had left him in
the morning, I little thought it was the last kiss, or I
could never have said good-bye, and I suppose he knew
that and wished to spare me pain. How many little
things I could have said or done that I did not ! We
met of course before my mother only as friends. He
appeared to me to be agitated, and I could not account
for his agitation. He stayed about an hour ; and when
he left I said purposely, " I hope we shall see you on
your return from Africa," and almost laughed outright,
because I thought we should meet on the morrow.
He gave me a long, long look at the door, and I ran
out on the balcony and kissed my hand to him, and
thus thoughtlessly took my last look, quite unprepared
for what followed.

I went to the theatre that evening quite happy, and
expected him. At 10.30 I thought I saw him at the
other side of the house looking into our box. I smiled,
and made a sign for him to come. I then ceased to
see him ; the minutes passed, and he did not come.
Something cold struck my heart ; I felt that I should
not see him again, and I moved to the back of the
box, and, unseen, the tears streamed down my face.
The old proverb kept haunting me like an air one
cannot get out of one's head, " There's many a true
word spoken in jest." The piece was *Pizarro*, and
happily for me Cora was bewailing her husband's loss
on the stage, and as I am invariably soft at tragedy
my distress caused no sensation.

I passed a feverish, restless night ; I could not sleep ; I felt that I could not wait till morning—I must see him. At last I dozed and started up, but I touched nothing, yet dreamt I could feel his arms round me. I understood him, and he said, " I am going now, my poor girl. My time is up, and I have gone ; but I will come again—I shall be back in less than three years. I am your Destiny."

He pointed to the clock, and it was two. He held up a letter, looked at me long with those gypsy eyes of his, put the letter down on the table, and said in the same way, " That is for your sister—not for you." He went to the door, gave me another of those long peculiar looks, and I saw him no more.

I sprang out of bed to the door into the passage (there was nothing), and thence I went to the room of one of my brothers, in whom I confided. I threw myself on the ground and cried my heart out. He got up and asked what ailed me, and tried to soothe and comfort me. " Richard is gone to Africa," I said, " and I shall not see him for three years." " Nonsense," he replied ; " you have only got a nightmare ; it was that lobster you had for supper ; you told me he was coming to-morrow." " So I did," I sobbed ; " but I have seen him in a dream, and he told me he had gone ; and if you will wait till the post comes in, you will see that I have told you truly."

I sat all night in my brother's armchair, and at eight o'clock in the morning when the post came in there was a letter for my sister Blanche, enclosing one for me. Richard had found it too painful to part from me, and

thought we should suffer less that way ; he begged her
to break it gently to me, and to give me the letter, which
assured me we should be reunited in 1859, as we were
on May 22 that year. He had received some secret
information, which caused him to leave England at once
and quietly, lest he should be detained as witness at some
trial. He had left his lodgings in London at 10.30
the preceding evening (when I saw him in the theatre),
and sailed at two o'clock from Southampton (when I
saw him in my room).

I believe there is a strong sympathy between some
people (it was not so well known then, but it is quite
recognized now)—so strong that, if they concentrate their
minds on each other at a particular moment and at the
same time, and each wills strongly to be together, the
will can produce this effect, though we do not yet
understand how or why. When I could collect my
scattered senses, I sat down and wrote to Richard all
about this, in the event of my being able to send it
to him.

But to return. At 8.30 Blanche came into the room
with the letter I have mentioned, to break the sad news
to me. "Good heavens ! " she said, " what has happened
to you? You look dreadful ! " " Richard is gone ! "
I gasped out. " How did you know?" she asked.
" Because I saw him here in the night ! " "That will
do you the most good now," she said. The tears
came into her eyes as she put a letter from Richard into
my hand, enclosed in one to herself, the one I had seen
in the night. The letter was a great comfort to me,
and I wore it round my neck in a little bag. Curiously

enough I had to post my letter to him to Trieste—the place where in after-life we spent many years—by his direction. It was the last exertion I was capable of ; the next few days I spent in my bed.

My happiness had been short and bright, and now I had to look forward to three years of my former patient endurance, only with this great change : before I was unloved and had no hope ; now the shame of loving unasked was taken from me, and I had the happiness of being loved, and some future to look forward to. When I got a little better, I wrote the following reflections to myself :

" A woman feels raised by the love of a man to whom she has given her whole heart, but not if she feels that she loves and does not respect, or that he fails in some point, and for such-and-such reasons she would not marry him. But when she loves without reserve, she holds her head more proudly, from the consciousness of being loved by him—no matter what the circumstances. So I felt with Richard, for he is above all men—so noble, so manly, with such a perfect absence of all meanness and hypocrisy. It is true I was captivated at first sight; but his immense talents and adventurous life compelled interest, and a master-mind like his exercises influence over all around it. But I *love* him, because I find in him depth of feeling, a generous heart, and because, though brave as a lion, he is yet a gentle, delicate, sensitive nature, and the soul of honour. Also he is calculated to appear as something unique and romantic in a woman's eyes, especially because he unites the wild, lawless creature

and the gentleman. He is the latter in every sense of
the word, a stamp of the man of the world of the best
sort, for he has seen things without the artificial
atmosphere of St. James's as well as within it. I
worship ambition. Fancy achieving a good which
affects millions, making your name a national name !
It is infamous the way half the men in the world live
and die, and are never missed, and, like a woman, leave
nothing behind them but a tombstone. By ambition
I mean men who have the will and power to change
the face of things. I wish I were a man : if I were, I
would be Richard Burton. But as I am a woman,
I would be Richard Burton's wife. I love him purely,
passionately, and devotedly : there is no void in my
heart ; it is at rest for ever with him. For six years
this has been part of my nature, part of myself, the
basis of all my actions, even part of my religion ; my
whole soul is absorbed in it. I have given my every
feeling to him, and kept back nothing for myself or
the world ; and I would this moment sacrifice and
leave all to follow his fortunes, were it his wish, or for
his good. Whatever the world may condemn in him
of lawless actions or strong opinions, whatever he is to
the world, he is perfect to me ; and I would not have
him otherwise than he is—except in spiritual matters.
This last point troubles me. I have been brought up
strictly, and have been given clear ideas on all subjects
of religion and principle, and have always tried to live
up to them. When I am in his presence, I am not
myself—he makes me for the time see things with his
own eyes, like a fever or a momentary madness ; and

when I am alone again, I recall my own belief and ways of thinking, which remain unchanged, and am frightened at my weak wavering and his dangerous but irresistible society.   He is gone ; but had I the chance now, I would give years of my life to hear that dear voice again, with all its devilry.   I have no right to love a man who calls himself a complete materialist, who has studied almost, I might say, beyond the depth of knowledge, who professes to acknowledge no God, no law, human or divine.   Yet I do feel a close suspicion that he has much more feeling and belief than he likes to have the credit of."

After Richard was gone I got a letter from him dated from Bruges, October 9, telling me to write to Trieste, and that he would write from Trieste and Bombay.   I sent three letters to Trieste and six to Bombay.   He asked me if I was offended at his abrupt departure.   Ah, no!   I take the following from my diary of that time :

"I have now got into a state of listening for every post, every knock making the heart bound, and the sickening disappointment that ensues making it sink ; but I say to myself, 'If I am true, nothing can harm me.'   My delight is to sit down and write to him all and everything, just as it enters my head, as I would if I were with him.   My letters are half miserable, half jocose, for I do not want to put him out of spirits, whatever I may be myself.   I feel that my letters are a sort of mixture of love, trust, anger, faith, sarcasm, tenderness, bullying, melancholy, all mixed up. . . . He has arrived at Alexandria. . . . At any rate

my heart and affections are my own to give, I rob
no one, and so I will remain. I have a happy home,
family, society, all I want, and I shall not clip my wings
of liberty except for him, whatever my lot may be. I
love and am loved, and so strike a balance in favour of
existence. No gilded misery for me. I was born for
love, and require it as air and light. Whatever harsh-
ness the future may bring, he has loved me, and my
future is bound up in him with all consequences. My
jealous heart spurns all compromise; it must have its
purpose or break. He thinks he is sacrificing me; but
I want pain, privations, danger with him. I have the
constitution and nerves for it. There are few places
I could not follow my husband, and be to him companion, friend, wife, and all. Where I could not so
follow him, I would not be a clog to him, for I am
tolerably independent."

Our friends used sometimes to talk about Richard at
this time and his expedition. Whilst they discussed
him as a public man, I was in downright pain lest they
should say something that I should not like. Father
told them that he was a friend of ours. I then practised
discussing him with the greatest *sang froid*, and of
course gave a vivid description of him, which inspired
great interest. His books, travels, and adventures
were talked of by many. I told Richard in one letter
that it was the case of the mouse and the lion ; but I
teased him by saying that when the mouse had nibbled
a hole big enough the lion forgot him because he was
so small, and put his big paw on him and crushed him
altogether. I knew that his hobby was reputation ; he

was great in the literary world, men's society, clubs,
and the Royal Geographical Society.   But I wished him
also to be great in the world of fashion, where my
despised sex is paramount.   I also knew that if a man
gets talked about in the right kind of way in handfuls
of the best society, here and there, his fame quickly
spreads.   I had plenty of opportunities to help him in
this way without his knowing it, and great was the
pleasure.   Again I fall back on my journal :

"I beg from God morning and night that Richard
may return safe.   Will the Almighty grant my prayer ?
I will not doubt, whether I hear from him or not.   I
believe that we often meet in spirit and often look at
the same star.   I have no doubt he often thinks of me ;
and when he returns and finds how faithful I have been,
all will be right.   There is another life if I lose this,
and there is always La Trappe left for the broken-
hearted.

"*Christmas Day*, 1856.—I was delighted to hear
father and mother praising Richard to-day ; mother
said he was so clever and agreeable and she liked him
so much, and they both seemed so interested about him.
They little knew how much they gratified me.   I was
reading a book ; but when the time came to put it away,
I found it had been upside-down all the time, so I fancy
I was more absorbed in their conversation than its
contents.   I have been trying to make out when it is
midnight in Eastern Africa, and when the morning star
shines there, and I have made out that at 10 p.m. it is
midnight there, and the morning star shines on him
two hours before it does on me.

" *January* 2, 1857.—I see by the papers that Richard left Bombay for Zanzibar with Lieutenant Speke on December 2 last. I am struck by the remembrance that it was on that very night that I was so ill and delirious. I dreamt I saw him sailing away and he spoke to me, but I thought my brain throbbed so loud that I could not hear him. I was quite taken off my guard to-day on hearing the news read out from the *Times*, so that even my mother asked me what was the matter. I have not had a letter; I might get one in a fortnight; but I must meet this uncertainty with confidence, and not let my love be dependent on any action of his, because he is a strange man and not as other men.

" *January* 18.—Unless to-morrow's mail brings me a letter, my hope is gone. What is the cause of his silence I cannot imagine. If he had not said he would write, I could understand it. But nothing shall alter my course. It is three months since he left, and I have only had two letters; yet I feel confident that Richard will be true, and I will try to deserve what I desire, so that I shall always have self-consolation. My only desire is that he may return safe to me with changed religious feelings, and that I may be his wife with my parents' consent. Suspense is a trial which I must bear for two years without a murmur. I must trust and pray to God ; I must keep my faith in Him, and live a quiet life, employ myself only in endeavouring to make myself worthy; and surely this conduct will bring its reward."

CHAPTER VII

MY CONTINENTAL TOUR: ITALY

(1857—1858)

Leave thy home for abroad an wouldst rise on high,
And travel whence benefits fivefold arise—
The soothing of sorrow and winning of bread,
Knowledge, manners, and commerce with good men and wise;
And they say that in travel are travail and care,
And disunion of friends and much hardship that tries.

ALF LAYLAH WA LAYLAH
(*Burton's "Arabian Nights"*).

IN August, 1857, nearly a year after Richard had gone, my sister Blanche married Mr. Smyth Pigott, of Brockley Court, Somerset, and after the honeymoon was over they asked me to travel abroad with them. I was glad to go, for it helped the weary waiting for Richard, who was far away in Central Africa.

On September 30 we all took a farewell dinner together, and were very much inclined to choke over it, as we were about to disperse for some time, and poor mother especially was upset at losing her two girls. On that occasion she indulged in a witticism. She told me that she had heard by a little bird that I was fond

of Richard ; but little thinking she was speaking anything in earnest, she said, " Well, if you marry that
man, you will have sold your birthright not for a mess
of pottage, but for Burton ale." I quickly answered her
back again, " Well, a little bird told me that you were
ordered an immense quantity of it all the time you
were in the family way with me, so that if anything
does happen we shall call it heredity," upon which we
both laughed. We all left home at six o'clock for
London Bridge Station : we—my sister, her husband,
and myself—to go on the journey, and the rest of the
family came with us to see us off.

We had a beautiful passage of six and a half hours,
and slept in rugs on deck. There was a splendid moon
and starlight. About three o'clock in the morning
the captain made friends with me, and talked about
yachting. He had been nearly all over the world.
The morning star was very brilliant, and I always
look at it with particular affection when I am on board
ship, thinking that what I love best lies under it. We
got to the station at Dieppe at 7.30 a.m. ; and then
ensued a tedious journey to Paris.

The next day we drove about Paris, and then went
to the Palais Royal, Trois Frères Provenceaux, where
we dined in a dear little place called a *cabinet*, very
like an opera-box. It was my first experience of that
sort of thing. The *cabinet* overlooked the arcade and
garden. We had a most *recherché* little dinner, and
only one thing was wanting to make it perfect enjoyment to me. The Pigotts sat together on one side of
the table, and I—alone on the other. I put a place

for Richard by me. After dinner we strolled along
the principal boulevards. I can easily understand a
Parisian not liking to live out of Paris. We saw it
to great advantage that night—a beautiful moon and
clear, sharp air.

This day (October 3) last year how wretched and
truly miserable I was ! On the evening of this day
Richard left ! We drove out and went to the Pré de
Catalan, where there was music, dancing, and other
performances. We went to the opera in the evening.
A *petit souper* afterwards. This night last year was a
memorable one. If Richard be living, he will remember
me now ; it was the night of my parting with him a
year ago when he went to Africa for three years.

We left Paris three days later ; arrived at Lyons 7 a.m.
The next morning breakfasted, dogs and all, and were at
Marseilles at 5 p.m. I should have been glad to stay
longer at Marseilles ; I thought it the most curious
and picturesque place I had ever seen. We arrived just
too late for the diligence. There was no steamer. A
veterino was so slow, and we could not remain till
Saturday, so we did not know what to do. At last we
discovered that a French merchant vessel was going to
sail at 8 o'clock p.m. ; but it was a pitch-dark night, and
there was a strong, hard wind, or mistral, with the sea
running very high. However, we held a consultation,
and agreed we would do it for economy ; so we got
our berths, and went and dined at the Hôtel des
Ambassadeurs, *table d'hôte*, where I sat by a cousin of
Billy Johnson, a traveller and linguist. We fraternized, and he made himself as agreeable as only such

men can.   After dinner we went on board, and all the
passengers went down to their berths.   I dressed myself
in nautical rig, and went on deck to see all that I could.
We passed the Isle d'Hyères and the Château d'If of
Monte Christo.   We could not go between the rocks,
owing to the mistral.   The moon arose, it blew hard,
and we shipped heavy seas.   The old tub creaked and
groaned and lurched, and every now and then bid fair
to stand on beam-ends.   Being afraid of going to sleep,
I lashed myself to a bench ; two Frenchmen joined me,
one a professor of music, the other rather a rough
diamond, who could speak a mouthful of several
languages, had travelled a little, and he treated me to a
description of India, and told me all the old stories
English girls hear from their military brothers and
cousins from the cradle.   Every time we shipped a sea
all the French, Italian, and Spanish passengers gave
prolonged howls and clung to each other ; it might
have been an Irish wake.   They were so frightfully sick,
poor things !   It hurt my inside to hear them, and it
was worse to see them.   Meanwhile my two companions
and I had pleasant conversation, not only on India,
but music and Paris.   By-and-by they too gradually
dropped off; so I went down and tumbled into my
berth, and slept soundly through the night.

I was aroused next morning by a steward redolent of
garlic.   Our maid shared the cabin with me, and treated
me to a scene like the deck of the preceding evening.
Why are maids always sick at sea, and have to be waited
on, poor things, by their mistresses who are not?   There
was such a noise, such heat and smells.   I slept till we

were in Nice Harbour. My sister and her husband
went off to find a house ; I cleared the baggage and
drove to the Hôtel Victoria, where we dined, and then
went to our new lodging.

I was not sorry to be housed, after being out two
days and two nights. I got up next morning at 6 a.m.;
there was a bright, beautiful sky, a dark blue sea, and
such a lightness in the air. I went out to look about
me. Nice is a very pretty town, tolerably clean, with
very high houses, beautiful mountains, and a perfect
sea, and balminess in the air. There is something
Moorish-looking about the people and place. I am
told there is no land between us and Tunis—three
hundred miles !—and that when the sirocco comes the
sand from the great desert blows across the sea on to
our windows. We have an African tree in our garden.
And Richard is over there in Africa.

My favourite occupation while at Nice was sitting
on the shingle with my face to the sea and towards
Africa. I hate myself because I cannot sketch. If
I could only exchange my musical talent for that,
I should be very happy. There is such a beautiful
variety in the Mediterranean : one day it looks like
undulating blue glass ; at others it is dark blue, rough,
and dashing, with white breakers on it ; but hardly
ever that dull yellowish green as in our Channel, which
makes one bilious to look at it. The sky is glorious,
so high and bright, so soft and clear, and the only
clouds you ever see are like little tufts of rose-coloured
wool. The best time to sit here is sunset. One does
not see the rays so distinctly in England ; and when the

sun sinks behind the hills of the frontier, there is such a purple, red, and gold tint on the sea and sky that many would pronounce it overdone or unnatural in a painting. A most exquisite pink shade is cast over the hills and town. There is one nice opera-house at Nice, one pretty church, a corso and terrace, where you go to hear the band and eat ices in the evening ; there is the reading club at Visconti's for ladies as well as men, where you can read and write and meet others and enjoy yourself. (I am talking of 1857.) Our apartments suit us very well. My portion consists of a nice lofty bedroom, a painted ceiling, furnished in English style, a little bathroom paved with red china, and a little sort of ante-drawing-room. My windows look over a little garden, where the African tree is, and the sea beyond, and beyond that again Africa and Richard.

We left Nice for Genoa at 5.30 on November 14, my sister, her husband, and self, in the *coupé*, which was very much like being packed as sardines—no room for legs. However, we were very jolly, only we got rather stiff during the twenty-four hours' journey ; for we only stopped twice—once for ten minutes at Oniglia at 4 a.m. for a cup of coffee, and once at noon next day for half an hour at another place to dine. However, I was too happy to grumble, having just received a letter saying that Richard would be home in next June, 1858 (he was not home for a year later) ; we smoked and chatted and slept alternately. The Cornice road is beautiful—a wild, lonely road in the mountains, with precipices, ravines, torrents, and passes of all descriptions : the sea beneath us on one side, and mountains covered with snow on the other. You seem to pass into all sorts of climates very speedily. On the land to our left was a fine starlight sky and clear, sharp air, and on the sea thunder and lightning and a white squall. There was always the excitement of imagining that a brigand might come or a torrent be impassable ; but alas ! not a ghost of an adventure, except once catching a milestone. I think the Whip Club would be puzzled at the driving : sometimes we have eleven horses, each with a different rein; to some the drivers whistle, to others they talk. It is tiresome work crawling up and down the mountains ; but when they do get a bit of plain ground, they seem to go ten miles an hour, tearing through narrow streets where there seems scarcely room for a sheet of paper between the diligence and the wall, whirling round sharp zigzag corners with not the width of a book between the wheel and the precipice, and that at full gallop. We created a great sensation at one of our halting-places, and indeed everywhere, for we were in our nautical rig; and what amused the natives immensely was that one of our terriers was a very long dog with short legs, and they talked of the yards of dog we had with us. We at last arrived at Genoa.

I liked Genoa far better than Nice : the sky is more Italian ; the sea looks as if it washed the town, or as if the town sprang out of it ; it is all so hilly. The town with its domes looks like white marble. The lower range of mountains is covered with monasteries, forts, pretty villas, and gardens ; the other ranges are covered with snow. There are six or seven fine streets, connected by a network of very narrow, oddly paved side-streets, whose tall houses nearly meet at the top ; they are picturesque, and look like the pictures of the Turkish bazaar. Mazzini is here, and the Government hourly expect an outbreak of the Republican party. The troops are under arms, and a transport with twelve hundred men from Turin and troops from Sardinia have arrived. The offer to the Neapolitan Government to expel the exiles is the cause. The police are hunting up Mazzini ; Garibaldi is here ; Lord Lyons' squadron is hourly expected.

I have been abroad now two months. I have had one unsatisfactory note from Richard ; he is coming back in June or July. Oh what a happiness and what anxiety ! In a few short months, please God, this dreadful separation will be over. Pray ! Pray ! ! Pray ! ! !

Monsieur Pernay spent an evening with me ; and seeing the picture on the wall of Richard in Meccan costume, he asked me what it was ; and on my telling him, he composed a valse on the spot, and called it " Richard in the Desert," and said he should compose a libretto on it. How I wish Richard were here ! It makes me quite envious when I see my sister and her husband. I am all alone, and Richard's place is vacant in the opera-box, in the carriage, and everywhere. Sometimes I dream he came back and would not speak to me, and I wake up with my pillow wet with tears.

My first exclamation as the clock struck twelve on St. Sylvester's night, 1857, as we all shook hands and

drank each other's health in a glass of punch at the
Café de la Concorde, was, " This year I shall see
Richard ! "

On the first Sunday of the year I went to hear Mass
at Saint Philip Neri, and then went to the post-office,
where a small boy pushed up against me and stole my
beloved picture of Richard out of my pocket. I did
not feel him do it, but a horrible idea of having lost
the picture came over me. I felt for it, and it was
gone ! I had a beautiful gold chain in my pocket, and
a purse with £25 ; yet the young rascal never touched
them, but seemed to know that I should care only for
the portrait. I instantly rushed off to every crier in
the town ; had two hundred *affiches* printed and stuck
up in every corner ; I put a paragraph in the papers ; I
asked every priest to give it out in the pulpit ; the
police, the post-office, every corner of the town was
warned. Of course I pretended it was a picture
of my brother. After three agonizing days and nights
an old woman brought it back, the frame gone, the
picture torn, rubbed, and smeared, which partly
effaced the expression of the face and made it look as
if it knew where it had been and how it had been
defiled. The story was that her little boy had found it
in that state in a dirty alley ; and thinking it was a
picture of Jesus Christ or a saint, took it home to his
little brother to keep him good when he was naughty,
and threw it in their toy cupboard. A poor priest
happened to dine with this poor family, and mentioned
the *affiche,* in which the words *ufficiale Inglese* as large
as my head appeared. The boys then produced the

wreck of the portrait, and asked if that could possibly be the article, and if it was really true that the Signorina was willing to give so much for it ; and the priest said " Yes," for the Signorina had wept much for the portrait of her favourite brother who was killed in the Crimea. So it was brought, and the simple Signorina gladly gave three napoleons to the old woman to know that she possessed all that remained of that much-loved face. But that boy—oh that boy !—got off scot-free, and the Signorina's reward did not induce any one to bring him to her. Doubtless, finding the stolen picture of no value to him, he had maltreated it and cast it in the gutter. How I could spank him !

We left Genoa at 9 a.m. on January 15. We wished good-bye to a crowd of friends inside and outside the hotel. We had a clean, roomy *veterino* with four capital little horses at the door charged with our luggage, a capital *vetturino* (coachman), and room for four inside and four out. A jolly party to fill it. It was agreed we should divide the expenses, take turns for the outside places, and be as good-humoured as possible. Luckily for me nobody cared for the box-seat, so I always got it. The first day we did thirty miles. Our halting-place for the day was Ruta, where something befell me. I lost my passport at Nervi, several miles back ; a village idiot to whom I gave a penny picked it up and sold it to a peasant woman for twelve sous, who happened to be riding on a mule into Ruta, and halted where we were feeding. Our *vetturino* (Emanuele) happened to see it and recognized it in her hand, bought it back again for twelve sous, and gave it to me. It would have been a fatal loss to me. Soon after sunset we halted for the night at Sestri ; the horses had done enough for the day. Four or five carriages had been attacked this winter, and there was a report of a large number of murders near Ancona, and there was no other sleeping-place to be reached that night. We soon had a capital fire, supper, and beds.

On this journey we planned out our day much as follows : We rose at daybreak and started ; we had breakfast in the carriage after three hours' drive. We passed our day in eating and drinking, laughing and talking, smoking and sleeping, and some mooning and sentimentalizing over the scenery : I the latter sort, and improving my Italian on the *vetturino*. We used to halt half-way two hours for the horses to rest and dinner, and then drive till dark where we halted for the night, ordered fire, supper, and beds, wrote out our journals, made our respective accounts, and smoked our cigarettes. The scenery and weather varied every day.

We slept a night at Sestri, and went on at daybreak. This day I had a terrible heartache ; to my horror we had a leader, the ghost of a white horse covered with sores, ridden by a fine, strapping wag of a youth, who told me his master was rich and stingy, and did not feed him, let alone the horse, which only had a mouthful when employed. I told him his master would go to hell, and he assured me smilingly that he was sure his soul was already there, and that it was only his body that was walking about. I asked him to sell the horse to me, and let me shoot him; but he shook his head and laughed. "You English treat your horses better than masters treat their servants in Italy," said he, as we topped the mountain. At my request Emanuele gave the poor beast a feed and sent him back, poor mass of skin and bones that it was. It was not fit to carry a fly, and I am told it was the best horse he had. That day our journey was a forty weary miles of black, barren ascent and descent, amongst snowy mountains, which looked as if man or beast had never trod there. Our halt was at Borghetto in the middle of the day. At the end of the forty miles came a delightful surprise. We were on a magnificent ridge of Maritime Alps covered with snow; a serpentine road led us down into a beautiful valley and Spezzia on the sea, the beautiful Gulf. The Croce di Malta was a comfortable little hotel. In half an hour we were round a roaring fire with a good supper.

Next morning we took a boat and explored the Gulf, the Source d'Eau, Lerici, where Byron and Shelley lived. That day was the Feast of Saint Anthony; the horses were blessed, which is a very amusing sight. It was the first night of the Carnival, and the Postilions' Ball, to which we were invited and went. It was full of peasant-girls and masqueraders; it was capital fun, and we danced all night. The costumes here are very pretty; they and the pronunciation change about every forty miles.

The day we went away we had great fun. The Magra had to be passed two hours from Spezzia;

it is a river with a bridge broken down. The peasants, working, look for all the world like diggers at the diggings; they are lawless enough to do anything. You get out and walk a mile amongst them; your carriage is embarked in a barge; it wades through and gets filled with water; the men at their pleasure upset it, or demand eighty francs or so. However, we were all game for anything that might occur, knowing how they treated others. Our *vetturino* was a regular brick—waded through with it without an accident; we walked through with all our money about us, dressing-cases in hand, our jackets with belts and daggers in them. One man became rather abusive; but we laughed at him, and gave him a universal chaffing. They followed us, and were annoying; but we swaggered along, and looked like people troubled with mosquitoes instead of ruffians, and not given to fainting and hysterics. So at last they were rather inclined to fraternize with us than otherwise. I suspect that they were accustomed to timid travellers. After this we passed Sarzana, a town of some consequence in these parts, with a castle and fortress. The weather this day was cold and biting, especially on the box-seat, and the scenery, except at Carrara, no great shakes. We found Carrara in a state of siege, and the troops occupied the hotel. Emanuele found a sort of stable, but we could get no food.

After this we proceeded by stages, and stopped some days at several places, and made long interior excursions, which I was often too tired to note. At last we arrived at Pisa. We had no trouble with the *douanier*.

When I entered the Tuscan frontier, I declared I would never say another word of French ; and Emanuele, who was a wag, sent all the *douaniers* to me ; but a franc, a smile, an assurance that we had nothing contraband, and the word was given to pass. We scarcely ever had our baggage touched ; but that was in 1858.

In Pisa we saw many things, including the Baptisteria, the Campanile or leaning tower, the Duomo, and the Sapienza, an object of interest to *me*, as Richard passed so much of his boyhood here, and that was his school. I regret to say the most debauched and ungentlemanly part of the population issued from this place, which distressed me, who held it sacred because of him. The Granda Bretagna was a very nice hotel, with a good *table d'hôte*, and all English. It had every comfort ; only, being full, we could only get small, dark rooms at the back, which was dull, and with nothing but stoves ; and the weather being bitter, we were petrified. We went a great deal to the Duomo and the Campo Santo, where the figures rather made us laugh, though I felt senti-mental enough about other things. At the top of the Campanile or leaning tower, or belfry, I found that Richard had chiselled his name, so I did the same. How curious it would have been if while he was doing it he could have said, " My future wife will also come and chisel hers, so many years later, in remembrance of me."

The man who shows the Campanile remembered Richard, and it was he who told me where he cut his name at the top of the tower.

The last day I was in Pisa (January 25) it was

our Princess Royal's wedding day. We had a grand dinner, champagne, toasts, and cheering. The *table d'hôte* was decorated with our yacht flags. One of the English ladies invited us to her rooms, where we had music and dancing, and I talked to one girl of seventeen, who proved to be an original after my own heart. After the *soirée*, we smoked a cigarette and discussed our plans. The next morning we had to leave Pisa. We were all sorry to part.

Half an hour's train brought us to Leghorn, where we got pretty rooms at the Victoria and Washington. It is quite spring weather, beautiful sky and sea ; again flat, ugly country, but the range of mountains shows to advantage ; the air is delicious, and we are all well and in spirits. The town is very fine, the people *tant-soit-peu-* Portsmouth-like. There is nothing to see at Leghorn. *Faute de mieux* we went to see an ugly duomo, which, however, contained Canova's Tempo, the one statue of which you hear from morning till night. We also visited the English Cemetery, which contained Smollett's tomb. There are the docks to see, and Habib's bazaar, a rogue, and not too civil, but he has beautiful Eastern things. The town is in a state of siege, and no Carnival is allowed.

We left Leghorn on February 1 for Florence, and visited successively many queer, little, out-of-the-way towns *en route*.

The first day at Florence we drove about to have a general view of the city, and after that we visited the principal palazzos, churches, and theatres—all of which have often been described before. We were at Florence nearly a month. We saw one Sunday's Carnival, one opera, one masked ball. We had several friends, who were anxious for us to stay, and go into society ; but time pressed, and we had to decline. Every evening we used to go to the theatre, and some of our friends would invite us to *petits soupers*. At Florence all Richard's friends, finding I knew his sister in England, were kind to us ; and we were very sorry to start at 3 a.m. on February 11 *en route* for Venice.

We were five individuals, with our baggage on our backs, turned into a rainy street, cutting a sorry figure and laughing at ourselves. The diligence started at once. We had twenty-one hours to Bologna, drawn by oxen at a foot's pace through the snow, which the *cantonniers* had cleared partially away, but which often lay in heaps of twelve or twenty feet untouched. I never saw such magnificent snow scenes as when crossing the Apennines. We slept at Bologna, saw it, and took a *vetturino* next day. The drive was a dreary, flat snow piece of forty miles in length. Malebergo was the only town. We here came across a horrid thing. Two men had fallen asleep in a hay-cart smoking ; it caught fire, burnt the men, cart, hay, and all. The horse ran away, had its hind-quarters burnt out, and they were all three dead, men and horse. It gave us a terrible turn, but we could do nothing. Next morning we were up at four o'clock. We crossed the river Po at seven o'clock ; it was bitter cold. We drove fifty miles that day ; the last twelve were very pretty. At length we reached Padua. The ground was like ice ; our off leader fell, and was dragged some little distance. (How

little I thought then that I should be a near neighbour
and frequent visitor of all these places during the
eighteen last years of my married life !)   When we left
Padua, we had twenty-seven miles more to go, where
we exchanged for the (to us girls) new wonder of a
gondola, which took us to the Hôtel Europa in Venice.
We were not sorry to have got through our journey,
and a blazing fire and a good supper and cigarette
soon effaced the memory of the cold, starvation, and
weariness we had gone through for so long.   We
wanted no rocking that night.

It is all very well writing ; but nothing I could
ever say would half express my enthusiasm for Venice.
It fulfils all the exigencies of romance; it is the
only thing that has never disappointed me.   I am so
happy at Venice.   Except for Richard's absence, I have
not another wish ungratified ; and I also like it because
this and Trieste were the last places he was in near
home when he started for Africa.

Not a night passes here that I do not dream that
Richard has come home and will not speak to me ; not
a day that I do not kneel down twice, praying that
God may send him a ray of divine grace, and bring
him to religion, and also, though I feel quite unworthy
of so high a mission, that I may be his wife, for I
so love and care for him that I should never have
courage to take upon myself the duties of married life
with any other man.   I have seen so much of married
life; have seen men so unjust, selfish, and provoking ;
and have always felt I never could receive an injury
from any man but him without everlasting resentment.

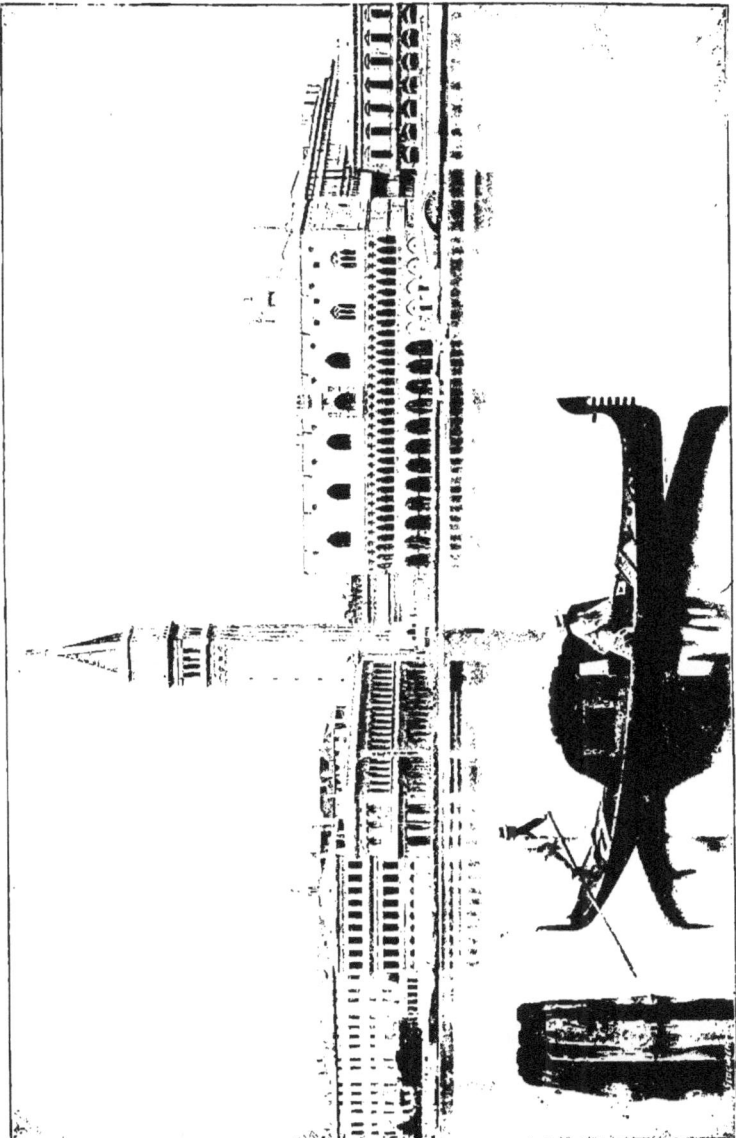

VENICE.

[Page 112.

Oh, if he should come home and have changed, it would break my heart! I would rather die than see that day!

We plan out our days here, rising at eight, breakfast nine, Mass, spending the morning with friends, music, reading, working, writing, reading French and Italian, and some sketching. At one o'clock we start to explore all the beautiful things to be seen here, then we go to a very cheerful *table d'hôte*, and afterwards spend a most agreeable evening in each other's apartments, or we gondola about to listen to the serenades by moonlight. I think we have walked and gondolaed the place all through by day and moon. How heavenly Venice would have been with Richard, we two floating about in these gondolas! Our friends are a charming Belgian couple named Hagemans, two little children, and a nice sister, and last, though not least, the Chevalier de St. Cheron. The Chevalier is a perfect French gentleman of noble family, good-looking, fascinating, brilliant in conversation ; has much heart, *esprit*, and *délicatesse* ; he is more solid than most Frenchmen, and better informed, and has noble sentiments, head and heart ; and yet, were he an Englishman, I should think him vain and ignorant. He has a few small prejudices and French tricks, which are, however, little faults of nationality, education, and circumstance, but not of nature. Henri V., the Bourbon King, called the Comte de Chambord, lives at the Palazzo Cavalli, and holds a small court, kept up in a little state by devoted partisans, who are under the surveillance of the police, and have three or four different lodgings everywhere.

St. Cheron is his right-hand man and devoted to him, and will be in the highest office when he comes to the throne. As we are devoted to the Bourbons he introduced us there, and the King helped to make our stay happy to us.

We arrived in Venice for the end of the Carnival. The last night of it we went to the masked ball at the Finice; it was the most brilliant sight I ever saw. We masked and dominoed, and it was there that the Chevalier and I first came in contact and spoke; he had been watching for an opportunity. The evening after the ball he came to *table d'hôte* and spoke to us, and asked leave to pay us an evening visit, which he did (the Hagemans were there too); and from that we spent all our evenings and days together.

One night we rowed in gondolas by moonlight to the Lido; we took the guitar. I never saw Venice look so beautiful. The water was like glass, and there was not a sound but the oars' splashing. We sang glees. Arrived at the Lido, we had tea and walked the whole length of the sands. That night was one of many such evenings in queenly Venice. I shall often remember the gondolier's serenades, the beautiful moon and starlight, the gliding about in the gondola in all the romantic parts of Venice, the soft air, the stillness of the night, hearing only the splash of oars, and nothing stirring except perhaps some dark and picturesque figure crossing the bridge, the little Madonna chapel on the banks of the Lido edging the Adriatic, the Piazza of San Marco with the band, and ices outside Florian's, the picturesque Armenians, Greeks, and

Moors, and the lovely water-girls with their *bigolo*, every language sounding in one's ears. I remember too all my favourite localities, too numerous to set down, but known doubtless to every lover of Venice.

On the days that were too bad for sight-seeing we and our friends read Byron, talked French, and sketched ; on indifferent days we lionized ; and on beautiful days we floated about round the islands. I had two particularly happy days ; they were the summer mornings when the sun shone and the birds sang ; and we were all so gay we sang too, and the Adriatic was so blue. There were two or three beautiful brigs sometimes sailing for Trieste.

One day Henri V. desired the Chevalier to bring us to a private audience. Blanche wore her wedding-dress with pearls and a slight veil ; my brother-in-law was in his best R.Y.S. uniform, and I in my bridesmaid's dress. We had a very smart gondola covered with our flags, the white one uppermost for the Bourbons, which did not escape the notice of the King, and the gondoliers in their Spanish-looking sashes and broad hats. Blanche looked like a small sultana in her bridal robes sitting amidst her flags. We were received by the Duc de Levis and the Comtesse de Chavannes ; there was also a Prince Somebody, and an emissary from the Pope waiting for an audience. As soon as the latter came out we were taken in, and most graciously received ; and the King invited us to sit. He was middle height and fair, a *beau-idéal* of a French gentleman, with winning manners. His consort was tall, gaunt, very dry and cold, but she was kind. They asked us a thousand

questions; and as my French was better than the others',
I told them all about our yachting, and all we had seen
and were going to see; and they were much interested.
I was also able to tell the King that when he was a little
boy he had condescended to ask my mother to dance,
and that it was one of the proudest souvenirs of her
life.   My brother-in-law behaved with great ease and
dignity; he put his yacht and his services at the King's
disposal, and expressed our respectful attachment to the
House of Bourbon.   We thanked them for receiving
us.   After about twenty minutes they saluted us; we
curtseyed to the ground, backed to the door, repeated
the curtsey, and disappeared.   We were received again
by the Duc de Levis and the Comtesse de Chavannes,
and conducted to the gondola.   I am proud to say that
we heard that the King was enthusiastic about Blanche
and myself, and subsequently that night at dinner and
many a day after he spoke of us.   We also heard
from the Chevalier and a Vicomte Simonet that the
King was charmed with my brother-in-law for turning
the white flag upwards and offering him the use of his
yacht.

CHAPTER VIII

MY CONTINENTAL TOUR: SWITZERLAND

(1858)

You're far, yet to my heart you're nearest near;
Absent, yet present in my sprite you appear.

ALF LAYLAH WA LAYLAH
(*Burton's "Arabian Nights"*).

WE left Venice one evening in early April at half-past nine, after six weeks' stay, and travelled by the night train to Padua. We then went through a terrible experience. We started on a twenty-four hours' drive without a stoppage, without a crumb of bread or a drop of water. We drove through Milan at 8.30 in the morning, and after leaving it we got a magnificent view of the Alps, and had a very trouble-some frontier. At last we came to Turin. We went on in a train with a diligence on it, and arrived at Susa, our last Italian town. Here the diligence was taken off the train. We had fourteen mules and two horses, and began to ascend Mont Cenis. These were the days when there were no trains there. Some of us with the conductor climbed up the shorter cuts (like ascending a chimney) until dark, and met the diligence. We had a splendid view. But what a night! The snow

in some places was twenty feet deep, and the wind and
sleet seemed as if they would sweep us over ; it was
wild and awful, one vast snow scene, and the scenery
magnificent.   At midnight we came to the top ; but
here was the worst part, where the smaller road begins.
Here, as before, we only went at a foot's pace, and the
horses could hardly stand.   The men kept tumbling
off, the vehicle was half buried in the snow, there were
drifts every few paces, and we had to be cut out.   At
Lans le Bourg at one o'clock we stopped, and they
gave us some bad soup, for which we gratefully paid
four francs.   The few travellers were ascending and
descending, asking all sorts of questions.   We tried to
sleep, but ever and anon some accident happened to
wake us.   Every here and there we tried to knock
somebody up for assistance ; but it appeared to me as
if most of the houses of refuge were shut up, thinking
that nobody would be mad enough to travel in such
weather.   We were so tired that it seemed as if the
horses were wandering about, not knowing where they
were going to.   Everything tumbled about most un-
comfortably in a snowy, dreamy state of confusion.
Some of the men roared with laughter at one of the
postilions sprawling off his horse into the snow, and
floundering about without being able to get up again.
Things went on like that till 7 a.m., when we pulled up
at the station, St. Jean de Marienne, where we ought to
have caught the 6 a.m. train, but it was gone ; so there
was nothing for it but to remain for the 10.20, and get
a good breakfast.   We took the 10.20 train, and arrived
at 12.20 at Chambéry.   Here a civil man convinced us

that we had to choose between two disagreeables ; so we took the lesser, remained at Chambéry till five o'clock, and then started by diligence, and (what we did not know) tired horses.

At midnight, when body and soul were worn out (we had not had our clothes off for three days and nights, hardly any food or other necessities; we had been sitting with our knees up to our chins in that blessed *coupé*, which was like a chimney-piece big enough for two, the windows close to our faces)— well, I say, when body and soul were worn out, they shot us down like so much rubbish at a miserable inn at Annecy at midnight, and swore they would go no farther. My brother-in-law stuck to his place, and refused to move till we had got another diligence and fresh horses ; so seeing there was no help for it, they did get them, and transferred our baggage. Then we took our places and drove off. The road was nearly impassable ; the driver frequently stopped at places to entreat that they would give him more horses, but all the inns were shut up and asleep, and nobody cared to hear him, so we lost half an hour every here and there. Morning came, but we stuck again, and were not near to the end of our journey. We turned into an inn, where we got some chocolate, and sat round a stove with the peasants, who chaffed our driver, his exploits, and his poor horses. That morning we passed an exquisite bridge over a chasm, of which I would give worlds to have a photograph. One seemed suspended between heaven and earth. I learnt afterwards that my bridge is between Crusie-Caille ; it is 636 feet long,

and 656 above the stream. The old road winds be-
neath it ; the Sardinians call it the Ponte Carlo Aberto.
A few more difficulties, and at 10.30 a.m., Wednesday,
April 7, we arrived at the Hôtel des Bergues, Geneva.
The poor horses were delighted the moment they saw
Geneva below, and put on a spurt of themselves.

The Hôtel des Bergues, Geneva (at the time I write),
is the second best hotel here ; we have three cheerful
rooms on the lake, and a dull *table d'hôte* at five o'clock.
The lake is like blue crystal, on which we have a
five-ton sailing-boat; the sky without a cloud; the
weather like May. The nights are exquisite. The
peasants are ugly ; they wear big hats, and speak bad
French. It is a terrible place for stomach-ache, owing
to the mountain water. The religion is a contrast to
Italy—little and good. As I am Number Three of
our party, I have had all along to make my own life
and never be in the way of the married couple. We
arrived here in time for the railway *fête* ; there were
flags and *feux de joie*, bands, and a magnificent peasant
ball. Our Minister for Switzerland, whose name was
Gordon, came for the *fête* (the French Minister refused).
He dined here, spent the evening with us, and took us
to the ball. The Union Jack floated at our windows
in his honour. A pretty place Geneva, but very dull.
The spring begins to show itself in the trees and
hedges. I long for the other side of the lake. We
walk and sail a great deal.

I have not heard a word from Richard, and I am
waiting like Patience on a monument in grand expecta-
tion of what the few months may bring, relying on

his sister having told me that he will be home this summer, when I feel that something decisive will take place. This day I have had an offer from an American, polished, handsome, fifty years of age, a widower, with £300,000 made in California ; but there is only one man in the world who could be master of such a spirit as mine. People may love (as it is called) a thousand times, but the real *feu sacré* only burns once in one's life. Perhaps some feel more than others ; but it seems to me that this love is the grandest thing in this nether world, and worth all the rest put together. If I succeed, I shall know how to prove myself worthy of it. If any woman wants to know what this *feu sacré* means, let her ascertain whether she loves fully and truly with brain, heart, and passion. If one iota is wanting in the balance of any of these three factors, let her cast her love aside as a spurious article—she will love again ; but if the investigation is satisfactory, let her hold it fast, and let nothing take it from her. For let her rest assured love is the one bright vision Heaven sends us in this wild, desolate, busy, selfish earth to cheer us on to the goal.

My American Crœsus is not my only chance. A Russian general here, a man of about forty years, with loads of decorations, who knows many languages, is a musician, and writes, has made me an offer. He is a man of family, has nine *châteaux*, and half a million of francs income. He saw me at the altar of the Madonna, Genoa, two months ago. He tells me he fell as much in love with me as if he were a boy of fifteen. He followed me, changed his hotel to come here,

came to dinner, and took the room next to me. He
serenades me on the violin at 6 a.m. and 11 p.m. and
at 7 a.m. He sent me a bouquet and a basket of fruit,
and a letter of about six pages long to tell me that the
Tsar is a great man, that he (the general) has bled for
his country, and that if I will marry him—" Que je serai
dans ses bras " (what a temptation!) " et qu'il me fera la
déesse du pays." I refused him of course.

On June 10, when we were in bed at one o'clock in
the morning, all the steamers set up a peal. I, who was
lying awake, rushed to the window, and then called up
the others. We looked out, and saw that apparently
the back of our hotel and the whole Quartier des
Bergues was in flames. We gave the alarm in the
house, ran down the corridors to arouse everybody,
and then to our rooms to put on what we could, collect
a few treasures and our animals. I took the bullfinch
(Toby) and Richard's picture, the Pigotts took each
a dog, and down we cut. By this time thousands of
people were running to the rescue, every bell in the
town was ringing, the whole fire brigade turned out,
and they even telegraphed to the borders of France to
send down reinforcements. Dozens of engines were
at work, and we soon learnt that our hotel was *not* on
fire, but that the fire was so extensive they could scarcely
distinguish what was on fire and what was not. In a
street at the back of us nine houses were burning,
a *café*, and an *entrepôt* of inflammables ; and the
pompiers said that if we had a north-east wind instead of a south-west one, nothing could have saved
our whole *quartier* from destruction. Every soul in

Geneva was there, and the roofs of the houses were crowded ; and we went up on the roof of the hotel to see the wonderful sight. The fire brigade was on the ground for thirty hours. They could do nothing for the houses already on fire, but only prevent its spreading by playing on the surrounding ones, which were red-hot, as was the back of our hotel. Fresh firemen and engines arrived from France. Among the animals destroyed were one horse and two cows, some sheep, and some goats, in their sheds. A cage of birds fell and opened, and the poor little things escaped, but in their fright flew about in the flames. A baby, whom the mother forgot in its bed (most unnatural), and two men were killed : one was crushed by the falling roof, and the other burned. Two firemen lost their lives : one in trying to save a woman (God bless him !), in which he succeeded, but fell in the flames himself ; another was mortally burnt ; and also two persons were lost whose bodies could never be found. It appeared that a Frenchman had a quarrel in the *café*, and out of spite went out and contrived to set it alight. The populace say (he is caught and in prison) that they will lynch him, and burn him at the stake. The loss of property is great. The flames arose above the whole town, and seemed to lick the whole *quartier*. It was a dark night, and everybody was in *déshabillé* from their beds, and there was a horrible smell of burnt flesh.

We started on July 1, a large and merry party, from Geneva one beautiful morning at the top of the diligence, and drove through an English-looking

country to Sallenches. Here we took some vehicles
that ought to have been built in the year 1 B.C., which
shook my sister quite ill ; but we who could walk much
preferred doing so, as well for ease as for seeing the
scenery, to which no pen of mine could ever do justice.
We arrived at Chamounix in the evening, bathed and
dined, and took a moonlight stroll through the town
and valley. Chamounix is the second thing that has
never disappointed me. I look around, and as far as
my eye can stretch up and down the valley are ranges
of grand mountains, covered with firs, Alpine roses, and
wild rhododendrons, and above these splendid peaks,
some covered with snow, almost overhanging us, and
standing out in bold relief against the bluest of skies.
I note it all—the peaceful hamlet in the vale at the
foot of Mont Blanc, the church spire distinct against
that background of firs on the opposite mountain-
side, the Orne rushing through the town, the balconies
and little gardens, the valley dotted with *châlets,* the
Glacier du Boisson and Mer de Glace sparkling in
the sun. How glorious it is !

We had to start next morning at daybreak before the
sun should become too hot. We dressed in little thick
boots, red petticoats that we might see each other at
a distance, brown Holland jackets and big hats, a pike
and a mule and a guide each, besides other guides. At
first the mule appears to step like an ostrich, and you
think of your mount at home, and you tremble as you
see the places he has to go up, or, worse, to go down.
In time you arrive at the top of the Flégère. From
here you see five glaciers, the best view of Mont Blanc

and other peaks too numerous to mention. We met some pleasant people, dined together at the *châlet*, and drew caricatures in the travellers' book. One or two of us went up as far as the Grands Mulets without guides, slept there, and descended early, where we picked up our party. In the descent we walked, and some of the mules ran away. Not finding ourselves quite pumped by the descent, we proposed ascending to the Chapeau the opposite side, to look at the Mer de Glace, which we did; and as we were mounting we had the pleasure of seeing an avalanche and some smaller falls. We were joined by a party of seven jolly Scotch girls, and we descended with them. We were very tired.

Our next excursion was to Montanvert, which ascent was most magnificent. The lower part of the mountain is a garden of wild flowers, roses, and firs, and between the mountains stood out wondrous peaks. Against the sky was the Aiguille Verte, leaning as much over as the Campanile at Pisa. It is wonderful to think of the commotion there must have been when these immense masses of rock were scattered there by the convulsions of Nature, and the trees were crushed. At Montanvert we fed, and were joined by others from the Mer de Glace. Here those who had weak heads went back, and those who feared not nor cared not went on. Every lady had her guide and alpenstock, every man had his alpenstock, and all of us were strapped round our waists to hold on to each other. A little cannon was fired to tell us the echo and announce our start. The first part was easy enough, and a man with a hatchet in advance cut us footsteps. (Albert Smith has opened this passage within five years.) Here and there is a stream of water, so pure one might fancy it to be melted diamonds. Thousands of chasms in the ice, five hundred or more feet deep, of a beautiful blue colour, and a torrent beneath, had to be passed by a plank thrown across. What is a precipice to-day is closed up to-morrow by the constant movement of the ice. Take the *tout ensemble*, it gives you the idea of a rebellious sea that had dared to run mountains high, in defiance of its Creator, who had struck it (while in motion) into ice. Here and there came a furious waterfall or torrent ; a plank was then thrown across in a safe part. Once I slipped, and my legs fell in, and my alpenstock ; but I clung to the stump till hauled up. Then came the Mauvais Pas. You descend the side of a precipice by holes cut for your feet, and let yourself down by a rope. If one has got a good head, it is worth while looking down. Hamlets look like a set of tea-things, men (if seen at all) like ants beneath one ; and how glorious ! one is suspended between heaven and earth, and one's immortal part soars higher than the prison carcase can ! As one loves to feel one's own nothingness by the side of the man to whom one has given one's heart, so does this feeling (the best we own) increase in magnitude when it relates to God. *He* holds you there, *He* guards against that false step which would dash you to pieces, and gives you the power of brain to look below, around, and upwards, to wonder and to thank. I think this was the most intense excitement of its sort that I had felt in my girl travelling life. At last we arrived at the Chapeau, and descended the same mountain as yesterday.

The next day we proposed ascending the Glacier du Boisson, and reascending Mont Blanc for a few hours ; but some of our party were anxious to get home, so we ordered some rackety vehicles for Argentières next morning, and there the strong betook themselves to their legs and alpenstocks, and the weak to mules. We strolled gaily along, making wreaths of wild flowers for our hats, singing the *Ranz des Vaches* and all that, though still in Savoy, and we mounted the Col de Balme. This is one of the darkest and sublimest views imaginable. On one side you look down the valley of Chamounix and the Savoy Mountains ; the Col seems like a high barrier with one hut on it. On the other side you look over the Bernese Alps, and you see a spectacle not of everyday occurrence. Turn to Switzerland, all is sunshiny, bright, and gay ; turn to Savoy, a thunder-storm is rolling along the valley beneath, and you stand there on the Col in winter, in snow, shivering, hail, wind, and sleet driving in your face. You see on one side, half a mile below, autumn ; on the other spring, with buttercups, daisies and all sorts of wild flowers, and forsooth the cuckoo ; and at the bottom of both valleys is summer, bright or stormy. At this place the ruffian who keeps the hut makes you pay twenty-eight francs for a slice of ham, and you come out rather amused at the people who are swearing on that account. Some delicate ladies are in semi-hysterics at the storm, or the black, frowning spot on which we find ourselves, and are rushing about, making tender inquiries after each other's sensitive feelings. After an hour's rest we start, the weak ones for Martigny, the strong by a steep path in the mountains, which brings us after a couple of hours to spring. But stop awhile in winter. A black range of mountains dark and desolate are dressed in thunder-clouds. You feel awed, yet you would rather see it so than in sunshine. A small bit of table-land is on the side; it makes you think of an exile in Siberia or Dante's Damned Soul in a Hell of Snow. We were all silent. No doubt we all made our reflections; and mine ran thus :

" If an angel from heaven came from Almighty God, and told you that Richard was condemned to be chained on that plateau for a hundred years in expiation of his sins before he could enter heaven, and gave you the choice between sharing his exile with him or a throne in the world beneath, which would you choose? "

My answer did not keep me long in suspense; it came in this form :

" A throne would be exile *without him*, and exile *with him* a home ! "

We reached spring, and passed the *châlets* where Gruyère cheese is made ; and I stopped the herdsman, and took a lesson in the *Ranz des Vaches* amidst much laughter, and to the evident amusement of a cuckoo, who chimed in. The descent of the Tête Noir is the most beautiful thing we have seen ; at any rate, it is the most graven on my memory. It is down the side of magnificently wooded mountains, with bridges of a primitive kind, overhanging precipices, and looks into the dark valley, part of which never sees the sun. Here we sang snatches of *Linda de Chamounix* ; the scenery reminds one of it, and comes up to, or even surpasses, all that I have read or thought. In one place we came to an immense rock that had fallen, and was just on the balance over a precipice, and there it has hung for hundreds and thousands of years. The peasants are *fait soit peu sauvage*, and they dealt us out plainly plenty of chaff, as they gave us water, in the fond belief that we did not understand French. At length we reached the *châlet* where travellers feed. After dinner at nine o'clock the moon rose, and we went through a splendid forest on a mountain-side, with a torrent dashing below. I lit my cigarette, and went a little ahead of my party. There are sacred moments and heavenly scenes I cannot share with the common herd. There was only one voice which I could have borne to break the silence, and that, like heaven, was so far off as to be like a fable now. At length we arrived at a hut at the top of the Mont Forclaz, a hut where we must have our passport *viséd*—why, I do not know, as we have long since been in Switzerland. The gendarme grumbled something about "eccentric English who scale the mountains in the night." A hint to be quick is all he gets, and we descend. Now we were so tired that we mounted our mules on the assurance that it would rest us ; but such a descent I should never care to do again. The road was steep and unfinished ; the moon was under a cloud ; there were precipices on each side. The step of the mule sends one upon a narrow, hard saddle, bumping one moment against the pommels, and the next on to the baggage here and there. There is a roll over a loose stone ; but the clever mule, snuffing and pawing its way, nimbly puts its feet together, and slides down a slab of rock. My companions got down and walked, tired as they were. I really could not ; and seeing the mule was so much cleverer than myself, I knotted the bridle and threw it on his back, and *in the dark* put my leg over the other side, and rode down straddle like a man, half an hour in advance of the rest. They said there were wolves on these mountains, but I did not see or hear any. I had only my pike to defend myself with, and should have been in an awful fright had I come across a wolf. At midnight I reached the hotel at Martigny, and went to bed.

Our next move was to charter a carriage that would hold us all inside and out. We had a splendid drive through the valley of the Rhone for some days, and visited many places.

I was immensely impressed by Chillon at night. The lake lies at our feet like a huge crystal with a broad track of moonlight on it. A moment ago it was fine starlight, and now the moon rises behind the Dent du Midi, lighting up those magnificent mountains too brightly for the stars. Vevey is asleep, and no noise is heard save the splash of an oar, or a bit of loose rock rolling with a crash down the mountain, or the buzz of some insect going home late. A bat flutters near my face now and then ; there is a distant note from a nightingale. How refreshing is the soft breeze and the sweet smell of the hay after the heat of the day ! And now crossing the moonlight track, westward bound, glides a lateen sail like a colossal swan. These are the scenes that, save for the God Who made them, let us know we are alone on earth. These are the moments when we miss the hand we want to clasp in ours without speaking, and yet be understood ; but my familiar spirit with whom I could share these moments is not here.

At last we received orders to be ready within an hour's notice to leave Geneva for Lausanne, and we were very glad to obey. We had been too long at Geneva, and were heartily tired of it, especially after all the beautiful things we had seen. It was, however, found that the cutter would not hold us all ; so the maid and I went with the baggage and animals, and also Mr. Richard Sykes (who brought a letter from my brother Jack, a charming, gentlemanly boy of twenty, who joined us for a few weeks), by steamer to Lausanne, and put up at an *auberge* at Ouchy on the water's edge, where we waited the sailing party. Ouchy consists (1858) of a humble street and an old-fashioned inn at the water's edge beneath Lausanne. Here we took three little rooms, one for Mr. Sykes, one for the maid, and one for me, which was half bedroom, half drawing-room, with a good view. The others arrived in a few days, having met the *bise* and had to put back to port. Here I found some one with whom I could begin German. I rowed and swam a great deal. There is a beautiful country for driving and walking, and our *chaloupe* is now at anchor. In this last we were able to make excursions.

Among other places we ran over to Evian, twelve miles across on the opposite coast. There were one hundred and twenty-five people in the hotel, who were very kind, and made a great fuss with us ; and we had great fun, though they had great difficulty in making room for us. Mr. Sykes had to go to an old tower in the garden, and my room was somewhere under the tiles. We often gave them supper and cigarettes at 11.30, after music and impromptu dancing in the evening. They were all vastly kind to us, and when we went away they came down to see us off in our cutter.

When we got half-way across the lake, I said to my brother-in-law, " Does it not look rather like wind out there ? " He gave a short, quick command at once to take every bit of sail down ; but we knew nothing of lake-sailing, though we knew sea-sailing, and before we had got it half down the wind came upon us like a wall, and threw us on our side. Our bobstay snapped like sealing-wax, our mainsail rent like ribbon, our foresail flew away, and she would not answer her helm, and we remained in the trough of the waves, which rose awfully high. We then cut away the jib. We had given up all hope, having beaten about for a long time, and two of us had been in the water for three-quarters of an hour. At length we spied five boats putting out to us, and we were truly thankful. It appeared that the fishermen had refused to come before, because they were convinced we had gone down long ago, and all the village people were on their knees praying for us. We were safely towed in by the five boats, much too disabled to help ourselves, and the cutter was smashed to pieces.

We rewarded the men liberally, got some brandy, dried our clothes, and went back by the next steamer.

There was a grand *fête* at Lausanne. The canteen of Swiss woodwork was decorated with branches, and there were shooting-galleries, the usual booths and whirligigs, a very respectable vagrant theatre, a dancing-circus and band. The streets were all festooned with garlands, and bits of sentiment such as, " Liberté et patrie," " Un bras pour la défendre, un cœur pour l'aimer," etc.

It was cloudless weather that evening at Lausanne, the sky clear and high, the country fresh, green, and sweet-smelling. The mountains surrounded one-half the lake with twenty different shades at the setting sun, from palest pink on the snow-peaks to the deepest purple on the rocks. It was all quiet enough after leaving the merriment of the fair, with only the noise of birds or bees, and the sweet smell of wild flowers in the fresh air. Later the evening star came out in the pale sky, and the glow-worms shone like brilliants in the grass. I thought of Richard in that far-away swamp in Central Africa, and a voiceless prayer rose to my lips. I wonder if he too is thinking of me at this time ? And as I thought an angelic whisper knocked at my heart and murmured, " Yes."

After we had been at Lausanne some time, I got ill. I was fretting because there was no news at all about Richard ; I had been hoping to hear from him for two months. I had enough of the climate too. I had a habit of rowing myself out a little way, undressing in the boat, jumping in for a swim, climbing

back into the boat, and rowing ashore ; and one day I
was too hot, and I just had the strength to give the last
pull to the oar ashore, when I fainted.   There were no
doctors, no medicines, and I lay ill on my very hard
bed with a dreadful pain in my side for three weeks.
But I was too strong to die ; and one day somebody got
me a bottle of Kirschwasser, and drinking it in small
quantities at a time seemed to take away the pain ;
but I was very pale and ill, and every one said I had
rheumatic fever.   We were all three more or less ill, and
did not like to part ; but it was a necessity, so I was
sent forward with twelve pieces of baggage and sixteen
napoleons to work my way from Ouchy to Honfleur,
where I was to wait for my brother-in-law and sister,
Honfleur being a quieter place than Havre.   Poor
Blanche looked so worn and sad!

I got in a railway-carriage by myself, and asked the
guard to look after me because I was alone ; but just
before the train started he put in a man, and begged
my pardon, saying it was inevitable, as there was not a
place in any other carriage.   In about twenty minutes
the man began to make horrible faces at me, and I was
so dreadfully frightened I felt I must speak ; so I
said, " I am afraid you are ill " ; and he said, " Yes ; I
am very sorry, but I am going to have an epileptic
fit."   He was almost immediately black, and in horrible
contortions.   It was an express train.   There was no
means of communicating with the guard (1858), and
there was no use in screaming ; so, frightened though
I was, I pulled the man down on the ground, undid
his cravat, and loosened all about his neck.   I had no

medicine with me, except a quarter of a bottle of sweet spirits of nitre, which I was taking for rheumatic fever. I poured it all down his throat, and then I covered his face over with a black silk handkerchief I had round my neck, that I might not see him, and squeezed myself up in the farthest corner. In about twenty minutes he came to, and asked me how long he had been like that. I told him, and he asked me if I was dreadfully frightened, and I said, " Yes." He said, " I am subject to these fits, but they generally last much longer ; this has been very slight." So I said, " I think it is my duty to tell you that I have put about three ounces of spirits of nitre down your throat." He said, " Well, I think it must have done me good, because I feel very comfortable." I called the guard the first station we arrived at, told him what had occurred, and begged him to move me into a carriage with other people, which he did. I never knew anything so slow as the trains were; and at the stations there seemed no one to help, nor to tell one where anything was. I got two seats with my back to the engine, so that I could lie down. The heat was intense. The carriage was crammed. There was a ladylike little woman, with a brawny nurse and two of the worst-behaved children I ever saw. They fought, and sang, and cried, and teased my bullfinch, and kicked my shins, and trod on my toes ; but the mother was too nice to offend, and so I bore it. At Mâcon at 8 p.m. we stopped to sup ; and then I felt I could bear no more of it, so I begged the guard to change me to a quiet carriage, and he put me in with two gentlemanly Spaniards. There was plenty of room, and we had a quiet night enough, only one of them was so long that every now and then in his sleep he put his feet into my lap or on the birdcage.

We arrived at 6 a.m., and drove for at least an hour to the Havre station in the pouring rain. Here my troubles began. It was past seven, the train was at 8.25 ; so I thought I had time to get a little breakfast at the *café*. I did so, and returned. The porters were very rude to me, and refused to weigh my baggage, saying I was too late. In vain I entreated, and I had to return to my *café* and sit in a miserable room from 8 o'clock to 1 p.m. I drank a bottle of gingerbeer, and did my accounts, but my head was too stupid to do them properly ; so with the idea that I had only forty-eight francs left, I had taken my ticket to Havre, but not paid the baggage, and I had still to get to Honfleur. I then got scared with fancying I had lost four napoleons, and sat looking at my purse in despair. Then I discovered I had lost a bunch of keys, that the turquoise had fallen out of my ring, that I had broken my back comb, and left behind part of my dressing-case. Then it suddenly occurred to me that I had no blessing because I had not said my morning prayers; so I at once knelt down, and during my prayers a light flashed on me that there were five napoleons to a hundred francs, and the money was right to a farthing, so I rose with a thankful heart heedless of smaller evils. I took the one o'clock train, which went fast. It was hot, windy, dusty, crowded; but no matter, I drove straight to the boat. Alas! it was gone, and I had only a few francs. There was nothing for it but to go to the hotel opposite the boats, and ask for a room, a hot bath, some tea and bread-and-butter (I had been out thirty-six hours without rest). I was on board the first boat, which steamed off at a quarter to seven in the morning, and at eight was safely housed at the Hôtel d'Angleterre, Honfleur, forty-eight hours after leaving Ouchy, with three-ha'pence in my pocket. Unfortunately at Havre there was a law by which the porters were not obliged to weigh your baggage unless you came half an hour before the time, but that nobody ever did, and they would not *dare* nor *think* of refusing a French person ; but because I was an English girl, and alone, they abused their power. I was only five minutes after time ; there was twenty-five minutes to spare, and they were rude into the bargain. They are not paid by Government (1858), and there is no tariff. They follow you like a flock of sheep, and say, " We will carry your baggage if you pay us, and if not we will not." My purse prevented my being very free-handed ; they would not take less than a franc and a half, and slang you for that ; and I spent eighteen francs on them between Lausanne and Honfleur.

Honfleur is a horrid place. It is a fishing town, con- taining about ten thousand people of an inferior class, as dull as the grave, no society, and, still worse, not the necessaries of life—the only good things are the fruit, the sea, and country. There are two hotels, which in England we should call public-houses ; not a room fit to sleep in, so I have had a bed put in a kind of observatory at the top of the house.   I can shut out all, and live with nature and my books.   There is a terrace, and at high tide the sea rolls under it, and at a stretch I could fancy myself on board a ship ; but, thank God, I am getting better.

They come and ask you what you would like for dinner :

" Ce que vous avez à la maison ; je ne suis pas difficile."   " Nous avons *tout* du melon, par exemple— des crevettes," etc.

What they want to feed me on here are melons and water.   An Englishman came the other day, very hungry, and wanted to dine.   " Voulez-vous une omelette, monsieur ? "   "Damn your omelette ! " he said ; " I want to dine."   He was obliged to go.   The servants are one remove from animals, and the family ditto, except madame, who is charming.   The weather is beastly, the sea is muddy, the sand all dirt; there is not a piano in the town.   The baths are half an hour from here, and the Basse gents are excessively *sauvage*.   But even in this fifth-rate society I found a grain of wheat among the chaff—a Parisian Spanish woman, the wife of a physician, here for her child's health, very *spirituelle*, not pretty, and devoted to Paris.   We smoke and read, and she gives me the benefit of her experience, which I really think I had better have been without ; but she is a jolly little creature, and I do not know how I should pass my time without her.

Blanche and my brother-in-law joined me at Honfleur a fortnight after my arrival ; and having received a draft for fresh supplies, we determined to start next

day. We had a delightful trip of six hours up the
Seine to Rouen ; we revisited the old cathedral, and
walked up to that little gem Notre Dame de bon
Secours.   I am very fond of Rouen; it is such a lovely
place.   We went on to Dieppe, and had a calm passage
to Southampton.   Once more I was in England.   We
went straight to London, and home.

CHAPTER IX

THEY MEET AGAIN

(1858—1860)

Allah guard a true lover, who strives with love
And hath borne the torments I still abide,
And seeing me bound in the cage with mind
Of ruth release me my love to find.

ALF LAYLAH WA LAYLAH
(*Burton's " Arabian Nights* ").

WHILE Isabel was touring through Italy and Switzerland, Burton was fighting his way through the Central African jungle to find the fabled lakes beyond the Usagara Mountains, which at that time the eye of the white man had never seen.

It is necessary to give a brief sketch of this expedition, and of the difference between Burton and Speke which arose from it, because these things influenced to a considerable degree Isabel's after-life. She was always defending her husband's position and fighting the case of Burton *versus* Speke.

As already stated, Burton left London in October, 1856. He went to Bombay, applied for Captain Speke to accompany him as second in command of his expedition into the unknown regions of Central Africa, and landed at Zanzibar in December. The Royal Geographical Society had obtained for him a grant of £1,000, and the Court of Directors of the East India Company had given him two years' leave.

On June 26, 1857, after an experimental trip, they set out in earnest on their journey into the far interior. Burton was handicapped by a very inadequate force, and he had to make his way through hostile savage tribes; yet he determined to risk it, and in eighteen days achieved the first stage of the journey. Despite sickness and every imaginable difficulty, the little band arrived at K'hutu.

Thence they marched to Zungomero, a pestilential Slough of Despond. Here they rested a fortnight, and then began the ascent of the Usagara Mountains. They managed to climb to the frontier of the second region, or Ghauts. They then pushed on, up and down the ranges of these mountains, sometimes through the dismal jungle, sometimes through marshy swamps, sometimes along roads strewn with corpses and victims of loathsome diseases, tormented always by insects and reptiles, and trembling with ague, with swimming heads, ears deafened by weakness, and legs that would scarcely support them, threatened by savages without and deserters within, until at last they reached the top of the third and westernmost range of the Usagara Mountains. The second stage of the journey was accomplished.

After a rest they went through the fiery heat of the Mdaburu jungle, where they were much troubled by their mutinous porters. At last they entered Kazeh.

The Arabs helped them here (Burton always got on well with Arabs), and they rested for a space. On January 10, 1858, they reached M'hali, and here Burton was smitten by partial paralysis, brought on by malaria ; his eyes were also afflicted, and death seemed imminent. But in a little time he was better, and again they pushed on through the wilderness. At last, on February 13, 1858, just when they were in despair, their longing eyes were gladdened by the first glimpse of the Lake Tanganyika, the sea of Ujiji, laying like an enchanted lake " in the lap of the mountains, basking in the gorgeous tropical sunshine."

For the first known time in the world's history European eyes rested on this loveliness. It is only fair therefore to remember that in the discovery of Lake Tanganyika Burton was the pioneer. His was the brain which planned and commanded the expedition, and it was he who first achieved with inadequate means and insufficient escort what Livingstone, Cameron, Speke, Grant, Baker, and Stanley achieved later. If he had possessed their advantages of men and money, what might he not have done !

At Ujiji they rested for some time ; they had travelled nine hundred and fifty miles, and had taken more than seven and a half months over the journey on account of the delay arising from danger and illness. They spent a month cruising about the lake, which, however, they were not able to explore thoroughly.

On May 28, 1858, Burton and Speke started on the homeward route. In due time they reached Kazeh again. Here, Burton being ill, and Speke not being able to get on with the Arabs, who abounded at Kazeh, it was decided that Burton should remain at Kazeh to prepare and send reports, and that Speke should go in search of the unknown lake (now called Nyanza) which the merchants had told them was some sixteen marches to the north. So Speke set out. After some six or seven weeks he returned to Kazeh. His flying trip had led him to the northern water, which he found to be an immense lake (Nyanza), and he announced that he had discovered the sources of the White Nile. On this point Burton was sceptical, and from this arose a controversy upon which it is unnecessary to enter. There were probably faults on both sides. The difference between Burton and Speke was much to be regretted ; I only allude to it here because it influenced the whole of Burton's subsequent career, and by so doing affected also that of his wife.

At Kazeh Burton decided that they must return to the seacoast by the way they came. So they beat their way back across the fiery field to the usual accompaniments of quarrels, mutinies, and desertions among the porters. At one place Speke was dangerously ill, but Burton nursed him through. They recrossed the Usagara Mountains, and struggled through mud and jungle, and at last caught sight of the sea. They made a triumphal entrance to Konduchi, the seaport village. They embarked and landed in Zanzibar on March 4, 1859. Here Burton wanted to get fresh leave of absence and additional funds ; but the evident desire of the British Consul to get rid of him (because he was too friendly with the Sultan), and the impatience

of Speke to return to England, caused him to abandon
the idea. Just then H.M.S. *Furious* arrived at Aden,
and passage homeward was offered to both of them.
Burton was too ill to go ; but Speke went, and his last
words, according to Burton, were : "Good-bye, old
fellow. You may be quite sure I shall not go up to
the Royal Geographical Society until you come to the
fore and we appear together. Make your mind quite
easy about that."

Nevertheless, when Burton arrived in England on
May 21, 1859 (having been absent two years and
eight months), he found the ground cut from under
his feet. Speke had arrived in London twelve days
before, and the day after his arrival had called at the
headquarters of the Royal Geographical Society, told
his own tale, and obtained the leadership of a new
expedition. Burton, who had originated and carried
out the expedition, found himself shelved, neglected,
and thrust aside by his lieutenant, who claimed and
received the whole credit for himself. Moreover,
Speke had spread all sorts of ugly—and I believe
untrue—reports about Burton. These coming on top
of certain other rumours—also, I believe, untrue—
which had originated in India,[1] were only too readily
believed. When Burton got home, he found that the
Government and the Royal Geographical Society
regarded him with disapproval, and society looked
askance at him. Instead of being honoured, he was

---

[1] Burton alludes to this prejudice against him in the original
(1886) edition of his *Arabian Nights*, "Alf Laylah wa Laylah,"
Terminal Essay, Section D, pp. 205, 206.

suspected and under a cloud. One may imagine how his spirit chafed under this treatment. He was indeed a most unlucky man. Yet in spite of the crowd of false friends and open enemies, in spite of all the calumny and suspicion and injustice, there was one heart which beat true to him. And then it was that Burton proved the strength of a woman's love.

Isabel had been back in England from her Continental tour just a year when Burton came home. It had been a terribly anxious year for her ; she had written to him regularly, and kept him well posted in all that was going on ; but naturally her letters only reached him at intervals. News of him had been meagre and infrequent, and there were long periods of silence which made her sick at heart with anxiety and dread. The novelty and excitement of her trip abroad had to some extent diverted her mind, but when she came home all her doubts and fears returned with threefold force. The monotony and inaction of her life chafed her active spirit ; the lack of sympathy and the want of some one in whom she could confide her love and her sorrow weighed her down. It was a sore probation, and in her trouble she turned, as it was her nature to turn, to the consolations of her religion. In the Lent of 1859 she went into a Retreat in the Convent at Norwich, and strove to banish worldly thoughts. She did not strive in vain, as the following extracts from one of her devotional books,[1] written when in retreat, will show.

[1] *Laméd*, one of Lady Burton's books of private devotion.

" I bewail my ordinary existence—the life that most girls lead—going out into society and belonging to the world.

" I must follow the ordinary little details of existence with patient endurance of suffering and resistance of evil. With courage I must fly at what I most dislike —grasp my nettle. There is good to be cultivated, there is religion to be uppermost; occupation and family cares must be my resources.

" And why must I do this? Other girls are not desirous of doing it. Because at a critical moment God snatched me from the world, when my heart bounded high for great things, and I was hard pressed by temptation. I said to myself, ' Why has He called such a being as myself into existence?'—seemingly to no purpose. And He has brought me to this quiet corner, and has showed me in a spiritual retreat (like in a holy lantern) things as they really are; He has recalled to me the holiest and purest of my childhood and my convent days, humbled me, and then, shutting out that view, once more He will send me forth to act from His fresh teaching. He seemed to say to me : ' You have but little time ; a long life is but eighty years or so—part of this is lost in childhood, part in old age, part in sleep. How few are the strong, mature years wherein to lay in store for death—the only store you can carry with you beyond the dreams of life, beyond the grave ! You, from defects in your upbringing, have allowed your heart to go before your head ; hence sharp twinges and bitter experience. These faults are forgiven you. Now enter on your mature years with a good spirit, and remember that the same excuses will not serve any more.'

" With these reflections I saw myself as an atom in this vast creation, chosen from thousands who would have served Him better, and brought safely through my nine months' imprisonment to my baptism. On what did I open my eyes? Not on the circle of a certain few, who are so covered with riches, honour, luxuries, and pleasures as to have their Paradise here. Not amongst the dregs of the unfortunate people who are the very spawn of vice, who never hear a good word or see a good action, who do not know that there is a God except in a curse. No! God gave me everything; but He chose a middle way for me, and each blessing that •surrounded me was immense in itself, and many were combined. Pure blood and good birth, health, youth, strength, beauty, talent, natural goodness—God and Nature gave me all, and the Devil and I spoiled the gift. Add to all this a happy home and good family, education, society, religion, and the true Church of Christ. He took from me the riches and the worldly success that might have damned me ; and having purified me, He sent me back only a sufficiency for needs and comforts. He gave me a noble incentive to good in the immense power of affection I have within me, which I may misuse, but not deprave or lose ; this power is as fresh as in my childhood, but saddened by experience. He preserves me from the multitude of hourly evils which I cannot see ; nay, more, He seems to watch every trifle to meet my needs and wants. He scarcely lets the wind visit me too roughly ;

He almost takes up the instruments He gave me, and works Himself. He seems to say, ' Toil for one short day, and in the evening come to Me for your reward.' He appointed to me, as to every one, an angel to protect me ; He has shown me the flowery paths that lead down—down to the Devil and Hell—and the rugged path that leads upward to Himself and Heaven. Shall I refuse to climb over my petty trials for this short time, when He is so merciful, when He has died for me ? ''

Isabel came out of her Retreat on Easter Day, and after visiting some friends for a few weeks returned to her parents' home in London. Here she was greeted with the news that Speke had come home alone. The air was full of Speke, and the rumour reached her ears that Burton was staying on in Zanzibar in the hope of being allowed to return to Africa. A sense of despair seized her ; and just as she was thinking whether she would not return to the Convent and become a Sister of Charity, she received six lines in a well-known hand by post from Zanzibar—no letter. This communication was long past date, and evidently had been slow in coming :

To Isabel.

That brow which rose before my sight,
As on the palmer's holy shrine ;
Those eyes—my life was in their light ;
Those lips—my sacramental wine ;
That voice whose flow was wont to seem
The music of an exile's dream.

She knew then it was all right.

Two days later she read in the paper that Burton would soon arrive. She writes in her diary:

"*May* 21.—I feel strange, frightened, sick, stupefied, dying to see him, and yet inclined to run away, lest, after all I have suffered and longed for, I should have to bear more."

But she did not run away. And here we leave her to tell her own tale.

On May 22 I chanced to call upon a friend. I was told she had gone out, but would be in to tea, and was asked if I would wait. I said, "Yes." In a few minutes another ring came to the door, and another visitor was also asked to wait. A voice that thrilled me through and through came up the stairs, saying, "I want Miss Arundell's address." The door opened, I turned round, and judge of my feelings when I beheld Richard ! For an instant we both stood dazed. I felt so intensely, that I fancied he must hear my heart beat, and see how every nerve was overtaxed. We rushed into each other's arms. I cannot attempt to describe the joy of that moment. He had landed the day before, and come to London, and had called here to know where I was living, where to find me. No one will wonder when I say that we forgot all about my hostess and her tea. We went downstairs, and Richard called a cab, and he put me in and told the man to drive about—anywhere. He put his arm round my waist, and I put my head on his shoulder. I felt quite stunned ; I could not speak or move, but felt like a person coming to after a fainting fit or a dream ; it was acute pain, and for the first half-hour I found no relief. I would have given worlds for tears, but none came. But it was absolute content, such as I fancy people must feel in the first few moments after the soul has quitted the body. When we were a little recovered, we mutually drew each other's pictures from our respective pockets at the same moment, to show how carefully we had always kept them.

After that we met constantly, and he called upon my parents. I now put our marriage *seriously* before them, but without success as regards my mother.

I shall never forget Richard as he was then. He had had twenty-one attacks of fever—had been partially paralyzed and partially blind. He was a mere skeleton, with brown-yellow skin hanging in bags, his eyes protruding, and his lips drawn away from his teeth. I used to give him my arm about the Botanical Gardens for fresh air, and sometimes convey him almost fainting in a cab to our house or friends' houses, who allowed and encouraged our meeting.

He told me that all the time he had been away the greatest consolation he had received were my fortnightly journals, in letter-form, to him, accompanied by all newspaper scraps, and public and private information, and accounts of books, such as I knew would interest him ; so that when he did get a mail, which was only in a huge batch now and then, he was as well posted up as if he were living in London.

Richard was looking so lank and thin. He was sadly altered ; his youth, health, spirits, and beauty were all gone for the time. He fully justified his fevers, his paralysis and blindness, and any amount of anxiety, peril, hardship, and privation in unhealthy latitudes. Never did I feel the strength of my love as then. He returned poorer, and dispirited by official rows and every species of annoyance ; but he was still—had he been ever so unsuccessful, and had every man's hand against him—my earthly god and king, and I could have knelt at his feet and worshipped him. I used to feel so proud of him ; I used to like to sit and look at him, and think, "You are mine, and there is no man on earth the least like you."[1]

Isabel tells us that she regretted bitterly not having been able to stay with and nurse the man she loved at this time. They were both most anxious that their marriage should take place, so that they might be together. But the great obstacle to their union was Mrs. Arundell's opposition. Isabel made a long and impassioned appeal to her mother ; but she would not relent, and turned a deaf ear to the lovers' pleadings. In justice to Mrs. Arundell, it must be admitted that she had apparently good reasons for refusing her consent to their marriage. Burton's niece says that she " vehemently objected to any daughter of hers espousing a Protestant."[2] But this is one of those half-truths

---

[1] At this point Lady Burton's autobiography ends—cut short by her death. Henceforward, when she speaks in the first person, it will be from her papers and letters, of which she left a great number. She was sorting them when she died. But I have felt justified in repeating the story of her marriage in her own words, as no other pen could do justice to it.

[2] Miss Stisted's *Life of Burton*.

which conceal a whole fallacy. Of course Mrs.
Arundell, who came of an old Roman Catholic family,
and who was a woman of strong religious convictions,
would have preferred her daughter to marry a man
of the same faith as herself. But it was not a question
between Catholicity and Protestantism, but between
Christianity and no religion at all. From all that was
publicly known of Burton at this time, from his writings
and his conversation, he was an Agnostic ; and so far
as the religious objection to the marriage entered, many
a Protestant Evangelical mother would have demurred
quite as much as Mrs. Arundell did. Religious prejudices may be just or unjust, but they are forces
which have to be reckoned with. And the religious
objection was not by any means the only one. At
this time there were unpleasant rumours flying about
concerning Burton, and some echo of them had reached
Mrs. Arundell's ears. The way in which the Royal
Geographical Society had passed him over in favour of
Speke had naturally lent colour to these reports ; and
although Burton had a few friends, he had many
enemies. He was under a cloud. The Government
ignored him ; the War Office disliked him ; his military
career had so far been a failure—there was no prospect
of promotion ; the Indian army had brought him under
the reduction ; he had not the means to keep a wife
in decent comfort, nor were his relations in a position
to help him, either with money or influence ; and
lastly, he was of a wild, roving disposition. All these
considerations combined to make Mrs. Arundell hesi-
tate in entrusting her daughter's happiness to his hands.

It must be remembered that Isabel was the eldest child. She was a very handsome and fascinating girl; she had many wealthy suitors, and might well have been expected to make "a good match." From a worldly point of view she was simply throwing herself away. From a higher point of view she was following her destiny, and marrying the man she loved with every fibre of her being. But Mrs. Arundell could hardly have been expected to see things in this light, and in opposing Isabel's marriage with Richard Burton she only acted as ninety-nine mothers out of every hundred would have done. No sooner were they married than she admitted that she had made a mistake, and did all in her power to atone for it; but at this time she was inexorable.[1]

Burton, who was very much in love, was not in the habit of brooking opposition, least of all from a woman; and he suggested to Isabel that they should take the law in their own hands, and make a runaway match of it. After all, they had arrived at years of discretion, and might fairly be expected to know their own minds. He was past forty, and Isabel was nearly thirty. More than three years had gone by since he declared his love to her in the Botanical Gardens; nearly ten years had passed since she had fallen in love with him on the Ramparts of Boulogne. Surely

[1] Lady Burton also, during the last years of her life, admitted that she had made a mistake in judging her mother's opposition too harshly. She often said to her sister, "I am so sorry I published those hard things I wrote of dear mother in my Life of Dick. It was her love for me which made her do it. I will cut it out in the next edition."

they had waited long enough. Isabel was swayed by his pleading; more than once she was on the point of yielding, but she resisted the temptation. Duty and obedience were always watchwords with her, and she could not bear the thought of going against her mother. Her sense of duty warred with her desire. So things see-sawed for nearly a year. And then:

"One day in April, 1860, I was walking out with two friends, and a tightening of the heart came over me that I had known before. I went home, and said to my sister, 'I am not going to see Richard for some time.' She said, 'Why, you will see him to-morrow!' 'No, I shall not,' I said; 'I don't know what is the matter.' A tap came at the door, and a note with the well-known writing was put into my hand. I knew my fate, and with a deep-drawn breath I opened it. He had left—could not bear the pain of saying good-bye; would be absent for nine months, on a journey to see Salt Lake City. He would then come back, and see whether I had made up my mind to choose between him or my mother, to marry me if I *would*; and if I had not the courage to risk it, he would go back to India, and thence to other explorations, and return no more. I was to take nine months to think about it." [1]

This was the last straw to Isabel, and for a time she broke down utterly. For some weeks she was ill in bed and delirious, heart-sick and hopeless, worn out with the mental conflict she was going through. Then she girded up her strength for one last struggle, and

[1] *Life of Sir Richard Burton*, by Isabel his wife, vol. i., p. 337.

when she arose from her bed her purpose was clear and
strong. The first thing she did showed that her mind
was made up. On the plea of change of air she went
into the country and stayed at a farmhouse. As she
had determined to marry a poor man and also to
accompany him in all his travels, she set herself to rough
it and to learn everything which might fit her for the
roving life she was afterwards to lead, so that in the
desert or the backwoods, with servants or without them,
she might be qualified for any emergency. In addition
to mastering all domestic duties at the farmhouse,
heavy and light, she tried her hand at outdoor work
as well, and learned how to look after the poultry-
yard and cattle, to groom the horses, and to milk the
cows. Nor did her efforts end here. When she came
back to London, she asked a friend (Dr. Bird) to teach
her to fence. He asked her why she wanted to learn
fencing. She answered, "Why? To defend Richard,
when he and I are attacked in the wilderness together."
Later on Burton himself taught her to fence, and she
became an expert fencer. At this time also she was
eager for books of all kinds. She wanted a wider range
of reading, so that she might, as she phrased it, "be
able to discuss things with Richard." This period of
waiting was, in effect, a period of preparation for her
marriage with the man she loved, and she pursued her
preparations steadily and quietly without a shadow of
wavering. Nevertheless she fretted a great deal during
this separation. A friend who knew her at this time has
told me she often looked wretched. She spent much
time in fasting and prayer, and there were days when

she would eat nothing but vegetable and drink water.
She used to call these her " marrow and water days."

One day she saw in the paper " Murder of Captain
Burton." Her anguish was intense. Her mother
went with her to the mail-office to make inquiries
and ascertain the truth. A Captain Burton had been
murdered by his crew, but it was not Isabel's Captain
Burton. She says, " My life seemed to hang on a
thread till he [the clerk] answered, and then my face
beamed so the man was quite startled." Great joy, like
great grief, is selfish. She gave little thought of the poor
man who was killed, the sense of relief was so great.
Burton—her Burton—was at that moment enjoying
himself with the Mormons in Salt Lake City, where he
stayed for some months. When his tour was completed,
he turned his face towards home again—and Isabel.

CHAPTER X[1]

AT LAST

(1860—1861)

My beloved is mine, and I am his.

Set me as a seal upon thine heart, as a seal upon thine arm :
For love is strong as death.

The Song of Solomon.

IT was Christmas, 1860, that I went to stop with my
relatives, Sir Clifford and Lady Constable (his *first*
wife, *née* Chichester), at Burton Constable—the father
and mother of the present baronet. There was a large
party in the house, and we were singing ; some one
propped up the music with the *Times*, which had just
arrived, and the first announcement that caught my
eye was that " Captain R. F. Burton had arrived from
America."

I was unable, except by great resolution, to continue
what I was doing. I soon retired to my room, and *sat*
up all night, packing, and conjecturing how I should
get away—all my numerous plans tending to a " bolt "
next morning—should I get an affectionate letter from

[1] This chapter is a condensed account of Lady Burton's marriage,
as related by herself in her Life of her husband, with some fresh
material added.

Richard. I received two ; one had been opened and read by somebody else, and one, as it afterwards turned out, had been burked at home before forwarding. It was not an easy matter. I was in a large country house in Yorkshire, with about twenty-five friends and relatives, amongst whom was one brother, and I had heaps of luggage. We were blocked up with snow, and nine miles from the station, and (*contra miglior noler voler mal pugna*) I had heard of his arrival only early in the evening, and twelve hours later I managed to get a telegram, ordering me to London, under the impression that it was of the most vital importance.

What a triumph it is to a woman's heart, when she has patiently and courageously worked and prayed and suffered, and the moment is realized that was the goal of her ambition !

As soon as we met, and had had our talk, he said :

" I have waited for five years. The first three were inevitable, on account of my journey to Africa, but the last two were not. Our lives are being spoiled by the unjust prejudice of your mother, and it is for you to consider whether you have not already done your duty in sacrificing two of the best years of your life out of respect to her. If *once* you *really* let me go, mind, I shall never come back, because I shall know that you have not got the strength of character which *my* wife must have. Now you must make up your mind to choose between your mother and me. If you choose me, we marry, and I stay ; if not, I go back to India, and on other explorations, and I return no more. Is your answer ready ? "

I said, " Quite. I marry you this day three weeks, let who will say nay."

When we fixed the date of our marriage, I wanted to be married on Wednesday, the 23rd, because it was the Espousals of Our Lady and St. Joseph ; but he would not, because Wednesday the 23rd and Friday the 13th were our unlucky days ; so we were married on the Vigil, Tuesday, January 22.

We pictured to ourselves much domestic happiness, with youth, health, courage, and talent to win honour, name, and position. We had the same tastes, and perfect confidence in each other. No one turns away from real happiness without some very strong temptation or delusion. I went straight to my father and mother, and told them what had occurred. My father said, " I consent with all my heart, if your mother consents"; and mother said, "*Never !*" I asked all my brothers and sisters, and they said they would receive him with delight. My mother offered me a marriage with my father and brothers present, my mother and sisters not. I felt that this was a slight upon *him*, a slight upon his family, and a slur upon me, which I did not deserve, and I refused it. I went to Cardinal Wiseman, and I told him the whole case as it stood, and he asked me if my mind was absolutely made up, and I said, " *Absolutely.*" Then he said, "Leave the matter to me." He requested Richard to call upon him, and asked him if he would give him three promises in writing—(1) that I should be allowed the free practice of my religion ; (2) that if we had any children they should be brought up Catholics ;

(3) that we should be married in the Catholic Church : which three promises Richard readily signed. He also amused the Cardinal, as the family afterwards learnt, by saying sharply, " Practise her religion indeed ! I should rather think she *shall.* A man without a religion may be excused, but a woman without a religion is not the woman for me." The Cardinal then sent for me, promised me his protection, said he would himself procure a special dispensation from Rome, and that he would perform the ceremony himself. He then saw my father, who told him how much opposed my mother was to it ; that she was threatened with paralysis ; that we had to consider her in every possible way, that she might receive no shocks, no agitation ; but that all the rest quite consented to the marriage. A big family council was then held ; and it was agreed far better for Richard and me and for every one to make all proper arrangements to be married and to be attended by friends, and for me to go away on a visit to some friends, that they might not come to the wedding, nor participate in it, in order not to agitate my mother ; that they would break it to her at a suitable time ; and that the secret of their knowing it should be kept up as long as mother lived. " Mind," said my father, " you must never bring a misunderstanding between mother and me, nor between her and her children."

I passed that three weeks preparing very solemnly and earnestly for my marriage day, but yet something differently to what many expectant brides do. I made a very solemn religious preparation, receiving the Sacraments. Gowns, presents, and wedding pageants had no part in it, had no place.

The following were my reflections [1] :

" The principal and leading features of my future life are going to be :

" Marriage with Richard.

" My parents' blessing and pardon.

" A man-child.

" An appointment, money earned by literature and publishing.

" A little society.

" Doing a great deal of good.

" Much travelling.

" I have always divided marriage into three classes—Love, Ambition, and Life. By Life I mean a particular style of life and second self that a peculiar disposition and strong character require to make life happy, and without which possibly neither Love alone nor Ambition alone would satisfy it. And I love a man in whom I can unite all three, Love, Life, and Ambition, of my own choice. Some understand Ambition as Title, Wealth, Estates ; I understand it as Fame, Name, Power. I have undertaken a very peculiar man ; I have asked a difficult mission of God, and that is to give me that man's body and soul. It is a grand mission ; and after ten years and a half of prayer God has given it to me. Now we must lead a good, useful, active, noble life, and be each other's salvation ; and if we have children, bring them up in the fear of God. The first thing to be done is to obtain my parents'

[1] From her devotional book *Laméd.*

pardon and blessing for going my own way; the next, to pray for a child to comfort me when he is absent and cannot take me; and, thirdly, to set to work with a good heart to work for an appointment or other means of living. We must do any amount of study and publishing, take society in moderation as a treat; we must do good according to our means; and when successful we will travel. My rules as a wife are as follows:

Rules for my Guidance as a Wife.

" 1. Let your husband find in you a companion, friend, and adviser, and *confidante*, that he may miss nothing at home; and let him find in the wife what he and many other men fancy is only to be found in a mistress, that he may seek nothing out of his home.

" 2. Be a careful nurse when he is ailing, that he may never be in low spirits about his health without a serious cause.

" 3. Make his home snug. If it be ever so small and poor, there can always be a certain *chic* about it. Men are always ashamed of a poverty-stricken home, and therefore prefer the club. Attend much to his creature comforts; allow smoking or anything else; for if you do not, *somebody else will*. Make it yourself cheerful and attractive, and draw relations and intimates about him, and the style of society (*literati*) that suits him, marking who are real friends to him and who are not.

" 4. Improve and educate yourself in every way, that you may enter into his pursuits and keep pace with the times, that he may not weary of you.

" 5. Be prepared at any moment to follow him at an hour's notice and rough it like a man.

" 6. Do not try to hide your affection for him, but let him see and feel it in every action. Never refuse him anything he asks. Observe a certain amount of reserve and delicacy before him. Keep up the honeymoon romance, whether at home or in the desert. At the same time do not make prudish bothers, which only disgust, and are not true modesty. Do not make the mistake of neglecting your personal appearance, but try to look well and dress well to please his eye.

" 7. Perpetually work up his interests with the world, whether for publishing or for appointments. Let him feel, when he has to go away, that he leaves a second self in charge of his affairs at home ; so that if sometimes he is obliged to leave you behind, he may have nothing of anxiety on his mind. Take an interest in everything that interests him. To be companionable, a woman must learn what interests her husband ; and if it is only planting turnips, she must try to understand turnips.

" 8. Never confide your domestic affairs to your female friends.

" 9. Hide his faults from *every one*, and back him up through every difficulty and trouble ; but with his peculiar temperament advocate peace whenever it is consistent with his honour before the world.

" 10. Never permit any one to speak disrespectfully of him before you ; and if any one does, no matter how difficult, leave the room. Never permit any one to tell you anything about him, especially of his conduct with regard to other women. Never hurt his feelings by a rude remark or jest. Never answer when he finds fault ; and never reproach him when he is in the wrong, *especially when he tells you of it*, nor take advantage of it when you are angry ; and always keep his heart up when he has made a failure.

" 11. Keep all disagreements for your own room, and never let others find them out.

" 12. Never ask him *not* to do anything—for instance, with regard to visiting other women, or any one you particularly dislike ; trust him, and tell him everything, except another person's secret.

" 13. Do not bother him with religious talk, be religious yourself and give good example, take life seriously and earnestly, pray for and procure prayers for him, and do all you can for him without his knowing it, and let all your life be something that will win mercy from God for him. You might *try* to say a little prayer *with* him every night before laying down to sleep, and gently draw him to be good to the poor and more gentle and forbearing to others.

" 14. Cultivate your own good health, spirits, and nerves, to counteract his naturally melancholy turn, and to enable you to carry out your mission.

" 15. Never open his letters, nor appear inquisitive about anything he does not volunteer to tell you.

" 16. Never interfere between him and his family ; encourage their being with him, and forward everything he wishes to do for them, and treat them in every respect (as far as they will let you) as if they were your own.

" 17. Keep everything going, and let nothing ever

be at a standstill : nothing would weary him like stagnation." [1]

Richard arranged with my own lawyer and my own priest that everything should be conducted in a strictly legal and strictly religious way, and the whole programme of the affair was prepared. A very solemn day to me was the eve of my marriage. The following day I was supposed to be going to pass a few weeks with a friend in the country.

At nine o'clock on Tuesday, January 22, 1861, my cab was at the door, with my box on it. I had to go and wish my father and mother good-bye before leaving. I went downstairs with a beating heart, after I had knelt in my own room, and said a fervent prayer that they might bless me, and if they did I would take it as a sign. I was so nervous, I could scarcely stand. When I went in mother kissed me, and said, "Good-bye, child ; God bless you ! " I went to my father's bedside, and knelt down and said good-bye. " God bless you, my darling ! " he said, and put his hand out of the bed and laid it on my head. I was too much overcome to speak, and one or two tears ran down my cheeks, and I remember as I passed down I kissed the door outside.

I then ran downstairs, and quickly got into my cab, and drove to the house of some friends (Dr. and

[1] She wrote in her book *Laméd* in 1864: "All has been carried out by God's help, with the only exception that He saw it was not good to give us children, for which we are now most grateful. Whatever happens to us is always for the best."

Miss Bird), where I changed my clothes—not wedding clothes (clothes which most brides of to-day would probably laugh at)—a fawn-coloured dress, a black-lace cloak, and a white bonnet—and they and I drove off to the Bavarian Catholic Church, Warwick Street. When assembled, we were altogether a party of eight. The Registrar was there for legality, as is customary. Richard was waiting on the doorstep for me, and as we went in he took holy water, and made a very large sign of the cross. The church doors were wide open, and full of people, and many were there who knew us. As the 10.30 Mass was about to begin we were called into the Sacristy, and we then found that the Cardinal in the night had been seized with an acute attack of the illness which carried him off four years later, and had deputed Dr. Hearne, his Vicar-General, to be his proxy.

After the ceremony was over and the names signed, we went back to the house of our friend Dr. Bird and his sister Alice, who have always been our best friends, where we had our wedding breakfast. During the time we were breakfasting Dr. Bird began to chaff Richard about the things that were sometimes said of him, and which were not true. "Now, Burton, tell me, how do you feel when you have killed a man?" Dr. Bird (being a physician) had given himself away without knowing it. Richard looked up quizzically, and drawled out, "Oh, quite jolly! How do you?"[1]

---

[1] Miss Alice Bird, who knew Sir Richard and Lady Burton for many years, has told me the following details about the wedding. The Birds were friends of the Arundell family, and Isabel came to them and told them how matters stood with regard to Mrs. Arundell's opposition and her ill-health, and asked if she might be married

LADY BURTON AT THE TIME OF HER MARRIAGE. [*Page* 166.

We then went to Richard's bachelor lodgings, where he had a bedroom, dressing-room, and sitting-room ; and we had very few pounds to bless ourselves with, but were as happy as it is given to any mortals out of heaven to be. The fact is, that the only clandestine thing about it—and that was quite contrary to *my* desire—was that my poor mother, with her health and her religious scruples, was kept in the dark ; but I must thank God, though paralysis came on two years later, it was not I that caused it.

To say that I was happy would be to say nothing. A peace came over me that I had never known. I felt that it was for eternity, an immortal repose, and I was in a bewilderment of wonder at the goodness of God, Who had almost worked miracles for me.

from their house, and so, to use her own phrase, " throw the mantle of respectability over the marriage," to prevent people saying that it was a runaway match. Dr. Bird and his sister gladly consented ; they accompanied her to the church, and when the ceremony was over the newly wedded couple returned to their house in Welbeck Street, where they had a simple luncheon, which did duty for the wedding breakfast.

After luncheon was over Isabel and her husband walked off down Welbeck Street to their lodging in St. James's, where they settled down without any fuss whatever. She had sent her boxes on ahead in a four-wheeler. That evening a bachelor friend of Burton's called in at the lodging in St. James's, and found Isabel seated there, in every sense mistress of the situation, and Burton proudly introduced her as " My wife." They did not send the friend away, but kept him there to smoke and have a chat with them.

BOOK II
WEDDED
(1861—1890)

" Ellati Zaujuhá ma'ahá b'tadir el Kamar b'asbiha."
(" The woman who has her husband with her can turn the moon
with her finger.")

169

CHAPTER I

FERNANDO PO

(1861—1863)

I praise thee while my days go on;
I love thee while my days go on;
Through dark and death, through fire and frost,
With emptied arms and treasure lost,
I thank thee while my days go on.

ELIZABETH BARRETT BROWNING.

I N fiction (though perhaps not now as much as formerly) marriage is often treated as the end of all things in a woman's life, and the last chapter winds up with the "happy ever after," like the concluding scene of a melodrama. But in this romance of Isabel Burton, this drama of real life, marriage was but the beginning of the second and more important half of her life. It was the blossoming of love's flower, the expanding of her womanhood, the fulfilment of her destiny. For such a marriage as hers was a sacrament consecrated by love; it was a knitting together, a oneness, a union of body, soul, and spirit, of thought, feeling, and inclination, such as is not often given to mortals to enjoy. But then Burton was no ordinary man, nor was his wife an ordinary woman. She often said he was

" the only man in the world who could manage me,"
and to this it may be added that she was the only
woman in the world who would have suited him.   No
other woman could have held him as she did.   The
very qualities which made her different to the ordinary
run of women were those which made her the ideal
wife for a man like Richard Burton.   The eagle does
not mate with the domestic hen, and in Isabel's unconventional and adventurous temperament Burton saw
the reflex of his own.   Though holding different views
on some things, they had the same basic principles; and
though their early environment and education had been
widely different, yet Nature, the greatest force of all,
had brought them together and blended them into one.
It was a union of affinities.   Isabel merged her life in
her husband's.   She sacrificed everything to him save
two things—her rare individuality, and her fervent faith
in her religion.   The first she could not an she would ;
the second she would not an she could ; and to his
honour be it said he never demanded it of her.   But
in all else she was his absolutely ; her passionate
ideals, the treasure of her love, her life's happiness—all
were his to cherish or to mar as he might please.   She
had a high ideal of the married state.   " I think," she
writes, " a true woman who is married to her proper
mate recognizes the fully performed mission, whether
prosperous or not, and no one can ever take his place
for her as an interpreter of that which is between her
and her Creator, to her the shadow of God's protection
here on earth."   And her conception of a wife's duty
was an equally unselfish one, for she wrote of the

beginning of her married life : " I began to feel, what I have always felt since, that he was a glorious, stately ship in full sail, commanding all attention and admiration, and sometimes, if the wind drops, she still sails gallantly, and no one sees the humble little steam-tug hidden on the other side, with her strong heart and faithful arms working forth, and glorying in her proud and stately ship."

Very soon after her marriage Isabel was reconciled to her mother. It came about in this wise. Mrs. Arundell thought she had gone away on a visit to some friends in the country, and told her friends so ; but a week or two after the marriage one of Isabel's aunts, Monica Lady Gerard, heard of her going into a lodging in St. James's, and immediately rushed off to tell Mrs. Arundell that Isabel could not be staying in the country, as was supposed, and she feared she had eloped or something of the kind. Mrs. Arundell, in an agony of fear, telegraphed to her husband, who was then staying with some friends, and he wired back to her, " She is married to Dick Burton, and thank God for it." He also wrote, enclosing a letter Burton had written to him on the day of the marriage, announcing the fact, and he asked his wife to send one of Isabel's brothers (who knew the Burtons' address) to them and be reconciled. Mrs. Arundell was so much relieved that a worse thing had not befallen Isabel that she sent for the truant pair at once. She was not a woman to do things by halves ; and recognizing that the inevitable had happened, and that for weal or woe the deed was done, she received both Isabel and her husband with the utmost kindness, and expressed her regret that she should have opposed the marriage. The statement that she never forgave Burton is incorrect. On the contrary, she forgave him at once, and grew to like him greatly, always treating him as a son. She gave a family party to introduce Burton to his wife's relations, and there was a general reconciliation all round.

For seven months after their marriage Isabel and her husband continued to live, off and on, at their little lodgings in St. James's, as happy as two birds in a nest. But the problem of ways and means had early to be considered. Now that Burton had taken unto himself a wife, it became imperatively necessary that he should to some extent forego his wandering habits and settle down to earn something to maintain her in the position in which she had been accustomed to live. He had a small patrimony and his pay; in all about £350 a year. With the help Isabel's friends would have given, this might have sufficed to begin matrimony in India. In the ordinary course of events, Burton, like any other officer in the service, would have returned to India, rejoined his regiment, and taken his wife out with him. The money difficulty alone would not have stood in the way. But there were other difficulties, as Burton knew well; the strong prejudice against him (an unjust one, I believe, but none the less real) made it hopeless for him to expect promotion in the Indian army. So he did what was undoubtedly the best thing under the circumstances. He determined not to return to India, and he applied for a post in the Consular Service, with the result that in March, some three months after his marriage, he was offered the post of Consul at Fernando Po, on the west coast of Africa—a deadly climate, and £700 a year. He cheerfully accepted it, as he was only too glad to get his foot on the lowest rung of the official ladder. He was told to hold himself in readiness to leave in August ; and as the climate of Fernando Po was almost certain death to a white woman, he would not allow his young wife to accompany him. So the bliss of the first months of their wedded life was overshadowed by the thought of approaching separation.

In accepting the offer of Fernando Po, Burton wrote to the Foreign Office[1] : " My connexion with H.M.'s Indian army has now lasted upwards of nineteen years, and I am unwilling to retire without pension or selling out of my corps. If therefore my name could be retained upon the list of my regiment—as, for instance, is the case with H.M.'s Consul at Zanzibar—I should feel deeply indebted." A reasonable request truly. Lord John Russell, who was then Secretary of State for Foreign Affairs, and who had given Burton the Consulship, caused his application to be forwarded to the proper quarter—the Bombay Government. But the authorities in India refused to entertain Burton's application ; they struck his name off the Indian Army List ; and in this way the whole of his nineteen years' service in India was swept away without pay or pension. If the brutal truth must be told, they were only too glad to seize on this excuse to get rid of him. But that does not palliate their conduct ; it was well said,

[1] Letter to Foreign Office, March 27, 1861.

"His enemies may be congratulated on their mingled malice and meanness."

With regard to Fernando Po, I cannot take the view that Burton was ill-treated in not getting a better post; on the contrary, taking all the circumstances into consideration, he was fortunate in obtaining this one. For what were the facts ? He had undoubtedly distinguished himself as an explorer, as a linguist, and as a writer ; but his Indian career had been a failure. He had managed to give offence in high quarters, and he was viewed with disfavour. On quitting one service under a cloud, he could not at once expect to receive a pick appointment in another. As a Consul he was yet an untried man. There is little doubt that even Fernando Po was given him through the influence of his wife. It was the same throughout his after-career ; his wife's unceasing efforts on his behalf helped him up every step of the official ladder, and shielded him more than once from the full force of the official displeasure. There is nothing like a brilliant and beautiful wife to help a man on ; and so Burton found it. He had done many clever and marvellous things during his life, but the best day's work he ever did for himself was when he married Isabel Arundell. His marriage was in fact his salvation. It steadied him down and gave him some one to work for and some one to love, and it did more than anything else to give the lie to the rumours against him which were floating about. No longer an Ishmael, he entered an ancient and honoured family. Many who would not have moved a finger to help Burton were willing to do

anything in their power for his wife ; and as she cared
for only one thing, her husband's interests, he secured
their influence in his favour.

When the London season came round, the Burtons,
despite their limited means, went a good deal into
society. The story of their romantic marriage got
abroad, and many friends were ready to take them by
the hand. The late Lord Houghton was especially
kind. He asked Lord Palmerston, who was then
Prime Minister, to give a party in their honour ; and
Isabel was the bride of the evening, and went down
to dinner on the Prime Minister's arm. Shortly after
this she was presented at Court, "on her marriage,"
by Lady John Russell.

There had been some little doubt in Isabel's mind
concerning her presentation, as the Queen made it a
rule then (and may do so now, for all I know) that
she would not receive at Court any bride who had
made a runaway marriage. Isabel's was hardly a
runaway marriage, as she married with her father's
knowledge and consent. Still it was not quite a usual
one, and she was very glad when her presentation at
Court removed any doubt in this respect, especially as
she looked forward to living abroad in the future, and
difficulties might arise as to her attending a foreign
court if she were not received at her own. She wanted
to help her husband in every way.

Concerning her presentation Mrs. Fitzgerald has
told me the following anecdote. Isabel's one thought
was how to please her husband, and she was always
yearning to win his approval. A word of praise from

him was the sweetest thing in life. Burton, however, though proud and fond of her, was of anything but an effusive nature, and his praises of any one were few and far between. When she was dressed for her first Drawing-Room—and very handsome she looked, a beautiful woman beautifully dressed—she went to show herself to her husband. He looked at her critically; and though he was evidently delighted with her appearance, said nothing, which was a great disappointment to her. But as she was leaving the room she overheard him say to her mother, "La jeune femme n'a rien à craindre"; and she went down to the carriage radiant and happy.

The Burtons were such an unconventional couple that there was a good deal of curiosity among their acquaintances as to how they would get on, and all sorts of conjectures were made. Many of Burton's bachelor friends told one another frankly, "It won't last. She will never be able to hold him." Shortly after her marriage one of her girl friends took her aside and asked her in confidence, "Well, Isabel, how *does* it work? Can you manage him? Does he ever come home at night?" "Oh," said Isabel, "it works very well indeed, and he always comes home with the milk in the morning." Of course this was only in joke, for Burton was a man of most temperate life, and after his marriage, at any rate, he literally forsook all others and cleaved only to his wife.

About this time a calamity befell them in Grindlay's fire, in which they lost everything they had in the world, except the few personal belongings in their lodgings. All Burton's manuscripts were destroyed. He took it philosophically enough, and said, "Well, it is a great bore ; but I dare say that the world will be none the worse for some of the manuscripts having been burnt." His wife notes this as "a prophetic speech"; and so it was, when we remember the fate of *The Scented Garden* thirty years after.

The London season came to an end sooner in those days than it does now, and the end of June found the Burtons embarked on a round of visits in country houses. One of the houses they visited at the time was Fryston, Lord Houghton's, and here they met many of the most celebrated people of the day; for wit and beauty, rank and talent, met on common ground around the table of him "whom men call Lord Houghton, but the gods Monckton Milnes." Isabel always looked back on these first seven months of her marriage as the happiest of her life. They were one long honeymoon, "a great oasis"; and she adds, "Even if I had had no other, it would have been worth living for." But alas! the evil day of parting came all too soon. In August Burton had to sail for Fernando Po—"the Foreign Office grave," as it was called—and had perforce to leave his young wife behind him. She went down to Liverpool with him to see him off, and the agony of that first parting is best expressed in her own words :

"I was to go out, not now, but later, and then perhaps not to land, and to return and ply up and down between Madeira and Teneriffe and London ; and I, knowing he had Africa at his back, was in a

constant agitation for fear of his doing more of these
explorations into unknown lands. There were about
eighteen men (West African merchants), and everybody
took him away from me, and he had made me promise
that if I was allowed to go on board and see him
off I would not cry and unman him. It was blowing
hard and raining. There was one man who was incon-
siderate enough to accompany and stick to us the whole
time, so that we could not exchange a word. (How I
hated him!) I went down below, and unpacked his
things, and settled his cabin, and saw to the arrangement of his luggage. My whole life and soul were in
that good-bye, and I found myself on board the tug,
which flew faster and faster from the steamer. I saw a
white handkerchief go up to his face. I then drove to
a spot where I could see the steamer till she became
a dot." [1]

Burton was absent eighteen months, working hard
at his duties as Consul on the west coast of Africa.
During that time Isabel lived with her parents at
14, Montagu Place, W. It was a hard thing to be
exiled from her husband ; but she did not waste her
time in idle repining. Burton left her plenty of work
to do, and she did it thoroughly. In the first place, she
fought hard, though unsuccessfully, against the decision
of the Bombay Government to remove Burton's name
from the Indian Army List. In the next place, she
arranged for the publication of his book on the
Mormons. Surely not a very congenial task for a

---

[1] *Life of Sir Richard Burton*, by Isabel his wife, vol. i.,
pp. 348, 349.

young wife of seven months with an absent husband, for the book was largely a defence of polygamy ! But whatever Burton told her to do she did. She also executed his divers commissions which came by every mail. One of them was to go to Paris in January, 1862, on a special mission, to present to the Emperor and Empress of the French some relics of the great Napoleon—a lock of his hair, a sketch of a plaster cast taken after his death—which had come into the possession of the Burton family, also a complete set of Burton's works, and to ask for an audience of them. She left her letter and presents at the Tuileries, and her audience was not granted. She blamed herself bitterly at the time, and put the failure of her mission of courtesy down to " want of experience and proper friends and protection." But the truth of the matter is, that she ought never to have been sent on such an unnecessary errand, for it was not one in which she or any one could have been expected to succeed. Nevertheless Burton's relatives made themselves very unpleasant about it, and worried Isabel most cruelly concerning the loss of their trifling relics. And it may be remarked here that Burton's near relatives, both his sister and his niece, always disliked Isabel, and never lost an opportunity of girding against her. One of them has even carried this rancorous hostility beyond the grave. These ladies were jealous of Isabel—jealous of her superior social position, of her beauty, her fascinations, and above all jealous of her influence over her husband. Why this should have been so it is impossible to say, for Burton did not get on very well with his relatives, and made a point of seeing as little of them as possible. Perhaps they thought it was Isabel who kept him away ; but it was not. Fortunately it is not necessary to enter into the details of a sordid family squabble. To do so would be to weary, and not to edify.

Following the annoyance to which she was subjected by her husband's relatives came another of a different nature. There were many who heard, and some who repeated, rumours against Burton which had been circulated by Speke and others. One candid friend made it his business to retail some of these to Isabel (one to the effect that her husband was " keeping a seraglio " out at Fernando Po), and gave her a good deal of gratuitous and sympathetic advice as to how she ought to act. But Isabel refused to listen to any- thing against her husband, and spurned the sympathy and advice, declaring that "any one who could listen to such lying tales was no friend of hers," and she closed the acquaintance forthwith.

Despite her brave words there is no doubt that she fretted a good deal through the months that fol- lowed. Her depression was further aggravated by a sharp attack of diphtheria. One day in October, when she could bear the loneliness and separation from her husband no longer, she went down to the Foreign Office, and cried her heart out to Sir Henry (then Mr.) Layard. Her distress touched the official's heart, for he asked her to wait while he went upstairs. Presently Mr. Layard came back, saying he had got four months' leave for Burton, and had ordered the dispatch to be sent off that very afternoon. She says,

" I could have thrown my arms around his neck and kissed him, but I did not ; he might have been surprised. I had to go and sit out in the Green Park till the excitement wore off; it was more to me than if he had given me a large fortune."

In December Burton returned home after an absence of eighteen months, and his wife went to Liverpool to meet him. We may imagine her joy. Christmas was spent at Wardour Castle (Lord Arundell's), a large family gathering ; then they went to Garswood to stay with Lord Gerard ; he was Isabel's uncle, and always her staunch friend.

Burton's leave sped all too soon ; and when the time came for his departure, his wife told him that she could not possibly go on living as she had been living. "One's husband in a place where I am not allowed to go, and I living with my mother like a girl. I am neither maid, nor wife, nor widow." So he arranged to take her with him as far as Teneriffe at any rate. As they were to leave from Liverpool, they stayed at Garswood, which was hard by, until the day came for them to sail.

CHAPTER II[1]

MADEIRA

(1863)

The smallest bark on life's tumultuous ocean
Will leave a track behind for evermore;
The slightest wave of influence set in motion
Extends and widens to the eternal shore.

I STARTED from Liverpool on a bleak morning in January with many a " God-speed," and in possession of many aids to enjoyment, youth, health, strength, and the society of a dearly loved husband, whose companionship is a boon not often bestowed upon mortals in this nether world.

After the inevitable wettings from spray, and the rope which gets wrong, and the hat which blows over, and the usual amount of hilarity—as if it were a new thing —at the dishevelled head of one's fellow-creature, we set foot on board the African steamship *Spartan* at 1 p.m. We had still two hours in the Mersey, so we formed a little knot on deck, and those who knew Richard gathered around us. There was much joking

---

[1] The chapters on Madeira and Teneriffe are compiled from manuscripts which Lady Burton wrote on her return from Teneriffe in 1863, but which her husband would not allow her to publish.

as to the dirty weather we should meet outside (how dirty we of the land little guessed), and as to Admiral Fitzroy's "biggest storm that was ever known," as duly announced in the *Times*, for the 30th, which we were to meet in "the Bay of Biscay, O!" There were pleasant speculations as to how I should enjoy my dinner, whether ham and eggs would become my favourite nourishment, and so forth. At 2.30 p.m. we nearly ran into a large brig; the steamer was in the pilot's charge, but our captain coming on deck saved us with a close shave. We should certainly have got the worst of it in two seconds more. *Of course* it was the brig's fault; she didn't answer her helm; and, to use the captain's phrase, the pilot and mate were a little "agitated" when his calm "Put the helm down" made us only slightly graze each other and glide off again. We put on full speed and out to sea, as six bells (three o'clock) told on my landlubber ears. Before four o'clock (dining hour) I had faintly asked the stewardess to help me to shake myself down in my berth, and unpack the few articles I might want during the voyage. *I did not dine.*

Sunday, 25th, 1 a.m.—It blew a whole gale, with tremendous sea; ship labouring heavily, and shipping very heavy seas on deck; pumps at work. We were making little or no way down Channel, when we suddenly shipped a heavy sea, washing overboard a quartermaster, and sending our captain into the lee scuppers with a sprained wrist. We stopped, and reversed engines, but could not see the poor fellow; and to lower a boat in such a sea was impossible.

He was a married man, and had left his wife at Liverpool.

I shall never forget the horrors of that night. Every berth was full; so much so that our captain, with a chivalry and forgetfulness of self which deserves recording in letters of gold, gave up his own cabin to Richard and myself, that we might not be separated an hour sooner than necessity compelled us to be, and encountered the fatigue of his long duties on deck, and the discomforts and anxieties of ten days' bad weather, with no shelter but a chance berth or the saloon sofa. During that night one tremendous sea stove in the doors of the main cabin, filling the saloon and berths with water. The lights were extinguished; things came unshipped; all the little comforts and treasures were floating at the top, leaving few dry garments out of the "hold," which would not be opened till our arrival at Madeira. There arose on that confused night a Babel of sounds; strong language from the men-sufferers, conjuring the steward to bring lights, and the weaker sex calling for their protectors, and endeavouring to find them in the dark. One young and pretty little woman, almost a child, recently married, in her fright rushed into the saloon in her nightdress, calling for her husband. A brutal voice answered her in the chaos that she need never hope to see him again, for he had "fallen overboard" and was "clinging on outside." The poor little creature (she was only sixteen) believed the voice, and, with the energy of despair, forced the door of her husband's cabin, and there she remained with him, and ere long had an

epileptic fit, and also another during the first ten days,
doubtless accelerated by this act of brutality.   I regret
to say it was committed by a naval officer who was
tipsy.   Another sonorous voice bid us " die like
Christians " ; but I don't think that was any sentiment
of the speaker's.   Ever and anon the dismal scene was
interlarded with " short and crisp " sentences, *not* com-
forting, such as, " We can't live long in such a sea as
this " ; " We're going to the bad " ; " Won't the captain
put into Holyhead ? " " There go the pumps—we've
seven feet of water in the hold " (when we stopped and
reversed, to try and rescue the quartermaster) ; " The
water has got into our engines, and we can't go on " ;
" There's the carpenter hammering—the captain's cabin
is stove in," etc., etc.   A rich lady gave the stewardess
£5 to hold her hand all night, so the rest of us poorer
ones had to do without that matron's ministrations.

I crawled to my cabin, and, as I lay there trembling
and sea-sick, something tumbled against the door,
rolled in, and sank on the floor.   It was the tipsy naval
officer.   I could not rise, I could not shut the door, I
could not tug him out; so I lay there.   When Richard,
who was lending a hand at the pumps, had finished his
work, he crawled along the decks till he got to the
cabin, where the sea had swamped through the open
door pretty considerably.   " Hullo !   What's that ? " he
said.   I managed faintly to ejaculate, " The tipsy naval
officer."   He picked him up by the scruff of the neck,
and, regardless of consequences, he propelled him with
a good kick behind all down the deck, and shut the
door.   He said, " The captain says we can't live more

than two hours in such a sea as this." At first I had been frightened that I should die, but now I was only frightened that I shouldn't, and I uttered feebly, "Oh, thank God it will be over so soon!" I shall never forget how angry he was with me because I was not frightened, and gave me quite a sermon.

On Thursday, the 29th, we skirted the Bay of Biscay, and the ship rolled heavily. I was very much impressed by the grandeur of the gigantic billows of the Atlantic while skirting the Bay, not short, chopping waves, such as I had seen in the Channel and Mediterranean, but more like the undulations of a prairie, a high rising ground surrounding you at a distance, and, while you are in its depression, shutting out all from your view, until the next long roller makes you reverse the position, and feel "monarch of all you survey," or, rather, liken yourself to a midge in a walnut shell—so deeply are you impressed by the size and force of the waves, the smallness of yourself and ship, and the magnitude of the Almighty power. About four o'clock the sea grew more and more inky, and it was evidently brewing up for Admiral Fitzroy's storm, which soon came and lasted us till Saturday; and those who had ventured to raise their heads from their sea-sick pillows had to lay them down again.

Saturday, 31*st*.—We had been a week at sea, and for the first time it began to get fine and enjoyable. We were due this day at Madeira; but on account of the gales delaying us, it was not possible that we should land before Monday. The next day, Sunday, was truly pleasant. Our passengers were a curious mixture. Out of the seven ladies on board, two were wives of Protestant missionaries, excellent men, who had done good service of their kind at Sierra Leone and Abeokuta, and were returning with young and pretty wives. The thirty-two men passengers were of all kinds—military, naval, official, clergymen, invalids, five black people, and "Coast Lambs," as the palm-oil merchants are ironically termed. We formed a little knot of a picked half-dozen at the top of the table, and "feeding time" was the principal event of the day.

A laughable incident occurred one day on board at dinner. There was a very simple-minded Quaker, with a large hat, who had evidently been browsing on the heather in the north all his life, and on this occasion a fine plum-pudding, swimming in lighted brandy, was put upon the table at second course. The poor Quaker had never seen this dish before, and in a great state of excitement he exclaimed, "Oh, my God! the pudding's on fire!" and clapped his large hat over the pudding, and put it out, amidst roars of laughter, which had to be explained to him when his fright was over. After dinner we formed whist parties. In fine weather cushions and railway-rugs covered the deck, and knots of loungers gathered under gigantic umbrellas, reading or talking or working, and also in the evening moon-light, when the missionaries chanted hymns. On Sunday there was Protestant service in the saloon, and those of other faiths did their private devotions on deck.

Monday morning, February 2. — We dropped our anchor a quarter of a mile from the town of Funchal.

We rose at six, had a cup of coffee, packed up our water-proof bags, and went on deck to get a first glimpse of Madeira. A glorious sight presented itself, producing a magical effect upon the cold, wet, dirty, sea-sick passenger who had emerged from his atrocious native climate but ten days before. Picture to yourself a deep blue sky, delicately tinted at the horizon, not a cloud to be seen, the ocean as blue as the Mediterranean. There was a warm sun, and a soft and sweet-smelling breeze from the land, as of aromatic herbs. Arising out of the bosom of the ocean in splendour, a quarter of a mile off, but looking infinitely less distant, were dark mountain masses with fantastic peaks and wild, rugged sides, sharply defined against the sky and streaked with snow, making them resemble the fanciful castles and peaks we can imagine in the clouds. The coast to the sea is thick with brilliant vegetation; dark soil—basalt and red tufa are its colours—with the variegated green of fir, chestnut, dark pine forests, and the gaudy sugar-cane. Here and there a belt of firs runs up a mountain, winding like a serpent, and is its only ornament. Wild geraniums, and other flowers which only grow in a hothouse in England, and badly too, are in wild luxuriance here. The island appears to be dotted everywhere with churches, villas, and hamlets —little gardens and patches of trees intermingled with them. There are three immense ravines, deep and dark ; and these with all the pleasant additions of birds, butterflies, and flowers of every sort and colour, a picturesque, good-humoured peasantry busy on the beach, and a little fleet of fishing-boats, with their large

THE BAY OF FUNCHAL, MADEIRA.

[Page 190.

white lagoon sails, like big white butterflies on the blue water. Most of the capes are immense precipices of rock.

Nestling at the foot of this mountain amphitheatre, and washed by the bay, straggling lengthways and up and down, is Funchal, with its brilliant white houses and green facings glittering in the sun. You almost wonder whether your last unpleasant three months in England and your ten days' voyage had been reality ; whether you had not been supping upon cold fish, and had just awakened from a clammy nightmare to a day such as the Almighty meant our days to be, such was one's sense of vitality and immense power of enjoyment at the change.

The landing was great fun, the running of the boats upon the beach being very difficult in a heavy surge. Richard and I managed to land, however, without a wetting, and went to the hotel.

When we had unpacked, eaten, and bathed, and had begun to shake off the *désagrémens* of our bad voyage, we had time to enjoy a pleasant, lazy day, lounging about, and luxuriating in our happy change from England and the ship. Later on in the day there was a little mist over the mountains, like the soft muslin veil thrown over a beautiful bride, shading her brilliant beauty, greatly to her advantage, leaving a little of it to the imagination. I beg a bride's pardon. How could there be a bride without a Brussels lace veil ? Shall I change the simile to that of a first communicant, and compare the belt of white thin cloud below the mountains, and that delicate mist, which throws such

enchanting shadows on the mountain-sides and precipices, to the " dim religious light " of the sunset hour,
when the lamp is replenished ?   For the sun is setting,
and bathes the sea and coast in a glorious light, deepens
the shade of the ravines, and shows off the dark, luxuriant foliage.

I can only venture upon describing a few of the
excursions we were able to make during our stay
at Madeira.

We started one fine morning in a boat with four
oars and rowed from Funchal, coasting along near
the cliff to Machico, which is twelve miles.   Our
men were chatty and communicative, and informed us
that the devil came there at night when they were out
fishing (I suppose originally the ingenious device of a
smuggler) ; and their superstition was genuine.   We
had two hours of rough walking, when we arrived
at Machico, and marched through the town with a
hundred followers, all clamouring for money.   We
rejoined our boat at 4 p.m., in the greatest clatter of
talk and laugh I ever heard.   Our sailors, elated by
two shillings'-worth of bad wine, were very chatty and
vocal.   We put up a sail, but there was not breeze
enough to fill it.   We chatted and read alternately;
watched the beautiful hour that struggles between day
and night—beautiful to the happy, and much to be
dreaded to the desolate.   The setting sun bathed the
dark basalt and red tufa cliffs in his red and purple
glory.   The straggling white town glittered in the clear
and brilliant light, with its dark green background.
The mountain-edges were sharp against the clear, soft

sky. That indescribable atmosphere which blackens the ravines and softens all the other beauties came over the island. The evening star was as large and brilliant as the Koh-i-noor ; and the full moon, rising gradually from behind Cape Garajão, poured its beams down the mountain, and threw its track upon the sea. As we neared Funchal the aromatic smell of the land was wafted toward us, and with it a sound of the tinkling of bells ; and a procession of torches wound like a serpent out of a church on a rock overhanging the sea. It was the Blessed Sacrament being carried to a dying man.

Our second boat excursion was to Cape Giram, a cliff some two thousand feet high, with the appearance of having been originally a high hill, cut in two by some convulsion of Nature. There was a lovely waterfall, and its silvery foam absolutely looked artificial, like the cascade of a theatre, as it streamed incessantly down a bed of long grass of a very pretty green, which it seemed to have made for itself to course down. I had no idea of the height; but having suddenly exclaimed to Richard, who was my *maître-d'armes*, " I wish I had brought my pistols with me, I should like to pick off those two gulls," to my horror, our boatman hailed somebody, and a small voice echoed back. The "gulls" were two Portuguese peasants gathering herbs for their cow.

Our last expedition, and best, was to Pico Arriere, the second highest point in the island. We had wished very much to ascend the highest, but that involved the six days' excursion, which we could not do; so we resolved to try the second, *faute de mieux*, which could be done without sleeping out. With the usual horses and guides we started from Funchal, and proceeded to ascend.

After an hour and a half we come to a little eminence, and the rough work is going to commence. The air begins to change wonderfully. The horizon now assumes the punch-bowl shape; and I, standing on one side of the imaginary basin, but not quite so high as the rim, describe my impressions. Behind and above us were the peaks, around us the mountains clad with forests; a fine, bold shore, with its high basalt and tufa cliffs; a long way below us the *quintas*, gardens, farms, thatched huts, little patches of sugar-cane of an enchanting green, fields looking very small, dwarf plains, watercourses, cascades, channels, and deep, abrupt ravines; the beautiful little town at the bottom of the basin, and the roadstead; the open sea, with white sails glittering on the blue water, appears to be running up the other side; the Desertas seemingly hanging midway between heaven and earth; and crowned by a glorious sky, warm sun, pure air, and sea-breeze. I feel so glad, I could shout Hallelujah for joy. The horses have breathed while I made these mental notes, and now we start again on the hard and broken road, which seems interminable. The horses don't like the cold, nor the men either. We do! (We have been some time in the snow, which descends to the unusual depth of three thousand feet.) The horses make a stand, and we dismount and walk (it appeared an immense way) till the road ceases and the actual mountain ascent begins. One guide wraps his head up in a red silk handkerchief, and will go no farther ; the other sulks, and says it is dangerous—the path is lost, and we shall fall into drifts ; but finding us resolved, Sulks consents to go, and Red Cap stops, shivering, with the horses, which are rearing and kicking, for the cold makes them playful.

So, pike in hand, Richard and I and Sulks begin the ascent, which lasts about one hour and a half—through two feet of snow, with several falls on my part, and sometimes crawling on hands and knees—during which, however, we could see Sta. Anna and the sea at the other side, and many of the mountains and gorges. When nearly at the top, we saw, with horror, thick black clouds rolling up to envelop us, travelling fast, and looking like a snowstorm. At last, when we were 5,593 feet high, only 300 feet below the summit of the Pico, which is 5,893 feet, there came a mighty wind. We threw ourselves down to prevent being blown off, and then the clouds rolled in upon us, and shut off all view of the Pico and our way, so that it was difficult to proceed without incurring danger of accidents. We scrambled to a projection of rock (the only thing we could see), and sat on it; and from our canteen, which had been slung to Sulks, we ate our lunch, and iced our claret ; and when we had finished we agreed to grope our way slowly down. We managed it (often in a sitting position), occasionally making some false step for want of being able to see ; we had no feeling in our hands and feet. We found Red Cap eventually, who had moved down to warmer latitudes, and was sulking and shivering, more so because, as he declined going, he forfeited his lunch, drink, and cigarette. We walked back until at some distance above the Mount church (feeling warmer and drier every moment as we descended), where we mounted and resumed those delightful baskets. The excursion occupied about seven and a half hours.

The time came all too soon for us to leave Madeira, and on March 4 we embarked for Santa Cruz, Teneriffe, whence alarming reports of yellow fever had reached our ears. By the same boat on which we had embarked came letters and papers from home. My news from home was very sad. My dear mother, who, though in weak health, had come down to Liverpool to see us off, and who bore up bravely till the last, had just time, after wishing us good-bye, to get back to Garswood (Uncle Gerard's), when the attack of paralysis, so long threatened, came upon her. Fortunately there was no immediate danger, but the news was a great shock to me. I spent the day apart from the rest, who were merry unto noisiness; and I was right glad when tea-time rang all hands below, and I occupied a quiet corner on deck, where I could shed my tears unseen, and enjoy my favourite twilight hour.

The sky was clear, with a rough sea, over which the white horses predominated. Men-of-war and fishing-boats were at anchor around us. The sun had just set ; the evening star's pale light was stealing over us. Presently the full moon rose behind Cape Garajāo. I bade good-bye to Madeira and every object with regret, straining my eyes from right to left, up and down, and all around, not from any silly sentiment, but because I always feel a species of gratitude to a place where I have been happy. The black and red cliffs, the straggling town, the sugar-canes, gardens, forests, flowers, the mountain-peaks and ravines—each separate, well-known object received its adieu.

I knew when I saw Madeira again it would be under far less happy circumstances. I should be alone, on my way back to England, and my beloved Richard at deadly Fernando Po. This fading, fairy panorama of Madeira, which had once made me so happy, now saddened me ; and the last track of moonlight, as it poured its beams down the mountains on the water, saw some useless tears.

CHAPTER III

(1863)

I went up into the infinite solitudes. I saw the sunrise gleaming on the mountain-peaks. I felt myself nearer the stars—I seemed almost to be in sympathy and communion with them.

IBSEN.

THE first sight of Santa Cruz (where we arrived next morning) is disappointing. When you see it from the deck of your ship, looking from right to left, you see a red, brown, and yellow coast, barren grey mountains, and ravines. The mountains, being exposed to much wind, present the most curious, harsh, and fantastic outline against the sky. These are called Passo Alto (a child would guess their volcanic origin); they are wide irregular masses of rock, as desolate and savage as can be imagined. Close to the water is a flat, whitewashed town, which always looks in a white heat. The only two high buildings are churches. The town bristled with cannon near the sea. The mountains, which are close to the town on the right, and shut it off, were covered with round, bushy, and compact green splotches, which were in reality good-sized fig trees. Behind the town is a steep rising mountain, with a good winding road; to the left of it is a regiment of windmills drawn up in line, as if waiting for Don Quixote; and in the distance, still on the left, and extending away from you, are masses of mountains, and hanging over them is a little haze in the sky, which might be a little woolly cloud, sugarloaf in shape, which you are told is the Peak of Teneriffe. The sky, the sea, the atmosphere are perfect, and far surpassing Madeira. Most exhilarating is the sensation thereof. The island, saving one pass, is covered with small barren hills, some of them conical, some like Primrose Hill, only much bigger, which are, I am told, the small disturbances of volcanoes.

These were my first impressions as we were rowed to a little quay in a little boat, and a dozen boys took our dozen packages; and a small walk brought us to Richardson's Hotel, *as it was*, a funny, old, brokendown place, with a curious interior, an uncomfortable picturesque remnant of Spanish-Moorish grandeur and style, better to sketch than to sleep and feed in. There was a large *patio*, or courtyard, and a broad carved oak staircase, and tiers of large balconies to correspond, running all round the interior of the house, into which galleries the rooms open. Green creepers covered the roof and balcony, and hung over, falling into the *patio*, giving it an ancient and picturesque look, like an old ruin. Rita, a peasant woman, came out to wait upon me, in a long white mantilla, topped by a black felt Spanish wide-awake, a comfortable-looking woman, but neither young nor pretty. The food was as poor and ancient as the hotel, and the servants to match. I could imagine the garlicked sausages to have been a remnant left in a mouldy cupboard by some impoverished hidalgo of a hundred years back.

Richard wanted to pass a few days here, but I suggested that, as the yellow fever was raging, and as Santa Cruz and all round could be seen in three or four days, we should do it on return, and meantime seek some purer abode, lest a yellow-fever bed or infected baggage should lay us low ; so we voted for Laguna, or rather San Christoval de la Laguna, a large town fifteen hundred feet above sea-level, and consequently above fever-range ; and we ordered the hotel carriage at once.

The vehicle was the skeleton of the first vehicle that was ever made—perhaps the one Noah provided in the Ark to drive his family down Mount Ararat when it became dry—no springs, windows, blinds, lining, or anything save the actual wood ; three mules abreast, rope, reins and driver all ancient to match. We found a crowd of men wringing their hands at the amount of small baggage to be packed away in it, swearing they could not and would not try to put it in. Always leave these men to themselves. After loud vociferation, swearing, and quarrelling, they packed it beautifully, and we were stowed away on the top of it, and rattled out of the town at a good pace, up a winding road, ascending the steep country behind Santa Cruz towards Laguna. As we rose higher we had a splendid view of the sea, and the white flat town with its two solitary towers lay at our feet. The winding road was propped up with walls to prevent landslip ; the mountains looked wild and rugged ; the weather was perfect. We met troops of pretty peasants with heavy loads, and every here and there a picturesque chapel or hermitage.

Our drive was pleasant enough, and I think at about 3 p.m. we were driving hard up and down the old Noah's-Ark-town called San Christoval de la Laguna. We drove to three inns. Number one was not possible. Number two, something like it ; where they were going to put us into the same room (perhaps the same bed—who knows ?) with a sick man (maybe a convalescent yellow-feverist). We held a parley and consultation. Was it possible to go on ? No, neither now nor to-morrow ; for the new road was being made, the old one broken up, and the coach (which, by-the-way, was the name given to a twin vehicle such as ours) was not allowed to run farther than Sausal, three miles off, from which we had twelve miles more to accomplish in order to reach the valley and town of Orotava—the El Dorado, and deservedly so, of Teneriffe. We did not like to descend again into the heat and pestilence of Santa Cruz. Moreover, we had made up our minds (not knowing Laguna) to pass a week there, and had ordered our muleteers to bring up and deposit our baggage there.

The coachman thought he knew of another house where we might get a room. So we drove to the " forlorn hope," which looked as bad as the rest, and were at first refused. The *patio* was a ruin, full of mud and broken plantains, the village idiot and the pig huddled up in one corner. In fact, the whole house was a ruin, and the inevitable carved-wood balcony

looked like tawdry finery on it. The landlady was
the most fiendish-looking old woman I have ever seen,
with sharp, bad, black eyes. She exchanged some words
in a whisper with three or four ruffianly looking men,
and said that she could let us have a room, but only
one. Richard went up to inspect it, and while he was
gone, and I was left alone, the village idiot worried
and frightened me. Our quarters consisted of a small
barnlike room with raftered ceiling, a floor with holes
big enough to slip your foot through into the courtyard, whitewashed walls, and a small latticed window
about two feet square near the ceiling. It was filthy,
and contained two small paillasses full of fleas, two hard
kitchen chairs, and a small kitchen table. For safety,
we had all our baggage brought up. We asked for a
light, and they gave us a rushlight, growling all the
time because we did not find the light of a dim oil-lamp
in the passage enough, and bread sufficient nourishment ;
but we clamoured for supper.

After three hours' preparation, during which we were
inspected by the whole band of ruffians composing the
establishment, and after loud, bewildering chatter about
what should become of us on the morrow, we were
asked with much pomp and ceremony into the kitchen.
We could not both go at once, as there was no key to
our door, and the baggage was unsafe. Richard was not
away five minutes, but returned with an exclamation of
disgust, threw himself on the paillasse, lit a cigar, and
opened a bottle of Santa Cruz wine we had brought
with us. I then started, and found it necessary to hold
the light close to the ground, in order not to put my

feet through the holes, or fall on the uneven boarding of the gallery. In a dirty kitchen, on a dirty cloth, was a pink mess in a saucer, smoking hot (which, if analysed, would have proved to be eggs, beetroot, garlic, and rancid oil), stale bread, dirty rancid butter, looking like melted tallow-grease ; and what I thought was a large vinegar-cruet, but in reality a bottle of wine, completed the repast. I tried to eat, but, though starved, soon desisted. When I returned to my room, Pepa, the dirty handmaiden—who was always gaping into the streets for excitement (which was not to be found in Laguna), but who proved more good-tempered and honest than her mistress—followed me, and, looking nervously around, put a large key into my hand, and told me to lock my door at night. I did not need a second hint, but also piled up the baggage and kitchen chairs and table against what looked to me like a second suspicious door, opening out on leads and locked outside. I then got out our arms—two revolvers and three bowie-knives—loaded the former, and put one of each close to our hands ready. Sleep was out of the question for me on account of the fleas, which were legion ; but I experienced nothing of a more alarming nature.

We were up betimes, and clamouring to get on to Orotava. They naturally wished to keep us, and so they invented every excuse. They all spoke loudly and at once. "The *public* coach was engaged by a *private* gentleman for several days ; there were no horses or mules to be had for some time" (they would almost have told us there was no hotel at Orotava, if they had dared); "the yellow fever raged everywhere except at Laguna, which was above its range." "Well, then," we said, "under all these circumstances we would *walk*." Now they never walk themselves, and a woman doing such a thing was incredible. They said, "*He* might walk; but what about the Señora and the baggage?" Seeing, finally, that we were determined, and offered good pay, the driver of the vehicle agreed to drive us three miles farther on to Sausal, and to furnish us with several mules for our baggage; but no *riding* mules, never thinking that we should accept such a proposition. To their surprise, we closed with it at once. They tried a last dodge in the shape of charging us the exorbitant price of five dollars, or £1, for our atrocious night's lodging and mess of eggs, and we gave it cheerfully. When we went to pack up, we discovered that, although we had been there but fifteen hours, and had never left the room at the same time without locking our door and taking the key, they had contrived to steal our best bowie-knife, but had touched nothing else. It were better to leave gold than a knife in the way of a Spaniard. We would not even stay to dispute this.

We finally started in the "coach," in high glee, through the melancholy streets, up a rising country, grand and hilly, and over a good road. Richard said that it was a most interesting mountain-pass, for reasons which were rather *au-dessus de ma portée*; and as I have no doubt of it, I will describe the trifles.

The chief travellers on this road were muleteers, picturesque men in blankets and sombreros, sitting on comfortable-looking and heavily laden pack-saddles, walking or galloping, and singing in a peculiar Moorish roulade, and smoking their little paper cigarillos. The only difference that I could see between them and a Spanish gentleman was, that the latter's mule was better bred and went a faster pace, and he had, in place of the blanket, a black cloak, with perhaps a bit of red sash or binding. Pretty peasant women, with a sturdy yet graceful walk and undulating figures, went by. They wore white flannel mantillas, topped by a sombrero, and carried enormous weights on their heads, and sang and chattered, not at all distressed by their burthens. We passed all the scenes of historical interest in our passage through the island. Our coach arrived finally at Sausal. Our aneroid marked nineteen hundred feet at the highest part of our drive through the pass. Here we dismounted, and the coach waited for an hour to see what passengers it might pick up.

We were in a very peculiar position, quite by ourselves (without even a servant), at a wayside house of refuge on a mountain-side, beyond which precincts no vehicle went at this time, and where it was impossible to remain, and without knowing a soul in the island. Luckily Richard spoke the language well. Still, we did not exactly know where we were going. We had an indistinct wish to go to Orotava ; but where it was, or how distant at that moment, we knew not ; nor did we know, when we got there, if we should find any accommodation, and if not, how we should be able to get back, or whether we should have to pass the night out .

of doors. Yet it was the happiest moment of my life.
I had been through two mortally dull years (without
travel), in commonplace, matter-of-fact Old England,
where one *can't* get into a difficulty. Independently
of this, our baggage—some twenty-five packages—was
scattered all over the place on mule-back, some coming
up from Santa Cruz, some from Laguna, and the
smaller ones with us. They would not know what
had become of us. And how were we to rid ourselves
of those we had with us? We saw several ·handsome,
proud, lazy-looking fellows, in blankets, sleeping about,
outside the cottage, and asked them if, for a couple of
dollars, they would carry these, and walk with us to
show us the way? Not a bit of it! They did not
want to earn two dollars (8*s*. 4*d*.) at such a price!
They *have* nothing, and *want* nothing but sleep and
independence. At last a party of muleteers came by.
Richard explained our difficulties, and one good-natured
old fellow put our small traps on the top of his pack,
and we left orders at the house of refuge with the girl
that any mules passing by laden with an Englishman's
luggage were to come on to Orotava, and then commenced our walk. And an uncommonly pretty, pleasant
walk it was. This path was only fit for mules ; and
the continuation of the good road we could not enter
upon, on account of the people at work, and incessant
blasting.

At the end of four hours a mere turn in the road
showed us the tropical valley in all its beauty, and the
effect was magical : the wealth of verdure and foliage,
wild flowers, and carolling birds of pretty plumage.

A horseshoe-shaped range of mountains shuts out the
Vale of Orotava from the rest of the world, enclosing
it entirely, except where open to the sea and its cool
breezes ; and we gradually wound down under its
eastern range, sloping to the beach.

A boy guide met us, and led us through many a
winding, paved street of Orotava, till the trickling of
the mountain stream reached our ears ; and then, following its course, he brought us to the door of our *fonda
gobea*, or inn, which, from its outward appearance,
charmed me inexpressibly. It is an ancient relic of
Spanish–Moorish grandeur—the palace of a defunct
Marchesa—a large building, of white stone, whitewashed
over, built in a square, the interior forming the *patio*,
or courtyard. Verandahed balconies run all around it
inside, in tiers of dark carved wood, and outside
windows, or wooden doors, empanelled, and with old
coats of arms above them. These open on to balconies
of the same. There is a flat roof, with garden or
terrace at the top. The inside balconies form the
passage. All the rooms open into the side next the
house ; the other looks into the court. We were very
weary and dusty as we entered the *patio*. The *amo*,
or master, made his appearance, and, much to our
chagrin, conducted us to a room very much like the
one we left at Laguna. I will not say that our spirits
fell, for we looked at each other and burst out laughing;
it was evident that the Canaries contained no better
accommodation ; but people who go in for travelling
laugh at the discomforts that make others miserable ;
so, with a glance at an upper skylight, a foot square,

we agreed that it would be a capital place for work, in the way of reading, writing, and study.

While Richard was settling something, and drinking a cup of coffee, I asked the *amo* to let me inspect the house, and see if I could not find better accommodation ; but he assured me that every nook and cranny was occupied. I explored an open belvedere at the top of the house, a garret half occupied by a photographer in the daytime, and the courtyard, and was going back in despair, when I came upon a long, lofty, dusty, deserted-looking loft, with thirty-two hard, straight-backed kitchen chairs in it. I counted them from curiosity.

"What," I asked, "is this ? "

" Oh," he replied, " we call this the *sala*, but no one ever comes into it ; so we use it as a lumber-room, and the workwomen sit here."

"Will you give me this ?" I asked again.

"Willingly," he replied, looking nevertheless as surprised as if I had asked to sleep in the courtyard ; "and, moreover, you can run over the house, and ask Bernardo [a peasant servant] to give you whatever furniture you may choose."

I was not long in thanking him and carrying his offer into execution. Bernardo and I speedily fraternized, and we soon had the place broomed and aired. It had evidently been the ballroom or reception-room of the defunct Marchesa in palmy days. Stone walls painted white, a wood floor with chinks in it, through which you could see the *patio* below, and through which " brave rats and mice " fearlessly came to play ; a raftered wood ceiling with a deep carved cornice (through the holes above the children overhead subsequently pelted us with nuts and cheese) ; three chains, with faded blue ribbons, suspended from the lofty ceiling, whereon chandeliers had evidently hung. Three carved-wood doors (rusty on their hinges) opened on to a verandah balcony, from which we had a splendid view. The hotel opened sideways, on the hillside, on to a perpendicular street, with a mountain torrent dashing down it beneath the windows. To the left, above, was the mountain range of Tigayga ; to the right was the town, or *villa* ; and below, and sideways to the right, was the cultivated valley, and the sea stretching broadly away, and, when clear, we could see the *white cone*—the immortal Peak. One double door, of cedar wood, opened on to the balcony overhanging the *patio* ; and one more into another room, which I had subsequently to barricade against an inquisitive old lady, who wanted to see if English people bathed and ate like Teneriffians.

Such was the aspect of the loft after a brooming. I then routed out an old screen, and ran it across the room, dividing it into two, thereby enabling the *amo* to charge me for bedroom and sitting-room. In the bedroom half I ran two straw paillasses together for a bed ; two little primitive washstands, capable of containing a pint of water ; and two tiny tables of like dimensions for our toilet. My next difficulty was to rig up a bath and a stove. Hunting about, I found a large wine-wash, as tall as myself. I rolled it in, and ordered it to be filled every day with sea water. The drawing-room contained two large kitchen tables (one for Richard's writing, one to dine on), and a smaller one for *my* occupations, a horsehair sofa, a pan of charcoal, kettles, and pots for hot water, tea, eggs, and minor cooking.

Presently mule after mule began to arrive with the baggage ; not a thing was missing. I divided the thirty-two hard-backed kitchen chairs between the two apartments. For want of drawers or wardrobe we kept most things in our trunks, hanging dresses, coats, and dressing-gown over the screen and chairs in lieu of wardrobe. Books, writing, and instruments strewed the whole place. I was delighted with my handiwork. We had arrived at seven, and at nine I went to fetch my philosophic husband, who had meanwhile got a book, and had quietly sat down, making up his mind for the worst. He was perfectly delighted with the fine old den, for we had good air, light, a splendid view, lots of room, and good water, both fresh and salt ; and here we intended to pass a happy month—to read, write, study, chat, walk, make excursions, and enjoy ourselves.

Saturday, March 21, 1863.—Of course we could not rest until we had " done " the Peak. We were in our saddles at nine. Our little caravan consisted of six persons and four animals—Richard and myself mounted on good horses, two mules laden with baggage, one guide, and three *arrieros*, or muleteers. Our distance varied (by different reports) between eighteen and thirty-two miles, from the Villa d'Orotava to the top of the great Peak and back ; and by the route we returned from choice—a longer, varied, and more difficult one—I dare say it was nearer the latter mark, and our time was thirty-five hours.

We clattered up the streets, and went out by a pretty road, studded with villages, gardens, cottages, *barrancos*, and geraniums falling in rich profusion over the walls into the main road. We turned abruptly from this road up the stony side of the Barranco de San Antonio, and proceeded through cultivated fields, but ever winding by the *barranco*, which becomes deeper and deeper. Here rushes a fierce mountain torrent. The stone at the sides is scooped as smoothly by its impetuous rush as a knife would carve a cake of soap, and you hear the rebounding in the gigantic caverns, which present all the appearance of being excavated by an immense body of water. On the borders of this mass of stone and of rushing waters, startling caverns, and mysterious rumblings, the edges were bound with rich belts of chestnut trees, wild flowers of every sort, myrtle and rosemary, looking as placid as in a garden ; and you do not expect to be awestruck—*as you are*—when you look into the depth of the ravine, into which you might have taken a step too far, deceived by the treacherous borders, if the strange sounds below had not induced you to look down. We were now about two thousand five hundred feet above the sea.

We ascended a very jagged and rough mountain, like a *barranco*, ever ascending, and came upon a beautiful slope of forest of mixed bay and broom. The soil, however, is a mass of loose stones as we wind through the forest, and again emerge on another barren, jagged, and stony mountain, like the one before the forest. It is now eleven o'clock, and we are four thousand five hundred feet above the sea, and the men ask for a halt. The valley rises like a hanging garden all the way till you come to the first cloud and mist, after which are no more houses ; the mist rests upon the woods, and ascends and descends for about the space of a league. We had now just got to the clouds. They usually descend to this distance, and, except on very clear days, hang there for several hours in the day—if not all day—shutting out the upper world of mountains like a curtain, though above and below it all may be clear. We dismounted in a thick, misty cloud, and looked about us, leaving the men to eat, drink, and breathe the animals.

The whole of our ascent appeared to me to be like ascending different mountains, one range higher than another, so that when you reached the top of one you found yourself unexpectedly at the foot of another ; only each varies as to soil : stones, vegetation ; stones, cinders, stones.

At one o'clock we passed the last vegetation, six thousand five hundred feet, with a shady clearing under the *retornas*, which our men told us was the Estancia della Cierra—the first station. The thermometer in shade was at 60°. Here we unloaded the mules, and tied them to the bushes, upon which they fed. We ate, drank, the men smoked, and then we reloaded and remounted, and soon emerged from the last vegetation, and entered upon Los Cañadas, through a gap, by the gate of Teora—a natural portico of lava. Here we ceased ascending for some time, the Cañadas being a

THE PEAK OF TENERIFFE, FROM THE VALE OF OROTAVA.

[*Page* 212.

sandy plain, extending fifteen miles in circumference round the base of the Peak. Richard wished to build him a house in this his peculiar element, wanted a good gallop, and all sorts of things. The hot sun literally rained fire, pouring down upon our heads and scorching the earth, and blistering our faces, hands, and lips, as if it spitefully begrudged us our pleasant excursion and boisterous spirits. There was water nowhere.

We rode along the plain laughing and chattering, and presently began to ascend again the same soil as on the plain, but steepening and more bleak and barren, with not a sign of life or vegetation. We came to the mountain, and put our poor beasts to the steep ascent, breasting the red pumice bed and thick bands of detached black blocks of lava. The soil, in fact, consists of loose pumice stones sprinkled with lava and broken bits of obsidian. Our animals sank knee-deep, and slid back several yards ; and we struggled upwards after this fashion for three-quarters of an hour, when we came to a little flat space on the right, with blocks of stone partially enclosing it, but open overhead and to one side.

This was the second station, called the Estancia de los Ingleses, nine thousand six hundred feet above the sea ; temperature 16°, only accessible on the southeastern side. Here we gladly dismounted, after eight hours' ride.

The *arrieros* unpacked and dismantled their beasts, let the mules roll, and put all four in shelter with their nosebags, and then went in search of fuel. Richard went off to take observations ; and I saw him with pleasure enjoying the indescribable atmospheric charm under the rose-pink blush of the upper sky. I knew mine was Martha's share of the business, and that I had better look sharp ; so I unpacked our panniers, and made the *estancia* ready for the night. In less than an hour our beds were made comfortable, and composed of railway-rugs, coats, and cloaks. There were two roaring fires, and tea and coffee ; and spread about were spirits, wine, fowls, bread, butter, hard eggs, and sausages. We could have spent a week there very comfortably ; and we sat round our camp-fire warming ourselves, eating, and talking over the day. The men brought out hard eggs, salt fish, and prepared *gofia*—the original Guanche food—which is corn roasted brown, then pounded fine, and put into a kid-skin bag with water and kneaded about in the hand into a sort of cake. They were immensely surprised at a sharp repeater which I had in my belt, and with which we tried to shoot a raven; but he would not come within shot, though we tried hard to tempt him with a chicken's leg stuck upon a stick at a distance.

We read and wrote till seven o'clock, and then it grew darker and colder, and I turned in, *i.e.* rolled myself round in the rugs with my feet to the camp-fire, and did not sleep, but watched. The *estancia*, or station, was a pile of wild rocks about twenty feet high, open overhead to one side, with a space in the middle big enough to camp in. At the head and down one side of our bed was a bank of snow ; two mules were tethered near our heads, but not near enough to kick and bite. The horses were a little farther off. There

were two capital fires of *retorna* wood; and strewed
all around were rugs, blankets, and wraps of all sorts,
kettles, canteens, bottles, books, instruments, eatables,
and kegs. It was dark at seven o'clock. The stars
shone brilliantly, but it was only the third night of the
moon, so we were badly off for that. But the day
had been brilliant, and our only drawback had been
that the curtain of clouds had shut out the under-world
from us about one o'clock for good and all. Our men
consisted of one guide, Manuel, and three *arrieros*.
They lay round the fire in their blankets and black
velvet sombreros in careless attitudes. (I did not
know a blanket could look so picturesque.) Their
dark hair and skins, white teeth, flashing eyes, and
handsome features, lit up by the lurid glare of the fire,
and animated by the conversation of Richard, to say
nothing of the spirits and tobacco with which he made
their hearts glad, made a first-rate bivouac scene, a
brigand-like group, for they are a fine and hardy race.
They held loud and long theological discussions, good-
humouredly anathematizing Richard as an infidel, and
showed their medals and crosses. He harangued them,
and completely baffled them with his Mohammedan
logic; and ended by opening his shirt, and showing
them a medal and cross like their own—the one I had
given him long ago. They looked at each other, shook
their fists, laughed, and were beside themselves with
excitement. I laughed and listened until the Great
Bear went down behind the mountain-side, and then
fell fast asleep. The men took it in turns to keep up
the fire, while they slept around it. The only sound

heard was once or twice the spiteful scream of a mule
trying to bite its neighbour, or a log of wood being
thrown on the fire; and outside the *estancia* the silence
was so profound as to fully realize "the last man."
The pleasant reminiscences of that night will live in
my memory when most other things are forgotten, or
trials and sorrows make me temporarily forget to be
grateful for past happiness. It was perfect repose and
full contentment. The tangled world below was forgotten, and the hand of him whom I cannot dispense
with through life was near to clasp mine.

At half-past three o'clock Manuel awoke us. It
was a pitch-dark night save the fires. The thermometer at 14°. We got up and crowded on every
warm thing possible, made some coffee, using brandy
for milk. Now one of the *arrieros* was to remain
behind to look after the fires, beasts, and *estancia*
generally. I mounted my horse, and Richard one of
the mules. Our guide went first. One *arriero* with a
pitch-pine torch, and one *arriero* to return with the
animals, made our party to start. At half-past four
o'clock we commenced upon what seemed the same
kind of thing as the last part of yesterday's ride—
steep, broken pumice, obsidian, and lava—only twenty
times more difficult and steep, with an occasional rock-
work or snowdrift. We were the first people who
had ascended in winter since 1797; and even the
guide did not exactly know what might happen for the
snow. Manuel went therefore first with a torch; then
Richard; then the second torch; then myself on my
poor Negro; and, lastly, a third torch. Our poor

beasts sank knee-deep, and slid tremendously. Once or twice my steed refused, and appeared to prefer descent to ascent, but fortunately changed his mind, or an inevitable roll to the bottom and broken bones would have been the result. Richard's mule went into a snowdrift, but emerged, with much pluck, without unseating him. I got a little frightened when it got to the steepest part, and found myself obliged to cling to the mane, for it was too dark, even with torches, to see much. In three-quarters of an hour we came to the highest and third *estancia*, ten thousand five hundred feet above sea-level, called Estancia de los Allemanes.

Here we dismounted, and our third *arriero* went down with the animals, while we, pike in hand, began the ascent of the Mal Pais, which is composed of what yesterday I had imagined to be walls of black stone, radiating from the ridge below the cone to the yellow mountain, but which are really very severe lava beds, about thirteen hundred feet high, consisting of immense blocks of lava ; some as big as a cottage, and some as small as a football ; some loose and rolling, others firm, with drifts of snow between, and piled up almost perpendicularly above you ; and when you have surmounted one ridge, and fancy yourself at the top, you find there is another still more difficult, until you have had so many disappointments that you cease to ask. It took me two hours, climbing on my hands and knees, with many rests. First I threw away my pike, then my outer coat, and gradually peeled, like the circus dancers do, who represent the seasons, army and navy, etc., until I absolutely arrived at the necessary blouse and petticoat. As there were no thieves, I dropped my things on the way as I climbed, and they served as so many landmarks on return. Every time we stopped to breathe I was obliged to fill my mouth with snow, and put it on my head and forehead—the sun had blistered me so, and the air was keen. At about 5.30 a.m. a truly soft light, preceding day, took the place of torchlight. The horizon gradually became like a rainbow, with that peculiar effect it always has of being on a level with one, and the world beneath curved like a bowl, which is very striking to a person who is on a great height for the first time. More toil, and we pass the icedrift at our right, and sight the Cone, which looks like a dirty-white sugar-loaf; which, I was told, was a low comparison! Every ten minutes I was obliged to rest; and the guides, after each few moments' rest, would urge me to a *toutine*—just a little more—to which I had manfully to make up my mind, though I felt very much fatigued.

At 6 a.m. the guides told us to turn round: a golden gleam was on the sea—the first of the sun; and gradually its edge appeared, and it rose majestically in pure golden glory; and we were hanging between heaven and earth—in solitude and silence—and were permitted to enjoy this beautiful moment. It was Sunday morning, March 22—Passion Sunday.[1] Out

[1 On reading through this manuscript with Mr. Wilkins, I am struck with the coincidence that it was on Passion Sunday, March 22, 1896 (thirty-three years later), that my dear sister, Lady Burton, died.—E. FITZGERALD.]

of the six souls there, five of us were Catholics, unable
to hear Mass. We knelt down, and I said aloud a
Paternoster, Ave Maria, and Gloria Patri, and offered
to our Lord the hearts of all present with genuine
thanksgiving, and with a silent prayer that the one dear
to me, the only unbeliever of our small party, might
one day receive the gift of faith.

We arose, and continued our now almost painful
way, and at 6.45 reached the base of the dirty-white
sugar-loaf. Here we breathed ; and what had seemed
to me to be a ridge from below was a small plain
space round the base of the Cone. The thermometer
stood at 120° in the steam, but there was no smell of
sulphur till we reached the top. Manuel and Richard
start, pike in hand. My muleteer took off his red
sash, tied it round my waist, and took the other end
over his shoulder, and with a pike in my hand we did
the last hard work ; and it was very hard after the
Mal Pais. The Cone is surrounded, as I have just
said, by a little plain base of pumice, and its own soil
is broken, fine pumice—out of which, from all parts,
issue jets of smoke, which burn you and your clothes :
I think I counted thirty-five. We had five hundred
and twelve feet more to accomplish, and we took three-
quarters of an hour. The top consists of masses of rock,
great and small, covered with bright, glistening, yellow
sulphur, and frost ; and from which issue powerful
jets of smoke from the volcano within. Richard helped
me up to stand on the corona, the top stone, at 7.40
a.m. It is so narrow there is only room for one person
to stand there at once. I stood there a minute or two.

I had reached the Peak. I was now, at the outside computation, twelve thousand three hundred feet high.

The guides again suggested a Gloria Patri, in thanksgiving—Richard a cigar. Both were accomplished. The guides had been a little anxious about this first winter attempt. They now told us it had been deemed impossible in Orotava to accomplish it; and as for the Señora, they had said, she could not even reach the second Estancia de los Ingleses, and lo! there she stood on the corona! From where we stood at this moment, it is said that on a clear day the eye can take in the unparalleled distance of eight hundred miles in circumference of ocean, grasping the whole of Teneriffe as from a balloon, and its coast, and the whole fourteen Canaries and coast of Africa. Unfortunately for us, the banks of clouds below were too thick for us to do more than obtain a view of the surrounding mountain-tops and country, and see the crater. The sea we could only behold at a great distance. We spent forty minutes at the top, examining the crater, and looking all around us; during the latter part of which operation, I am sorry to say, I fell fast asleep from sheer fatigue, and was aroused by Richard hallooing to me that my clothes were on fire, which, alas! was too true. I pocketed specimens of obsidian, sulphur, and pumice. It was piercing cold, with a burning sun; and we experienced a nasty, choking, sickening smell of sulphur, which arose in fetid puffs from the many-coloured surface — dead white, purple, dull red, green, and brilliant yellow. A sense of awe stole over me as Richard almost poked his head into the holes whence issued the jets of smoke. I could not help thinking of the fearful catastrophes that had taken place—how eruptions, perhaps from that very hole, had desolated Teneriffe— how, perhaps, it was that which had caused Hanno to say that on the coast of Africa it rained fire ; and yet here we were fearlessly poking our heads inquisitively into it. What if this should be the instant of another great convulsion?

I did not experience any of the sensations described by most travellers on the Peak, such as sickness, pains in the head or inside, or faintness and difficulty of breathing, though the air was rare in the extreme, and although I am of a highly sensitive and nervous temperament, and suffer all this when obliged to lead a sedentary life and deprived of open air and hard exercise. I found my brain clear and the air and height delightfully exhilarating, and could have travelled so for a month with much pleasure. The only inconvenience that I did experience was a sun that appeared to concentrate itself upon me as a focus (as, I suppose, it appeared to do the same to each of us), and a piercing cold and severe wind besides, which combined to heat and yet freeze my head and face, until the latter became like a perfect mask of hard, red skin, likewise my lips and inside of my mouth. My hands, feet, and knees also were torn by the rocks, and I was a little bruised by sleeping on stones; but that was all ; and my only difficulty about breathing proceeded from the labour of climbing on hands and feet, and had no connexion with the rarity of the atmosphere ; and as we were, I believe, the first winter travellers living who had ascended at that season, we had an excellent opportunity of judging. My guide also told me that I was the only señora who had performed some feat or other ; but I could not exactly understand what.

At 8.30 we began the descent, planting our pikes and our heels in the soft stuff, sliding down ten or twelve yards at a time, and arrived in a quarter of an hour at the little plain base. Here we breathed for a few moments, and then started again for the descent of that truly Mal Pais. It was even *worse* to descend. I only wondered how we got up in the dark without breaking our ankles or legs over those colossal ruins, called the "Hobberings," of the Peak. Twice twisting my ankle in the loose masses, though not badly, warned me that it was better to take my time than get a bad hurt ; and the others were most considerate to me, both going and coming, begging me not to be ashamed to stop as often and as long as I liked. We were therefore two hours coming down, picking up the discarded garments on the way, and inclining a little to the right, to see the ice cave—Cueva de Zelo—which occupied twenty minutes. It is a large cavern in the rock, hung with huge icicles, and covered over with ice inside. We now descended to the place we had mounted on horse-back in the night. How the poor beast ever came up it is my astonishment ; and I am sure, if it had been daylight, I should have been a great deal more frightened than I was. It was a case of " poling " down on our heels again ; and our two guides hailed the two below with a Guanche whistle, which meant " Put the kettle on."

We reached the next stage at 10.11. I was now rather "done up," so I drank a bowl of strong green tea, and performed a kind of toilet, etc., under the lee of a rock, taking off the remnants of my gloves, boots, and stockings, and replacing them with others, which I fortunately had taken the precaution to bring ; washed, brushed, and combed ; dressed a little more tidily ; and glycerined my hands, feet, and face. I then wanted to lie down and sleep ; but alas ! there was no shade except in the snowdrifts; so I tied a wet towel round my head, and erected an umbrella over it, and slept for half an hour, while Richard and the men breakfasted and reloaded. We sent the animals down the remainder of the steep ascent which had taken up our last three-quarters of an hour yesterday—that is, from the *estancia* where we slept to the commencement of the Cañadas—and we followed on foot, and were down in about half an hour. This is the bottom of the actual mountain out of which the Cone rises. Once more being on almost level ground, we soon passed the desert, fifteen miles in circumference, surrounding the mountain. There were still ranges of mountains and country to descend, below it, to reach Orotava. We accomplished them all after a hot but pleasant ride, broken by rests, and arrived safe home at Orotava at 7 p.m.

We spent a thoroughly happy month at Orotava, in the wilds, amongst the peasantry. No trammels of society, no world, *no post*, out of civilization, *en bourgeois*, and doing everything for ourselves, with the bare necessaries of life. All our days were much alike, except excursion days.

We rose at seven, cup of tea, and toilet. Then came my domestic work (Richard had plunged into literature at half-past seven): this consisted of what, I suppose, Shakspeare meant by "chronicling small beer"; but I had no fine lady's maid to do it for me—she would have been sadly out of place—ordering dinner, market, and accounts, needlework, doing the room, the washing, small cookery on the pan of charcoal, and superintending the roughest of the work as performed by Bernardo. Husbands are uncomfortable without "Chronicle," though they never see the *petit détail* going on, and like to keep up the pleasant illusion that it is done by magic. *I* thought it very good fun, this kind of gypsying. Breakfast at ten, write till two (journals and diaries kept up, etc.), dinner at two; then walk or ride or make an excursion; cup of tea on coming in, literature till ten, with a break of supper at eight, and at ten to bed: a delightfully healthy and wholesome life, both for mind and body, but one which I can't recommend to any one who cannot rough it, or who has no serious occupation, or lacks a very agreeable companion.

Sometimes, when Richard was busy writing, I would stroll far away into the valley to enjoy the sweet, balmy sea-breeze and smell of flowers, and drink in the soft, clear air, and would get far away from our little straggling, up-and-down town on its perch, and cross over *barrancos* and ravines and enjoy myself. One day, so occupied, I came upon a lovely *quinta* in a garden, full of fruits and flowers, a perfect forest of tall rose trees and geranium bushes, which hung over the garden hedge into the path. Two charming old ladies caught me prigging—Los Senhoras T. They came out and asked me in, showed me all over their garden, gave me fruit and sweetmeats and flowers, and kissed me. They did not know what five o'clock tea meant, but I often wandered there about that time, and found a charming substitute in the above articles, and I quite struck up a friendship with them.

We put off leaving our peaceful retreat until the last possible day, when we went down to Santa Cruz. When we had been at Santa Cruz three or four days, the fatal gun boomed—the signal of our separation. It was midday, and there was my detestable steamer at anchor—the steamer by which I was to return to England. I felt as I did when I was a child, and the cab stopped at the dentist's door. I may pass over this miserable day and our most miserable parting. Richard was going again to pestilential Fernando Po. I should not see him for many, many weary months, and perhaps never again. How gladly would I have gone with him ; even to the eleventh hour I had hoped that he would relent and let me go. But the climate was death to a white woman, and he was inexorable. He would not even let me sleep one night at Fernando Po. So we parted, he to his consulate, and I to go back home—which was no home without *him*. I pass over the pain of that parting. With many tears and a heavy heart I embarked on my steamer for England.

CHAPTER IV

A TRIP TO PORTUGAL

(1863—1865)

Containeth Time a twain of days—this of blessing, that of bane;
And holdeth Life a twain of halves—this of pleasure, that of pain.

ALF LAYLAH WA LAYLAH
(*Burton's "Arabian Nights"*).

O N returning to England, a long and dreary interval of fifteen months ensued. Isabel spent it for the most part with her parents in London, working all the time for her husband in one way or another. The separation was broken this time by one or two voyages which she made from England to Teneriffe, where she and her husband met for a space when he could snatch a week or two from Fernando Po. She had one very anxious time; it was when Burton was sent on a special mission to the King of Dahomé, to impress upon that potentate the importance the British Government attached to the cessation of the slave-trade, and to endeavour by every possible means to induce him to discontinue the Dahoman customs, which were abominable cruelties. Burton succeeded in some things, and his dusky majesty took a great fancy to him, and he made him a brigadier-

general of his Amazons. When the news of this un-
looked-for honour reached Isabel, she became " madly
jealous from afar," for she pictured to herself her
husband surrounded by lovely houris in flowing robes
mounted on matchless Arab steeds. Burton, however,
allayed her pangs by sending her a little sketch of the
chief officer of his brigade, as a type of the rest. Even
Isabel, who owns that she was influenced occasionally
by the green-eyed monster, could not be jealous of this
enchantress.

The mission to the King of Dahomé was a difficult
and dangerous one; but Burton acquitted himself well.
Isabel at home lost no time in bringing her husband's
services before Lord Russell, the Foreign Secretary, and
she seized this opportunity to ask for his promotion
to a less deadly climate, where she might join him.
In reply she received the following letter :

"MINTO, *October* 6, 1863.
"DEAR MRS. BURTON,
    " I know the climate in which your husband
is working so zealously and so well is an unhealthy
one, but it is not true to say that he is the smallest of
consuls in the worst part of the world. Many have
inferior salaries, and some are in more unhealthy places.

    " However, if I find a vacancy of a post with an equal
salary and a better position, I will not forget his services.
I do not imagine he would wish for a less active post.

    " He has performed his mission to Dahomé very
creditably, to my entire satisfaction.

                    " I remain, yours truly,
                        " RUSSELL."

With this answer she was fain to be content for a space. In August, 1864, the time came round again for Burton's second leave home. His wife, rejoicing, travelled down to meet him at Liverpool, this time to part no more, as previously. A few weeks after his return they went to Mortlake Cemetery and chose the place for their grave, the very spot where the stone tent now is, beneath which they both are sleeping. Very quickly after that came the British Association meeting at Bath and the tragic incident of Speke's death. [1]

---

[1] "Laurence Oliphant conveyed to Richard that Speke had said that 'if Burton appeared on the platform at Bath' (which was, as it were, Speke's native town) 'he would kick him.' I remember Richard's answer—'Well, *that* settles it! By God! he *shall* kick me'; and so to Bath we went. There was to be no speaking on Africa the first day, but the next day was fixed for the 'great discussion between Burton and Speke.' The first day we went on the platform close to Speke. He looked at Richard and at me, and we at him. I shall never forget his face. It was full of sorrow, of yearning and perplexity. Then he seemed to turn to stone. After a while he began to fidget a great deal, and exclaimed half aloud, 'Oh, I cannot stand this any longer!' He got up to go out. The man nearest him said, 'Shall you want your chair again, sir? May I have it? Shall you come back?' and he answered, 'I hope not,' and left the hall. The next day a large crowd was assembled for this famous discussion. All the distinguished people were with the Council; Richard *alone was excluded*, and stood on the platform—*we two alone*, he with his notes in his hand. There was a delay of about twenty-five minutes, and then the Council and speakers filed in and announced the terrible accident out shooting that had befallen poor Speke shortly after his leaving the hall the day before. Richard sank into a chair, and I saw by the workings of his face the terrible emotion he was controlling and the shock he had received. When called upon to speak, in a voice that trembled, he spoke of other things and as briefly as he could. When we got home he wept long and bitterly, and I was for many a day trying to comfort him" (*Life of Sir Richard Burton*, by Isabel his wife, vol. i., p. 389).

Apart from the sad circumstance of Speke's death, which cast a shadow over their joy, the Burtons passed a very pleasant winter. They stayed at several country houses, as was their wont, and found many hospitable friends glad to receive them, and met many interesting people, notably Professor Jowett. Early in 1864 they went on a two months' driving tour in Ireland, which they explored by degrees from end to end after their own fashion in an Irish car. They paid many visits *en route* ; and it may be mentioned in passing that Isabel always used to see the little horse which took them over Ireland had his midday feed, *washed down by a pint of whisky and water.* She always declared that this was what kept him so frisky and fresh ! This Irish tour also brings out the restless, roving spirit of both Burton and his wife. Even when on leave at home, and in the midst of civilization, they could never remain any length of time in one place, but preferred to be on the move and rough it in their own fashion. At Dublin they met with an unusual amount of hospitality ; and while they were staying in that city Isabel met Lentaigne, the great convict philanthropist. He had such a passion for taking convicts in and trying to reform them that Lord Carlisle once said to him, " Why, Lentaigne, you will wake up some morning and find you are the only spoon in the house." He took Isabel to see all the prisons and reformatories in Dublin, and endeavoured to arouse in her something of his enthusiasm for their inhabitants. Knowing that she would soon be bound for foreign parts, he implored her to take one with her, a convict woman of about thirty-four, who was just being discharged after fifteen years in prison. " Why, Mr. Lentaigne, what did she do ? " asked Isabel. " Poor girl ! " he answered—" the sweetest creature !—she murdered her baby when she was sixteen." " Well," answered Isabel, " I would do anything to oblige you ; but if I took her, I dare say I should often be left alone with her, and at thirty-four she *might* like larger game."

It was about this time that the Burtons again represented to Lord Russell how miserable their lives were, in consequence of being continually separated by the deadly climate of Fernando Po. Isabel's repeated petitions so moved the Foreign Secretary that he transferred Burton to the Consulate of Santos in the Brazils. It was not much of a post, it is true, and with a treacherous climate ; but still his wife could accompany him there, and they hailed the change with gratitude. Before their departure a complimentary dinner was given by the Anthropological Society to Burton, with Lord Stanley (afterwards Lord Derby) in the chair. Lord Stanley made a very complimentary speech about the guest of the evening, and the President of the Society proposed Mrs. Burton's health, and spoke of the " respect and admiration " with which they all regarded her. The dinner was a capital send-off, and the Burtons may be said to have entered upon the second stage of their married life with the omens set fair.

Husband and wife arranged that they should go out to Portugal together for a little tour ; that he should go on from there to Brazil ; and she should return to London to wind up affairs, and as soon as

that was done join him at Rio. In accordance with
this programme they embarked at Southampton for
Lisbon on May 10, 1865. The passage out was
uneventful. Isabel in her journal thus describes their
experiences on arriving at Lisbon :

" As soon as our vessel dropped her anchor a crowd
of boats came alongside, and there ensued a wonderful
scene. In their anxiety to secure employment the
porters almost dragged the passengers in half, and tore
the baggage from each other as dogs fight for a bone,
screaming themselves hoarse the while, and scarcely
intelligible from excitement. The noise was so great
we could not hear ourselves speak, and our great difficulty was to prevent any one of them from fingering
our baggage. We made up our minds to wait till the
great rush was over. We sent some baggage on with
the steamer, and kept some to go ashore. I am sure
I do not exaggerate when I say that, as I sat and
watched one bag, I told fifteen men, one after another,
to let it alone. We saw some friends go off in the
clutches of many fingers, and amid scenes of confusion
and excitement ; but not caring to do likewise, we
chose a boat, and went round to the custom-house.
The landing was most disagreeable, and in a bad gale
not to be done at all—merely a few dirty steps on the
river-side. In wind and pelting rain we walked to
our hotel, followed closely at our heels by men and
famished-looking dogs. We proceeded at once to the
best-looking hotel in the place, the Braganza, which
makes some show from the river—a large, square, red
building, several storeys high, with tiers of balconies

all round the house. On account of the diplomats occupying this hotel on a special mission from England to give the Garter to the King of Portugal, it was still crowded, and we were put up in the garrets at first. After two days we were given a very pleasant suite of rooms—bedroom, dining- and drawing-room— with wide windows overlooking the Tagus and a great part of Lisbon.

"These quarters were, however, not without drawbacks, for here occurred an incident which gave me a foretaste of the sort of thing I was to expect in Brazil. Our bedroom was a large whitewashed place ; there were three holes in the wall, one at the bedside bristling with horns, and these were cockroaches some three inches long. The drawing-room was gorgeous with yellow satin, and the magnificent yellow curtains were sprinkled with these crawling things. The consequence was that I used to stand on a chair and scream. This annoyed Richard very much. 'A nice sort of traveller and companion *you* are going to make,' he said ; 'I suppose you think you look very pretty and interesting standing on that chair and howling at those innocent creatures.' This hurt me so much that, without descending from the chair, I stopped screaming, and made a meditation like St. Simon Stylites on his pillar ; and it was, 'That if I was going to live in a country always in contact with these and worse things, though I had a perfect horror of anything black and crawling, it would never do to go on like that.' So I got down, fetched a basin of water and a slipper, and in two hours, by the watch, I had knocked ninety-seven of them into it. It cured me. From that day I had no more fear of vermin and reptiles, which is just as well in a country where nature is over-luxuriant. A little while after we changed our rooms we were succeeded by Lord and Lady Lytton, and, to my infinite delight, I heard the same screams coming from the same room a little while after. 'There!' I said in triumph, 'you see I am not the *only* woman who does not like cockroaches.'"

The Burtons tarried two months in Portugal, and explored it from end to end, and Isabel made notes of everything she saw in her characteristic way. Space does not permit of giving the account of her Portuguese tour in full, but we are fain to find room for the following descriptions of a bull-fight and procession at Lisbon. Burton insisted on taking his wife (whose loathing of cruelty to animals was intense) to see it, probably to accustom her betimes to the savage sights and sounds which might await her in the semi-civilized country whither they were bound. "At first," she says, "I crouched down with my hands over my face, but I gradually peeped through one finger and then another until I saw the whole of it." And this is what she saw :

"On Sunday afternoon at half-past four we drove to the Campo di Sta. Anna, where stands the Praça dos Touros, or Bull Circus, a wooden edifice built in the time of Dom Miguel. It is fitted with five hundred boxes, and can contain ten thousand persons. It is a high, round, red building, ornamented. The circle has a barrier and then a space all round, and a second and higher barrier where the people begin. They were watering the ring when we entered, crackers were fizzing, and the band was playing. At five o'clock the circle was filled.

" A blast from the trumpets announced the entry of the *cavalleiro*, a knight on a prancing steed richly caparisoned, which performed all the steps and evolutions of the old Spanish horsemanship—*i.e.* saluting the public and curveting all about in steps. The *cavalleiro* then announced the deeds to be performed, and this ceremony was called 'the greeting of the knight.' Before him marched the bull-fighters, who ranged themselves for inspection in ranks. They were sixteen in number. Eight *gallegos* were dressed in white stockings to the knee, flesh-coloured tights, green caps lined with red, red sashes, and gay, chintz-patterned jackets, and were armed with long pronged forks like pitchforks, called *homens de forçado*. They were Portuguese, fit and hearty. Two boys in chocolate-coloured velvet and gold attended as pages, and six Spaniards, who really did all the work, completed the number. They were tall, straight, slim, proud, and graceful, and they strutted about with cool jauntiness. Their dress began with dandy shoes, then flesh-coloured stockings, velvet tights slashed with gold or silver, a scarlet sash, and a short jacket that was a mass of gold or silver, and a sombrero of fanciful make. Their hair was as short as possible, save for a pigtail rolled up like a woman's back hair and knotted with ribbon. There was one in green and gold, one in pale blue and silver, one in purple and silver, one in dark blue and silver, one in chocolate and silver, and one in maroon and silver. The green and gold was the favourite man, on account of his coolness, jaunty demeanour, and his graceful carelessness. The *cavalleiro* having inspected them, retired. Another man then came out, the *piccador*.

"At a fresh blast of the horn the door of the arena flew open, and in rushed a bull. For an instant he stopped, stared wildly round in surprise, and gave a wild roar of rage. Then he made at the horseman, whose duty it was to receive him at full gallop and to plant the barb in his neck before his horns reached the horse's hind-quarters, which he would otherwise have ripped up. When the bull had received several barbs from the *piccador*, he was tired of pursuing the horse. It was then the duty of the Spaniards to run so as to draw the bull after them, when on foot they planted two barbs in his neck. The instant he received them he roared and turned off for an instant, during which the man flew over the barrier as lightly as possible. This went on for some time, the bull bounding about with his tail in the air and roaring as he sought another victim. The prettiest part of it was the skill of the *matador* or *espada*, who shook a cloak at the bull. The beast immediately rushed at it as quick as a flash of lightning ; the *espada* darted aside, twisted the cloak, and changed places with the bull, who could never get at him. It was as if he rushed at a shadow. It was most graceful. In the case of our green-and-gold *espada* the bulls seemed afraid of him. They retired before his gaze as he knelt down before them, begging of them to come on; after a few rounds they seemed to acknowledge a master, for he appeared to terrify them.

The last act was that in which the *gallegos* tease the bull
to run at them.   One, when the bull was charging with
bowed head, jumped between the horns and clung on,
allowing himself to be flung about, and the others
caught hold of the tail and jumped on his back, and he
pranced about till tired.   This is literally ' seizing the
bull by the horns.'   Then oxen with bells were turned
in, and the bull was supposed to go off quietly with
them.   We had thirteen bulls, and the performance
lasted two hours.   The programmes were crammed
with high-flown language.

   " Women were there in full war-paint, green and
pink silk and white mantillas.   Little children of four
and five years old were there too.   No wonder they grow
hardened !   A few English tourists were present also,
and a lot of dirty-looking people dressed in Sunday.
best.   Our first bull would go back with the cows ;
the second bull jumped over the barrier, and gave a
great deal of trouble, and very nearly succeeded in
getting amongst the people.   Every now and then
a bull would fly over the head of the *bandahille* and
jump the barrier to escape him.   One bull flew at the
barrier, and, failing to clear it, fell backwards ; one bull
would not fight, and was fearfully hissed ; one had to
be lassoed to get him out of the ring.   Once or twice
gallegos would have been gored but for the balls on
the bulls' horns.

   " After the first terror I found the fight very
exciting.   If it had been a bit more cruel no woman
ought to have seen it.   I heard some who were
accustomed to Spanish bull-fights say it was very tame.

The bulls' horns were muffled, so that they could not gore the horses or men. Hence there were no disembowelled horses and dogs lying dead, and a bull which has fought well is not unfairly killed. The men were bruised though, and perhaps the horses. The bull had some twenty barbs sticking in the fleshy part of his neck. When he is lassoed and made fast in the stable, the men take out the barbs, wash the wounds in vinegar and salt, and the bull returns to his herd.

"The day before we left Portugal—Richard for Brazil and I for England—I had also the good fortune to witness a royal procession.

"Early in the day Lisbon presented an appearance as if something unusual was about to take place. The streets were strewed thickly with soft red sand. The corridors were hung with festoons of gay-coloured drapery, and silk cloths and carpets hung from the balconies, of blue and scarlet and yellow. The cathedral had a grand box erected outside, of scarlet and green velvet.

"Being Corpus Christi, the great day of all the year, there was grand High Mass and Exposition. All the bishops, priests, and the Royal Family attended. In the afternoon the streets were crowded with people on foot, curious groups lined the sides, and carriages were drawn up at all available places. At four o'clock a flourish of trumpets announced that the procession had issued from the cathedral. Officers, covered with decorations, passed to and fro on horseback. Water-carriers plied their *aqua fresca* trade. Bands played in all the streets. While waiting, Portuguese men, with brazen effrontery, asked permission to get into my carriage to see the procession better ; the rude shopboys clambered up the wheels, hiding the view with their hats. I dispersed the men, but took in the children. They did not attempt this with any of the Portuguese carriages, but only with mine.

" The procession occupied two hours and a half. First came a troop of black men, and a dragon (*i.e.* a man in scaly armour) mounted on an elephant in their midst. The next group was St. George on his horse, followed by Britannia—a small girl astride dressed like Britannia. The military presented arms to Britannia. These groups were both followed by led chargers caparisoned with scarlet velvet trappings, their manes and tails plaited with blue silk, and with blue plumes on their heads. They were led by grooms in the royal livery of red and gold. These were followed by all the different religious orders, carrying tall candles mounted in silver, and a large silver crucifix in the centre, and surrounded by acolytes in red cloth. Then came golden canopies, surmounted by gold and silver crosses. Then all the clergy surrounding some great ecclesiastical dignitary—the bishop probably—to whom the soldiers presented arms. Then came an official with a gold bell in a large gold frame, which was rung three times at every few hundred yards, followed by a huge red-and-yellow canopy, under which were the relics of St. Vincent. Then, carried on cushions, were seven mitres covered with jewels, representing the seven archbishops, more crosses and candles, clergy in copes, and all the great people of the Church. Then

came the last and important group. It was headed
by a procession of silver lanterns carried by the bishops
and chief priests. Then followed a magnificent canopy,
under which the Cardinal Patriarch carried the Blessed
Sacrament. The corners of the canopy were held by
members of the Royal Family, and immediately behind
it came the King. The troops brought up the rear.
The soldiers knelt as the Blessed Sacrament passed,
and we all went on our knees and bowed our heads.
The King was tall, dark, and majestic, with a long
nose and piercing black eyes, and he walked with
grace and dignity. He wore uniform of dark blue
with gold epaulettes, and the Order of the Garter,
which had just been given him."

The day after the royal procession Burton sailed
from Lisbon for Brazil. His wife went on board with
him, inspected his cabin, and saw that everything was
comfortable, and then "with a heavy heart returned in a
boat to the pier, and watched the vessel slowly steaming
away out of the Tagus." She attempted to drive after
her along the shore, but the steamer went too fast ; so
she went to the nearest church, and prayed for strength
to bear the separation. Burton had told his wife to
return to England by the next steamer. As she was
in the habit of obeying his commands very literally,
and as a few hours after he left Lisbon a little cockle-
shell of a steamer came in, she embarked in this most
unseaworthy boat the afternoon of the same day, though
she had no proper accommodation for passengers. They
had a terrible time of it crossing the Bay of Biscay, to
all the accompaniments of a raging storm, violent sea-

sickness, and a cabin "like the Black Hole of Calcutta."
Her experiences were so unpleasant that she dubbed the
vessel *Ye Shippe of Hell*.   Nevertheless, as was her wont,
she managed to see the ludicrous side.   She writes :

" Our passengers were some fun.   There was not a
single man who could have been called a gentleman
among the passengers, and only two ladies.   They
were Donna Maria Bita Tenario y Moscoso (a
Portuguese marquise), travelling for her health with a
maid-companion, and myself returning with my maid
to England.   There were two other ladies (so called)
with children, each of them a little girl, and the girls
were as troublesome as the monkey and the dog who
were with them.   They trod on our toes, rubbed their
jammy fingers on our dresses, tore our leaves out of
our books, screamed, wanted everything, and fought
like the monkey and the dog.   Their papas were quiet,
worthy men.   We had also on board a captain and
mate whose ship had been burnt in Morocco with a full
cargo on the eve of returning to England ; a gentleman
returning from Teneriffe (where he has spent twenty-
five years) to England, his native land, whom everybody
hoaxed and persuaded him almost that the moon was
made of green cheese in England ; a Jew who ate,
drank, was sick, and then began to gorge again, laughed
and talked and was sick with greatest good humour
and unconcern ;   an intelligent and well-mannered
young fellow, English born, but naturalized in Portugal,
going out to the Consulate at Liverpool ; and, lastly,
a Russian gentleman, who looked like an old ball of
worsted thrown under the grate.   Nothing was talked

of but sickness and so forth ; but I must say they were all good-hearted, good-humoured, and good-natured, and their kindness to each other on the voyage nothing could exceed. The two terrible children aforesaid were a great amusement in *Ye Shippe*. One used to tease a monkey by boiling an egg hard and giving it him hot, to see him toss it from paw to paw, and then holding a looking-glass before him, for him to see his grimaces and antics and other tricks ; and the other child was always teasing a poor Armenian priest born in Jerusalem. He had taken a second-class passage amongst the sailors and common men. The first class was bad enough. God help the second ! They would not give the poor man anything to eat, and bullied and teased him. He bore up in such a manly way my heart ached for him and made me blush for the British snob. I used to load my pockets with things for him when I left the table, and got the first class to admit him to our society under an awning ; but the captain would not have him in the cabin or on the upper deck. Our skipper was a rough man, having risen from a common sailor, but pleasant enough when in a polite humour. The third amusement was the fallals of our maids, who were much more ill and helpless than their mistresses. They were always ' dying,' ' wouldn't get up,' ' couldn't walk,' but had to be supported by the gentlemen. There was great joy on the sixth day because we thought we saw land. It might have been a fog-bank; it might have been Portland Bill ; anyway, we began to pack and prepare and bet who would sleep ashore. We awoke on the seventh day in a fog off Beachy

Head at 4.30 a.m., and lay to and whistled. Some
time after we passed Eastbourne, and then ran plank
along the coast.   How pretty the white walls of
England looked in the morning sun ! At night we
reached Gravesend ; but there was too little water, and
we went aground at Erith, where we were obliged
to stay till next morning, owing to the bad fog and
no water.   However, we made our way up to St.
Katherine's wharf at ten.   There was an awful bustle ;
but I disturbed the whole ship to land ; and taking my
Portuguese marquise under my wing, I fought my way
to shore.   I arrived home at noon—a happy meeting in
the bosom of my family."

Arrived in London, Isabel at once set to work to
complete her preparations for her departure to Brazil.
It was a habit with the Burtons all through their lives
that, whenever they were leaving England for any length
of time, Burton started first in light marching order to
prospect the place, leaving his wife behind to pay,
pack, and bring up the heavy baggage in the rear.   This
was the case in the present instance.   When her work
was done, Isabel found she had still ten days on her
hands before the steamer sailed from Southampton for
Rio.   So temporal affairs being settled for the nonce,
she turned her attention to her spiritual needs, and
prepared herself for her new life by prayer and other
religious exercise.   She went into retreat for a week
at the Convent of the Assumption, Kensington Square.
The following meditation is taken from her devotional
book of that period :

" I am to bear *all* joyfully, as an atonement to save

Richard. How thoughtful for me has been God's dispensation! He rescued me from a fate which, though it was a happy one, I pined in, because I was intended for a higher destiny and yearned for it. Let me not think that my lot is to be exempt from trials, nor shrink from them, but let me take pain and pleasure alike. Let me summon health and spirits and nerves to my aid, for I have asked and obtained a most difficult mission, and I must acquire patient endurance of suffering, resistance of evil, and take difficulties and pain with courage and even with avidity. My mission and my religion must be uppermost. As I asked ardently for this mission—none other than to be Richard's wife—let me not forget to ask as ardently for grace to carry it out, and let me do all I can to lay up such store as will remain with me beyond the grave. I have bought bitter experiences, but much has, I hope, been forgiven me. I belong to God—the God who made all this beautiful world which perpetually makes my heart so glad. I cannot see Him, but I feel Him; He is with me, within me, around me, everywhere. If I lost Him, what would become of me? How I have bowed down before my husband's intellect! If I lost Richard, life would be worthless. Yet he and I and life are perishable, and will soon be over; but God and my soul and eternity are everlasting. I pray to be better moulded to the will of God, and for love of Him to become indifferent to what may befall me."

The next week Isabel sailed from Southampton to join her husband at Rio.

CHAPTER V

BRAZIL

(1865—1867)

For to share is the bliss of heaven, as it is the joy of earth;
And the unshared bread lacks savour, and the wine unshared lacks zest;
And the joy of the soul redeemed would be little, little worth,
If, content with its own security, it could forget the rest.

ISABEL had a pleasant voyage out to Brazil, and witnessed for the first time the ceremonies of "crossing the Line," Neptune, and the tubbing, shaving, climbing the greasy pole, sack races, and all the rest of it. When the ship arrived at Pernambuco, on August 27, Isabel found all the letters she had written to her husband since they had parted at Lisbon accumulated at the post-office. This upset her so much that, while the other passengers were dancing and making merry, she stole on deck and passed the evening in tears, or, to use her own phrase, she had "a good boohoo in the moonlight."

A few days later the ship reached Rio de Janeiro. Burton came on board to meet her, and she had the joy of personally delivering the overdue letters into his hands.

They stayed five or six weeks in Rio, at the Estran-

geiros Hotel, and enjoyed a good deal of society, and
made several excursions into the country round about.
They were well received by the European society of the
place, which was chiefly naval and diplomatic. This
was pleasant for Isabel, who could never quite accommodate herself to the somewhat second-rate position to
which the English Consul and his wife are generally
relegated by foreign courts (more so then than now).
Isabel was always sensitive about the position abroad
of her husband and herself. In the ordinary way, at
many foreign capitals, the consul and his wife are not
permitted to attend court, and the line of demarca-
tion between the Consular and Diplomatic service is
rigidly drawn. But Isabel would have none of this,
and she demanded and obtained the position which
belonged to her by birth, and to her husband by
reason of his famous and distinguished public services.
Burton himself cared nothing for these things, and
his wife only cared for them because she had an idea
they would help him on in his career. That her
efforts in this direction did help him there is no doubt ;
but in some ways they may have hindered too, for they
aroused jealousy in certain small minds among his
colleagues in the Consular service, who disliked to see
the Burtons taking a social position superior to their
own. The fact is that both Richard Burton and his
wife were simply thrown away in the Consular service ;
they were too big for their position, in energy, in ability,
in every way. They had no field for their activities,
and their large and ardent natures perpetually chafed
at the restraints and petty annoyances resulting from

their semi-inferior position. Except at Damascus, they were round pegs in square holes. Burton was not of the stuff to make a good consul; and the same, relatively speaking, may be said of his wife. They were both of them in a false position from the start.

The following extract from a letter which Isabel wrote home shortly after her arrival in Brazil is of interest in this connexion:

"I dare say some of my friends do not know what a consul is. I am sure I had not the remotest idea until I came here, and then I find it is very much what Lady Augusta thinks in *The Bramleighs*, written by a much-respected member of our cloth, Charles Lever, consul at Trieste. 'Isn't a consul,' she asks, 'a horrid creature that lives in a seaport, and worries merchant seamen, and imprisons people who have no passports? Papa always wrote to the consul about getting heavy baggage through the custom-house; and when our servants quarrelled with the porters, or the hotel people, it was the consul sent some of them to jail. But you are aware, darling, he isn't a creature one knows. They are simply impossible, dear—impossible! The moment a gentleman touches an *emploi* it's all over with him—from that hour he becomes the Customs creature, or the consul, or the factor, or whatever it be, irrevocably. Do you know that is the only way to keep men of family out of small official life? We should see them keeping lighthouses if it were not for the obloquy.' Now, alas! dear, as you are well aware, I *do* know what a consul is, and what it is to be settled down in a place that my Irish maid calls the 'end of God's speed,' whatever that

may be ; but which I interpret that, after Providence
made the world, being Saturday night, all the rubbish
was thrown down here and forgotten."

She was over-sensitive on this point, and keenly alive
to slights from those who, though inferior in other
respects, were superior in official position, and who were
jealous when they saw " only the Consul's wife " playing
the *grande dame*. They were unable to understand that
a woman of Isabel's calibre could hardly play any other
part in whatever position she found herself. Fortunately, through the kindness of Sir Edward and Lady
Thornton (Sir Edward was then British Minister at
Rio), she experienced very few of these annoyances
at Rio ; and she always remembered their goodness to
her in this respect. The Emperor and Empress also
took the Burtons up, and made much of them.

On this their first sojourn in Rio everything was
most pleasant. The Diplomatic society, thanks to Sir
Edward and Lady Thornton, welcomed the Burtons
with open arms. A lady who occupied a prominent
position in the Diplomatic circle of Rio at that time
has told me the following about Isabel: " We liked
her from the first, and we were always glad to see
her when she came up to Rio or Petropolis from São
Paulo. She was a handsome, fascinating woman, full
of fun and high spirits, and the very best of good
company. It was impossible to be dull with her, for
she was a brilliant talker, and always had some witty
anecdotes or tales of her adventures to tell us. She
was devoted to her husband and his interests, and was
never tired of singing his praises. She was a great

help to him in every way, for he by no means shared her popularity."

At Rio Isabel gave her first dinner-party—the first since her marriage; and here she got a touch of fever, which lasted for some time.

When she was sufficiently recovered, the Burtons left Rio for Santos (their consulate, one hundred and twenty miles to the south). They went down on board H.M.S. *Triton*, and on arrival were saluted by the usual number of guns. The Consular Corps were in attendance, and the Brazilian local magnates came to visit them. Thus began Isabel's first experience of official life.

Santos was only a mangrove swamp, and in many respects as unhealthy as Fernando Po. Burton had come down and inspected the place before the arrival of his wife at Rio; and he had arranged, as there were two places equally requiring the presence of a consul— São Paulo on the top of the Serra, and Santos low down on the coast—that Isabel should live for the most part at São Paulo, which was comparatively healthy, and that they should ride up and down between Santos and São Paulo as need required. For an Englishwoman to have lived always at Santos would have been fatal to her health. The railway between Santos and São Paulo was then in process of being made. As they had determined not to sleep at Santos, the Burtons went the same day on trolleys along the new line as far as Mugis, where they stayed the night. The next day, by dint of mules, walking, riding, and occasional trolleys, they got to the top of the Serra, a very precipitous climb. At the top

SANTOS.

[*Page* 248.

a locomotive took them to São Paulo, where they put up at a small inn. The next day Burton had to go down to Santos to establish his consulate; but his wife remained at São Paulo to look for a house, and, as she said, "set up our first real home."

In about a fortnight she followed him down to Santos in the diligence, and remained there until the swamps gave her a touch of fever. She then went up to São Paulo again, and after some difficulty found a house. This was in the latter part of 1865. The whole of the next eighteen months was spent between São Paulo and Santos, varied at long intervals by a trip to Rio, or a visit to Barra, the watering-place, or excursions in the country round São Paulo. Burton was often away on his consular duties or on expeditions to far-away places, and his wife was necessarily left much alone at São Paulo, where she led a life more like "farmhouse life," to use her own phrase, than anything else. There were many and great drawbacks arising from the unhealthy climate, the insects and vermin, and the want of congenial society. But Isabel was one of those who manage to get enjoyment out of the most unlikely surroundings, and she always made the best of circumstances and the material at her disposal. As one has said of her, "If she had found herself in a coal-hole, she would immediately have set to work to arrange the coals to the best possible advantage."

On the whole, this period of her life (December, 1865, to June, 1867) was a happy one. The story of it is best told in a series of letters which she wrote to her mother ; and from them I have been permitted to make the following extracts :

"SÃO PAULO, *December* 15, 1865.

"I do hate Santos. The climate is beastly, the people fluffy. The stinks, the vermin, the food, the niggers are all of a piece. There are no walks ; and if you go one way, you sink knee-deep in mangrove swamps ; another you are covered with sand-flies ; and a third is crawling up a steep mountain by a mule-path to get a glimpse of the sea beyond the lagoons which surround Santos. I stayed there a fortnight and some days, and I got quite ill and peevish. At last Richard was to go to Ignipe, and I to São Paulo again. I started on Tuesday, the 12th, at one in the day ; and as it was so fine I sent all my cloaks and warm wraps away, and started in a boat, as for two hours from Santos the roads had overflowed. Then I took the diligence, which is an open van with seven mules, and got the box-seat to enjoy the country. It rained in buckets, and thundered and lightened all the way. We dined in a roadside hut on black beans and garlic, I and strange travelling companions, and arrived in eleven and a half hours. I had only a cotton gown on and no shawl, and Kier (my maid) said I came to the door like a shivering charity-girl, with the rain streaming off the brim of my hat. Kier gave me some tea with brandy, groomed me down with brandy and water, and put me between blankets. They think me a wonderful person here for being so independent, as all the ladies are namby-pamby. To go up and down by myself between Santos and São

Paulo is quite a masculine feat. I am the only woman who ever crossed the Serra outside the diligence, and the only lady or woman who ever walked across the viaduct, which is now a couple of planks wide across the valley, with one hundred and eighty feet to fall if you slip or get giddy. I saw every one staring at me and holding up their hands ; and I was not aware I had done anything odd, till I landed safely the other side, and saw all the rest going round. The next day two of the workmen fell off and were killed.

" You asked me to tell you about São Paulo.

" I have taken a house in the town itself, because if Richard has to be away often, I should not feel very safe with only Kier, out in the country amongst lawless people and beasts. The part of the town I am in is very high, on a good eminence, and therefore dry and healthy, a nice little street, though narrow. I have an *appartement* furnished ; four rooms to myself and the use of three others, and the kitchen, the servant of the house, and everything but food, for 150 milreis, or £15 a month.

" Behind is a yard and a patch of flowers, which people of sanguine temperaments might call a garden, where we keep barrels of water for washing or drinking. We have to buy water at threepence a gallon.

" As to furniture, in the Brazils they put many things into a house which you do not want, and nothing you do. I have had their hard, lumbering, buggy beds removed, and have put up our own little iron English bedsteads with spring mattresses. I slept in my own cosy little bed from Montagu Place last night for the

first time since it left my room there (now Dilly's) ; I
kissed it with delight, and jumped in it. I also bought
one in London for Richard.

"My servants consist of Kier, and one black boy, a
very curious dwarf as black as the grate, named Chico.
He is honest and sharp as a needle, and can do everything. All the English here wanted him, and did their
best to prevent his coming to me ; but he ran away,
and came to me for less than half the money he asked
them ; and he watches me like a dog, and flies for everything I want. I shall bring him home with me when
I come. The slaves here have to work night and day,
and people treat them like mules, with an utter dis-
regard for their personal comforts. There is something
superior and refined in my dwarf, and I treat him with
the same consideration as I would a white servant; I
see that he has plenty of good food, a good bed, and
proper exercise and sleep, and he works none the worse
for it.

"São Paulo itself is a pretty, white, straggling town
on a hill and running down into a high table-land,
which is well wooded and watered, and mountains all
round in the distance. We are about three thousand
feet above sea-level. It is a fine climate, too hot from
nine till four in summer, but fairly cool all the other
hours. No cockroaches, fleas, bugs, and sand-flies, but
only mosquitoes and jiggers. Out in the country there
are snakes, monkeys, jaguars, and wild cats, scorpion-
centipedes, and spiders, but not in the town. Of course
it is dull for those who have time to be dull, and very
expensive. For those who are launched in Brazilian

society, it is a fast and immoral place, without any *chic* or style. It is full of students, and no one is religious or honest in money matters ; and I should never be surprised if fire were rained down upon it, as in a city of the Old Testament, for want of a just Brazilian. *En revanche* it is very healthy, and only one month's journey to England.

" I have had my first jigger since I wrote. A jigger is a little dirty insect like a white tick that gets into your foot, under your toe-nail if possible, burrows, and makes a large bag of eggs. It itches ; and if you are wise, you send at once for a negress, and she picks it out with a common pin : if you do it yourself, you break its bag, and your foot festers. I knew nothing about it, and left it for eight days, and found I could not walk for a little black lump in my foot, which spurted fluid like ink when I touched it. At last my nigger asked me to let him look at it, and he got a sharp pair of scissors and took it out. It was like a white bag this size ⊙, with a black head, and it left quite a hole in my foot. You cannot walk about here without your shoes, and they must be full of camphor, or the jiggers get into your feet, and people have their nails taken off to extract them, and sometimes their toes and feet cut off."

" São Paulo, *January* 3, 1866.

" I have had twelve hard days' work, from six in the morning till late at night, with Kier and my black boy. We have had to unpack fifty-nine pieces of baggage, wash the dirty trunks and stow them away, sort, dry, and clean all their contents, and arrange ourselves in our rooms. We are now comfortable for the moment ; but we shall not stay here very long. There are many disagreeables in the house which I did not know till I had settled in it and taken it for four months. For example, I have rented it from a French family who are composed, it appears, of odds and ends, and they have the same right as myself to two of these rooms, the salon and the storeroom, so I am not alone and cannot do as I like ; and, worst of all, one of them is a lady who will come up and call on me. I am obliged to send to her and beg to be excused, which is disagreeable. She is, it appears, a notorious personage. Richard is gone to the mines, and has been away now nearly three weeks ; and I have taken it upon myself to rent a very nice house opposite this one. The English here mislead one about expenses ; I am obliged to buy my own experience, and I do not expect to shake down into my income for three or four months more. The English like to appear grand, saving all the while ; and they like to show me off as their lady consul, and make me run into expenses, while I want honestly to live within £700 a year, and have as much comfort as that will allow us. It will only go as far as £300 in England."

"São Paulo, *January* 17, 1866.

"I have settled down in my furnished apartments with Kier and Chico, and am chiefly employed in arranging domestic expenses, studying Portuguese, and practising my music. Richard has been gone to the mines a month, and returned to Santos yesterday ; so I conclude he will be up here in a few days. It is our fifth wedding day on the 22nd. Here every one wants to let his own especial dog-hole to us, so it is very hard to get settled. The house is a nice, large, roomy one, with good views. Kier and I and Chico, with the assistance of a friend's servant, are painting, white-washing, and papering it ourselves. Only fancy, the Brazilians are dreadfully shocked at me for working ! They never do anything but live in rags, filth, and dis-comfort at the back of their houses, and have one show-room and one show-dress for strangers, eat *fejão* (black beans), and pretend they are spending the deuce and all. The eighth deadly sin here is to be poor, or worse, economical. They say I am economical, because I work myself. I said to one of the principal ladies yesterday : ' Yes, I am economical ; but I spend all I have, and do not save ; I pay my debts, and make my husband com-fortable ; and we are always well fed and well dressed, and clean at both ends of our house. That's English way ! ' So she shut up."

"São Paulo, *March* 9, 1866.

" I got the same crying fit about you, dear mother, last week, as I did at Lisbon, starting up in the night and screaming out that you were dead ; I find I do it whenever I am over-fatigued and weak. The chance of losing you is what weighs most on my mind, and it is therefore my nightmare when I am not strong; not but what when awake I am perfectly confident that we shall meet again before another year is out.

" I caught a cobra snake yesterday in our garden, and bottled it in spirits, and also heaps of spiders, whose bite is like a cobra's—they are about the size of half a crown."

"São Paulo, *April* 18, 1866.

" I have had a great row in my house last night ; but when you write back, you must not mention it, because Richard was fortunately out, and I do not want him to know it.   Chico has taken a great dislike to the young gentleman who lodges in my house downstairs, because he has called him names ; so last night, Richard being away, he got a pail full of slops and watched for him like a monkey to fling it all over him ; but the young man caught sight of him, and gave him a kick that sent him and the pail flying into the air.   I heard a great noise and went down, ill as I was, and found the little imp chattering like a monkey, and showing his teeth ; so I made him go down on his knees and beg the young man's pardon.   I was going to send him away ; but to-day he came and knelt and kissed the ground before me, and implored me to forgive him this once, and he would never do such a thing again ; so I have promised this time, and will not tell Richard.   Richard would half kill him if he knew it; so you must none of you write back any jokes."

"São Paulo, *May* 14, 1866.

" My house is now completely finished, and looks very pretty and comfortable in a barnlike way.   I shall be so pleased to receive the candlesticks and vases for my altar as a birthday present, and the Mater Dolorosa. My chapel is the only really pretty and refined part of my house, except the terrace ; the rooms are rough and coarse with holes and chinks, but with all that is absolutely necessary in them, and they are large and airy. I painted my chapel myself, white with a blue border and a blue domed ceiling and a gilt border. I first nailed thin bits of wood over the rat-holes in the floor, and then covered it with Indian matting. I have painted inscriptions on the walls in blue. I have always a lamp burning, and the altar is a mass of flowers. It is of plain wood with the Holy Stone let in, and covered with an Indian cloth, and again with a piece of lace. I have white muslin curtains in a semicircle opening in the middle.

"On May 5 my landlord's child was christened in my chapel. They asked me to lend it to them for the occasion, so I decorated the chapel and made it very pretty. I thought they would christen the child, take a glass of wine and a bit of cake, and depart within an hour. To my discomfort they brought a lot of friends, children, and niggers, and they stopped six hours, during which I had to entertain them (in Portuguese). They ran all over my house, pulled about everything, ate and drank everything, spat on my clean floors, made me hold the child to be christened, and it was a year old, and kicked and screamed like a young colt all the time. Part of the ceremony was that I had to present a silver sword about the size of a dagger, orna-mented with mock jewels, to the statue of Our Lady for the child. I had a very pleasant day !

"One day we walked almost six miles out of São Paulo up the mountains to make a pilgrimage to a small wayside chapel ; and there we had São Paulo like a map at our feet, and all the glorious mountains round us, and we sat under a banana tree and spread our lunch and ate it, and stayed all day and walked back in the cool of the evening. Some of these South American evening scenes are very lovely and on a magnificent scale. The canoes paddling down the river, the sun setting on the mountains, the large foliage and big insects, the cool, sweet-scented atmosphere, and a sort of evening hum in the air, the angelus in the distance, the thrum of the guitars from the blacks going home from work—all add to the charm. Richard came home on Saturday, the 12th, after a pleasant nine-teen days' ride in the interior. He went to pay a visit to some French *savants* in some village, and they took him for a Brazilian Government spy, and were very rude to him, and finding afterwards who he was wrote him an humble apology. On June 1 I am going up to Rio. Richard is going to read his travels before the Emperor. The Comte and Comtesse d'Eu have asked us to their palace ; but I do not think we shall go there, as there will be too much etiquette to permit of our attending to our affairs."

"PETROPOLIS, ABOVE RIO, *June* 22, 1866.

" Petropolis is a bit of table-land about three thousand feet high in the mountains, just big enough to contain a pretty, white, straggling town, with a river running through it—a town composed of villas and gardens, and

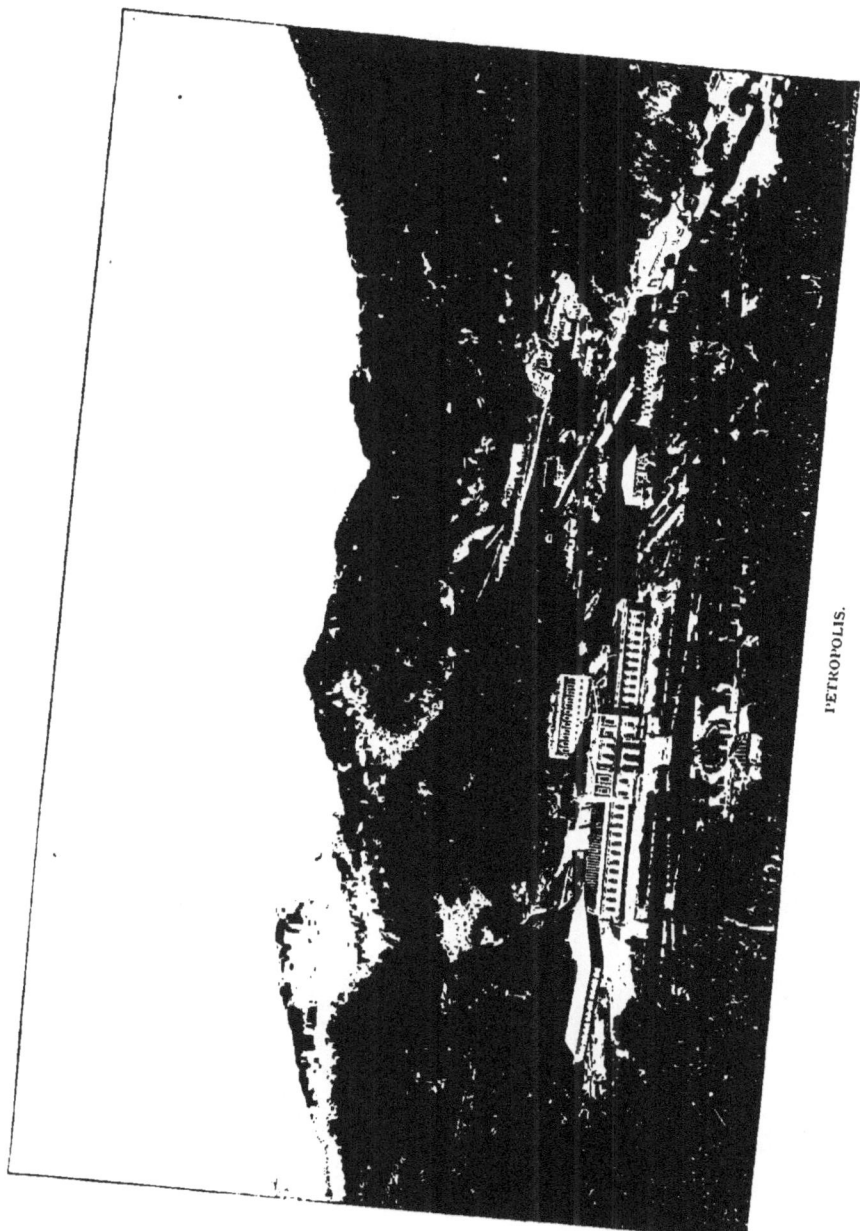

PETROPOLIS.

[*Page* 258.

inhabited by the Diplomatic Corps. It is a Diplomatic nest, in fact. This small settlement is surrounded by the mountain-tops, and on all sides between them are wild panoramic views. We went the other day to be presented to the Emperor and Empress. The first time we were taken by the Vicomte and Vicomtesse Barbaçena. She is one of the Empress's favourites. I was in grand toilet, and Richard in uniform. The palace is in a beautiful locality, but not grander than Crewe, or any English country gentleman's place. We were ushered through lines of corridors by successions of chamberlains, and in a few moments into the imperial presence. The Emperor is a fine man, about six feet two inches, with chestnut hair, blue eyes, and broad shoulders, and has manly manners. He was very cordial to us, and after a short audience we were passed on to the Empress's reception-room, where, after the usual kissing of hands, we sat down and conversed for about twenty minutes (always in French). She is a daughter of Ferdinand II. of Naples; and the Emperor, as you know, is Pedro, the son of Pedro I., the first Emperor of Brazil and King of Portugal.

" The second time the Emperor kept Richard two hours and a half talking on important affairs and asking his opinion of the resources of the country. The third time we visited the Comte d'Eu and the Duc de Saxe, who have each married daughters of the Emperor. The former (Comte d'Eu) is an old and kind patron of Richard ; and we were received quite in a friendly way by him, like any other morning visit, and we are now in a position to go whenever we like to the palace *sans cérémonie*. None of the other English here have the privilege. While we were with the Comte d'Eu and his wife, their pet terrier came and sat up and begged ; it looked so ridiculous, so like a subject before royalty, that we all roared with laughter. I am reported to have gone to Court with a magnificent tiara of diamonds (you remember my crystals !). The Emperor has taken a great fancy to Richard, and has put him in communication with him, and all the Ministers of State here make a great fuss with him (Richard).

" The society in Rio is entirely Diplomatic. There are the Ministers from every Court in the world with their *attachés*."

"RIO DE JANEIRO, *June*, 1866.

" I have been again to the palace (this time to the birthday drawing-room), and to-morrow am going to see the Empress in the evening. I am very fond of our Minister and his wife, Mr.[1] and Mrs. Thornton, and I am very proud of them ; they are people we can look up to.

"Since I wrote Richard has given two lectures before a room full of people. The Emperor and Empress, Comte d'Eu, and the Princesse Impériale were present ; we had to receive them, and to entertain them after in the room prepared for them. I have seen them three times since I wrote, and they always

---

[1] Afterwards the Right Hon. Sir Edward Thornton, H.B.M. Minister at Washington, sometime Ambassador at St. Petersburg, etc.

make us sit down and talk to us for some time. I
told the Empress all about your paralysis, and how
anxious I was about you; and she is so sympathetic
and kind, and always asks what news I have of you.
She appears to take an interest in me, and asks me
every sort of question. Most of my time in Rio has
been occupied in going to dinners."

"Rio de Janeiro, *July* 8, 1866.

" Yes, I am still covered with boils, and I cannot sit
or stand, walk or lie down, without a moan, and I am
irritated and depressed beyond words. I do not know
if my blood be too poor or too hot, and there is nobody
here to ask; but Kier makes me drink porter, which I
can get at Rio. I have a few days well, and then I
burst out in crops of boils ; and if an animal sting me,
the place festers directly, and after I get well again for
a few days. I am very thin, and my nose like a cut-
water ; and people who saw me on my arrival from
England say I look very delicate ; but I feel very well
when I have no boils.

" Since I wrote the flag-ship has come in, and I am
greatly distressed because I am going to lose nearly the
only nice lady friend I have, Mrs. Elliot, who was a
daughter of Sir John Plackett, and married Admiral
Elliot, the son of Lord Minto ; he has got his
promotion."

" Rio de Janeiro, *July* 23, 1866.

" I am still here. Richard left me a fortnight ago, and
I am still at the Patent work. You have no idea how

heartbreaking it is to have anything to do with the Ministers. When last I wrote to you, we were informed that we had obtained our concession. I was in high glee about it, and Richard went away as jolly as a sandboy, only leaving me to receive the papers ; and no sooner was he gone than I got a letter to tell me the Council of State had raised an objection to its being printed, and I have been obliged to remain in the hotel at Rio at great expense, and all alone to fight the case as best I may. Richard is gone to look after the sea-serpent (but I do not tell this, as it might get him into a row with the F. O.). I forgot to tell you there is said to be a sea-serpent here one hundred and sixty feet long. No English person can have any idea of the way matters are conducted at Rio. I am receiving the greatest kindness from the Emperor, Empress, Comte d'Eu, and the Imperial Princess, and the Ministers, and you would think I should be able to get anything. They offer me and promise me everything; but when I accept it, and think next day I shall receive my Patent papers signed, there is always some little hitch that will take a few days more. I have been here seven weeks like this, and of course have no redress. On July 10 the *Meida* went away, taking the Elliots, the Admiral and his wife. I went out a little way with them ; and it was most affecting to see the parting between them and the fleet. The ships all manned their rigging, cheered, and played 'God save the Queen' and 'I am leaving thee in sorrow.' I never saw any one look so distressed as the Admiral ; and Mrs. Elliot cried, and so did I."

" On Saturday, the 11th, I left Rio, much to my regret for some things, and to that of the friends I made there, who wanted me to stay for a ball on the 14th. However, I knew Richard's travels would be finished about that day, and he would feel dull and lonely at home alone, so I thought *bonne épouse avant tout*, and that the rest could take care of itself. I sailed on the 11th, and was rewarded, as at four o'clock in the morning of the 12th poor Richard came off from the coast in a canoe in a gale of wind, and the captain obliged me by laying to and taking him in. His canoe had been upset, and he was two days in the water, but not deep water. We then came home together. It blew very hard, and I was sick all the way. I find it very dull here after Rio. It is like farmhouse life up the country, with no one to speak to ; but I shall soon get reconciled, and have plenty to do to make the place comfortable again, and resume my *bourgeoise* life."

" SÃO PAULO, *September* 2, 1866.

" To-morrow a little Englishman and woman are to be married. Richard has to marry them. It seems so strange. Fancy him doing parson ! We shall muster about eighty people, Brazilian and English. I shall wear my poplin, black and white lace, and crystal coronet. People marry at five in the evening, and dance after, and sleep in the house. Richard says, ' I won't say, " Let us pray." ' He is going to begin with, ' Do any of you know any reason why this man and woman should not be married ? Have any of you got anything to say?' Then, shaking his finger at them in a threatening way, he is going to plunge into it. I know I shall burst out laughing."

"SÃO PAULO, *September* 15, 1866.

" I do not think the climate disagrees with me. Of course one does not feel buoyant in great heat; but it is more money affairs and local miseries that worry me, and you know we all have them in every latitude. I should not feel justified, I think, in coming home for anything but *serious* illness. I have just domesticated and tamed Richard a little; and it would not do to give him an excuse for becoming a wandering vagabond again. He requires a comfortable and respectable home, and a tight hand upon his purse-strings; and I feel that I have a mission which amply fills my hands. Nobody knows all the difficulties in a colonial or tropical home till she has tried them—the difficulty of giving and taking, of being charitable and sweet-tempered, and yet being mistress with proper dignity, as here we are all on a par. I often think a *parvenue*, or half-bred woman, would burst if she had to do as I do. But do not notice any of this writing back.

" I have had a ride on my new horse: a wretched animal to look at; but he went like the wind across the country, which is very wild and beautiful. The riding here is very different to English riding. If the animal is to walk or trot, he goes a sort of ambling jiggle, which I think most uncomfortable. You cannot rise, nor do even a military trot, but sit down in your saddle like a jelly and let him go. The only other pace is a

[*Page* 264.

hard gallop, which is the best ; you go like the wind over prairie and valley, up and down hill, all the same. The horses here are trained so that if your animal puts his foot in a hole you shoot off over his head, and he turns head over heels, and then stands up and waits for you, and never breaks his leg. In the wilds women ride straddle-leg like a man ; but one does not like to do it here. We are a shade too civilized. We are leading a very regular life : up at 5 a.m. and out for a walk ; I then go to Mass, market, and home ; Richard gives me a fencing lesson and Indian clubs ; then cold bath and dress ; breakfast at 11 a.m., and then look after my house ; practise singing, Portuguese, help Richard with literature, dine at six o'clock, and to bed at nine or ten.

" I am at present engaged with the F. O. Reports : I have to copy (1) thirty-two pages on Cotton Report ; (2) one hundred and twenty-five pages Geographical Report ; (3) eighty pages General Trade Report. This for Lord Stanley, so I do it cheerfully."

" Rio de Janeiro, *December* 8, 1866.

" We are nearly all down with cholera. I have had a very mild attack. Our *Chargé d'affaires* has nearly died of it, and also our Secretary of Legation ; Kier has had it also mildly. Here people cannot drink or be indolent with impunity. If I did not fence, do gymnastics, ride and bathe in the sea, eat and drink but little, attend to my internal arrangements, and occupy myself from early till late, to keep my mind free from the depression that comes upon us all in these latitudes, especially those who are not in clover like us, I could not live for six months. As it is, I do not think I have lost anything, except one's skin darkens from the sun, and one feels weak from the heat ; but I could recover in six months in England.

" When I got the cholera, it was three in the morning. I thought I was dying, so I got up, went to my desk and settled all my worldly affairs, carried my last instructions to Kier in her bed, put on my clothes, and went out to confession and communion."

" RIO DE JANEIRO, *December* 22, 1866.

" I have come down to Rio again to try and sell a book of Richard's, and am still at work about the gold concession. Richard is travelling (with leave) in the interior. I accompanied Richard part of the way on his travels. We parted on a little mountain with a church on the top—a most romantic spot. He started with two companions, three horse-boys, and a long string of mules. I rode my black horse, and returned alone with one mounted slave. We had fearful weather all the time, torrents of tropical rain, thunder and lightning, and our horses were often knee-deep in the slush and mud. You cannot imagine how beautiful the forests are. The trees are all interlaced with beautiful creepers, things that would be cultivated in a hot-house, and then be a failure, and all wild, tangled, and luxuriant, and in a virgin forest ; you must force your horse through these to make your way.

" You need not be frightened about me and my riding, though every one says I am sure to be thrown some day; but I never ride a Rio Grande horse for that reason. Only a man can shoot off properly when they turn head over heels. I am getting very well up in all that concerns stables and horses, and ride every day. The other day I went off to ride, and I lost myself for four and a half hours in a forest, and got quite frightened. I met two bulls and a large snake (cobra); I rode away from the two former, and the latter wriggled away under my horse's belly; he was frightened at it. The ladies' society here is awful; they have all risen out of unknown depths. Chico is still with me, and likely to be, as we are both very fond of him. I have made a smart lad of him, and he would make a great sensation in London as a tiger. He is so proud of the buttons Rody sent me for him, and shows them to every one."

"São Paulo, *March* 10, 1867.

"When Richard is away, it is not always safe here. For instance, last night a drunken English sailor, who had run away from his ship, got into the house, and insisted on having a passport and his papers made out. I could not persuade him that the Consul was absent, and had to give him food and money to get him out. Still, if he had used any violence, I would have gone down to the lodgers. At the same time, I never see or hear of *them* unless I wish it. Do not mention about the drunken sailor writing back, as Richard would say it was my own fault, because I will not allow any one to be turned away from my door who is in need, and so my house is open to all the poor of the neighbourhood, and he scolds me for

it. I sometimes suffer for it, but only one case out
of twenty.

"Brazilians never give charity; and how can the
poor judge between a true Catholic and a Brazilian
one, if some of us do not act up to our religion in
the only way that speaks home to them? I certainly
felt rather frightened last night, as the sailor told me
he was 'a damned scoundrel and a murderer,' and
wanted a bed in the house; but I coaxed him off
with a milreis, and then barred the door."

"THE BARRA, *April* 13, 1867.

"I write to you from a fresh place. In São Paulo
they have been making a new road, and have enclosed
a piece of marsh with water five feet deep. The new
road prevents this discharging itself into the river
beneath, and the enclosed water is stagnant and putrid,
and causes a malaria in my house. Richard has just
returned—knocked up by six weeks in the wilds—
and he broke out with fever. I felt affected and the
whole house squeamish. I rushed off with Richard
to the sea-border, about fifty miles from São Paulo.
Kier begged to be left. We have got a magnificent
sand-beach, and rose-coloured shells, and spacious bay,
and mountain scenery all around ; but we have some
other disadvantages. It would be intensely pleasant if
Richard would get better. One might walk on the
beach in one's nightgown ; and we walked from our
ranco, or shed, to the sea, and can bathe and walk as
we like. We are in what they dare to call the hotel.
It is a shed, Swiss-shape, and as good inside as a poor

cottage at home, with fare to match. It is as hot as the lower regions; and if one could take off one's flesh and sit in one's bones, one would be too glad. The very sea-breeze dries you up, and the vermin numbers about twenty species. The flies of various kinds, mosquitoes, sand-flies, and *borruchutes*, are at you day and night; and if you jump up in the night, it is only to squash beetles. A woman here had a snake round her leg yesterday. Behind the house and up to the first range of mountains is one vast mangrove swamp, full of fevers and vermin. I will not sleep in the beds about in strange houses (there is so much leprosy in the country), and so I always carry my hammock with me, and sling it. Last night it blew so hard that Chico and I had to get up and nail all the old things they call windows. I thought the old shanty was going to be carried away. I must tell you this is our sanatorium or fashionable watering-place here.

" I have had another bad boil since I wrote to you. We have had a Brazilian friend of Richard's lodging with us, who kept saying, 'If you ride with that boil, in a few days you will fall down dead'; or, 'Oh! don't leave that jigger in your foot; in a week it will have to be cut off.' Such was his mania; and he used to go to bed all tied up with towels and things for fear his ears should catch cold. He was quite a young man too !

" You know I have often told you that people here think me shockingly independent because I ride with Chico behind me. So what do you think I did the other

day? They have, at last, something to talk about now.
I rode out about a league and a half, where I met four
fine geese. I must tell you I have never seen a goose ;
they do not eat them here, but only use them as an
ornamental bird. Well, Chico and I caught them,
and slung one at each side of my saddle, and one at
each side of his, and rode with them cackling and
squawking all the way through the town ; and whenever
I met any woman I thought would be ashamed of me,
I stopped and was ever so civil to her. When I got
up to our house, Richard, hearing the noise, ran out
on the balcony ; and seeing what was the matter, he
laughed and shook his fist, and said, 'Oh, you delightful
blackguard—how like you !' "

Two months later Burton obtained leave of absence
from his consulate, and he and his wife started on
an expedition into the interior. This expedition was
the most memorable event of Isabel's life in Brazil.
On her return she wrote a full account of her adventures, intending to publish it later. She never did so,
and we found the manuscript among her papers after
her death. This unpublished manuscript, revised and
condensed, forms the next three chapters.

CHAPTER VI

OUR EXPEDITION INTO THE INTERIOR

(1867)

S'il existe un pays qui jamais puisse se passer du reste du monde, ce sera certainement la Province des Mines.

ST. HILAIRE.

WE had been in Brazil now nearly two years, vegetating between Santos and São Paulo, with an occasional trip to Rio de Janeiro. Though Richard had made several expeditions on his own account, I had never yet been able to go very far afield or to see life in the wilds. It was therefore with no small delight that I received the news that we had a short leave of absence, admitting of three months' wandering. The hammocks and saddle-bags were soon ready, and we sailed for Rio, which was about two hundred miles from our consulate. At Rio we received some friendly hints concerning our tour from exalted quarters, where brain and personal merit met with courtesy, despite official grade and tropical bile. We determined in consequence to prospect the great and wealthy province of Minas Geraes, and not to do simply the beaten track, but to go off the roads and to see what the province really was like. We wanted to visit the gold-mines, and to report concerning the new railway—about the proper line of which two parties were contending—a question of private or public benefit. We also intended to go down the São Francisco River, the Brazilian Mississippi, from Sabará to the sea, and to visit the Paulo Affonso Rapids, the Niagara of Brazil.

We left Rio on June 12, 1867, and sailed from the Prainha in a little steamer, which paddled across the Bay of Rio in fine style, and deposited us in about two hours on a rickety little wharf at the northern end called the Maná landing-place, whence the well-known financial firm of that name.

Whoever has not seen the Bay of Rio would do well to see it before he dies; it would repay him. All great travellers say that it competes with the Golden Horn. It is like a broad and long lake surrounded by mountains and studded with islands and boulders. But it is absurd to try and describe the bay with the pen; one might paint it; for much of its beauty (like a golden-haired, blue-eyed English girl of the barley-sugar description) lies in the colouring.

At the rickety landing-place begins a little railroad, which runs for eleven miles through a mangrove and papyrus flat to the foot of the Estrella range of mountains. Here we changed the train for a carriage drawn by four mules, and commenced a zigzag ascent up the mountains, which are grand. We wound round and round a colossal amphitheatre, the shaggy walls of which were clothed with a tropical forest, rich with bamboos and ferns, each zigzag showing exquisite

[*Page 272.*]

THE BAY OF RIO.

panoramas of the bay beneath. The ascent occupied
two hours ; and at last, at the height of three thousand
feet, we arrived at a table-land like a tropical Chamounix. Here was Petropolis, where we tarried for
some days.

Petropolis is a pretty, white, straggling settlement,
chiefly inhabited by Germans. It has two streets, with
a river running between, across which are many little
bridges, a church, a theatre, four or five hotels, the
Emperor's palace, and villas dotted everywhere. It
is the Imperial and Diplomatic health resort, and the
people attached to the Court and the Diplomatic
Corps have snuggeries scattered all about the table-
land of Petropolis, and form a pleasant little society.
The cottages are like Swiss *châlets*. It is a paradise
of mountains, rocks, cascades, and bold panoramas.
Here abounded the usual mysterious *châlet* of the
bachelor *attaché*. I will take you up that ridgy path
and show you a type of the class : four little rooms
strewed with guns, pistols, foils, and fishing-tackle, a
hammock, books, writing materials, pictures of lovely
woman dressing or kissing a bird or looking in the
glass, pretty curtains, frescoes on the walls drawn in
a bold hand of sporting subjects, *enfantillage*—and
other things ! This is the *châlet* of the Vicomte de
B——, *attaché* to the French Legation, a fair type of
the rest.

We left Petropolis for Juiz de Fóra at daybreak
on a fine, cold morning ; the grey mist was still clinging to the mountains. We had a large *char-à-banc*,
holding eight, in two and two, all facing the horses.

We took our small bags with us, but everything
heavier had gone on in the public coach. Our party,
besides Richard and myself, consisted of Mr. Morritt,
proprietor of the hotel and the *char-à-banc,* and three
other Englishmen, who with the driver and my negret
Chico made up the eight. The four mules were so
fresh that they were with difficulty harnessed, and
were held in by four men. When the horn sounded,
they sprang on all fours and started with a rush,
with a runner at either side for a few yards till clear of
the bridge. We simply tore along the mountain-side.

I shall save a great deal of trouble if I describe
the scenery wholesale for a hundred miles and specify
afterwards. Our trap dashed along at pleasant speed
through splendid amphitheatres of wooded mountains,
with broad rivers sweeping down through the valleys,
with rapids here and there, and boulders of rock and
waterfalls. The drive was along a first-rate road,
winding over the mountain-side. The roads on the
other side of the Parahybuna River were as high, as
beautiful, and as well wooded as the one along which
we drove. In all my Brazilian travelling this description of the scenery would mostly serve for every
day, but here and there we found a special bit of
beauty or more exquisite peep between the ridges.
At first you think your eyes will never tire of admiring
such trees and such foliage, but at last they hardly
elicit an observation. A circumstance that created
a laugh against us was that, like true Britishers,
Richard and I had our note-books, and we beset
poor Mr. Morritt with five questions at once. He

was so good and patient, and when he had finished
with one of us would turn to the other and say,
" Well, and what can I do for you?"

Our first stage was the " Farm of Padre Carrea,"
a hollow in the hills, where we changed mules. We
drove for forty miles downhill ; then we had fifteen
or twenty on the level when crossing the river valley;
then we ascended again for thirty-nine miles. The
road was splendid ; it was made by two French
engineers. Our second station was Pedro do Rio.
The third was Posse, the most important station on
the road for receiving coffee. Here thousands of mules
meet to load and unload, rest and go their ways. This
scene was very picturesque.

After Posse we began to see more fertile land, and
we passed a mountain of granite which, if it were in
England or France, would have a special excursion
train to it (here no one thinks anything about it) ; it
looked like a huge rampart, and its smooth walls were
sun-scorched. After this we passed a region of coffee
plantations, and thence to Entre Rios (" Betwixt the
Rivers"), the half-way house. It is a very unhealthy
station, and there is a dreadful smell of bad water ;
otherwise it would be a first-rate place for any one
wanting to speculate in starting a hotel. The last
ten miles before coming to Entre Rios lay through
virgin forest. We saw *tucanos* (birds with big beaks
and gorgeous plumage of black, green, scarlet, and
orange), wonderful trees, orange groves, bamboos (most
luxuriant ; they would grow on a box if they were
thrown at it), plants of every kind, coffee and sugar-

cane plantations, tobacco plants, castor-oil plants, acacias, and mimosa. What invariably attracts the English eye, accustomed to laurel and holly, are the *trepaderas* ; and the masses of bamboo form natural arches and festoons, and take every fantastic form. We crossed the rivers over bridges of iron.

We breakfasted at noon at Entre Rios ; we then mounted our *char-à-banc* once more, and drove on eight miles to the next station, called Serraria, where we sighted the province of Minas Geraes on the opposite side of the valley of Parahybuna. At Serraria we got a wicked mule, which nearly upset us three times. A wicked mule is a *beau-idéal* fiend ; the way he tucks his head under his body and sends all his legs out at once, like a spider, is wonderful to see ; and when all four mules do it, it is like a fancy sketch in *Punch.* They drive none but wild mules along this road, and after three months they sell them, for they become too tame for their work. Soon after this last station we passed through the " Pumpkin " chain of hills. We had ten miles to go uphill, and it was the hottest drive of the day, not only on account of the time of day, but because we were at the base of another huge granite mountain, much bigger than the last, like a colossal church.

We were not very tired when we sighted Juiz de Fóra, considering that we had driven nearly one hundred miles in twelve hours. We drove up to a *châlet* built by the French engineers just at sunset, and were guests in an empty house, and were well lodged. After supper the moon was nearly full, and the scene was lovely. There was a fine road; nearly all the buildings were on the same side of it as our *châlet*; opposite us was a chapel, farther down a hotel, and farther up, the thing that made all the beauty of Juiz de Fóra, the house of Commendador Mariano Procopio Ferreira Lage. It appeared like a castle on the summit of a wooded mountain. We were serenaded by a band of villagers. The evening air was exquisite, and the moon made the night as light as day.

The following day we inspected Juiz de Fóra. The town is a pretty situation, two thousand feet above sea-level, and the climate cool and temperate. The wonder of the place is the *château* of Commendador Mariano Procopio, who is a Brazilian planter who has travelled, and his wealth is the result of his energy and success. He built this castle on the top of a wooded eminence. This land eight years ago (I believe) was a waste marsh. He spent £40,000 on it, and made a beautiful lake, with islands, bridges, swans, and a little boat paddled by negroes instead of steam. He made mysterious walks, bordered by tropical and European plants, amongst which the most striking to an English eye were enormous arums with leaves five feet long and three broad, and acacias, mimosas, umbrella trees in full flower. He also erected Chinese-looking arbours, benches, and grotesque designs in wood. I believe the man carries out all his nightmare visions there. In another part of the grounds was a mena-gerie full of deer, monkeys, emu, silver and gold pheasants, and Brazilian beasts and birds. He has

an aqueduct to his house and fountains everywhere.
There is an especially beautiful fountain on the highest
point of Juiz de Fóra, in the centre of his grounds,
and from there is a splendid view. There is a white
cottage in his gardens for his aged mother. He has
also an orangery of huge extent, different species of
oranges growing luxuriantly, and we reclined on the grass
for an hour picking and eating them. All the land
around was his; he built the chapel; even our *châlet*
was his property; and besides he has a model farm.
Altogether Juiz de Fóra appeared a thriving town,
and the Commendador was the pivot on which it
all moved. It seemed so strange to find in the
interior of Brazil a place like that of an English
gentleman. One cannot give this generous and enter-
prising planter enough praise. If there were more
like him, Brazil would soon be properly exploited.
Some object that the arrangement of his place is
too fantastic. There is no doubt it is fantastic, but
it is so because he is giving the natives a model of
everything on a tiny scale, and collecting in addition
his native tropical luxuriance around him, as an English
gentleman would delight to collect things on his estate,
if he could get the same vegetation to grow in
England.

On leaving Juiz de Fóra, I was obliged to leave
my baggage behind, which appeared to me rather
unreasonable, as it only consisted of the usual little
canisters, a pair of long, narrow boxes for the mule's
back. If the ladies who travel with big baskets the
size of a small cottage had seen my tiny bundle and

a little leather case just big enough for brush, comb,
and a very small change, they would have pitied me.
We mounted the coach on a cold, raw morning—this
time a public coach. Only one man of our party
accompanied us on to Barbacena ; the rest were
homeward bound. The two coaches stood side by
side, ready packed, facing different ways, at 6 a.m., to
start at the same moment. We had a small, strong
coach with four mules. A handsome, strapping
German youth, named Godfrey, was our driver, and
we boasted a good guard. Inside was a lady with
negresses and babies, and an Austrian lieutenant.
Outside on a dicky my negret and a large number
of small packages—only such could go. The driver
and guard were in front, and above and behind them
on the highest part of the coach was a seat for three,
which held Richard, Mr. E——, and myself in the
middle, the warmest and safest place in event of a
spill. The partings ensued between the two coaches,
and the last words were, " Remember by twelve o'clock
we shall be a hundred miles apart." The horn
sounded ; there was the usual fling of mules' heads
and legs in the air, and we made the start as if we
had been shot out of a gun. We proceeded on our
drive of sixty-six miles in twelve hours, including
stoppages, constantly changing mules, for the roads
between Juiz de Fóra and Barbacena were infamous, and
all up and down hill. The country was very poor in
comparison with what we had left behind, but I should
have admired it if I had not seen the other. The road-
sides are adorned with quaint pillars, mounds of yellow

clay, the palaces of the *cupims*, or white ants, which they are said to desert when finished. They must be very fond of building. The *sabiá* (the Brazilian nightingale) sang loud in the waving tops of the " roast-fish tree." We passed over wooded hills, broad plains, and across running streams and small falls. At last we reached the bottom of the great Serra Mantiqueira. The ascent was very bad and steep for ten miles, and through a Scotch mist and rain. All the men had to get down and walk, and even so we often stuck in deep mud-holes, and appeared as if we were going to fall over on one side. I now comprehended why my baggage could not come ; my heart ached for the mules. Travelling on the top of that coach was a very peculiar sensation. When we were on plain ground and in full gallop we heaved to and fro as if in a rolling sea, and when going fast it was like a perpetual succession of buck-jumping, especially over the *caldeiroês*, lines of mud like a corduroy across the road. On the descent our coach-man entertained us with a history of how he once broke his legs and the guard his ribs and the whole coach came to grief at that particular spot.

Our next station (and it seemed so far) was Nas-cisuento Novo; then came Registro Velho, where travellers used to be searched for gold and diamonds, and amusing stories are told how they used to conceal them in their food or keep them in their mouths. Here we had our last change of mules, and here the Morro Velho Company from the mines halted for the night, and we found to our delight that we should find a special troop of them waiting at Barbacena to convey us where we liked.   This was our last league, and the weather was frosty.

We arrived at the Barbacena hotel when it was dusk, and found it a decent but not luxurious inn, kept by an unfortunate family named Paes.   At the door we saw a good-humoured Irish face, which proved to be that of our master of the horse, Mr. James Fitzpatrick, of the Morro Velho Company, who was awaiting Richard and myself with two blacks and ten animals. We therefore asked for one of the spare mules and saddles for Mr. E——, who had decided to accompany us to the mines.   The town appeared quite deserted, but I thought it was because it was dark and cold and the people were all dining or supping.   We were tired, and went to bed directly after dinner.

Next day we inspected Barbacena, a white town upon an eminence.   The town is built in the form of a cross, the arms being long.   It is three thousand eight hundred feet above sea-level, and is very cold except in the sun.   There was little to see except four churches, all poor and miserable except the Matriz, which was the usual whitewashed barn with a few gaudy figures. It was a dead-alive kind of place, with all the houses shut up and to be bought for very little.   All the young men were gone to the war.   There was no one about : no society, not even a market; no carriage save the public coach, with its skeleton horses eating the grass in the streets.

After dinner that evening we saw a black corpse on a stretcher.   The porters were laughing and talking and merrily jolting it from side to side, and I was considered rather sentimental for calling it disrespect to the dead. Our *table d'hôte* was a motley and amusing group. There were the driver and guard of our coach, the Austrian lieutenant, ourselves, several Brazilians, and Mr. Fitzpatrick. We all got on together very well. There was some punch made ; and as the conversation turned upon mesmerism for that night's discussion, a delicate subject, I withdrew to a hard couch in an inner room.

On Wednesday, June 19, we left the last remnant of civilization behind us at Barbacena, and that remnant was so little it should not be called by that name. We shall now not see a carriage for some months, nor a road that can be called a road, but must take to the saddle and the bridle for the country. Our party consisted of Richard and myself, Mr. E——, Mr. James Fitzpatrick, captain of our stud, Chico, my negret, mounted, and two slaves on foot as guides, three cargo mules, and two spare animals as change.

Our first ride was to be twenty miles, or five leagues, across country. We did it in five hours, and one more half-hour we employed in losing our way. The country was poor, and through what is called *campos* —*i.e.* rolling plains, with a coarse pasturage. Near dusk we reached Barroso, a village with a ranch, a small chapel, and a few huts. The ranch was small and dirty, and smelt of *tropeiros* (muleteers) and mules. The ranch was a shed-like cottage with a porch or verandah. It had one room with a ceiling of bamboo matting, whitewashed mud walls, no window, and a mud floor. The only thing in it was a wooden bedstead without a bed on it. This was ours ; the rest had to sleep in the verandah or on the floor with rugs amongst the *tropeiros*, picturesque-looking muleteers. They gave us rice, chicken, and beans. I prepared the food and slung the hammocks, and after eating we lay ourselves down to rest.

We rose at three o'clock in the morning, before it was light, and at 4.30 we were in our saddles again. We rode twenty-four miles. We breakfasted under a hedge at a place written " Elvas," pronounced " Hervas," and got a cup of coffee from a neighbouring gypsy camp. Shortly after we passed a ranch, with a curious old arched bridge made of wood. To-day's journey was very like yesterday's in point of country, but we were a little tired the last few miles, as we had been somewhat dilatory, and had been eight hours in hard saddles on rough animals ; the sun also broke out very hot. At last, however, we were cheered by arriving at a pretty village, and shortly afterwards sighted a beautiful-looking town on a hill, with many spires. We rode up to the bridge to enter the town, tired, hot, torn, and dusty, just as the procession of the Blessed Sacrament was passing, followed by the friars and a military band. We bent our heads and bowed down to the saddle. This was the town of São João d'El Rei, and it was the Feast of Corpus Christi.

São João d'El Rei is five thousand two hundred feet above sea-level. It was June 21 (here the shortest as in England it is the longest day), and the climate was delicious. We met two English faces in the streets, and hailed them at once. They proved to be Mr. Charles Copsey, who had been at Cambridge with my husband's brother, in command of the Brazilian Rifle Volunteer Brigade (I knew many of the same men), and Dr. Lee, a man of Kent. Dr. Lee had been there thirty-five years. These two compatriots were most kind to us. They introduced us to all the best families, and showed us all the lions of the place.

The churches of São João were so numerous that we only " did " the three best. We walked about the principal streets, getting the best views of the white, spiral, hilly, little city, which looked beautiful at sunset. We visited one Brazilian's general collection, another's books, another's pictures, and the only place we did not go to see was the hospital. We loafed about, and everybody dined with us at the hotel—very little better than a ranch.

We left our hotel, or rather ranch, at 10.30 a.m. the next morning, and rode to Matosinhos, the suburb at the entrance, where we breakfasted at the house of Dr. Lee and made the acquaintance of his Brazilian wife, a sweet-mannered woman, whose kindness and hospitality charmed us. After a sumptuous breakfast we walked about his grounds, and he gave us a *cão de féla*, an ugly, toad-coloured, long dog, with a big head, broad shoulders, and lanky body, answering in breed to our bull-dog.

Here Mr. Copsey could not make up his mind to part with us so soon, and actually forsook his wife and children and cottage to accompany us for a few days.

Our ride was a pretty easy two leagues, or eight miles, over mountains, bringing us to a small white village or town, which we should call a village, nestled among them, called São José. This village contains a running brook, a bridge, and a handsome fountain. Our ranch was a miserable affair, without any pretension to bedding, and if possible less to a washing-basin; so the rest preferred sitting up all night; but as my experience has taught me to take all the little comforts that Providence throws to me, in order to endure the more, I slung my hammock and slept the sleep of good conscience, in spite of the clinking of glasses and twanging of guitars.

We intended to leave São José at one o'clock a.m., but those who foolishly sat up had all sorts of mishaps. There had been a little too much conviviality; the animals had strayed; so, though we started before light, it was much later than we intended. Our road was a terrible one; we could not keep together, and got lost in parties of two and three. At first the road was very pretty, through woods; but as dawn appeared we had to climb a wall of steep rock, terrible to climb and worse to descend. Two of our party unwillingly vacated their saddles before we got clear of it, and Mr. E——'s saddle slipped off behind from the steepness and bad girths. We then had a long ride over *campos*, and stopped to breakfast at a deserted ranch. We were then supposed to be about twelve miles from our destination, Lagôa Dourada. The rest of our day was full of misfortunes. The valiant people who would dance and drink all night dropped asleep upon the road. We lost our way for six miles, and had to ride back and take another track. Our black guides had not laid a branch across the road for us. (It is an African custom to place a twig or branch on the road, to convey any intelligence to those who are coming after you.) We came to a Slough of Despond, a mud-hole across the road, which looked only a little wet and dirty, but a mule or rider may be engulfed in it. Mr. Fitzpatrick luckily preceded me, and fell into it. My mule jumped it, and in the jump my pistol fell out of my belt into it, and was never seen more. We had a very hard day of it up and down hill through virgin forest with several of these swamps. At sunset we arrived very tired at the top of a hill, and found an aboriginal-looking settlement of huts. We then descended into the valley by a steep, winding road for some distance, and came to a long, straggling, hilly, but pretty and more civilized village, with a few churches and a running brook, with a decent ranch at its extreme end, where there was a party of English engineers, who kindly attended to our creature comforts while at Lagôa Dourada.

It was Sunday, the Eve of St. John, and there were big bonfires and a village band. Our ranch was a cottage. The brook with the gold-washings ran by it, and the purling thereof made pleasant music that night.

The great object of our visit to Lagôa Dourada was to see with disinterested eyes which course the continuation of the Dom Pedro Segunda Railway should run through Minas—that is, to see which course would be for the greatest public advantage, regardless of private intrigue. The English engineers and Richard having quite agreed upon the subject, they kindly invited us to celebrate the Feast of St. John by assisting to "lay the first chain." It was a day likely to be remembered by the Brazilians, for it connoted their pet feast—the " Feast of Fire "—and the commencement of a work to be of great benefit to them.

At twelve o'clock (noon) the next day the English engineers, with a party comprising all the Brazilian swells of Lagôa Dourada, proceeded to a valley within the village to lay the first chain for the exploration of the mountains which divide the watershed of the Rio São Francisco and the Paraopéba from the Carandahy and Rio Grande, for the prolongation of the Dom Pedro Segunda Railway.

I had the honour of giving the first blow to the stake and breaking a bottle of wine over it. The sights taken were S. 73° W. and N. 74° W. The engineers made me write this in their books. (The following day all were to break up, our party of engineers bound northward, and ourselves on our march.) The inauguration passed off very favourably. It was a beautiful day. The village band played, flags were flying, wine was produced, glasses clinked, and we drank the health of " The Emperor," " The Queen," " Brazil," " England," " Unity," " Future Railway," and most of the principal people present ; speeches were made, and *vivas* shouted, and last the Brazilians proposed the health of St. John with *vivas*.

When these ceremonies were over, we marched back to the ranch with the band playing and colours flying.

In the afternoon we walked a little way up and down the stream, and saw some gold-washing on a homœopathic scale. The land belongs to a Brazilian, who gets three or four milreis a day out of it (about eight shillings). We then sat down in the village on benches in the shade. The men drank beer and smoked cigarettes, and I took my needlework and talked with them.

In the evening the English engineers gave us a big dinner in the ranch, and how they managed to do it so well I cannot imagine. It was like a big picnic. The village padre sat at the head of the long wooden table, and I at the bottom, and on wooden benches at each side were eight Englishmen and seventeen Brazilian local magnates. We had chickens, messes of rice and meat, *feijão* (beans) and *farinha* (flour), bread, cheese, beer, port, and other drinks— all out of the engineers' stores. It was great fun. Directly after dinner they began speechifying, and each man ended his speech with a little nasal stanza to friendship, the audience taking up the last word. At last somebody drank the health of the married men, and then some one else proposed the health of the single, and then every one began to quarrel as to which was the better and happier state. Richard and Mr. Copsey loudly stood up for the single, and urged them on to greater frenzy, and I would have done the same thing only I was afraid of shocking the padre. The wordy war lasted fully half an hour, and terribly distressed one spoony Englishman, who gave us a homily from his corner on the sanctity of the married state. If it had been in France, there would have been half-a-dozen duels, and I fully expected to see some kniving; but with them it was only hilarity and good spirits, and they embraced across the table at the very moment I thought they were going to hit one another. We finished up by repairing to our room and having some punch there, and we all parted happy and pleased with our day. After we were in bed we were serenaded by the band. The people walked about with music, and twanged their guitars all night. It is a great day for marriage —for lovers, and all that sort of pleasant thing. The girls dress in their best, and put the flowers of São João in their hair, and one likes to see the young people happy. A pleasant remembrance of this place lingers with me yet.

The next morning we proposed starting at four o'clock, and got up early. Our white horse, however, knew the ground, and strayed six miles away, so we could not start till 9 a.m. Moreover, Mr. Copsey, who was on duty at São João d'El Rei for next day, was obliged to wish us good-bye and return.

When at last we started, we rode for two leagues and a half, accompanied by several of our friends of the evening before, and at last came to a brook, where we sat under the shade of a tree and breakfasted, after which our friends wished us good-bye and returned. We then rode on, uncertain as to our course. The scenery was pretty; the weather was very hot. We had no road, but found our way over the hills through bits of forest, and towards evening we came to a village called Camapoão.

We had been detained by bad road and accidents, and had been five hours doing only fifteen miles ; so, though we could only find an infamous ranch (the worst we had ever seen), we thought it best to risk it for the night. We had been obliged to pass one by, as it looked really dangerous with damp, filth, and reptiles. The owner of the ranch, one José Antonio d'Azevedo, was a character, and a very bad one— original in rudeness, independence, and suspicion. There was not a basin or any kind of cooking-pot, nor a fire nor hot water. There was, however, one bed (José's), and no amount of entreaty to let me rest my aching limbs on it would induce him to allow me to do so. I had almost to go on my knees to be allowed to swing my hammock, lest I should spoil his mud-and-stick walls ; but after a glass of cognac from our stock and much flattering and coaxing, he did permit that, and gave us some beans and flour, rice and onions, to eat. Richard slept on a wooden table, I in the hammock, and the rest of our party with the mules on the ground round a fire. It was a bitterly cold night, and we got full of vermin. At about one in the morning I was aroused by a loud whispering, apparently close to my head, and a low growl from my dog underneath my hammock, and I could distinctly hear the old man say, " Pode facil- mente matar a todas " ("It would be very easy to kill the whole lot "). I felt quite cold and weak with fright; but I stretched out my hand in the dark to where I knew my weapons were, and got hold of a bowie-knife and loaded revolver. I then whispered to Richard, and we got some matches and struck a light. There was no one in the room, and the whispering and laughing still went on as if the old man and his negroes were conversing and joking behind the thin partition wall. Nothing occurred. In the morning we thought he was only alluding to his chickens ; yet, as we learnt afterwards, he did bear an ugly name.

We were very glad to get up at 4 a.m., though pitch dark, and to set out. The old man did his best to keep us by talking of the *atoleiros* on the road, which we must pass, and were sure to fall into. And indeed an *atoleiro* is an ugly thing ; for you only expect a passage of wet mud in the road, whereas you and your horse go plump in over head, and sometimes do not get out. We passed a fearful one a mile past his house, but sent the blacks on first, and they brought us a long round through brushwood, which was not dangerous, but unpleasant to fight through ; and Chico stuck in it, and we were fully ten minutes extricating him. We then rode up and down mountains and waded several rivers, and moonlight passed away, and dawn came with a welcome. By nine o'clock we had accomplished twelve miles, and arrived at Suasuhy, a long, big village, with a church and about three hundred houses and fifteen hundred inhabitants. We were quite overcome with the luxury of being able to wash our hands and faces *in a basin*. We had too a better breakfast than usual. The ranch was kept by a handsome family—father, mother, and four daughters. After this we rode on again through beautiful scenery up and down mountains, through shallow rivers and bits of virgin forest. Yet, though the scenery is magnificent, it is so alike, that one description describes all, and what you see to-day you will to-morrow and for the next three months, with the exception of every here and there a startling feature. After another three leagues we sighted the Serra d'Ouro Branco, a grand pile of rock, and presently caught sight of a convent and a large square and church seated on an eminence below the mountain. We were descending. We turned a corner down a steep, stone hill, and beheld a beautiful white village in the valley, and silvery, winding river, called Maronhão, running through it, and another smaller one discharging itself into the larger. A striking church, the Matriz, rose on the opposite hill. In the distance were the two Serras, straight ranges like a wall, one shorter than the other. Ouro Branco is so called because the gold found there was mixed with platina. It was three o'clock, and we had now travelled six leagues and a half, and were glad to rest. The sunset was lovely.

This village was Congonhas do Campo. We got into a comfortable ranch, and then called on the padre. That is the best thing to do at these places, as he is the man who shows you hospitality, points out the lions, and introduces you and gives you all the information you want. The padre showed us great kindness, and took us to see the college and the church, the most striking part of the village and valley. Walking through the streets, we saw the arms of some noble Portuguese family, well carved in stone, over a small deserted house—doubtless the arms of some of the first colonists.

The padre breakfasted with us at the ranch next morning, and saw us set out from Congonhas at twelve o'clock. We rode three leagues, or twelve miles, which seemed more like five, up and down mountains, through rivers and virgin forests, and on ridges running round steep precipices and mountain-sides for many a mile. On our way we met a small white dog with a black ear, looking wet and tired and ownerless. Mr. E—— hit at it with a hunting-whip ; it did not cry nor move, but stared at our passing troop. Towards night we arrived at a little sort of private family settlement, consisting of four or five ranches belonging to a man of the same name as the place—to wit, Teixeira. Here we found the villagers in a great state of excitement, armed with guns to kill a mad dog, which had been rabid for some days, and had bitten everything it saw, communicating the disease, and had after all escaped them. He was a small white dog with a black ear !

We had great difficulty in finding a night's rest at Teixeira. Four or five houses would not take us in. One man was especially surly ; but at last a cobbler and his wife took us in, and were kind and hospitable to us. Here I had a little bed of sticks and straw, and slept soundly.

Next morning we had a shot at a flock of small green parrots before starting for Coche d'Agua at 8.30, and we rode till 10.30. We crossed the Rio da Plata six times (it was so tortuous) before nine o'clock, and twice the Bassão later. After crossing the Bassão the second time, we sat under a shady tree on its banks, and ate our breakfast out of our provision basket—cold pork, onions, and biscuit, and drank from the river.

We had been told that the remainder of our ride to Coche d'Agua from this spot was four leagues ; but it was nearer eight leagues (thirty-two miles), and we arrived after dusk at 6.15. It was a very poor place ; there was nothing to eat, and no beds, and we were dead tired.

The people were kind, and lit an enormous fire in the centre of the ranch, and let me lie down upon their sleeping-place till 3 a.m., " because I was a Catholic and spoke Portuguese." It was a slab of wood with a straw sacking, and even so I thought it a great luxury. We rose next morning at 3.30. The mules were called in, and we rode four leagues, first by moonlight and then dawn. We passed through two valleys, and arrived at 8.45 a.m. at another settlement. This was the village outside of the Morro Velho colony, and as the bells rang nine we alighted at the entrance of the Casa Grande, and were most cordially and hospitably received by the Superintendent of the São João d'El Rei Mining Company and Mrs. Gordon, and conducted into their most comfortable English home.

CHAPTER VII

Earth's crammed with heaven,
And every common bush afire with God;
But only he who sees takes off his shoes;
The rest sit round it, and pick blackberries.

ELIZABETH BARRETT BROWNING.

MORRO VELHO, where is the queen of the Minas Geraes Mines, is a very curious and interesting place, unlike any other I have seen in Brazil. It has a good deal of bustle, life, and cheerfulness about it which one scarcely sees elsewhere. It is an extensive, elevated valley, surrounded by mountains and divided into districts or settlements, each consisting of villages made up of detached cottages without streets, after the manner of most villages in Minas Geraes. Congonhas must be excepted, as that is a regular village with shops ; we passed through it on the outskirts of the gold-mining colony ; although it is independent of, still it is supported by, its wealthy neighbour.

Mr. Gordon, the English superintendent of the mines, was like a local king at Morro Velho and all over

295

the province. He was consulted and petitioned by every one, beloved, respected, and depended upon ; in short, a universal father ; and well he deserved respect.

The first Sunday we were with the Gordons at Casa Grande we witnessed the slave muster ; and when it was over the slaves gave us an Indian representation of a sham palaver, war-dance, and fight. They were dressed in war-paint and feathers. The King and his son were enthroned on chairs, and the courtiers came and seated themselves around on the grass, and the attendants carried umbrellas. First there was a council. The King was dissatisfied with his Minister of War, who was seized and brought before him. Then the Minister made a speech in his own praise. Then there was a fight, in which the Captain of War took every one prisoner, and gave the swords to the King. Then the Minister was poisoned by the enemy, but cured by a nut which the King gave him. Then all the captives crawled on the ground like snakes to the King's feet to do him homage. The King's jesters were great fun. They had a gong and bells and tom-tom, and sang and danced at the same time. They danced a curious step—little steps in which they adhered to a peculiar time.

On Wednesday, July 10, we left Morro Velho for a space in light marching order. Mr. Gordon wished Richard to inspect a seam of ore of disputed substance, and he organized a trip for us to the place. It was to last eleven days, and we were then to return to Morro Velho. We set out from the Casa Grande at 8.15. Our road was very bad, chiefly over moun-

THE SLAVE MUSTER AT MORRO VELHO.

[Page 296.

tains and through rivers, but incessantly up and down, without any repose of level ground.

We rode for more than four hours, and then stopped at a village called Morro Vermelho, where we stopped an hour for breakfast and to change animals.

Our road after this, till six o'clock in the evening, lay through the most exquisite forests, but with terrible footing for the mules—thick, pudding-like, wet mud, and loose, slippery stones, corduroys of hard mud striping some of the most difficult places, where only a sure-footed mule can tread. We stopped, in passing, at the house of a Mr. Brockenshaw, an English miner. It was a tumbledown ranch, but in the wildest, most desolate, and most beautiful spot imaginable. The chief features of the scenery were mountain-peaks, virgin forests, and rivers. And oh the foliage of the forest ! The immense avenues of leafage looked like mysterious labyrinths, with castles and arches of ferns forty feet high. We crossed an awful *serra* all in ruts, and full of scarped rock, mud-holes, or *atoleiros* ; the highest point was four thousand two hundred feet. Just as we were at the worst of our difficulties, and Mr. E—— had broken his crupper, we heard a cheery English voice shouting behind us, "O ! da casa?" ("Any one at home?"), which is what people say in Brazil when they enter a house apparently empty and want to make some-body hear at the back. Turning, we beheld a Scotch gentleman with a merry face and snow-white hair, and a beard like floss silk down to his waist. The Brazilians call him "O Padre Eterno," as he is like the picture of God the Father. He was Mr. Brown,

Superintendent of the Cuiabá Mine. After cordial greetings he joined our party.

We eventually arrived at Gongo Soco, the original peat-mining village, once gay and rich, now worked out, abandoned, and poor. The river of the same name runs through it. It was now a little before five o'clock, and we came to a better track, and rode on some miles farther to the house and iron foundry of Senhor Antonio Marcos, the Ranger of Woods and Forests, who had prepared hospitality for us. We dismounted at six o'clock very stiff. We had been nine hours and a quarter in the saddle, and had ridden thirty-two miles of difficult country, which did not, however, prevent us from passing a merry evening with Mr. Brown's assistance.

After a good night, yet still aching from the rough road, we went out early to see the iron business. The soil is a mixture of *iacutinga* (iron and charcoal). and the process, slow and primitive, is known as the "Catalan process." We saw the whole thing done from beginning to end. We left the foundry at 10.15, and went down the watershed of the river Gongo Soco, crossing it twice, and in an hour and a quarter arrived at São João do Morro Grande. Thence we rode to Brumado, a decayed village. Here we stopped for an hour in the great house of the Commendador João Alves de Sousa Continho, where we changed animals. This was once a gay and high house in great repute. It looked now as if withered; it has fallen into decay, and is inhabited by the old ex-courtier, once a favourite of the first Emperor. We proceeded across the ridge to the Santa Barbara, or main road. As we wound down a hill, in a somewhat romantic spot, we espied descending from the opposite height a troop of people dressed in black and white, and my conventual eye at once detected them to be Sisters of Charity. The rest of our party could not make them out, and were quite in a state of excitement at seeing these pilgrims. We met upon the bridge crossing the river. There were eleven sisters and two priests, all in religious habit and mounted on poor hack mules. They were going to form a new house at Dimantina, there being only one other convent in the interior, and that at Marianna. I recognized some old friends amongst them. They presented a very curious and pretty sight, as they came round a corner on the mountain-side, with their black habits and white bonnets. After stopping and talking for a little while, we rode on, and arrived at 4 p.m. at Catas Altas, having done twenty miles in five hours. Here we called on the padre and saw the church.

In the evening the good old padre came to visit us, but could not be persuaded to take a glass of champagne, of which we had a bottle in the provision basket.

We left Catas Altas next morning at 6.20, and rode for two miles till we reached Agua Quente ("hot water"). Here we had to make divers arrangements. We stayed there less than an hour, and rode on to a place about three hours' ride from Agua Quente, through forests and a mountain ascent, in a heavy rain.

We eventually arrived at a piece of country that

appeared like a gigantic basin with a mountain-ridge running nearly all round it. The soil was lumpy and ferruginous, and covered with a coarse, high grass, and very difficult of passage. At the top of this ridge we had to ride till we came successively to two places with small mountain torrents, which had sliced through the rock, and the bits that were broken away were like cakes of coal. There we had to sit and breakfast, while Richard went to examine this curious coal formation, which it was supposed might some day be valuable. This operation over, we mounted again, and at about one o'clock arrived at a little ranch called Moreira. We had left one change of mules and horses to follow us, and we missed them terribly, as we had to ride the same wretched animals all day.

Then Mr. Gordon, who had accompanied us thus far, wished us good-bye for a few days, as his business took him another way, and we rode through pretty woods to Inficionado ("Infected"), twenty-four miles in all, and reached it at 3.30. It is a long village, with several ranches and a few churches, very pretty, but remarkable for its number of idiots and deformities.

It was pleasant after the day's fatigues to sit by a running brook opposite the ranch. The sun was not quite set yet; the almost full moon was visible. Richard and Mr. E—— were sitting by the ranch door, and herds of mules were picketed in front. It was a most picturesque scene.

We left Inficionado next morning at 9.30, and rode along a bad road, which reminded me of the common pictures of Napoleon on an impossible horse crossing

the Alps. We reached a ranch called Camargos at
12.15. To-day we ate while riding, and did not stop;
the ride was hot and steep. We never drew rein till
we reached Sant' Anna, where we expected friends to
take us in. We had fortunately sent on a black
messenger with our letters of introduction, and to
apprise them of our coming ; and he ran to meet us
a few hundred yards before we reached the house, and
told us that the owner, Captain Treloar, superintendent
of these mines, could not receive us, as his wife
was dying. Much grieved and shocked, we returned
to a neighbouring *vendha* for a few minutes to write
a note of sympathy and apology for our untimely
intrusion, and also to consult as to what we had
better do with ourselves, since we had " counted our
chickens " prematurely, certain of the never-failing
hospitality of our compatriots, and had given away
all our provisions. Now we were thrown on the wide
world without so much as a biscuit. We soon decided
to prospect the place we were in, and then ride to
Marianna, where we had a letter of introduction to a
Dr. Mockett. Sant' Anna looked a desolate, dead-
alive place, and consisted of the Casa Grande, or
Superintendent's house, a chapel on the hill, a big
universal kitchen, and a hospital. These were the
only four large buildings; but there were plenty of
small white cottages, which looked like dots on the
hill, for the English, and for the black settlers a line
of huts. The valley, which was pretty, was occupied by
the houses, which appeared small after Morro Velho.

When we returned to our *vendha*, we found waiting

for us Mr. Symmonds, son-in-law of Captain Treloar who insisted on our going to-morrow to his house. He said it was empty, all the family being together at Sant' Anna during their affliction; but as he kindly remarked we should be more comfortable there, we agreed, and mounted and rode with him along a pleasant, sandy road—not track—for two miles or more, till we passed a pretty villa in the centre of some wild-looking mountains. There lived Captain Treloar and his wife with a large family of nine daughters, six of whom were married, and three sons. All the men of the family, sons and sons-in-law, are connected with the mine.

We had a pretty ride of two miles more, and arrived on the brink of a height, and suddenly viewed a mass of spires and domes in the valley beneath, which we at once knew was the pretty cathedral town of Marianna. We rode down into it, and sent our letter to Dr. Mockett; but he too was absent attending Mrs. Treloar—a second disappointment; but we found a ranch. Marianna has nine churches, a seminary, a bishop's palace, a convent, hospital, college, and orphanage of Sisters of Charity, but no hotel save a miserable ranch. It is a regular cathedral city, and so dead-alive, so unvisited by strangers, that I suppose it would not pay to have one. Our fare was of the worst description. My feet stuck out of the end of my miserable, short, straw bed, and it was a bitterly cold night. We sent round all our letters of introduction; but that night no one seemed to wake up to the fact of our arrival.

The next day, Sunday, was a wet and miserable morning. However, later Captain Treloar's son-in-law came and rescued us, and took us to his house. This was a comfortable English home, where we found nicely furnished rooms, and were cheered with the sight of Bass's ale, sherry, and everything imaginable to eat and drink, a piano, and plenty of books. We did not tear ourselves away from these luxuries for three days—from Sunday to Wednesday.

From here we went to visit the Passagem Mine. We changed our clothes, and each with a lantern and stick descended a steep, dark, slippery tunnel of forty-five fathoms deep—the caverns large and vaulted, and in some places propped up with beams and dripping with water. The stone is a mixture of quartz and gold. The miners were all black slaves. They were chanting a wild air in chorus in time to the strokes of the hammer. They work with an iron crowbar called a drill and a hammer, and each one bores away four *palmes* a day. If they do six, they get paid for the two over. They were streaming with perspiration, but yet seemed very merry. The mine was lit up with torches for us. We then descended thirty-two fathoms deeper, seeing all the different openings and channels. To the uninitiated like myself, it looked probable that the caverns of stone, apparently supported by nothing, would fall in. I took down my negret Chico. He showed great symptoms of fear, and exclaimed, " Parece O inferno! " I was rather struck by the justice of the observation. The darkness, the depth of the caverns, the glare of the torches lighting up the black figures humming against the walls, the heat and want of air, the horrid smells, the wild chant, reminded me of Dante. I wonder if he took some of his hells out of a mine?

Next day poor Mrs. Treloar died, after fifteen days of bilious attack. In this country, if you are well and strong, in good nerve and spirits, and can fight your own way, you do very well ; but the moment you are sick, down with you, fall out of the ranks and die, unless you have some one who values your life as his own. But even this could not save poor Mrs. Treloar. Mr. Symmonds requested Richard, as English Consul, to perform the funeral service, as they had no church, no clergyman, no burial-ground ; so they would not distress her mind by the knowledge that she was dying. My husband seemed to have been sent by Providence to perform this sad affair, as the English here hold greatly to their consuls performing a ceremony in the absence of a clergyman. The Treloars were to have gone home to England for good the previous month, having several of their children at school in England, and only put it off for that "little while" often so fatal in the tropics. She was buried on the hilltop, and was followed by all the men in the neighbourhood, black and white. Women do not attend funerals, nor sales, nor shops, nor post-offices in Brazil. Richard read the service, and I was left in charge of the house and blacks while they were all absent. A little before the funeral I heard a tremendous noise in the kitchen like the crashing of crockery, black women screaming, and men swearing angry oaths. I ran in and found two of the men kniving each other over a piece of money which we had given the servants for their attention to us. Blood was upon the ground. I rushed in between them and wrenched their knives away, and ordered them all out upon the grass upon their knees, and they obeyed. The funeral was now winding up the hill opposite the house, and I read prayers for the dead.

Directly after the funeral we mounted our animals and rode for six miles along a pretty mountainous road to Ouro Preto. We rode down into the town (which looked rather imposing from the height we viewed it) as the clock struck six. It was now dark, and we were received into the house of Commendador Paula Santos, Director of the Bank, and were made very comfortable.

Ouro Preto is the capital of Minas Geraes. It is by far the most hilly town I ever saw ; walking up and down the streets is quite as difficult as ascending and descending ladders, and there is an equal danger of falling. I think one could throw a stone from the top of a street to the bottom without its touching anything *en route*. The President of the Province lives here, and has a white palace like a little fortress. There is a small theatre, a bank, two tramways (one provincial and one imperial), a prison and large police barrack, a townhall, several carved stone fountains, and fifteen churches. We found the one usual English family, a general shopkeeper and watchmaker, with a wife and children, brother and sister. They were very hospitable. We stayed here two days.

We left Ouro Preto at 9.40 on Saturday morning, and rode along a neither very good nor very bad road, with fine mountain scenery, and the wind rather too cool. We were now turning our faces back again towards Morro Velho. We followed the course of the river, riding in the dry bed. We arrived at Casa Branca (a few ranches) at 1.15, and came up with a party of American immigrants. Here we only changed animals, and mounted again at two o'clock, as we had a long, weary ride facing wind and rain on the mountain-tops. We at last arrived at the house of Mr. Treloar (brother of the Mr. Treloar of Sant' Anna). Here we hoped to find hospitality ; but he too was in affliction, so we rode on to Rio das Pedras, and dismounted at 3 p.m. The hamlet was a few huts and a burnt-down church. We luckily got in fifteen minutes before the Americans, and secured some rough beds and food. Here we had an amusing evening with the immigrants. They were an old father with an oldish daughter, two young married couples, and one stray man, one old, grey-haired, swallowed-tailed gentleman, and a young woman with a lot of chicks. They were wandering about in search of land to settle down and be farmers, and were amusing, clever, and intelligent.

Richard awoke us at 3 a.m. It rained in torrents all night, and there was a succession of bad storms of thunder and lightning ; so I was very loath to get up. But whether I liked it or not I was ordered to mount at 6 a.m.

We had a long, muddy, rainy, weary, up and down

hill ride, slipping back two steps for every one forward, and going downhill much faster than we wished, which made the journey appear double the distance. After eight miles we arrived at our old sleeping-place on the borders of Morro Velho, Coche d'Agua. The old people were gone, and the new ones were not very civil, and we had great difficulty in getting even a cup of coffee. We had some amusement coming along. Mr. E—— was strongly in favour of riding with a loose rein. We were scaling a greasy hill, and his animal, after slithering about several minutes, fell on its stomach. Chico and I dismounted, for our beasts couldn't stand ; but when we were off neither could we. Mr. E——'s mule got up and ran away; and Richard, through wicked fun, though safe at the top, would not catch it. Chico's mule was only donkey size. Mr. E—— jumped upon it, and being tall he looked as if he were riding a dog and trailing his legs on the ground. He rode after his mule and caught it in half an hour, and we were all right again.

From Coche d'Agua next morning we rode on to Morro Velho, and found the church bells ringing, and pretty girls with sprays of flowers in their hair going to hear Mass. I was not allowed to go, so I paid two old women to go and hear Mass for me, much to the amusement of the party. We breakfasted by the roadside, and rode into Morro Velho and to the Gordons. The journey, though only twenty-four miles, had been long and tedious on account of the rain and mud and constant steep ascents and descents. We arrived looking like wet dogs at our kind host's door ;

and my appearance especially created mirth, as my
skirt up to my waist was heavy with mud, my hat torn
to ribbons, with the rain running down the tatters.   A
big bath was prepared for each of us.   We changed our
clothes, and sat down to a comfortable and excellent
dinner, thankful to be in the hospitable shelter of the
Casa Grande again.   Here we tarried for a fortnight, and
thoroughly explored Morro Velho this time.

Among other things, I determined to go down into
the mine, which has the reputation of being the largest,
deepest, and richest gold-mine in Brazil.   We had been
very anxious to visit its depths when we were at Morro
Velho before, but Mr. Gordon had put us off until
our return.

It was considered rather an event for a lady to go
down the mine, especially as Mrs. Gordon, the Superintendent's wife, who had been at Morro Velho nine
years and a half, had never been down.   However, she
consented to accompany me.   She said, "I have never
yet taken courage ; I am sure if I don't do it now, I
never shall."   So the end of it was that a crowd of
miners and their families and blacks collected along the
road and at the top of the mine to see us descend.
One lady staying in the house with us (Casa Grande)
could not make up her mind to go ; and when I asked
Chico, he wrung his hands, and implored me not to go,
weeping piteously.   As we went along we could hear
the miners' delighted remarks, and their wives wondering : "Well, to be sure now, to think of they two
going down a mile and a quarter in the dark, and they
not obliged to, and don't know but that they may never

come up again! I'd rather it was they than me!"
"Aye, that's our countrywomen; they's not afeared
of nothing! I'd like to see some o' they Brazzys put
into that 'ere kibble."

We were dressed in brown Holland trousers, blouse,
belt, and miner's cap, and a candle was stuck on our
heads with a dab of clay. The party to go down
consisted of Mr. Gordon, Richard, Mr. E——, and
Mr. John Whitaker, an engineer. There are two
ways of going down, by ladders and by a bucket.
The ladders are nearly a thousand yards long. If you
see lights moving like sparks at enormous distances
beneath, it is apt to make you giddy. Should your
clothes catch in anything, should you make a false
step, you fall into unknown space. The miners
consider this safe. They do it in half an hour, running
down like cats, do their day's work, and run up again
in three-quarters of an hour; but to a new-comer
it is dreadfully fatiguing, and may occupy four hours
—to a woman it is next to impossible.

The other way is easy, but considered by the miners
excessively unsafe. It is to be put into an iron
bucket called a kibble, which is like a huge gypsy-
pot (big enough to hold two ordinary-sized people
thinly clad), suspended by three chains. It is unwound
by machinery, and let down by an iron rope or chain
as the lifts are in London. It takes about twenty
minutes, and is only used for hauling tons of stone
out of the mine or hauling up wounded men. The
miners said to me, "We make it a point of honour
to go down by the ladders; for the fact is, on the

ladder we depend on ourselves, but in the kibble we depend on every link of the chain, which breaks from time to time." If the slightest accident happens, you can do nothing to help yourself, but are dashed into an apparently fathomless abyss in darkness. The opening where we first embarked was a narrow, dark hole, very hot and oppressive. The kibble was suspended over the abyss. Richard and Mr. E—— went first. Mr. Gordon and Mr. Whitaker, being superintendent and engineer, went by the ladders.

In due time the kibble returned, and Mrs. Gordon and I were put into it, with some candles fastened to the side by a dab of clay, a piece of lighted tow in the chain above us that we might see the beauties of the lower regions, and a flask of brandy in case we got faint, which I am proud to say we did not touch. As we looked up many jokes were exchanged, and word was given to lower away. We waved a temporary farewell to the sea of faces, and the last thing we saw was Chico and Mrs. Gordon's black maid weeping bitterly and wringing their hands. A tremendous cheer reached us, even when some distance below.

We began to descend slowly, and by means of our rough illuminations we saw all that we passed through. Lower and lower on all sides were dark abysses like Dante's Inferno. The huge mountain-sides were kept apart by giant tree trunks. How they came there or how fastened up is one of the wonders of man's power and God's permission. As we went down, down into the bowels of the earth, each dark, yawning cavern looked uglier than its neighbour. Every here and there was a forest of timber. Whenever we passed any works, the miners lifted their lighted caps, which looked like sparks in the immensity, and spoke or gave us a *viva*, that we might not be frightened. It was a comfort to hear a human voice, though it could do us no good if anything went wrong. Suddenly in a dark, desolate place our kibble touched some projecting thing and tilted partly over. I clutched at the chains above my head, and Mrs. Gordon held me. It righted itself in a second. In their anxiety to do well they had put us into the wrong kibble, which had a superfluity of chain, and had played out a little too much of it above. This happened three times, and they were three moments of agony— such moments as make people's hair turn grey. I was too full of life and hope to want to die. Every one ought to experience some such moments in his life, when his heart flies up in supplication to God. It was wonderful, when half-way down, to look below and see the lights, like fireflies in the forest, moving about. At length the kibble stood still, and began to roll like a boat. Then it began to descend perpendicularly ; and after a little while we saw the glare of lights, and friendly voices bid us welcome to the mines. Loud *vivas* greeted us from the workmen.

I cannot describe how kind and thoughtful all the rough workmen were. Everything was done to show us how much they were pleased and flattered by our visit, to allay fear, to amuse us, and to show us everything of interest. It would have been a good lesson

in manners to many London drawing-rooms.   We
each had two men to guide us about.

It was a stupendous scene of its kind.   Caverns
of quartz pyrites and gold, whose vaulted roofs, walls,
and floors swarmed with blacks with lighted candles
on their heads, looked excessively infernal.   Each man
had drill and hammer, and was singing a wild song and
beating in time with his hammer.   Each man bores
eight *palmes* (pounds) a day, and is paid accordingly,
though a slave.   If he bores more, he is paid for his
over-work.   Some are suspended to the vaulted roof
by chains, and in frightful-looking positions ; others
are on the perpendicular walls.

After seeing the whole of this splendid palace of
darkness in the bowels of the earth, we sat on a
slab of stone and had some wine.   Richard said to
Mr. Gordon, "Suppose this timber should ever catch
fire, what would you do ? "   Mr. Gordon laughed, and
said, "Oh, that is impossible ; the whole place is
dripping with water, and the wood is all damp, and
it would not take ; and we have no chance of fire-
damp and other dangers of explosion as in other mines
—coal-mines, for instance.   Oh, I'm not afraid of
that." [1]

At this time the mine was at its climax of greatness
and perfection, perfectly worked and regulated, and
paying enormously.

We mounted as we came.   I found it a much more
unpleasant sensation and more frightening to ascend

[1] Yet the mine was almost destroyed by fire some six months
after our visit.

than to descend. Yet sometimes out of some caverns of horror on the way up would pop an urchin of ten or twelve laughing, and hop across a beam like a frog without the least fear. The Brazilian authorities wanted to interfere to prevent children being employed in the mine, and Mr. Gordon to please them stopped it; but whole families came and implored on their knees to be taken back. They earned much, and their lives were rendered respectable and well regulated, and their condition superior under the existing *régime*. But there is no doubt that this part of the province would degenerate terribly, should the colony be broken up, or the present Superintendent leave.

In the evening the miners and their officers gave us a concert. A large room in the stores was very prettily decorated with palm and the flower of Saint John (which is a creeper like a rich orange honeysuckle and dark green leaves), and chandeliers were intermixed. There was a little stage for the performers, adorned with a large painted representation of the British arms, and a place for the band. The room, though large, was crowded; all the little colony was present. We had comic performances, Christy Minstrels, and sentimental songs for about two hours, wound up by a dance, and at midnight broke up with "God save the Queen."

We were now preparing for the second half of our trip—to canoe down the Rio São Francisco (thirteen hundred miles) from Sabará to the sea. The expedition was to be Richard, myself (if permitted), and Mr. E——, who was to choose whether he would go or not (as it turned out, fortunately for him, he preferred to return to Rio with the Gold Troop on July 28). I was entreating to go, and my fate was hanging in the balance, when the question was settled for me by an accident.

Richard had been requested to give a lecture on his travels. The night of July 27 was fixed. The room was arranged as before. Richard spoke of the pleasure he had in becoming acquainted with them all, and told them his impressions about Morro Velho. He thanked the officers, captains, miners, and all for their kindness and attention, and touched upon his travels generally, especially the Nile, Mecca, and Dahomé. Mr. Gordon then spoke, and Mr. E——, and many pretty little speeches were made. It lasted about an hour, and then we had a short concert. I sang four times ; and Chico was dressed up, and sang very prettily with the guitar, and danced. All the singers did something, and a little dancing, and "God save the Queen" as usual terminated the festivities. Unfortunately for me, after my first song, as I was going off the platform there was a deep step to take in the dark, and I fell off and sprained my ankle severely ; but I managed to perform my part to the end by sitting still, excepting when I had to sing ; so that it was not found out until all was over, and I had to be carried home. This was a dreadful bore for Richard, who could not take me, and did not like to leave me ; so he good-naturedly put off his journey for ten days.

The doctor at first thought my leg was broken,

but it turned out to be only a severe contusion. I was five days in bed, and then was promoted to crutches, litter, and sofa, which lasted me twenty days.

At last the day came to see Richard off on his important journey in a canoe from Sabará down the Rio das Velhas and Rio São Francisco to the sea, visiting the diamond-mines at Diamantina from the nearest point (to that city) of the river. Mr. E—— had already started for Rio. I did not think it *convenable* to travel alone with the *jeune brigand*, so he did not wait for me. We set out from Morro Velho on August 6, a large party on horse and mule back, poor me in a litter, and of course ordered to return with the party. The litter is a covered stretcher, with a mule in front and one behind, in shafts, and it takes two men to manage it. It is expensive travelling, and a great luxury for those who tire soon in the saddle ; but I would rather ride any distance, as the motion makes me ill. It is not easy like the hammock. We rode for twelve miles over a pretty mountainous road to Sabará, a very picturesque, ancient-looking town, with eight churches and some important houses, and with a decent *vendha*, or ranch. It is on a head of the Rio das Velhas, and seems to be the centre of North American emigration here. The first view of the town and winding river is exceedingly pretty. A church on a hilltop is the first indication or landmark of Sabará, the town being immediately below it. We arrived, ranched ourselves, and got a good dinner. We went to the only shop, and bought

some French jewellery for a few coppers, as parting
presents for each other, by way of "chaff"; and after
seeing the town, ended the evening as usual seated
round an empty ranch on the floor or on our boxes,
and drank execrable tea, which tasted like hot brandy-
and-water without sugar, and some beer presented
to us by the great man of the place. As I was told
he was very rich and stingy, I asked him to make me
a present of a few bottles of beer for my party, as we
were thirsty; but if I remember right, he sent me in
a bill for it next morning.

In the morning we got a good ranch breakfast,
during which we were visited by all the "swells" of
Sabará. We set out for the river, where the canoes were.
Two canoes were lashed together, boarded, and covered
over with an awning just like a tent. There was a
little brick stove, benches, and a writing-table erected.
Richard and I went on board, and the young lady of
the party, Miss Dundas, niece of "Uncle Brown,"
the before-mentioned "Padre Eterno," broke a bottle
of *caxassi* over her bows, exclaiming, "Brig *Eliza*,"
whereby hangs an untold joke. Besides our own
party, nearly all the village followed us. So there
arose respectable cheers for the "Brig *Eliza*," "Captain
and Mrs. Burton," "Success to the expedition," "The
Superintendent and his wife," "Prosperity to Sabará,"
"The Emperor of Brazil," "The Queen of England,"
with many *vivas*. We then took all our own party
on board, and sent the animals forward to meet us,
and shoved off. There were two blacks in the stern,
and two in the bows to paddle and pole, and one black

to cook for Richard and attend upon him. One old
black was disagreeably nervous, and begged Richard
to exchange him at the next town, which he did. We
spooned down with the stream, which ran very fast,
and went down two rapids, and got aground twice, and
towards sunset arrived at Roça Grande. Here they
all took leave of Richard—I need not say how sadly.
They kindly left me behind for a space to follow, as
it was a more serious business for me to say "good-
bye " than for them. "I was not to expect him till
I saw him. It might be two months, or four, or
six." He did not know what might happen. The
dangers were Indians, *piranhas* (a sort of river pike),
fever and ague, and of course the rapids. At last
I parted from him on his ' brig,' with the old
swallow-tailed gentleman (before mentioned), who had
begged a two-days' passage, and a savage *cão de féla*
and his five blacks ; and from a bank I watched
the barque with dim eyes round a winding of the
river, which hid it from my sight. The sun was
sinking as I turned away. I was put into my litter,
and taken back to Sabará, where I fell in with my
party, and we returned to Morro Velho as we came.
This was August 7.

I remained with my kind friends the Gordons
till I got well enough to ride all day without injury.
On one occasion I was able to be of use to Mr.
Gordon in a small matter which required a little
diplomacy and a gallop of three leagues, twelve miles
either way, out and in within a given time, the
message he had sent having failed. I asked to go ; I

wanted to try if I was fit for my long ride, and he gave me my choice of all the stables. I selected a white horse of remarkable speed and endurance, with a strong cross of the Arab in him, and it certainly would have been my own fault if I had failed as to time. I rode there, found the desired decision, and walked into his office with the answer long before the time, which pleased him very much. After that I thought I was fit to set out on my return journey to Rio. I had already stayed so long in their house, receiving great kindness and hospitality; and though they begged of me to continue with them until it was time to meet Richard at Rio, I felt that life was too serious to pass my days in the pleasant *dolce far niente* of catching butterflies, which really was my principal occupation at Morro Velho. There was too much to be done elsewhere, so I begged Mr. Gordon to lend me seven animals, two slaves, and one of his *tropeiro* captains, or muleteers, and I prepared to leave this hospitable family on the coming August 25.

Before this date, as I felt sufficiently recovered, I had gradually emancipated myself from litter and sofa, and tried my strength as usual. I had one very pleasant and amusing excursion.

There was a village called Santa Rita, about five miles from Morro Velho, where they have a church, but no priest; and being the Feast of the Assumption of Our Lady, a great day, the villages had sent over to borrow the Morro Velho padre. They sent a mounted attendant and a horse saddled with silver

trappings to bring him there and back. I asked
him to take me. Mr. Gordon lent me a horse and
a mounted attendant, and we set out on a most lovely
morning for our pretty mountain ride. The padre
was in the height of Minas fashion and elegance.
He wore jack-boots, white corduroys, a very smart
coat, waistcoat, watch-chain, embroidered Roman
collar, a white *pouche* with tassels and silk cravat,
and enormous silver spurs. On arriving, we were
received by upwards of forty people in a private
house on the way to the church. From there we
went on to the church, a small, tawdry, roadside chapel,
where the padre said Mass ; and though the people
were very devout, the children and dogs were very
distracting. We then went to a *vendha*, and spread
our basket of provisions. This made the people
furious. The padre had passed me off as his niece,
so everybody was anxious to have the honour of
doing hospitality to the padre and his niece. About
fifteen messages were sent to us, so we said we would
go round and take coffee with them after our breakfast.
The great attraction of the place was a handsome old
lady, Donna Floris Vella, civilized and intelligent by
nature. She petted me a good deal at first for
being the padre's niece, and called me *bena moca*
(here to be young and *fat* is the highest personal
compliment they can pay you), and quarrelled with
us for going off into the *mato*—the forest, as she
called the *vendha*—to breakfast, instead of coming
to her. But I suddenly forgot that I was the padre's
niece, and turned round and spoke to Mr. Fitzpatrick,

the Morro Velho Master of Horse, who had been
sent to attend upon me, in English. When she heard
me speaking English so fluently, she flew at the
padre and punched him in the ribs in a friendly
way, and told him he was a liar ; but she kept
up the joke with the rest ; so we had coffee and
very interesting general conversation about England
and civilization, church matters and marriages, and
were taken round to several houses. They would
have been jealous if we had only visited one ;
so we did not reach home till late in the afternoon.

One day afterwards, as I was sitting at the church
door at Morro Velho, I saw some hammocks with
bodies lying in them. They were carried by others,
all dripping with blood. The kibble—the same one
we had been down the mine in—had broken a link
of its chain and fallen. How sorry it made me feel,
and how thankful that it did not happen on our
day, as it easily might ! Mr. Gordon is so careful
about accidents that he has the chain hauled over
and examined every twelve hours, and a prize is
given to any one who can find a faulty link ; yet in
spite of all this from time to time it will break away.
I think it happened twice during my stay. There
is not the smallest occurrence that happens in that
large colony that does not come under Mr. Gordon's
eye between nine and ten o'clock every morning.
The wonder is how he finds time for everything and
every one with so much ease to himself.

While I was at Morro Velho he allowed me to

organize little singing parties every night. All who could sing used to assemble, and he would join us, and we learnt duets, trios, quartettes, chorus glees, and so on. It brought people together ; and he said it was refreshing after the day's work, instead of sitting reading or writing in a corner, always tired.

So passed the time at Morro Velho, until the day of my departure dawned.

CHAPTER VIII

MY LONELY RIDE TO RIO

(1867)

The day of my delight is the day when you draw near,
And the day of mine affright is the day you turn away.

ALF LAYLAH WA LAYLAH

(*Burton's " Arabian Nights "*).

ON Sunday, August 25, we had a sad dinner at the Casa Grande at midday, on account of the breaking up our little party, which had been so pleasant off and on for the past two months. We should probably never meet again. I bade Mrs. Gordon farewell, and at 3.30 a considerable cavalcade set out from Mr. Gordon's hospitable door. I had to pass through the village of Morro Velho. There appeared many a waving handkerchief, and I received many a warm handshake and " God-speed."

At the top of the village hill I turned to take a last grateful farewell of valley, church, and village—the little colony, with its white settlements and pretty bungalows, where I had passed so many pleasant days. We rode along one of the beautiful roads, which I have before described, for about six miles, often silent or trying to make cheerful remarks. Mr. Gordon accompanied me.

322

A little before five o'clock the sun's rays were beginning to fade away into the pleasant, illuminated coolness of late afternoon, and we stopped at a house agreed upon as the parting-place, the house of the same Donna Floris Vella before mentioned, an old widow lady with a delicate son. Though already grey and aged, she was very buxom and clever, though deprived by circumstances of cultivation. She was what we would call "a good fellow." Here we stayed half an hour, and looked at her flowers. Then we remounted, and rode on for a few hundred yards. My host, Mr. Gordon, who commanded our party, here anticipated a little mutiny, as all in their kindness of heart wanted to accompany the lone woman, and some begged to go with me for one day and some even for one stage. So we suddenly stopped in a tract of low brushwood, and he gently but firmly said, "It was here that I parted with my daughter when her husband took her to England, and it is here that I will part with you." I shook hands silently with him, and then with the others all round, and as the sun's last rays faded into evening I turned the head of my "gallant grey" towards my long ride ; but I turned myself in the saddle, and watched them all retreating across the tract homewards until the last waving handkerchief had disappeared.

It was one of those beautiful South American evenings, cool and fresh after the day's heat; and twilight was succeeded by a brilliant starlight such as England's denizens have never dreamt of. There was perfect stillness, save the hum of late insects and a noise like distant rain ; sweet smells from the forest were wafted

across my path ; and dark, brown birds of magpie shape
flitted along the ground like big bats or moths, sometimes perching for an instant, and disappearing without
noise in a ghostlike fashion.   I felt very sad.   I was
sorry to leave my friends.   Two months even " off
and on " is like twelve months to a wanderer and an
Englishwoman in exile, and above all in the wilds.
She is glad to meet her country people *when they are
kind*; and they had been so very kind.   Moreover,
I was returning after a taste of bush life, not to my
eyrie in São Paulo, but to the cab shafts of semi-
civilization in Rio de Janeiro.

My retinue consisted of the Captain of the Gold
Troop, a kind, attentive man.   He rode down with
the Gold Troop from the mines, and protected it with
an old two-barrelled horse-pistol, which would never
go off when we wanted to shoot anything (and by
way of parenthesis I may remark that, with the assistance of a small boy to look after the mules, I would
undertake for a bet to rob the troop myself).   My
capitão, whom for the future I shall call Senhor Jorge,
spoke but little, and that in Brazilian.   I should call
him a very silent youth, which was an advantage in
passing beautiful scenery, or when taking notes, or
feeling inclined for thought ; but there were moments
when I wanted to glean information about the country,
and then I used to draw him out with success.
Besides this stalwart there was my faithful Chico, two
slaves to take care of the animals, six mules for baggage
and riding, and my grey horse.

We arrived at the ranch of Sant' Antonio d'Acima

at about eight o'clock. Here I got a comfortable straw bed and some milk. Some of the inhabitants, about fifteen in number, came over to our ranch, which consisted of four bare, whitewashed walls, a ceiling of plaited bamboo, a mud floor, a wooden shutter for a window, two wooden benches and table, and three tallow dips. These good people sang songs and glees, and danced Minas dances for me to the native wire guitar, snapping their fingers, and beating time with their feet. They sing and dance at the same time. They were all very merry. At ten I retired to try and sleep, leaving them to continue their festivities ; but what with the excitement of the day, and the still twanging guitars at the other side of the partition, I did not succeed.

At 2 a.m. I rose, and, calling to Senhor Jorge, asked him to send for the animals. The two slaves were sent to the pasture to look for them, drive them in, and feed them. While this operation was going on, I paid the master for my night's entertainment the sum of seven milreis, or fourteen shillings. When I mounted, it was 4 a.m. It was quite dark and foggy, but this I did not mind. I had heard from all quarters that the country was execrable. My mule, like Byron's corsair, possessed one virtue to a thousand crimes, and that was surefootedness, and had an objection to deep holes ; and were the whole journey to have been performed on a single plank, I would have ridden him in the dark without a bridle. I threw it on his neck, and tried to keep my hands warm. Soon the fog lifted, and the moon's last crescent showed us the way, aided by starlight. The dawn grew upon us at 5.30, and at 6.30 the sun gilded the mountain-tops. At eight we arrived at Rio das Pedras, our old station, breakfasted from our basket, and changed animals. I had arranged to ride my mule in the dark, but my good grey horse in the daylight, for he trotted well, and this would relieve the journey greatly. We had now ridden twelve miles. My mule was lazy, I had no spur, and besides the country was difficult. I had still twelve miles to go. So I changed for the grey. I passed over several bits of prairie ground, where I gave my grey "spirits." I arrived at twelve o'clock, two hours later than I had intended, at Casa Branca, the station where we had stopped five weeks previously. The sun had already been fierce for two hours. It is an excellent plan in Brazil to start early and ride your twenty-four or thirty miles before ten or eleven, and rest during the great heat of the day under shelter. It saves both man and beast, and enables them to last longer; and on a moonlight or starlight morning in the tropics you lose nothing of scenery, it is so bright. Casa Branca was an old broken-down house in a valley near a river. The only available room was occupied by an invalid. The woman of the house, be it remarked, had twenty-four children, and a cat for each child; so we had scanty room, but decent food—*canjica* (a rice mess), fowl roast and stewed, *farinha* (flour), *coves* (cabbage), with *tocinho* (bacon fat), and *feijão* (black beans). My sleeping-place was a room with four narrow mud walls, a rush ceiling, mud floor, a door which only kept shut by planting a stake against it, and a bit of sacking covered the hole representing a window. Every day, on arriving at my ranch, I first looked after the animals and their comforts, for on this all depends; then settled my own, wrote up this journal, saw that the men had all they wanted, dined, and then inspected the place, and read till falling asleep, always rising at 1 or 2 a.m. This evening I took a stroll down the partially dried-up bed of the river by twilight, and met herds of cattle being driven home. The picture would have made a good Turner. On my return Chico brought me a *caxassi* bath; this is, literally, a grog of native rum and hot water, without sugar, which gives a refreshing sleep. In these countries there is a minute tick, which covers you by millions, burrowing into your flesh; you cannot extract it, and it maddens you. At night you derive an inexpressible relief from having the grog bath.

Next morning we rose at 2.20, but did not get off till 4 a.m. It was pitch dark, raining, with high wind, and altogether a decidedly suicidal kind of morning. Instead of going *down* the bed of the river, we struck away to the right (N.W.), on a new road to any I had been formerly. We groped our way through rain and biting wind. At 7 a.m. we took a last view of the cross of Morro Velho from a height forty-six miles off, having passed through Cachoeira do Campo, a long, straggling village which climbed a hill and possessed a church and one or two respectable houses. It should be remarked that in Minas Geraes there are a great number of large black crosses, with all the instruments of the Passion, erected either before the parish church or on heights ; they were introduced by the Jesuit missionaries. An Englishman having any great enterprise on hand will say as an incentive to the blacks, " When such a work is completed, I will plant a cross in your village " ; and the hope of this makes them anxious and hard-working. We passed a deserted house and ranch. The country all about was ugly, wild, and desolate, and composed chiefly of barren *campos*. At 9 a.m. we arrived at Chiquero, a little village and ranch on a hill. We picnicked in the open ranch with the mules, not liking to go into a hot shelter and come out again in the wind. Meantime the sun came out and scorched us up. We changed animals, and left Chiquero at ten. My mule " Camondongo " trotted after us like a dog. Our road was bad, but a little less ugly than hitherto. We saw a fox in the wood, and Senhor Jorge tried to shoot it with the old horse-pistol, but failed. Later on we passed through some woods, and finally saw Ouro Branco quite close to us from a height on the other side of the serra. I was quite delighted, and exclaimed, " Oh, we shall get in early to-day." " Patience," said my *capitão* ; " wait a little." We had to make an enormous *détour* of at least two leagues to get to Ouro Branco, which seemed close to us, because we could not cut straight across the serra, which was impassable. It was very irritating always seeing the town near us, and yet always unable to reach it. I wanted to ride straight down the serra, but Senhor Jorge wouldn't let me, and so we eventually passed round under the rocks beneath it. I saw that

he was right, though it seemed such a waste of time.
Still, the delay was not to be regretted, as the only
curious feature of this part is in this turn, which is
full of curious hills covered with stones of a wonderful and natural formation, starting out of the earth in
a slanting position.   The only idea it conveys to the
mind is that of a hilly churchyard, overstocked with
tombstones all blown on one side by the wind.   They
are intersected with a curious stunted tree or shrub,
with a tuft at the end of each branch ; and every here
and there was a small patch or forest of them, and
they presented a very weird look in the surrounding
desolation.   I did not know, nor could Senhor Jorge
inform me, what these stones were made of, nor why
this curious formation.   Though he had travelled the
road for seven years, and been in the country since
his birth, he had never remarked them before.   Coming
in we saw a peasant with a stick and a pistol fighting
a cobra.   It appeared a long day, as we had had five
hours of darkness, biting wind, and rain, followed by
four hours of scorching sun.

We arrived at Ouro Branco at one o'clock.   It is
a long, straggling village, with a church and a few
nice, respectable, white houses.   A wall of green serra
faces the village, which runs round on the top of a
semicircular eminence under the serra.   It had several
old houses, one marked 1759, a Minas cross, and
an old stone fountain.   The ranch was respectable,
but very dirty behind the scenes.   I went into the
inner part to prepare food myself, and was thankful
that I did so.   The women were unwashed, dirtily

clad, covered with snuff, and with hair streaming down their backs; and the kitchen utensils cannot be described. It is almost impossible for an English-woman in any part of the world, no matter how rough she may become, even in bushranging, to view dirt with calm and indifference.

I left Ouro Branco at 4.30 a.m. It was then pitch dark, but finally the heavy clouds and small rain cleared away, and we enjoyed starlight, then a delicious dawn and bright morning. We first rode through a long, straggling village, called Carreiras, and afterwards passed a small *fazenda*, where there were evidences of a refined mind; it was radiant with flowers, and trellised with creepers. Our road to-day was prettier. We passed through well-wooded lanes with pretty foliage— the umbrella tree and feathery mimosa. The next feature worth remarking was a small river, which had overhanging trees of a white-and-pink feathery flower which yields an edible bean. I sent one of our men to pick some. They have a branch of green buds in the middle, and the external ones sprout forth in feather, which is magenta pink at its base and snow white at the ends, terminating in a yellow knob. We then met some men hunting peccary; the master with a horse and gun, and the beaters with dogs in couples and hatchets. At 8 a.m. we arrived at a small ranch, in a forest called Holaria, kept by an Italian and a Portuguese. The former keeps his original grind-organ, which attracted all the birds in the neighbour-hood, who perched and sang loudly in the tree-tops surrounding it. He had, however, forgotten his native tongue. We picketed the animals, and breakfasted in the open.

The gigantic earth-slips in this part of the world present a very remarkable appearance. They appeared like yawning gulfs, as if some awful convulsion of Nature had just taken place ; and one can hardly believe the hubbub that is effected by little streams of water wearing away and causing the earth to fall. Some appeared as if a vast plain had sunk, leaving gigantic walls, fanciful castles, and pyramids of earth standing alone in the middle. They are of a bright red clay, which the sun variegates like a kaleidoscope.

We left Holaria at nine, and came to Quelsez, a long village with shops and a few decent houses. I stopped at the shop of a Portuguese Jew to look at violas. We then rode along a rather pretty and level road, where we met mules and *tropeiros,* which indicated that we were joining the civilized world again, and suggested more of highway and traffic than we had as yet seen. We stopped at Bandeirinho, a few huts and farm, and had a glass of water and witnessed great excitement amongst the juvenile population because a cobra was killing all their chickens. All along the road to-day our way was lined with a beautiful sort of lilac laburnum. We had plenty of level ground for galloping.

We arrived at 12.30 at a village called Ribeirão do Inferno, a few straggling houses and ranch, poor but clean. In the ranch and its surroundings lay a sick girl, an old woman, two young married women, and a man. As I was known to be European, they came to ask me if I had any remedies ; sickness was rare here, and doctor or medicines unknown. I produced a little medicine chest, with which they were quite surprised and delighted. First I went to the old woman. She was seventy ; she had been travelling along on a mule, when she was suddenly seized with spasms, was unable to proceed, and was carried into the first house. She was shut up in the dark, and would not allow any light in the room, where about a dozen sympathizers were collected, till I absolutely refused to prescribe for her in the dark. She then consented to a candle being brought. She then, after some beating about the bush, confessed to me that she had eaten too much cabbage, upon which I prescribed for her to take a cup of " English " tea which I had with me with milk and sugar, and left her quite happy. The girl had a serious chill. I made her some hot punch of *caxassi* water and sugar, with a large lump of hog's lard in it, in default of butter, and covered her up with six blankets and rugs to produce perspiration. The family fought very hard about it, and declared that she should not and would not drink it ; but I insisted that she must, and she helped me by taking to it very kindly. She was quite well, but weak, after a few hours. The two young women had head-aches from other causes, and I gave them carbonate of soda, which they insisted was sea-salt, and imagination made them sea-sick. But the worst of all was the man, who was seriously ill, and I found out at last it resulted from decayed teeth, upon which I told him that only a dentist could cure him. His wife told

me with tears that it was death to have a tooth out,
and I must give him some medicine that would make
the decayed teeth drop out without pain ; but I told
her that that was beyond my, or any one's, power.   I
wonder what a London doctor would have given for
my reputation that night !

It is worth noticing that to-day the *carapatos* (ticks)
were on the decrease.   This seems to be the border
or barrier of their country ; but I do believe this place
to be unhealthy, for we were all slightly ailing that
night.   A young Portuguese engineer who has been
educated in France arrived at the ranch in the evening
en route for Ouro Preto.   He told me he had been in
Ouro Preto when we had passed through it on our way
out, and had much wished to make our acquaintance.

We were rather lazy the next morning, and did not
leave Ribeirao until a few minutes to six.   My invalids
were all well ; but I only saw the master.   My four
men and myself were all suffering from headache, so
the place must have been unhealthy.   We had nothing
to regret in starting so late, for it was darker, colder,
and more mizzly than ever.   We rode two and a
half leagues, or ten miles, before breakfast.   Neither
our road nor any events were worthy of remark.   The
scenery would have been very beautiful for England,
but it was tame for South America.   We passed at
intervals a few cottages or a solitary *fazenda*.   We
breakfasted in the open ground of a pretty ranch, called
Floresta, surrounded by wooded mountains.   There
we found several men lassoing a struggling bull, who
would not consent to leave his birthplace and little

friends, and gave them about twenty minutes' trouble over every hundred yards, tearing men and trees down with his lasso. Senhor Jorge would go inside the ranch, but I persisted in seeing the sport. We then passed a few straggling houses; then an old *fazenda* ; then we came to a stream with one plank, which we made our animals cross.

We reached Gama at 1.10 p.m., having been out for seven hours. I felt a little tired, and declined to ride any farther, as there was no necessity. Gama is a ranch, and a poor, dirty one, in a desolate spot. It was fortunate for me that I arrived when I did, for half an hour later arrived *en route* for some distant *fazenda* Senhor Nicolão Netto Carneiro Seão, a polished and travelled man who spoke excellent English. He was travelling with his wife, children, and servants, numbering sixteen persons, some splendid animals, and a *liteira*. We had a long conversation over a gypsy fire which his servant made on the ranch floor, during which he told me he had served for five years in the British navy. He appeared to be anxious to import everything European, and to civilize his country. He was kind enough to say that he longed to meet Richard, and gave us a general invitation to visit his *fazenda*, and we exchanged cards.

The next morning we got up at 1.30 a.m., but did not start till 3.30. The morning was starlight, with a biting wind, but it soon grew dark and cloudy. We had no end of petty misfortunes. My change horse, being allowed to run loose, that we might go faster, instead of following us, ran back to his pasturage of last night. The mule I was riding insisted on following him, and heeded neither bit nor whip, but nearly left me in a ditch. Our cargo mule took advantage of the scrimmage to bolt in an opposite direction. And it was at this crisis especially dark and cloudy. We lost nearly an hour in collecting again, as we could not see each other nor any path. It seemed a very long two leagues (eight miles) before breakfast. As soon as it was light we could see a church tower of Barbacena on a neighbouring hill, apparently about three miles from us, but in reality fifteen miles distant.

At 7.10 we encamped in a clearing. My grey horse (the change) was tied up to a tree preparatory to being saddled, and got the staggers, threw himself down, and rolled and kicked so that, when we left again at eight o'clock, I had to remount my mule "Camondongo." We passed a village outside Barbacena, and met a very large Brazilian family travelling somewhere with horses, mules, and *liteiras*. There were so many girls that it looked like a school. We stopped at the ranch of Boa Vista that I might change saddles. The grey seemed all right again. The mule was done up. I sent the cargo mules, servants, and animals on to Registro, a league farther than Barbacena, and rode to Hermlano's Hotel, where we had originally put up at Barbacena when we started. Here I found Godfrey, our former German coach-driver, and arranged my passage, and found that Hermlano or some other scoundrel had changed my *cão de féla* pup for a white mongrel, which I presented to Godfrey. I paid a visit of twenty minutes to a

former hospitable acquaintance, Dr. Regnault, and then
rode on five miles farther to Registro, and arrived at
1.15 very tired, having been out ten hours.

Registro, which I have cursorily noticed before, is a
picturesque *fazenda* on the roadside, all constructed in
a rude wooden style, and is a mule station.   It is a fine,
large building, and the coach, after leaving Barbacena,
stops here first to pick up passengers and baggage.
There is also a celebrated cigarette manufactory, which
contains two rooms full of workers, one for men and the
other for women slaves.   I went to visit them, and
bought a packet for half a milreis, or thirteenpence
(then).   The cigarettes are hard and strong, and do not
draw well.   I did not like them.   The master makes
about 1,600 milreis, or about £160, a month by them;
so some people evidently find them good.

I rose at 3.30 the next morning.   Whilst dressing I
heard what I supposed was threshing grain or beating
sacks; it went on for about thirty minutes, and I did
not pay any attention to it till at last I heard a sob issue
from the beaten mass at the other side of a thin partition
wall.   I then knew what was taking place, and turned
so sick I could hardly reach the door.   I roused the
whole house, and called out to the man to cease.   I begged
the girl slave off, and besought the master to stop, for
I felt quite ill; but it was fully ten minutes before I
could awaken any one's pity or sympathy; they seemed
to be so used to it they would hardly take the trouble
to get up, and the man who was beating only laughed
and beat on.   I nearly fainted, though I could only hear
and not see the operation.   I thought the poor wretch

must have been pounded to a jelly before he left off; but she turned out to be a fine, strapping black girl, with marvellous recuperative powers, for when the man ceased she just gave herself a shake and walked away.

I left Registro at 7 a.m.   Here I was to lose my escort. Senhor Jorge and the slaves accompanied me to see me off, and appeared very sorry that our pleasant ride was over.   They were to start at the same time to ride back home to Morro Velho.   It was quite a curious sensation, after three months' absence, to find myself once more on a road, and a road with a coach going to civilized haunts.   I found the motion of the coach as unpleasant as a steamer in a gale of wind after a long stay on land.

We descended the Serra de Mantiqueira so quickly that I did not recognize our former laborious ascent. I noticed the trees and ferns were very beautiful in the forests as we dashed along—all festoons and arches. We had a most beautiful and extensive view of the Serra de Mantiqueira and the surrounding mountains. We then came to our last station, just outside Juiz de Fóra.   The country is very much the same during all this journey, perpetual mountain, valley, forest, and river, and the only great feature is the serra.

We drove up to the hotel of Juiz de Fóra at 3.30, having done our sixty-four miles in eight hours and twenty-three minutes.   I asked Godfrey how it was that we had come back so much faster than we made the journey out.   It transpired that he had got married in the interval, and now had somebody waiting for him at home.

Some of my coach companions came to the hotel, one a very much esteemed old man ; a French engineer, with a pretty, delicate wife and child ; and three Southerners—General Hawthorne, of the Southern army, an intelligent and very remarkable man, with two companions. We had rather a pleasant dinner.

Next day was Sunday, and I called on the padre and went to church. After this I spent a pleasant afternoon under the Commendador's orange trees with the *tangerines*. I collected plants and roots to send back to Mrs. Gordon at Morro Velho, and was escorted by the padre, the chief manager of the company, and the head gardener, who cut them for me. Here we found the three Southerners, who joined us, and we had a violent political discussion.

The coach left Juiz de Fóra the next morning at 6.30. To-day as well as yesterday I was compelled, much against the grain, to go inside by Richard's express wish at parting. At the station I met Captain Treloar on his way home, much better in spirits. He wished me very much to return with him, which I declined with thanks.

We soon came upon the winding river Parahybuna. We took up three Brazilian ladies, who were dreadfully frightened of the wild mules and speed, and also of the dust, and wanted to close the windows in spite of the sickening heat ; but I persuaded them otherwise. They wanted my place because it faced the mules, and also wished that I should make them a present of my aromatic vinegar. They consisted of a young married woman, whose husband, a mere boy, was on the top of the coach, and she was chaperoning two raw young girl cousins on a visit to her *fazenda* at some distance. By-and-by the boy husband got too hot outside, and was crammed in with us, five persons when three were more than enough, especially young people, who sprawl about.

Once more we arrived under the great granite mountain which overshadows the station of Parahybuna. At 2.30 we put down the Brazilian ladies, who mounted horses and rode somewhere into the interior, and I was thankful for the space and coolness.

Then we reached Posse, where we took in a strapping German girl with big, flat feet, who trod all the way upon mine. The German Protestant parson had started with me from Juiz de Fóra, but he had to give up his place to the Brazilian ladies, and gladly resumed it when they left, as the heat outside was considerable, and besides which he practised his little English upon me. Soon after Posse arose the second wall of granite, and the scenery became doubly beautiful and the air cooler. We saw the sun set behind the mountains, and the scenery was fairyland and the air delicious; it was an evening one could not forget for many weeks.

I arrived at Petropolis at 7 p.m., where I got a hearty welcome and a good dinner, went to bed, and slept as soundly as a person would who had been out in the sun for twelve hours and had driven one hundred miles. This did not prevent my starting for Rio the next morning at 6 a.m.

The morning was clear, and we had a pleasant drive down the mountains. When I got on board the little steamer to cross the Bay of Rio, I hid in the ladies' cabin, for I was ashamed of the state of my clothes. I could not explain to people why I was so remarkable, and I was well stared at. My boots were in shreds, my only dress had about forty slits in it, my hat was in ribbons, while my face was of a reddish mahogany hue and much swollen with exposure. I was harassed by an old Brazilian lady in the cabin, who asked me every possible question on earth about England ; and at last, when she asked me if we had got any *bacalhão* (dried cod), to get rid of her I said "No!" Then she said she could not think much of a country that had no *bacalhão*, to which I returned no reply.

On arriving at Rio, I was told that the Estrangeiros Hotel, where I had left my maid and my luggage before starting for the interior three months previously, was full. As I did not want to be seen about Rio in such a plight, I waited till dusk, and then went to the next best hotel in the town. The landlord, seeing a ragged woman, did not recognize me, and he pointed to a little tavern across the road where sailors' wives were wont to lodge, and said, "I think that will be about your place, my good woman, not here." "Well," I said, "I think I am coming in here all the same." Wondering, he took me upstairs and showed me a garret ; but I would have none of it, and insisted on seeing his best rooms. There I stopped and said, "This will do. Be kind enough to send this letter for me to the Estrangeiros."

Presently down came my maid, who was a great swell, with my luggage and letters. After a bath and change of garments I rang the bell and ordered supper. The landlord came up himself, as I was so strange a being. When he saw me, he said, "Did that woman come to take apartments for you, madam? I beg your pardon, I am afraid I was rather rude to her." "Well," I said, "I am 'that woman' myself; but you need not apologize, because I saw myself in the glass, and I don't wonder at it." He nearly tumbled down; and when I explained how I came to be in such a plight, he begged my pardon till I was quite tired of hearing him.

I spent the next few days resting my still weak foot, and reading and answering a sackful of welcome letters from home, which had accumulated during my three months' absence. Then I went down to Santos.

CHAPTER IX

HOME AGAIN

(1867—1869)

Home! there is magic in that little word;
It is a mystic circle that surrounds
Pleasures and comforts never known beyond
Its hallowed limits.

ISABEL did not remain long at Santos. At the end of October she went up to Rio to gain news of her husband, of whom she had heard nothing since they parted at Roça Grande nearly four months before, when he started in his canoe down the Rio São Francisco. As he did not return, she was naturally anxious. She wrote to her mother :

"I have come down to Rio to meet Richard. The English steamer from Bahia came in on November 1. I was in a great state of joyful excitement ; went on board in a man-of-war's boat. But, as once before when I went to Liverpool, Richard was not there, nor was there any letter or anything. I am very uneasy, and unless within two or three weeks some news comes I shall start to Bahia by steamer, change for the small one to Penedo Alagoas, and thence to a tiny one just put on from Penedo up the river to the falls, which are scarcely known yet [Paulo Affonso Falls, the Niagara of Brazil]. Here my difficulties would be great, as I should have to buy mules and ride round an unnavigable port and then canoe up. I fear Richard is ill, or taken prisoner, or has his money stolen. He always would carry gigantic sums in his pockets, hanging half out ; and he only has four slaves with him, and has to sleep amongst them. I am not afraid of anything except the wild Indians, fever, ague, and a vicious fish which can be easily avoided ; there are no other dangers. However, I trust that news may soon come. I cannot remain here so long by myself as another month. I had a narrow escape bathing the day before yesterday. What I thought was a big piece of seaweed was a ground shark a few yards from me ; but it receded instead of coming at me. I shall feel rather shy of the water in future."

As the steamers came in from Bahia Isabel went on board them one after another in the hope of greeting her husband ; but still he did not come. At last, when she had made herself quite ill with anxiety, and when she had fully determined to start in search of him, he turned up unexpectedly—of course by the one steamer which she did not meet—and he was quite angry that she had not come on board to greet him. After telling her all his adventures while canoeing down the river (which have been fully described elsewhere [1]), they went down to Santos.

They moved about between Santos and São Paulo for the next four months, until, in April, 1868, Burton broke

[1] *The Highlands of Brazil*, by Richard Burton.

down. The climate at last proved too much even for
his iron frame, and he had a very severe illness ; how
severe it was may be gathered from the following letter :

"São Paulo, *May* 3, 1868.

"My dearest Mother,
"I have been in the greatest trouble since I last
wrote. You may remember Richard was very ill with
a pain in the side. At last he took to incessant
paroxysms of screaming, and seemed to be dying, and I
knew not what to do. Fortunately a doctor came from
Rio on the eighth day of his illness. I sent at once to
him, and he kindly took up his quarters in our house.
On hearing my account, and examining Richard, he
said he did not know if he could save him, but would
do his best. He put twelve leeches on, and cupped
him on the right breast, lanced him in thirty-eight
places, and put on a powerful blister on the whole of
that side. He lost an immense deal of black clotted
blood. It would be impossible to detail all we have
gone through. This is the tenth day the doctor has
had him in hand, and the seventeenth of his illness.
Suffice it to say that the remedies have been legion, and
there has been something to do every quarter of an
hour day and night. For three days the doctor was
uncertain if he could live. The disease is one that grows
upon you unconsciously, and you only know it when it
knocks you down. It was congestion of the liver,
combined with inflammation of the lung, where they
join. The agony was fearful, and poor Richard could
not move hand or foot, nor speak, swallow, or breathe

without a paroxysm of pain that made him scream for a quarter of an hour. When I thought he was dying, I took the scapulars and some holy water, and I said, ' The doctor has tried all his remedies ; now let me try one of mine.' I put some holy water on his head, and knelt down and said some prayers, and put on the blessed scapulars. He had not been able to raise his head for days to have the pillow turned, but he raised it of his own accord sufficiently to let the string pass under his head, and had no pain. It was a silent consent. He was quite still for about an hour, and then he said in a whisper, ' Zoo, I think I'm a little better.' From then to now he slowly and painfully got better, and has never had a *bad* paroxysm since. Day and night I have watched by his bed for seventeen days and nights, and I begin to feel very nervous, as I am quite alone ; he won't let any one do anything for him but me. Now, however, thank God! all the symptoms are disappearing ; he is out of danger ; he can speak better, swallow, and turn a little in bed with my help. To-day I got him up in a chair for half an hour for the first time, and he has had chicken broth. For fifteen days nothing passed his lips but medicine. He is awfully thin and grey, and looks about sixty. He is quite gaunt, and it is sad to look at him. The worst of it is that I'm afraid that his lungs will never be quite right again. He can't get the affected lung well at all. His breathing is still impeded, and he has a twinge in it. He cannot go to England because of the cold ; but if he is well enough in three months from this to spare me, I am to go and remain till Easter. He has given up his expedition (I am afraid he will never make another), but will take a quiet trip down to the River Plata and Paraguay (a civilized trip). My servants have all been very kind and attentive, and our doctor excellent, and the neighbours have all shown the greatest kindness and sympathy. I have not been out of the house for ages, but I believe there have been all sorts of religious *fêtes* going on, and our poor old bishop has died and was buried with great pomp. I tried to go out in the garden yesterday, but I nearly fainted, and had to come back. Don't mention my fatigue or health in writing back."

Burton recovered slowly. His illness, however, had the effect of disgusting him with Brazil, and of making him decide to throw up his consulate, a thing he had long been wishing to do, if a favourable opportunity presented itself. The present was a decidedly unfavourable opportunity, but nevertheless he came to the conclusion that he could not stand Brazil any longer. " It had given him his illness ; it was far from the world ; it was no advancement ; it led to nothing." He had been there three years, and he wanted to be on the move again.

His slightest wish was his wife's law. Though she was in a way sorry, for São Paulo had been the only home she had ever enjoyed with her husband so far, she at once set to work to carry out his desire. She sold up everything at São Paulo. Burton applied to the Foreign Office for leave ; and that obtained, they went down to Santos together. Here it was decided that

they should part for a time. He was to go to the Pacific
coast for a trip, and return by way of the Straits of
Magellan, Buenos Ayres, and Rio to London. Isabel
was to go direct to London, see if she could not induce
the Foreign Office to give him another post, transact
certain business concerning mines and company pro-
moters, arrange for the publication of certain books,
and await the arrival of her husband.

While they were at Santos Isabel wrote the following
letter to her mother :

"THE COAST NEAR SANTOS, *June* 16, 1868.

" In this country, if you are well, all right ; but
the moment you are ailing, lie down and die, for it is
no use trying to live. I kept Richard alive by never
taking my eyes off him for eight weeks, and perpetually
standing at the bedside with one thing or another. But
who in a general way will get any one to do that for
them ? I would now like to pass to something more
cheerful.

" The first regatta ever known took place at Santos
last Sunday for all nations—English, American, French,
German, Portuguese, and Brazilian, and native *caiques* :
English and American in white flannel and black belts ;
German, scarlet ; French, blue ; Portuguese, white
with blue belts and caps ; Brazilians, like parrots, in
national costume, all green, with yellow fixings and
scarlet caps. Our boat was of course expected to win.
It was manned by four railway clerks, who had ordered
a big supper on the strength of the winnings ; but, poor
things ! they had such weak arms, and they boasted

and talked so much, that they were exhausted before they started. The 'English ladies' (?) objected to their rowing in jerseys, as improper! And they did not know how to feather their oars (had perhaps never heard of it), so they came in *last*. The Portuguese, who stepped quietly into their boat without a word, came in first, Brazil second, German third, and the three big nations, French, American, and English, last. We *last* by half a boat's length! Tremendous fighting and quarrelling ensued, red and angry faces, and 'bargee' language. I am very glad; it will produce a good feeling on the Brazilian side, a general emulation, and take our English snobs down a peg, which they sadly want. The native *caiques* were really pretty—black men with paddles standing upright, and all moving together like a machine.

"I leave São Paulo on the 31st, Santos on the 1st, Rio on the 9th, and will reach home early in September. I could not stay here any longer without a change. I think you had better leave town for your country change now, as I *cannot* leave London earlier than the middle of October. All my wealth depends on my editing a book and a poem of Richard's and two things of my own for the October press; and, moreover, I am grown so fat and coarse and vulgar I must brush myself up in town a little before appearing, and I have no clothes, and I am sure you will faint when you see my complexion and my hands. So try and start early out of town, and return early. I can join in any fun in October. I got your little note from Cossy. I dare say the woods are very nice; but I think if you saw the

virgin forests of South America in which I am now
sitting alone, far from any human creature, with gaudy
butterflies and birds fluttering around me, big vegetation, and a shark playing in the boiling green sea, which
washes up to my feet, and the bold mountain background on a very blue sky, the thick foliage covered
with wild flowers and creepers such as no hothouse in
England could grow, arum leaves, one alone bigger
than me, which shade me from the burning sun, the
distant clatter of monkeys, the aromatic smells and
mysterious whisperings of the forest, you would own
that even the Cossy woods were tame ; for to be
thoroughly alone thus with Nature is glorious. Chico
is cooking a mysterious mess in a gypsy kettle for me;
my pony is browsing near ; and I, your affectionate
child, am sitting in a short petticoat and jacket, bare-
legged to the knees, writing to you and others to catch
the next mail.

" Richard starts with me, and turns the opposite way
from Rio. He goes *via* Rosario, Rio Grande do Sul,
Buenos Ayres, Monte Video, the Plata River, and
Paraguay, to see the war. A *voyage de luxe* for him,
for these places are all within writing latitudes and
some little civilization."

On July 24 Isabel embarked for London, and arrived
at Southampton on September 1, after a rough voyage.
Her mother and two of her sisters came down to
Southampton to meet her ; and great was the joy of
their meeting.

As soon as Isabel had settled down at home she

turned to her work, and good luck attended her. She carried through all her husband's mining business, and arranged for the publication of his books, notably for the one he had just written on *The Highlands of Brazil*. As it was to be brought out at once, she was also commissioned to correct and pass the proofs for press. She did so ; but as the book contained certain things of which she did not approve, she inserted the following preface in the book by way of protest. It is quoted in full, because it illustrates a much-vexed question—the attitude which she adopted towards her husband's writings. Her action in these matters has called down upon her the fiercest criticism ; but this brief preface shows that her views were consistent throughout, and her husband was fully aware of them when he left her his sole literary executor.

Before the reader dives into the interior of Brazil with my husband as a medium, let me address two words to him.

I have returned home, on six months' leave of absence, after three years in Brazil. One of the many commissions I am to execute for Captain Burton is to see the following pages through the press.

It has been my privilege, during those three years, to have been his almost constant companion ; and I consider that to travel, write, read, and study under such a master is no small boon to any one desirous of seeing and learning.

Although he frequently informs me, in a certain oriental way, that "the Moslem can permit no equality with women," yet he has chosen me, his pupil, for this distinction, in preference to a more competent stranger.

As long as there is anything difficult to do, a risk to be incurred, or any chance of improving the mind and of educating oneself, I am a very faithful disciple ; but I now begin to feel that, while

LADY BURTON IN 1869.   [*Page* 350.

he and his readers are old friends, I am humbly standing unknown in the shadow of his glory. It is therefore time for me respectfully but firmly to assert that, although I proudly accept of the trust confided to me, and pledge myself not to avail myself of my discretionary powers to alter one word of the original text, I protest vehemently against his religious and moral sentiments, which belie a good and chivalrous life. I point the finger of indignation particularly at what misrepresents our Holy Roman Catholic Church, and at what upholds that unnatural and repulsive law, Polygamy, which the Author is careful not to practise himself, but from a high moral pedestal he preaches to the ignorant as a means of population in young countries.

I am compelled to differ with him on many other subjects; but, be it understood, not in the common spirit of domestic jar, but with a mutual agreement to differ and enjoy our differences, whence points of interest never flag.

Having now justified myself, and given a friendly warning to a fair or gentle reader—the rest must take care of themselves— I leave him or her to steer through these anthropological sand-banks and hidden rocks as best he or she may.

Isabel's greatest achievement at this time was the obtaining for her husband the long-coveted Consulship of Damascus from Lord Stanley, who was an old friend and neighbour of her uncle, Lord Gerard. Lord Stanley (afterwards Lord Derby) was then Foreign Secretary in Disraeli's brief first Administration. He was a friend of the Burtons, and had a high opinion of them both. To him Isabel repaired, and brought the whole of her eloquence and influence to bear : no light thing, as Burton's enemies—and he had many—guessing what she was after, endeavoured to influence the Foreign Secretary by representing that his appointment would be unpopular, both with the Moslems and the

Christian missionaries in Syria. In Lord Stanley's opinion, however, Burton was the man for the post, and he appointed him Consul of Damascus, with a salary of £1,000 a year. Isabel telegraphed and wrote the glad news; but neither her letter nor her telegram reached her husband, who was then roving about South America. Burton heard the news of his appointment accidentally in a *café* at Lucca. He telegraphed at once accepting it, and started for England.

In the meantime there had been a change of Government, and Lord Clarendon succeeded Lord Stanley at the Foreign Office. Burton's enemies renewed their opposition to his appointment, and besought Lord Clarendon to cancel it. Isabel, whose vigilance never slumbered for one moment, got wind of this, and immediately dispatched copies of the following letter to her husband at Rio, Buenos Ayres, and Valparaiso :

"LONDON, *January* 7, 1869.

"MY DARLING,

"If you get this, come home at once by shortest way. Telegraph from Lisbon and Southampton, and I will meet you at latter and have all snug.

"*Strictly private.* The new Government have tried to upset some of the appointments made by the last. There is no little jealousy about yours. Others wanted it even at £700 a year, and were refused. Lord Stanley thinks, and so do I, that you may as well be on the ground as soon as possible.

"Your faithful and attached wife."

Burton did not receive this letter, as he had already started for home with all speed. His wife met him at Southampton. Burton went to the Foreign Office, and had a long interview with Lord Clarendon, who told him that the objections to his appointment at Damascus were "very serious." Burton assured Lord Clarendon that the objections raised were unfounded. Lord Clarendon then let the appointment go forward, though he plainly warned Burton that, if the feeling stated to exist against him at Damascus should prevent the proper performance of his official duties, he would immediately recall him. It is necessary to call attention to this, as it has a direct bearing on the vexed question of Burton's recall two years later.

No shadow of that untoward event, however, dimmed the brightness of Burton's prospects just now. He gave an assurance that he would act with "unusual prudence," and it was hinted that if he succeeded at Damascus he might eventually get Morocco or Teheran or Constantinople. Isabel writes : "We were, in fact, at the zenith of our career." She might well think so, for they were basking in the unaccustomed light of the official favour ; they received a most enthusiastic welcome from their friends, and were dined and *fêted* everywhere. The new year (1869) opened most auspiciously for them.

They spent the spring in London and in paying a round of visits to many friends. Later they crossed over to Boulogne, and visited the old haunts where they met for the first time eighteen years before.

Burton's leave was now running short, and the time was drawing near when he was due at Damascus. He decided to go to Vichy and take a month's course of the waters, and then proceed *viâ* Brindisi to Damascus. His wife was to come out to Damascus later. At Boulogne therefore they parted; he went to Vichy, and she was to return to London and carry out the usual plan of " pay, pack, and follow."

Isabel went round by way of Paris, and then she began to feel unhappy at being separated from her husband, and to want to join him at Vichy. "I did not see why I could not have the month there with him, and make up double-quick time after." So instead of returning to London, she started off for Vichy, and spent the month there with her husband. Algernon Swinburne and Frederick Leighton (both great friends of the Burtons) were there also, and they made many excursions together. When Burton's "cure" was at an end, his wife accompanied him as far as Turin. Here they parted, he going to catch the P. & O. at Brindisi, *en route* for Damascus, and she returning to London to arrange and settle everything for a long sojourn in the East.

She was in England for some weeks (the autumn of 1869), and up to her eyes in work. She had to see a great many publishers for one thing, and for another she was busy in every way preparing herself for Damascus. She went down to Essex to see the tube-wells worked, and mastered the detail of them, as Burton was anxious, if possible, to produce water in the desert. She also took lessons in taking off wheels and

axles, oiling and putting them on again ; and lessons.
in taking her own guns and pistols to pieces, cleaning
and putting them together again. Then she had to
buy a heap of useful and necessary things to stock the
house at Damascus with. One of her purchases almost
rivalled her famous "jungle suit." She invested in a
pony-carriage, a thing unheard of in Syria ; and her
uncle, Lord Gerard, also made her a present of an old
family chariot. This tickled the late Lord Houghton
immensely, and he made so many jokes about "Isabel
driving through the desert in a chariot drawn by
camels" that she left it. But she took out the pony-
carriage ; and as there was only one road in the country,
she found it useless, though she was lucky enough to
sell it to some one at Damascus, who bought it not
for use, but as a curio.

Other work of a different nature also came to
her hand, the work of vindicating her husband and
defending his position. At a meeting of the Royal
Geographical Society, at which she was present, Sir
Roderick Murchison, who was in the chair, spoke of
"Central or Equatorial Africa, in which lie those great
water-basins which, thanks to the labours of *Speke,
Grant, and Baker*, are known to feed the Nile." After
the meeting was over she went up to Sir Roderick
and asked him why Burton had not been mentioned
with the others. He replied it was an oversight, and
he would see that it was rectified in the reports to
the press. It was not. So she wrote to *The Times*,
protesting against the omission of her husband's name,
and to *The Athenæum*. These letters have been

published in her Life of Sir Richard. But the
following letter from Sir Roderick Murchison, called
forth by her letter to *The Times*, and her reply thereto,
have not been published :

" 16, BELGRAVE SQUARE, *November* 14, 1869.

" MY DEAR MRS. BURTON,

" I regret that you did not call on me as you
proposed, instead of making your *complaint* in *The
Times*.

" No change in the wording of the address could
have been made when you appealed to me ; for the
printed article was in the hands of several reporters.

" Nor can I, in looking at the address (as now
before me), see why you should be offended at my
speaking of ' the great Lake Tanganyika, first visited
by Burton and Speke.'

" My little opening address was not a history of all
African discoveries ; and if you will only refer to the
twenty-ninth volume of *The Journal of the Royal
Geographical Society* (1859), you will see how, in
presenting the medal to your husband as the chief of the
East African Expedition, I strove to do him all justice
for his successful and bold explorations. But I was
under the necessity of coupling Speke with Burton as
joint discoverers of the Lake Tanganyika, inasmuch as
they both worked together until prostrated by illness ;
and whilst your husband was blind or almost so, Speke
made all the astronomical observations which fixed the
real position of places near the lake.

" Thus your husband, in his reply to me after receiving the medal, says, 'Whilst I undertook the history, ethnography, the languages and peculiarities of the people, to Captain Speke fell the arduous task of delineating the exact topography and of laying down our positions by astronomical observations, a labour to which at times even the undaunted Livingstone found himself unequal' (*Journal R. G. S.*, vol. xxix., p. 97).

"I beg you also to read your husband's masterly and eloquent description of the lake regions of Central Equatorial Africa in the same volume. No memoir in our journal is more striking than this, and I think it will gratify you to have Captain Burton's most effective writing brought once more to the notice of geographers. I will with great pleasure add a full footnote to the paragraph in which I first allude to the Tanganyika, and point out how admirably Captain Burton has illustrated that portion of Lake Tanganyika which he and his companion visited ; though, as you know, he was then prostrated by illness and almost blind.

"With this explanation, which will appear in all the official and public copies of my little, imperfect, opening address, I hope you will be satisfied, and exonerate me from any thought of not doing full justice to your meritorious husband, who, if he had been in health, would doubtless have worked out the path which Livingstone is still engaged in discovering : the settlement of whether the waters of Tanganyika flow into the said discovered Albert Nyanza by Baker.

"Believe me to be ever, dear Mrs. Burton,
"Yours sincerely,
"RODERICK MURCHISON."

"14, MONTAGU PLACE, MONTAGU SQUARE, W.,
"*November* 15, 1869.

"DEAR SIR RODERICK,

"I have every intention of calling upon you, and
I think you know I have always looked upon you as a
very sincere and particular friend ; nor had I the slightest
idea of being offended with *you* ; and if you have read
my letter, you will have seen that I particularly laid a
stress upon *your* kindness ; but what you and I know
on this subject, and perhaps many connected with the
Royal Geographical Society, is now, considering the
fast flow of events, almost ancient history, unless brought
before the public. I *did* feel nettled the other night ;
but I might have kept quiet, had I not had many visits
and letters of condolence on my husband having been
passed over. I then felt myself *obliged* to remind the
public what the Society the other night had forgotten.
Had I visited you, and had we talked it over, and had
the reports been run over and corrected, it would hardly
have set the large number of people right who were at
the meeting of last Monday, who heard Captain Burton
mentioned only once, and the other four twenty times.
Indeed, I was not offended at the *only* mention you
did make of him, but at the mention of the other
three, excluding him. I shall be truly grateful for your
proposed notice of him. And do not think I grudge
anything to any other traveller. I am glad you mentioned Speke with him. Speke was a brave man, and
full of fine qualities. I grudge his memory no honour
that can be paid ; I never wish to detract from any of
the great merits of the other four. I only ask to

maintain my husband's right place amongst them, which is only second to Livingstone. I hope I shall see you in a few days, and

> " Believe me, most sincerely yours,
> "Isabel Burton."

A month later all her business was completed, and Isabel left London for Damascus, to enter upon the most eventful epoch of her eventful life.

CHAPTER X[1]

MY JOURNEY TO DAMASCUS

(1869—1870)

The East is a Career.

DISRAELI's "*Tancred.*"

I SHALL not readily forget the evening of Thursday, December 16, 1869. I had a terrible parting from my dear ones, especially from my mother. As a Frenchman would say, " Je quittais ma mère." We all dined together—the last dinner—at five o'clock, and three hours later I set out for the station. My brothers and sister came down to Victoria to see me off, and at the last moment my brother Rudolph decided to accompany me to Dover, for which I was truly thankful. It was a wild night, and the express to Dover rushed through the raging winter storm. My mind was a curious mixture of exultation and depression, and with it all was a sense of supernormal consciousness that something of this had been enacted before. About a fortnight previously I dreamed one of my curious dreams. I thought that I came to a small harbour,

---

[1] The chapters on Damascus are compiled from letters and diaries of Lady Burton, and from some of the rough manuscript notes from which she wrote her *Inner Life of Syria.*

and it was as black as night, and the wind was sobbing up mournfully, and there were two steamers in the harbour, waiting. One refused to go out, but the other went, and came to grief. So in the train, as we tore along, I prayed silently that I might have a sign from Heaven, and it should be that one captain should refuse to go. Between my prayers my spirits rose and fell. They rose because my destination was Damascus, the dream of my childhood. I should follow the footsteps of Lady Mary Wortley Montagu, Lady Hester Stanhope, the Princess de la Tour d'Auvergne, that trio of famous European women who lived of their own choice a thoroughly Eastern life, and of whom I looked to make a fourth. They fell because I was leaving behind me my home, my family, and many dear ties in England, without any definite hope of return.

We arrived at Dover, and walked to the boat, and could hardly keep on our legs for the wind. When I set out to embark, lo ! there were two steamers. The Ostend boat refused to go out ; the other one was preparing to start. Now I was most anxious to sail without an hour's delay, but I turned to my brother and said, " Rody, if it is my duty to go I will go, for I do not like to stay on my own responsibility. I am scrupulous about Dick's time and money, and he told me to lose no time." The answer was, " Duty be damned ! I won't let you go." Still I hesitated, and as I was between the ways an old sailor stepped out of the darkness as I stood on the quay, and said, " Go home, missie ; I haven't seen such a night this forty year." I remembered my dream, and decided.

I turned into the nearest shelter, a small inn opposite the boats, so as to be able to start at daylight; and the result justified my foresight. The captain of the first vessel, by which I had intended to go, went out. After shipping awful seas, and being frightfully knocked about, he moored some way off Calais Pier; but the sea and the wind drove the boat right on to it, and carried away one of the paddles, the tiller, and hurt several passengers. The waves drove her backwards and forwards on to the pier like a nutshell for half an hour, and she was nearly going down, but some smacks hauled her off and out to sea again. She beat about all night, and returned to Dover in a pitiable plight, having neither landed the passengers nor the baggage.

It was thus I met her when I embarked on the other boat at nine o'clock the next morning. The weather was terribly rough even then, but at least we had the advantage of daylight. We had a rough passage, the sea mountains high; but we reached Calais eventually, where I managed to get some food at the buffet, such as it was, but I had to sit on the floor with a plate on my lap, so great and rude was the crowd. The boat accident caused me to miss my proper train to Marseilles, and to lose two of my many trunks. It would almost seem as if some malignant spirit had picked these two trunks out, for the one contained nearly all my money, and the other all my little comforts for the journey. I had to decide at once between missing my passage at Marseilles and forsaking my missing trunks. I decided to go on, and leave them to look after themselves. Six months later they turned up at Damascus safe and sound. We travelled through the weary night and most of the next day, and only reached Marseilles at 5 p.m., after having met with many *contretemps* and discomforts. I at once went on board, arranged my cabin, did all my little business, and went back alone to the hotel to have a hot bath and a cutlet, having been nearly forty-eight hours on the road without rest or stopping.

Our ship was one of the P. & O. floating hotels, superbly fitted. We steamed out from Marseilles at half-past nine the next morning. It was a great pleasure to exchange the fogs and cold of England for the climate of the sunny, smiling south, the olive groves, and the mother-o'-pearl sea ; yet these beauties of Nature have no meaning in them when the heart feels lonely and desolate, as mine did then.

Yet on the whole I had a very pleasant passage from Marseilles to Alexandria. We had not more than fifty passengers on board, all Anglo-Indians, and middling class. I got a very nice cabin forward, all to myself, with my maid. The ship was full of young married couples going out to India. They were not used to ships, and were evidently unaware of the ventilators at the top of the cabin, so at night one got the full benefit of their love-making. One night, for instance, I heard a young bride fervently calling upon her "Joey" to kiss her. It was amusing at first, but afterwards it became rather monotonous. I did not know a soul on board with whom I could exchange ideas, and I kept as much as possible to myself without appearing rude. I was asked to choose my place at table, and I humbly

chose one some way down; but the captain asked me to
move up to the seat of honour on his right hand, and I
felt quite at a loss to account for the distinction, because
not a soul on board knew anything about me.   I did
not find the captain, though, a bad companion.   He was
a short, fat, dark, brisk little man, just the sort of man a
captain and a sailor should be.   I am glad to say he
had not the slightest idea of being unduly attentive.
The conversation was dull at table.   The ladies talked
chiefly about Colonel "This" and Captain "That,"
peppering their conversation with an occasional
Hindustani word, a spice of Anglo-Indian gossip, and
plentiful regimentalisms, such as "griffin," "tiffen,"
"the Staff," and "gymkhana," all of which was Greek
to me.

Take it all round, the six days' passage was not so
bad.   I particularly admired the coast of Sicily, the
mountains rising one above another, Etna smoking in
the distance, the sea like glass, and the air adding a
sensuous charm, a soft, balmy breeze like the Arabian
seas.   Yet, as I had been spoiled by Brazilian scenery,
I did not go into the same ecstasies over it as my
fellow-passengers.   We spent Christmas Eve as our
last night on board.   In the evening we went in for
snapdragon and other festivities of the season, and
tried to be as merry as we could.   The ship could
not go into the harbour of Alexandria at night; it has a
dangerous entrance; so we sent up our rockets and blue-
lights, and remained outside the lighthouse till dawn.

On Christmas Day morning I first set my foot on
Eastern ground.   We steamed into the harbour of

THE BOULEVART, ALEXANDRIA.

[*Page* 364.

Alexandria slowly; everybody was going on to India
except me, and I landed. The first thing I did was
to go straight to a telegraph office and pay nineteen
shillings and sixpence for a telegram to Richard at
Beyrout, which of course arrived there after I did. I
cannot say that I was struck with Alexandria; in point
of fact, I mentally called it "a hole," in vulgar parlance.
I went to the Hôtel de l'Europe, a second-rate hotel,
though one of the best in Alexandria. It was not so
bad as might have been expected. In the afternoon
we made a party up to see Pompey's Pillar and
Cleopatra's Needle and the bazars and other things.
But I am bound to say that, on the whole, I thought
Alexandria "neither fish, flesh, fowl, nor good red
herring." It was a sort of a jumble of Eastern
and Western, and the worst of each. The only
amusing incident which happened to me there was
when two dragomans got up a fictitious quarrel as to
who should take me to the bazars. Of course they
appealed to me, and I said, "You may both come, but
I shall only pay one." Whereupon they fastened upon
each other tooth and nail, tore each other's clothes,
and bit each other's cheeks. These two, though I
never suspected it at the time, were, it appeared, in
the habit of thus dealing with ladies and missionaries
and amiable English tourists; and they always got up
this farce, because, to avoid a street fight, the kind-
hearted looker-on would generally employ and pay
them both, and perhaps give them a tip in addition
to calm them down. But I innocently did the right
thing without knowing it. I had so often seen negroes

fight with knives in Brazil that the spectacle of two dragomans biting each other's cheeks appeared to me to be supremely ridiculous. I laughed, and waited patiently until one of them pretended to be very much hurt. Then turning to the other, I said, "You seem the better man ; I will take you"; and they were both very much crestfallen.

I spent the evening alone in my small room at the hotel. A strange Christmas truly.

Next morning I went on board the Russian *Ceres*, which was bound for Beyrout, a three days' passage. It was an uneventful journey. The best thing about the boat was the *caviare*, which was delicious. The deck was simply filthy, as it was crowded with Orientals from every part of the East, all nations and creeds and tongues. But it was the most interesting part of the ship to me, as I had always been dreaming of the East. Each of these Eastern families had their mattresses and their prayer-carpets, on which they seemed to squat night and day. No matter how rough or how sea-sick, they were always there saying their prayers, or devouring their food, or dozing, or reclining on their backs. Occasionally they chanted their devotions through their noses. I could not help laughing at the sound ; and when I laughed they did the same. I used to bring all the sweets out of the saloon for the children, so they were always glad to see me. The other passengers thought it passing strange that I should elect to spend the whole of my days with "Eastern rabble."

We passed Port Said and got to Jaffa in about two

days. I was not impressed with Jaffa. The town looks like dirty, well-rubbed dice running down the side of a conical-shaped, green hill. Here I sent another telegram to Damascus to Richard—the Russian Vice-Consul kindly took charge of it—but all the same it never reached its destination, though I am certain it was not the Consul's fault. At Jaffa we picked up an Effendi and his harím, and two Italian musicians, who played the concertina and guitar. The latter pair confided in me, and said they had made a *mariage de cœur*, and were really very hard up, in fact dependent on their talent ; so I hit on a plan to help them. I asked the captain to let us have a little music after breakfast and dinner. They played, and I carried round the plate, and my gleanings paid their passage and something more. As for the Effendi's harím she was carefully veiled and wrapped up in an *izár*, or sheet, and confined to her cabin, except when she was permitted at rare intervals to appear on deck. Her Effendi jealously watched her door, to see that nobody went in but the stewardess. However, she freely unveiled before me. I was not impressed with her charms, and I thought what a fine thing the sheet and the veil would be to some of our European women. There is an irresistible suggestion of concealed charm about them. It was my first experience of a real harím.

On the third day, very early, we anchored off Beyrout. The town as viewed from the water's edge is beautiful. Its base is washed by the blue Mediterranean. It straggles along the coast and crawls up part of the lower hills. The yellow sand beyond the town, and the dark green pine forests which surround it, contrast well with the deep blue bay and the turquoise skies. It is backed by the splendid range of the Lebanon. The air is redolent with the smell of pine wood. Every town in the East has its peculiar odour, and when once you have been in one you can tell it blindfold afterwards. I went ashore, and put up at a clean and comfortable hotel facing the sea, which was kept by a Greek. This hotel later on came to be to my eyes the very centre of civilization ; for during our sojourn at Damascus Beyrout was our Biarritz, and this little hotel the most luxurious house in Syria. Here I had breakfast, and after that I called on our Consul-General. His wife was ill in bed, but he asked me kindly to remain to luncheon, and showed me how to smoke my first narghíleh. I was very anxious to start at once for Damascus, but the diligence had gone. So I had to stop, willy-nilly, for the night at Beyrout. In the evening the Duchesse de Persigny arrived from Damascus, and sent me word that she would like to dine with me. Of course I was delighted. She gave me some news of Richard, and enlivened my dinner very much by anecdotes of Damascus. She was a very witty, eccentric woman, as every one knows who had to do with her when she was in England. She had many adventures in Damascus, which she related to me in her racy, inimitable way. It didn't sound so bad in French, but I fear her humour was a trifle too spicy to bear translation into plain English prose. When I got to Damascus, I heard a good deal more about her "goings on" there.

I went to bed, but not to sleep, for it seemed to me that I was at the parting of the ways. To-morrow I was to realize the dream of my life. I was to leave behind me everything connected with Europe and its petty civilization, and wend my way to "The Pearl of the East." As soon as you cross the Lebanon Range you quit an old life for a new life, you forsake the new world and make acquaintance with the old world, you relapse into a purely oriental and primitive phase of existence.

Early the next morning "the private carriage" which the Consul-General had kindly obtained for me, a shabby omnibus drawn by three old screws, made its appearance. I was to drive in it over the Lebanons, seventy-two miles, to Damascus; so I naturally viewed it with interest, not unmingled with apprehension. Quite a little crowd assembled to see me off, and watched with interest while my English maid, a large pet St. Bernard dog, my baggage, and myself were all squeezed into the omnibus or on top of it. The Consul-General sent his kawwass as guard. This official appeared a most gorgeous creature, with silver-mounted pistols and all sorts of knives and dangling things hanging about him. He rejoiced in the name of Sakharaddín, which I pronounced "Sardine," and this seemed to afford great amusement to the gaping crowd which had assembled to see me off.

The drive from Beyrout to Damascus was charming, and it lasted two days.

First we drove over the Plain of Beyrout, behind the town. The roadside was lined with cactus hedges and rude *cafés*, which are filled on Sundays and holidays by all classes. They go to smoke, sip coffee and *raki*, and watch the passers-by. Immediately on arriving at the foot of the Lebanon, we commenced a winding, steep ascent, every turn of which gave charming views of the sea and of Beyrout, which we did not lose sight of for several hours. We wound round and round the ascent until Beyrout and the sea became invisible. The cold made me hungry, and I refreshed myself with some bread, hard-boiled eggs, and a cigarette. "Sardine" was keeping Ramadan, but the sight of these luxuries tempted him, and he broke his fast. I couldn't help offering him something, he looked so wistful! At last we reached the top, and a glorious wintry sunset gave us a splendid view. It was of course midwinter, and one saw little of the boasted fertility of the Lebanon. After the beauties of Brazil the scenery looked to me like a wilderness of rock and sand, treeless and barren ; the very mountains were only hills. I could not help contrasting the new world and the old. In Brazil, though rich in luxuriant vegetable and animal life, there is no history—all is new and progressive, but vulgar and *parvenu* ; whereas Syria, in her abomination of desolation, is the old land, and she teems with relics of departed glory. I felt that I would rather abide with her, and mourn the past amid her barren rocks and sandy desert, than rush into the progress and the hurry of the new world.

We descended the Lebanon at a full canter into the

Buká'a Plain.   On the road I met three strangers, who offered me a little civility when I was searching for a glass of water at a khan, or inn.   As I was better mounted than they, I said that in the event of my reaching our night-halt first I would order supper and beds for them, and they informed me that every house on the road had been *retenue* for me, so that I was really making quite a royal progress.   I was able to keep my promise to them.   The halt was at Shtora, a little half-way inn kept by a Greek.   The three travellers soon came up.   We supped together and spent a pleasant evening.   They turned out to be a French *employé* at the Foreign Office, a Bavarian minister on his travels, and a Swedish officer on leave.

The next morning we parted.   My new acquaintances set out in an opposite direction, and I went on to Damascus.   We trotted cheerfully across the rest of the Buká'a Plain, and then commenced the ascent of the Anti-Lebanon.   To my mind the Anti-Lebanon, off the beaten track, is wilder and more picturesque than the other range.   The descent of the Anti-Lebanon we did at a good pace, but it seemed a long time until we landed on the plain Es Sáhará.   That reached, compensation for the ugly scenery we had to pass through began when we entered a beautiful mountain defile, about two hours from Damascus.   Here, between mountains, runs the road ; and the Barada—the ancient Abana, they say—rushes through the mountains and by the roadside to water the gardens of Damascus.

Between Salahíyyeh and Damascus is a quarter of an hour's ride through gardens and orchards.   I had heard of them often, and of the beautiful white city, with her swelling domes, tapering minarets, and glittering golden crescents looming against the far horizon of the distant hills. So I had heard of Damascus, so I had pictured it, and so I often saw it later; but I did not see it thus on this my first entrance to it, for it was winter. As we rumbled along the carriage road I asked ever and again, "Where are the beautiful gardens of Damascus?" "Here," said the kawwass, pointing to what in winter-time and to English eyes appeared only ugly shrubberies, wood clumps, and orchards. I saw merely scrubby woods bordered by green, which made a contrast to the utter sterility of Es Sáhará. We passed Dummar, a village which contains several summer villas belonging to the Wali (the Governor-General of Syria) and other personages. The Barada ran along the right of the road, and gradually broadened into the green Merj, which looked then like a village common. And thus I entered Damascus.

We passed a beautiful mosque, with the dome flanked by two slender minarets. I scarcely noticed it at the time, for I drove with all haste to the only hotel in Damascus—"Demetri's." It is a good house with a fine courtyard, which has orange and lemon trees, a fountain full of goldfish in it, and a covered gallery running round it. All this would have been cool and pleasant in the summer, but it was dark, damp, and dreary that winter evening. I must own frankly that my first impression of Damascus was not favourable, and a feeling of disappointment stole over me. It was very cold; and driving into the city as I did tired out,

DAMASCUS, FROM THE DESERT.

[*Page* 372.

the shaky trap heaving and pitching heavily through the thick mire and slushy, narrow streets, filled with refuse and wild dogs, is, to speak mildly, not liable to give one a pleasant impression.

However, all my discomfort, depression, and disappointment were soon swallowed up in the joy of meeting Richard, who had also put up, pending my appearance, at this hotel. He came in about an hour after my arrival, and I found him looking ill and worn. After our first greetings were over he told me his reception at Damascus had been most cordial, but he had been dispirited by not getting any letters from me or telegrams. They all arrived in a heap some days after I came. And this explained how it was that he had not come to meet me at Beyrout, as I had expected him to do. In fact, I had felt sorely hurt that he had not come. But he told me he had gone to Beyrout over and over again to meet me, and I had not turned up, and now the steamer by which I had arrived was the only one which he had not gone to meet. He was feeling very low and sad about my non-appearance. It was therefore a joyful surprise for him when he came in from his lonely walk to find me settled down comfortably in his room. Though he greeted me in that matter-of-fact way with which he was wont to repress his emotions, I could *feel* that he was both surprised and overjoyed. He had already been three months at Damascus, and the climate and loneliness had had a bad effect upon him, both mentally and physically. However, we had a comfortable little dinner, the best that " Demetri's " could give us, which was nothing special, and after dinner was over we warmed ourselves over a *mangal*, a large brass dish on a stand, full of live charcoal embers. Then we had a smoke, and began to discuss our plans for our new home.

It had taken me fifteen days and nights without stopping to come from London to Damascus.

END OF VOL. I.